Esther's Sling

- Bonus Edition -

A Novel

Ben Brunson

For more information about the author and to learn more about the weapons, units and places in this novel, please visit

www.benbrunson.com

Esther's Sling is a work of fiction. All events and characters contained herein are a product of the author's imagination.

Published by Interact Press, LLC

ISBN: 978-1-939893-01-7

Also by Ben Brunson:

The Falstaff Enigma

To Robert Brunson, my father and inspiration

Table of Contents

Prelude

"It is the mission of the Islamic Republic of Iran to erase Israel from the map of the region."

> **- Mahmoud Ahmadinejad**, Assistant Professor of Transportation Engineering, *Elm-o Sanat University;* at a meeting of the International Conference for Support of the Intifada; as quoted by the Fars News Agency of Iran on January 15, 2001.

"We declare explicitly that we will not be satisfied with anything less than the complete obliteration of the Zionist regime from the political map of the world."

> **- Hossein Shariatmadari**, Confidant to Ayatollah Ali Hoseini Khamenei, Supreme Leader of the Islamic Republic of Iran; in a written editorial in the Iran Daily *Kayhan* published on October 30, 2005.

"With God's help, the countdown button for the destruction of the Zionist regime has been pushed by the hands of the children of Lebanon and Palestine. By God's will, we will witness the destruction of this regime in the near future."

> **- Mahmoud Ahmadinejad**, President of the Islamic Republic of Iran; as quoted by the Fars News Agency of Iran on June 3, 2007.

"Throughout history, Allah has imposed upon the Jews, people who would punish them for their corruption. The last punishment was carried out by Hitler by means of all the things he did to them – even though they exaggerated this issue – he managed to put them in their place. This was divine punishment for them. Allah willing, the next time will be at the hands of the believers."

> **- Youssef al-Qaradawi**, Muslim Brotherhood intellectual leader; Cairo, Egypt, January 30, 2009.

"The Zionist regime wants to establish its base upon the ruins of the civilizations of the region. The uniform shout of the Iranian nation is forever 'Death to Israel.'"

> **- Mahmoud Ahmadinejad**, President of the Islamic Republic of Iran; as quoted by the Fars News Agency of Iran on October 10, 2009.

"See what has become of Israel. They gathered the most criminal people in the world and stationed them in our region with lies and fabricated scenarios. They waged wars, committed massive aggression and made millions of people homeless. Today, it is clear that Israel is the most hated regime in the world. It is not useful for its masters anymore. They are in doubt now. They wonder whether to continue spending money on this regime or not. But whether they want it or not, with God's grace, this regime will be annihilated and Palestinians and other regional nations will be rid of its bad omen."

- **Mahmoud Ahmadinejad**, President of the Islamic Republic of Iran; in a speech inside Iran on March 11, 2010.

"I am telling you that a new and greater Middle East will be established without the existence of the U.S. and the Zionist regime."

- **Mahmoud Ahmadinejad**, President of the Islamic Republic of Iran; in a speech inside Iran on April 20, 2010.

"Zionists, who have no faith in religion or even God, now claim piety and intend to take away the Islamic identity of the Holy Quds. This ridiculous move is in fact the continuation of the colonialist polices of oppressors, which will not save the Zionist regime, but also take the regime closer to the endpoint of its existence."

- **Mahmoud Ahmadinejad**, President of the Islamic Republic of Iran; in a speech inside Iran on January 3, 2012.

"The Iranian nation is standing for its cause and that is the full annihilation of Israel."

- **Major General Seyed Hassan Firuzabadi**, Chief of Staff of the Armed Forces of Iran; in a speech to a defense meeting inside Iran on May 20, 2012

Part I
Decisions

1 – Seeds

If war is hell, then covert war is purgatory. Or so thought Amit Margolis as he waited in room 901 of the Ramada Pudong Airport Hotel just outside Shanghai, China. For over a year he had been wheeling and dealing as a businessman based in Moscow, fully embracing the free spending style of connected capitalism that infused life into the capital of the Russian Federation. Brains and knowledge helped, but success was really correlated to the degrees of separation between your circle of friends and the center of power. And the power center around which everyone with aspirations orbited was clear to all: Vladimir Putin.

Margolis was not sure if his nineteen months of investment would have a satisfactory ending. Today he would find out. Success meant that the nation he served would be a little safer tomorrow and he could think about going home. Failure meant that he would have to rethink his approach to his work and maybe, if his managers willed it, start over on a process that could keep him away from home for another year or longer. He picked up the morning's issue of Shanghai Daily, a business newspaper published in English.

The date was Thursday, September 28, 2006. Outside, summer continued its grip on the weather. The forecast high was over 90 degrees Fahrenheit. Through his window Amit could see the early formation of dark clouds that would bring afternoon rain. He was happy to be stuck in his room this day, even if the reason was nerve racking. He was eager to turn his mind to any subject other than the pending knock on his door that, if it came, would be his first sign that today would bring a happy outcome. As he read the lead story about the dismissal of a previously high-flying Communist Party leader in Shanghai, Amit looked at his watch. It was almost one in the afternoon.

At that moment, Mikhail Gordienko stepped out of the back seat of a taxi and onto the curb in front of the Ramada lobby entrance. The taxi had picked him up an hour earlier at the headquarters of the Semiconductor Materials International Company, known simply as SMIC in the world of integrated microprocessor chip design and manufacture.

Gordienko, the 45-year-old Director General of Phase Technologies Corporation, a company based in Moscow, had flown to Shanghai the day before to take delivery of 120 integrated circuits designed by his company and fabricated by SMIC, one of the world's most advanced chip foundries. His job now was to transport this valuable cargo back to Moscow and he had about four hours to kill before he would board a nonstop flight home. Six weeks earlier five engineering chips – the prototypes of the chips now in Gordienko's possession – had been delivered to the test lab of Phase Technologies in Moscow by Federal Express. They were put through a series of tests, each chip performing exactly as designed. But only Gordienko knew that SMIC had shipped only three chips for testing, not five.

The Russian executive was in his room on the seventh floor of the Ramada within a couple of minutes. His overnight bag was already packed as he took one last look around the room. He paused in the bathroom and looked at himself in the mirror. This was his last opportunity to back out of the bargain he had struck months earlier. This was the point when second thoughts were supposed to play on one's conscience, challenging concepts of integrity and duty. He wondered how his life would be different tomorrow. But as he pondered these questions, the face that looked back at him in the mirror was not his own. He could only see the face of his younger brother Yuri, the brother he had taught to curve a soccer ball with both feet. The brother he had tutored in math. The brother who came to his defense when a high school bully demanded Mikhail's money.

While Mikhail earned his PhD in Computer Science and Engineering at Lomonosov Moscow State University, Yuri Gordienko had gone on to become a pilot in the Russian Air Force, flying Sukhoi Su-25 ground attack aircraft. Yuri's love of flying kept him in the Air Force, where he was called to duty during the Second Chechen War.

Yuri Gordienko was on a combat mission when a shoulder fired infrared missile shot down his plane on May 29, 2002. Yuri was fortunate; he survived a low altitude ejection, something that was far from certain given the poorly maintained aircraft of the Russian military at the time. But his good fortune had lasted only the time it took for his parachute to float him down to earth. He was taken prisoner by Chechen guerillas under the command of Dokka Umerov, the Islamic warlord and ally of al Qaeda.

Yuri's family had no information about his fate until the afternoon of June 8 when a videotape was delivered by mail to the studios of NTV in Moscow. Mikhail, his parents and siblings learned that night, along with the rest of Russia, that Yuri Gordienko had been executed two days earlier. The video was aired on TV, Mikhail only seeing it later that evening after receiving phone calls from family and friends. The beaten body of Yuri Gordienko was barely alive as he knelt down facing the camera. His head was bowed and his eyes closed as three men stood behind him wearing camouflage combat jackets. His wrists were bound behind his back. But what burned into Mikhail's mind was the thick black beards of each man, the white Jihadist scarves wrapped around their foreheads and the pure evil in their eyes. The video was stopped as the man in the middle pulled Yuri's head back with his left hand while he began to raise a long-bladed knife in his right hand. There was no need for the news commentator to say what happened next, but the details still were reported with the faux intonation of concern and pity that was belied by the station's desire for ratings.

Mikhail went through the full range of emotion that night, from disbelief when his friends first called him, to the shedding of tears, to a feeling of rage and anger that he had never before known. It was the last emotion that lingered. And as he looked into the mirror of this Shanghai hotel room, his hatred of the Muslim killers of his brother was as intense as it had been that summer night in 2002. That hatred made what he was about to do very easy. He would probably have done this for free. At least that is what he told himself. But he was still more than happy to make a profit in this transaction.

Five minutes later the knock on the door to room 901 penetrated the thoughts of Amit Margolis. He put down his newspaper and opened the door to his erstwhile business partner, now his official partner in espionage. "Good to see you, Mikhail," said Amit as he reached out to grab the travel bag in the Russian's left hand. Amit's Russian was fluent, even if his accent was indeterminate.

Gordienko offered the bag and quickly walked into the suite, suddenly self-conscious about being in the hall. Once the door closed behind him, he relaxed enough to talk. "How are you, Mike?" The Russian knew Margolis only as Mike Jenkins, a Canadian businessman.

Margolis placed the bag on the floor in front of the door and walked across the room to a desk that jutted out from the wall. He sat down as the Russian executive settled in the seat across from him. "Good, good. I am very happy to see you. I assume everything went well this morning?"

"Yes, I have the ICs," replied the Russian. Gordienko placed an aluminum briefcase on the desk and opened it. Inside were 128 integrated circuit chips, each in a sealed pink electrostatic discharge shielding poly bag, forming a flexible Faraday cage.

"Wait," said Amit. He reached down to grab hold of his own aluminum briefcase that was sitting on the floor next to the wall. He lifted it up and placed it on the desk next to Gordienko's briefcase. He opened up the case and removed two wrist bracelets attached to each other by a thin wire. Gordienko immediately recognized the anti-static devices commonly used to protect sensitive electronics. Attached to the center of the connecting wire was another wire about twenty feet in length that had a large alligator clip at the end.

Margolis stood up, walked into the bathroom and attached the clip to the copper pipe under the sink. He returned to his seat and each man wrapped one of the Velcro-secured bracelets around his wrist. The men were now grounded, helping to ensure that their bodies would not build-up an excess number of electrons to be suddenly discharged into the delicate integrated circuit chips they were about to handle.

Margolis reached into his open case and lifted up one pink poly bag with a single integrated circuit chip in it. "I have one hundred and twenty of these, per the terms of your contract," he said. The bag that contained the chip was identical to the sealed bags in Mikhail's case.

"There's a problem."

"What?"

"Well, they ... um," Mikhail said, looking into his case, "gave me a hundred twenty-eight." The Russian looked at Margolis and shrugged his shoulders. "The eight extra were bonus."

"No problem. Just take my one-twenty."

"I can't do that. They gave me an invoice that says they delivered a hundred twenty-eight ICs. They already emailed the invoice to accounting."

Amit Margolis thought for a moment. "I guess we will swap out one twenty and you can keep eight originals."

"I can't think of anything else. Let's do it."

The pair spent the next fifteen minutes carefully substituting 120 legitimate ball grid array chips with perfect forgeries manufactured by Citadel Semiconductors in Migdal Haemek, Israel – complete with the logo of SMIC on the military grade gold/tin alloy packaging lids that sealed the circuits from the elements.

Half way through the process, Gordienko spoke. "How did you pull off the thing with the prototype chips?"

"What, adding the two chips?"

"Yes."

"Not very hard. Intercepting a FedEx package and adding our two chips was no problem. We needed our chips tested alongside the Chinese chips."

"What about the email?"

"What email?"

"SMIC sent an email to our engineers saying they shipped five chips. They copied me and just about everyone else."

"Oh, that." Amit just shrugged his shoulders. "IT nerds. Nothing I understand really."

Gordienko shook his head in amazement. "Do you like what you do? Being a spy? James Bond?"

Amit replied with a harsh look at his friend. He wanted him to know that the question was out of bounds. The Russian returned the look, unwilling to retract his query. Finally Amit stated flatly, "It's a job, Mikhail. Just a job."

When they were done, 120 of the original chips were now in Amit's case and all of the fake Citadel chips plus six originals were in the metallic briefcase of Mikhail Gordienko.

Mikhail left two original SMIC chips on the desk and lifted both of them up between the thumb and forefinger of his left hand to show them to Amit. "You don't know why I left these out, do you?"

Amit did not know. He simply gazed at the Russian with a quizzical look that clearly answered the question.

The Russian smiled and shook his head. "Tsk, tsk. You see Mike, this is the type of detail that gives you away. It's a good thing you and I are partners." Margolis was thinking exactly the same thing. "These will be our 'randomly' selected sacrificial chips. We pick one chip at random per hundred to take apart and put under the microscope. My engineers will scan the circuits to ensure that they are exactly as designed. It is a key part of our certification standards. Of course, the chips are destroyed in the process."

Margolis struggled to maintain his composure. This was the type of oversight that he knew could destroy years of effort. Internally he was cursing himself. At the same time, in that instant, he was certain for the first time that Mikhail Gordienko was fully on his team. "Thank you, Mikhail Andreievich. I am very glad we are on the same side."

Gordienko put the two integrated circuits into a separated area of his aluminum case and closed it.

Amit removed his anti-static wrist bracelet, stood and walked into the bedroom of the suite. He returned with two glasses and a bottle of Moët & Chandon Brut Imperial champagne. "I had room service bring this up earlier today," he said. The bottle was dripping water from the ice bucket it had been in until a moment before. Amit was careful to keep the bottle over the rug.

Gordienko smiled as he peeled the bracelet from his wrist. "You remembered." The tension in his body eased for the first time since he entered the room.

"I don't forget important things, my friend." Amit put the glasses down on the desk, popped the cork and poured some champagne.

Mikhail lifted his glass, no stranger to alcohol consumption. "To your health."

Amit lifted his glass up. "To health."

Amit sipped his champagne in western fashion. Mikhail chugged his beverage in one gulp, returning the glass to the desk top with a relish that announced his Russian heritage.

"Ah, that is good," said the Russian. He looked into Amit's eyes. "Who are you, really?"

"I am Michael Jenkins."

"No. Really."

Amit took another sip and put the glass down. "You know all you need to know about me, my friend. Anything else is counterproductive."

Gordienko lifted the bottle of Moët and filled his glass back up. He took a sip this time. "When can you pay?" The request by the Russian was blunt, much in keeping with his temperament. The offer from Margolis that enticed the Russian to show up at this hotel room was a deal that guaranteed a tidy profit margin for Gordienko's company. Times had been tough, with Russian arms exporters losing a lot of business to American companies in the wake of yet another Russian-supplied military having been easily destroyed by the U.S. Army. The latest victim, Iraq, was the second time in a dozen years that the country had been knocked off. The spectacle of a large paper army trained and supplied by Moscow being so handily defeated by the U.S. with minimal losses made it a hard sell for Russian arms makers in the competitive global marketplace. Gordienko's company, despite its ties into the Kremlin, could not thrive when Russian weapon systems were not selling. The result was that the cash flow of Phase Technologies Corporation, or PTC, was extremely tight and the offer from Margolis had to be considered.

The deal offered by Margolis allowed PTC to aggressively bid as a subcontractor to design dedicated chips for a Tor M-1E surface-to-air missile system being built for the Islamic Republic of Iran. Margolis would guarantee a nice profit for PTC if the company bid for the contract at cost, ensuring a win. Behind the scenes, a Canadian company controlled by "Michael Jenkins" entered into a technology consulting project with PTC that guaranteed a nice profit for no real work. For Gordienko the money was welcome. But the real motivation was the chance to inflict harm on an Islamic nation. He only hoped that whatever the real purpose was for the chips now in his briefcase, it would wreak massive destruction on Iran.

"I will pay you half of what I owe next week. The balance will be paid when the chips are inside the Tor computers."

Gordienko nodded. He was satisfied with the business response, but still far from satisfied with his knowledge of the man across from him. "At least tell me what country. I know you are either American or Israeli or British, but I think American."

"I am Canadian. You have seen my passport many times." Amit smiled at the man he had successfully recruited into the service of Mossad eight months earlier.

"Come on Mike. I deserve to know at least this much. I deserve to know who I am working for right now."

Amit looked out the window. If this same series of questions had occurred in Moscow, he would be very nervous about a setup. In the distance, a rain shower was moving in their direction. "I have friends in Washington. That's as much as I will say."

"American. I knew it."

Amit Margolis smiled. He had not lied to his Russian friend, at least not directly. Disinformation was the ancient art of intelligence agencies and he was an artist. *Seeds*, he thought to himself. *I am planting seeds.*

The chips fabricated by Citadel would soon be on their way to Moscow to be tested, certified and then delivered by Phase Technologies Corporation to Diamond-Alnay Concern, the leading manufacturer of high-technology military equipment in Russia. The chips were destined for the command, control and network integration computers for 29 batteries of the mobile Tor M-1E systems purchased by Iran and scheduled for delivery in early 2007.

The Application Specific Integrated Circuits, or ASIC chips, were subcontracted to a Chinese chip foundry instead of being sourced inside Russia because the Russian government would not let the latest generation of Field Programmable Gate Array chips be sold for export. As designed by PTC, these specific ASIC chips would prohibit the Iranians from using symmetric enciphering keys longer than 110 bits and limit the number of targets that the system could track simultaneously – a safety valve for the remote possibility that the Russian Air Force might someday need to attack Iran, or the more likely risk that Iran might deliver one of these systems to an enemy of Russia. This type of degradation of cutting edge technology was a routine practice of both the U.S. and Russia when selling military hardware. Every country wanted to retain a qualitative military advantage if at all possible.

2 – The Kitchen Cabinet

"Gentlemen, please be seated." These had become the trademark words of Eli Cohen to signal the start of any meeting. He would use this phrase even when, as now, everyone present was already seated. As the long-serving prime minister of Israel, Cohen commanded the full attention and respect of the small gathering. The date was Wednesday, May 20, 2009, and Prime Minister Cohen had just returned from Washington, where he held his first face-to-face meeting in the White House with the new President of the United States. He had no need to tell the men in this room just how poorly that meeting had gone; it had been the only news story occupying Israel's attention for the last three days.

Cohen and the six other men in the room formed Israel's unofficial "Kitchen" Cabinet – the small group that made the most critical decisions facing the tiny nation of almost 6 million Jews and 1.7 million Arabs. The discussions of this group were always important. Sometimes the words being exchanged probed the very issue of Israel's continued existence as a nation-state. Today was one of those days. The sense of isolation for these men was only accentuated by the meter of reinforced concrete that formed the walls and roof of this room in the basement of the prime minister's office building located at 3 Kaplan Street in Jerusalem.

Cohen sat at the head of the conference table and opened a new bottle of water. He averaged about a bottle every hour – three liters over the course of his typically long work days, the end point of a habit started as a young Army sergeant in command of a Sherman tank during the Six Day War. At age 62 he still looked like he would be right at home inside a tank, his strong physique obvious despite his full head of gray hair and the lines that etched deeper on his face during times like this.

The prime minister took a long swig of water. "I will start by saying that my trip was as bad as you are all thinking," he began. "If anything, the headlines understate the problem. The man who came here as a candidate last summer and gave that speech on Iran was just bullshitting for votes. Unfortunately I learned the man's real thoughts on Monday. Frankly, I am not even sure we have an ally in the White House anymore."

A thump interrupted the prime minister's words. Zvi Avner sat two seats to his left. The 56-year-old Israeli defense minister had pounded his fist on the table, a reaction which surprised no one. "We should have gone while Bush was president," he said. "We had the chance in December. I told everybody this. We knew this!"

"Please calm down Zvi," the prime minister responded. "We all know that we had a friend, but we know equally well that he had not yet been convinced that a strike was necessary. And let's face the facts here – we have been floating along and relying upon the U.S. Air Force as our strike force. We do not even have a plan yet. At least not one that, in my opinion, offers the right odds of success without relying upon the Americans. We have to change our thinking and develop a plan that assumes we are acting alone." He paused for a second before adding, "And that works!"

Heads nodded around the room signifying unanimous consent on Cohen's last point. The prime minister understood that his point was uncontroversial. But he also realized that reaching a plan the extended Israeli Cabinet would support and that didn't include the armed forces of the greatest military power on earth would be a great challenge. He was not at all sure he would achieve this goal.

Benjamin Raibani shifted in his chair as he always did when preparing to speak. He sat between Cohen and Avner, a symbolic position for the minister who had no real portfolio to worry about. As the oldest man in the room, Raibani was responsible for imparting wisdom and caution into the discussions and thinking of the Israeli Cabinet, especially when it came to Iran. Without any practical duties, the 71-year-old minister of strategic affairs was free to apply his considerable brain power to any situation without the constraints that come from daily obligations. He had been a friend and confidant of Eli Cohen for more than four decades and there was no secret left unknown between the two men. "Please, Eli, can you summarize where we stand with the Americans and especially the president?"

On a lighter day Cohen would joke about his nickname for Raibani, the "Metronome" – the man who always returned the group to topics at hand and maintained the proper pace. But right now, Cohen welcomed this quality in Raibani. "Yes, you're right. Let me hit the ... well I would say highlights, but in this case the right word is lowlights. First, we have all read the Mossad file on the president. I have to give kudos to the Mossad analyst or analysts who wrote the summary. Now that I have met the man one-on-one, I realize that they were spot on. I made a couple of pages of notes on the flight home that I gave to Ami. I am sure these will help update the profile." Amichai "Ami" Levy was the director of Mossad and, in the mind of Eli Cohen, the most important man in Israel not present in this room at that moment.

The prime minister continued. "I am going to be charitable and refrain from calling the man an anti-Semite, but there is no doubt that he is a product of the decades long tilt toward the Palestinian cause among the academic left in America. I went to Washington hopeful that the weight of the office would overcome his background. I left disappointed. We had the predictable dialogue on the Palestinians." Cohen paused, his eyes staring at nothing, his lip quivered slightly. "No. It was no dialogue. I received a fifteen minute lecture on the importance of a Palestinian state and the ... um ... I am trying to recall the word. Ah, yes, the 'intransigence' of Israel in general and me in particular." Cohen drank more water. "This discussion is not important. After the lecture I defended myself, of course, but then I asked him specifically about Iran. He referred to his CIA reports and told me that Iran was at least three to four years away from a bomb. He stated flatly that he believes that under his administration the U.S. and Iran will be able to negotiate honestly and fairly – these were his words – 'honestly and fairly'. The man is incredibly naïve." Cohen stabbed his finger into the air as he spoke to emphasize his point.

"I tried to nail him down so that I could judge where we stand now. So I asked him a hypothetical. I said 'Mister President, assume the CIA walks into your office tomorrow and tells you that they have absolute proof that the Iranians will have a working bomb in six months. Will you then join us in using military force to remove this program?'" The prime minister took the time to look each man in the room briefly in the eye. He leaned forward in his chair, his right elbow on the table in front of him supporting his weight. His index finger pointed outward to the opposite wall as if facing the President of the United States. "Do you know what that man said to me?" he asked rhetorically. "He said 'you are asking me a hypothetical question. All I can tell you is that it is the policy of the United States to insist that all signatories to the Non-Proliferation Treaty abide by their obligations.'" Eli Cohen was now reliving the moment when he came to the conclusion that Israel stood alone in the world. His face was reddening and everyone in the room could see it. "'If Iran fails in its obligations, then the United States will work with you and all other nations to contain any threat.'"

Cohen leaned further forward, assuming the posture he wished he could have assumed three days earlier with the president. "I replied, 'Mister President, with all due respect, we are not in a theoretical debate at Harvard. We are discussing life and death for eight million Israeli citizens. We are discussing in real terms whether or not the world will stand by as it did in the Thirties while darkness overwhelms the Jewish people. We are discussing the next Holocaust.'" Cohen relaxed slightly, his right arm returning to a rested position on the table. His eyes shifted downward. "Well that man was clearly angered at my tone. And I freely admit that perhaps I was somewhat condescending to the most powerful man on the planet." Cohen offered the hint of a smile, breaking the tension of the moment. The other men in the room all knew Eli Cohen intimately, including his strengths and weaknesses. Some of them even smiled. "All he would say to me in response was something like 'I will continue to review this situation in a rational and restrained manner.' Without saying it directly, the message was clear. This man will not join us in a military strike. We are on our own."

"To hell with him," blurted out Zvi Avner. "What about our friends?"

"To hell with him?" admonished Cohen. "He is the goddamn president. There will be no U.S. military action without his orders."

"And most of our 'friends' worked to get him elected!" the prime minister continued. "Here, I will tell you a story. I had dinner Monday night with Senator Schein of New York. I relayed to him just what I have told you. Maybe I was even more blunt in my view of the motives of this president. He then spent five minutes reassuring me that the president will be a friend of Israel in the long-run and chalked our discussion up to his political inexperience. I don't know, gentlemen. But I think our friends in America are in denial over this guy. I wonder if we have lost American Jews."

The prime minister then spent another ten minutes highlighting his meetings with senior American leaders, both Jew and Gentile. He summed up the situation. "We maintain deep support in the U.S. military and intelligence community. But we have lost the president. And that loss means we are alone in our struggle with Iran, at least when it comes to overt military support. I tell each of you here and now, we will develop a working plan over the next few months that assumes we are alone and addresses every contingency. If the day comes when we must strike Iran, we will have a plan that will succeed. This process starts right now. Zvi, please review the military issues as you see them."

Eli Cohen finally leaned his weight back against his chair. He was no longer red. He had calmed and now was in his analytical mode, his mind focused on the enormous challenge that fell upon his shoulders. He swiveled his chair to reach back to the credenza behind him. Everyone in the room knew what he was reaching for. But for those who would soon be offended, they would suffer in silence as their prime minister indulged his famous addiction. Cohen swiveled back to the conference table. In his right hand he had a cigar cutter. In his left hand he held a Cohiba Espléndidos cigar. He clipped the tip and immediately began rolling the now truncated end between his lips. He placed the cutter on the table and reached into his right pocket to remove a cheap lighter, expertly applying the flame to the far end of the cigar.

The only man in the room comfortable enough to respond stood and took two steps over to the wall, turning on an upgraded air filtration system. The system had been added specifically for this prime minister and these occasions. Benjamin Raibani returned to his seat, rolling his eyes for the amusement of the other men in the room. "I thought you were giving up cigars?"

Cohen exhaled. "That is obviously an Arab disinformation campaign designed to undermine the morale of Israel." Most in the room laughed.

"I hope you at least offered the president one of those," replied Raibani.

"Well, at least he is a smoker. Of course, I could only offer him a cheap Dominican," Cohen answered with a smile, to the bemusement of the room. The prime minister had publicly switched to cigars rolled in the Dominican Republic to avoid offending his American benefactors. The conference room they now occupied was not public.

Zvi Avner cleared his throat. He had not been laughing, his mind fully absorbed by the subject of this meeting. Along with the man seated to his right, Benjamin Raibani, Avner had once served as the chief of staff of the Israeli Defense Force, only more recently than the older Raibani. For the prior three years, Avner had been retired from the military and serving in the Likud Party as a member of the Knesset. He had embraced political life in Jerusalem fully, including indulging himself in the endless cocktail parties and dinners that were the province of the powerful and connected. His waistline reflected his newly adopted lifestyle, no longer the reflection of fitness expected in a senior Israeli military officer. When Cohen asked him to become the minister of defense two months earlier, Avner did not hesitate. It was the post that he had always believed he was uniquely suited for.

"Thank you, Prime Minister." Avner opened a manila folder. He picked up a pen and held it like a drum stick in his right hand. It was a long time mannerism of his that no one could understand or get him to change. He had to have a pen in his hand while he spoke. "You are indeed right that our planning has, unfortunately, been U.S. centric," Avner began. "We have hoped all along to be able to have a strike force led by B-2 Spirit bombers of the U.S. Air Force. They are a unique asset of the United States that we simply cannot reproduce.

"With the U.S. out of the picture, I have to start with a question that this group needs to answer. What is our strategic goal now? Our planning up to now has assumed at least ninety percent destruction of Persian nuclear infrastructure and significant damage to the Persian air defense network, ballistic missile inventory, electrical grid and military command and control." Avner had an odd custom of referring to Iran as Persia and the Iranians as Persians. "Of course, most of this destruction was coming from the American Air Force. So if it is just us alone, I need to know what we are trying to achieve." Avner was talking directly to his boss.

"This is a fair question," Cohen replied. "I am open to discussion on this, but I will say that if we are being realistic then we have to narrow the scope of our goals. First, forget everything other than the nuclear program itself. The question is how do we define success?" No one in the room wanted to step onto that landmine. Prime Minister Cohen scanned the room but wasn't surprised by the silence. "Okay, I will take a crack at it. I say if we go, then we must set back their program by at least a decade. Comments?"

Benjamin Raibani spoke first. "Actually I think that is exactly right. That's what I had in mind."

Avi Gresch, Minister of Foreign Affairs, sat the farthest away from Cohen. He was not a military man, but was a politician with a keen sense of public relations. His response reflected his expertise. "I like it. It makes sense. It will make sense to the rest of the world."

Eli Cohen didn't respect a man without a strong military background. He brushed off the advice despite the fact that it was supportive. "Who else? Yavi?" Unlike his feelings for Gresch, Cohen had tremendous respect for Yavi Aitan, the up and coming star of the Israeli Defense Force.

"It makes sense as a political statement," responded the minister of intelligence and atomic affairs. "We can claim victory if all we do is destroy Natanz and Isfahan. Of course, what it will take to achieve that goal in reality is, in my opinion, something well beyond just destroying those two targets. But we will have to come back to that."

Cohen leaned back in his chair. Once again, the commentary of Yavi Aitan had earned the respect of his boss. "Yes, I think you are right. If no one else objects, then Zvi, you have your strategic objective."

Avner had the green light to proceed. "I will plan for that strategic outcome and let you handle the political aspects," the defense minister said. He paused to review his thoughts. "Everybody here understands the make-up of the IAF." The most professional of the three branches of the Israeli Defense Force, the Israeli Air Force reflected both the tactical history of Israel's wars and the practical realities of Israeli defense budgets. Israel had to defend its existence against a hostile neighboring population of over 145 million Arabs on an annual budget smaller than what the United States spends annually just to care for and support its veterans.

"We have built a potent force designed for fighter superiority and strike missions that are geographically very close to Israel," Avner continued. "Our Air Force excels at fast sortie turn-around. We are ready to confront Hezbollah or the Syrian Army or the Egyptians." Avner waved his pen-loaded hand in the air as he ticked off Israel's adversaries. He knew when he watched the video of Prime Minister Cohen and the U.S. president meeting the press in the White House – and saw the animosity between these two men who should be allies – that this meeting would be about how Israel could destroy the Iranian nuclear program without direct U.S. military support. He had been practicing his speech.

"But none of this represents the tactical challenge posed by Persia. Our targets in Persia average sixteen hundred kilometers distance, each way. We have so far identified over twenty-five targets that must be successfully hit in order to destroy their nuclear program. Of these, most are targets that the IAF can destroy in one sortie. But two of them, Natanz and Fordow, are underground and hardened. These two targets are especially challenging as they both require bunker busting bombs. Plus we expect Persia to increase their tunnel construction as they have done in Isfahan, so time does not help us.

"Layer on top of the size and complexity of the target list, we must assume that the moment we strike, we will face a barrage of missiles from Hezbollah. We estimate their total missile arsenal at close to forty thousand. That compares to about fifteen thousand missiles in their arsenal at the start of the second Lebanon war, during which they fired about forty- two hundred missiles into Israel. If ..."

"Wait now." Benjamin Raibani interrupted. His age, experience and proven wisdom made him the most respected man in the room. His words carried weight that was second only to Cohen's. "That forty thousand number is misleading. Almost all of those are combat missiles or katyushas. How many are real threats?"

"I was going to get to that." The defense minister was not happy. He had been on the pace he had practiced and did not want interruptions. He paused deliberately to express his displeasure. "May I continue?"

"Yes. Of course," replied Raibani.

"Of those, Hezbollah has, by our best intelligence" – Avner looked at a sheet of paper he pulled out of his folder – "two hundred and forty missiles with a range greater than fifty kilometers. That consists of one hundred twenty Fajr-5 missiles with a range of seventy-five kilometers, ten Scud Ds with guidance and a seven hundred kilometer range and, unfortunately, one hundred and ten M-600 missiles. These are Syrian built, use programmed inertial guidance and have a range of just over three hundred kilometers."

"A hundred ten?" Cohen was perplexed and angry as he rhetorically expressed his feelings. "When did this happen? Hell, how did this happen?"

This was the type of discussion Avner feared. "We have only recently identified one hundred of these missiles delivered into the control of Hezbollah by Syria. However, they are stored inside Syria for the time being. We are thinking through options, including a strike similar to the Zelzal operation." Avner was referring to an Israeli commando operation inside Lebanon during 2007 that destroyed an underground storage facility in the Bekaa Valley that had housed 54 Iranian built Zelzal-2 missiles. "This gift from Syria was done to replace those Zelzal missiles. The bad news is that the M-600, which is a Syrian copy of Persia's Fateh-110, is a step up in range and accuracy."

"Gift?" replied Eli Cohen. "That son-of-a-bitch Assad wouldn't give Hezbollah a single bullet unless he was paid by the Iranians. I've read his Mossad file. He has to pay his wife's MasterCard bill." Everyone in the room except Avner laughed.

"Please Mister Prime Minister," implored Zvi Avner. "I have a lot to cover." Cohen waved his cigar in the air, ceding the floor to his colleague. "Thank you." Avner took a breath. "Regardless of the number of long-range missiles, we should assume that Hezbollah will respond when called upon by Persia. They will fire hundreds of missiles daily and the target list this time will include Tel Aviv and maybe even Dimona. I will not go into the state of development of our missile defense systems other than to say we are very happy with the progress of Iron Dome and Arrow 2. But the point is that we will have to launch a ground offensive into Lebanon to stop this barrage when it comes. And we will need to have our strike aircraft available – all of them."

"Aren't they burying everything in Lebanon now?" The question this time came from Yavi Aitan. It was rhetorical. At 42, Aitan was the youngest man in the room and the cerebral whiz kid who earned a PhD in mathematics from MIT when he was only 24. From there he was recruited into Unit 8200, Israel's version of America's National Security Agency. Unit 8200 was growing rapidly and the intelligence and analytical insight of Yavi Aitan immediately stood out even among the outsized brainpower of the organization. Aitan had advanced quickly. On his 32nd birthday, Aitan was transferred from the operational side of Unit 8200 into the managerial side of its parent, the Directorate of Military Intelligence, known as Aman.

Aitan continued to advance rapidly and was promoted to the rank of general in the aftermath of the second Lebanon war, when it was revealed that his correct written assessment of the presence of Iranian anti-ship missiles in Lebanon had been intentionally buried by senior Aman and Israel Defense Force staff officers. When a C-802 missile struck the INS Hanit on July 14, 2006, killing four crew members and nearly sinking the frigate, the strength of Aitan's analysis was revealed and became legendary within the Israeli intelligence community. He was like the Wall Street analyst who predicts the next stock market crash, enduring ridicule until proven right. In the housecleaning that followed the poorest showing ever by the IDF, Aitan had been elevated to prominence. Eli Cohen immediately became a fan of the penetrating mental capabilities of General Aitan and had only him in mind when time came to name a new minister of intelligence and atomic affairs.

"Yes. Hezbollah is turning Lebanon into a big bunker network," Avner responded. "It was bad three years ago. It is getting worse all the time now."

"So we will need to significantly upgrade our bunker buster munitions in both quality and quantity." Aitan had beaten the defense minister to his point.

"Yes, I will get to that. Now, let me state the obvious about our tactical situation." Avner felt like he was going to punch the next person who interrupted him, an action that would not be entirely out of character. "The planning for a Persian strike has to assume that we have one full-out sortie to achieve our strategic goal because as soon as those aircraft return to Israel, we will need them in Lebanon and Gaza. I have to assume that Hamas will join in with everything they have. In addition, I cannot be prudent without at least planning for the possibility that Syria, at the behest of Persia, will attack – even if it is just an attempt to retake the Golan Heights."

Aitan was compelled to respond. "Based on our sources, Basher Assad is very unlikely to take overt military action."

Avner was expecting this comment. "That may be the case and we all hope that it will be the case. But I do not have the luxury of making that assumption. The point is that if Syrian units start to move while we are simultaneously dealing with Hezbollah and Hamas, the air force will be fully engaged with virtually zero reserve. It will be the same situation as the Six Day War. From the perspective of the IAF, we are all-in once we strike Persia. This has been our working assumption and our planning to date. We would be intimately involved in the first strike, especially suppressing Persian air defense. Then the Americans would drop the heavy hardware, leaving us free to deal with our neighbors."

Eli Cohen blew a cloud of cigar smoke toward the center of the table. "You made your point Zvi. What are you driving at?"

This was the question Avner was waiting for. "Look, just because the Americans are out of the equation doesn't change anything for us. We have the exact same tactical considerations. We have one sortie for the IAF over Persia and then they have to be available right here to deal with the fallout.

"Here are the practical challenges. First, we have two primary targets now and a third emerging rapidly. Isfahan we can destroy with conventional bombing – although the Iranians have added a tunnel complex at Isfahan that is a secondary target. Natanz is underground and hardened. Now we have this site north of Qom under construction and I am assuming that we will have to deal with it too. The weapon we are relying on to penetrate and destroy these targets is the American GBU-28, which is seven and a half meters long and weighs over two thousand kilograms. We only have one airplane that can deliver it: the F-15I Ra'am. We can modify them to carry two bombs each, but we lose the central external fuel tank in the process. We have twenty-five Ra'ams, so we can deliver fifty of these bombs in the first sortie assuming one hundred percent mission availability."

Yavi Aitan jumped in. "We have the plans for Fordow in some detail." He was using the name for the site north of Qom that would soon become widely known. He was not aware of it, but he was about to help Avner make the point he was really vectoring toward. "They are building two underground complexes that are twenty-two and a half kilometers apart. The main complex has an underground chamber that is a rectangle one hundred fifty-seven by ninety-six meters. It is designed with a primary and secondary enrichment hall and what we think is a fabrication room to convert highly enriched uranium from the cascades into uranium dioxide powder and then into uranium tetraflouride, or green salt.

"This room could include machinery to convert green salt into metallic form," Aitan continued, "but if they go that route, it will be a tight fit. They would have to bring in kilns to melt the green salt and fuse it with magnesium. To accomplish that they will need to add a lot of ventilation that is not reflected in their plans. Also, there is a smaller room that could have several possible uses, including storage of depleted uranium hexafluoride, or storage of highly enriched uranium dioxide or green salt, or even warhead storage. Plus they have a separate processing hall which is being built above ground but will probably be buried in the future. This hall will receive shipments of uranium hexafluoride that is enriched up to twenty percent. The hall will have an autoclave to heat granular hexafluoride into gaseous form and feed it through piping directly into the centrifuge cascades in the main chamber.

"Interestingly, the plans show that the secondary enrichment hall, which is designed for less than three thousand centrifuges, will be separated from the rest of the rooms by a thick wall. My guess is that the secondary hall is for inspection purposes if they have to let in the IAEA." Aitan referred to the International Atomic Energy Agency, the organization that oversees publicly declared nuclear programs on behalf of the United Nations.

"Why do you say that?" asked Raibani.

"Because the main complex has six entrances into the mountain which funnel into three openings into the chamber," Aitan replied. "All three openings are into the secondary enrichment hall area. The main chamber is separated by a wall that has a couple of openings that look like they will be hidden. So call it an educated guess. Does that answer your question?"

Raibani nodded.

"The primary enrichment hall is designed for 8,856 centrifuges."

"What about this second complex you mentioned?" asked the prime minister. "How long have we known about this?"

"Well, we learned about the second complex when we obtained the engineering plans in September 2007. I have discussed the second complex before," Aitan answered.

"With me?"

"Yes, sir. Right here in this room."

Cohen shrugged his shoulders. "I must have misunderstood what you were saying." He placed his cigar between his lips to inhale the smoke.

"I apologize for any lack of clarity. The second complex is six kilometers southwest of Manzariyeh Airport. It is on the northern edge of the Baqarebad military complex, built by Iran to store missiles and warheads. The tunnel complex here was originally dug out ten years ago to store important government documents. But the new plans are for a smaller version of complex one. My guess is this is intended to be the final warhead fabrication, assembly and storage facility, but it could just be a back-up to complex one. To date, we haven't seen any construction, but the plans call for a tripling in the size of the underground chamber."

"What is the timing for each complex to come online?" asked the defense minister, making sure his unwitting surrogate made the right points.

"Their focus is on the first complex and we estimate construction and the placement of centrifuges to be completed in about eighteen months. The second complex is clearly a low priority for them. Our best guess is that they are waiting to begin real work on it after they are finished with the first."

"How deep is the first complex?" continued Avner.

"Well, the entrances are all at the nine hundred twenty meter contour line." Aitan raised his left hand up in the air. His fingers were straight and his palm was face down and parallel to the table. "The floor of the main chamber is eight hundred and eighty-six meters above sea level." He dropped the level of his hand a few inches to visualize the drop in altitude from the entrances to the level of the chamber. "The finished height of the chamber is four meters. The minimum amount of earth above the chamber is the point over the southwest corner. At that point, there is fifty-two meters of volcanic basalt. Fordow is part of a geological formation known as the Oromeieh-Dokhtar belt. It is the end result of ancient volcanic flows." Aitan had no notes. All of the information was stored in his head. Everyone in the room knew that if Yavi Aitan read it once and committed it to memory, then the information would be locked away as if on a hard drive.

Aitan turned his face to look at Avner. The younger man continued. "That depth is equal to one hundred fifty-five feet of earth at a minimum at the southwest corner. The maximum depth to reach the chamber is seventy-eight meters, or two hundred fifty-seven feet of basalt rock above the primary enrichment hall. If I recall correctly, the GBU-28 can penetrate, at best, only one hundred twenty feet of earth. And that assumes the bomb is dropped from at least fifty thousand feet."

"How long?" The words were in the direct style of Benjamin Raibani. The metronome was ticking again.

"Eighteen months as …" Aitan was cut off again.

"No," Raibani interjected. "Once they have Fordow operational, how long to get to ninety percent enrichment?"

Yavi Aitan pursed his lips. "That depends. Let me make a couple of assumptions." Aitan pivoted his left forearm upward from the table on its elbow. He stuck his thumb upward. "First, assume that they enrich to twenty percent at Natanz, which I must point out they have not yet done to our knowledge." Aitan extended his left forefinger. "Second, assume that we are right on the number of centrifuges inside Fordow and that they are all operational." Aitan extended his middle finger. "Third, assume they are using their first generation centrifuges inside Fordow, what they call the IR-1. This last assumption is key and is in our favor. The IR-1 is not very efficient." Aitan extended his next finger, his pinky finger now struggling to stay folded. "And finally, assume that they have a reasonably advanced implosion design that only needs twenty kilograms of ninety percent uranium."

Raibani interjected. "How do you know the efficiency of their centrifuges?"

"Well, we have a lot of data on Natanz from both the IAEA and other sources. We know the statistics for the amount of base feedstock, the product, which has been three point five percent enriched uranium and the tail. We have even been able to get some of the tailings from Natanz to Dimona for analysis." Aitan paused. The look in Raibani's eyes asked the question that he didn't need to verbalize. "Excuse me, I am hanging around with too many nuclear scientists and physicists these days. The tailings are the depleted uranium byproduct of the enrichment process.

"In a nutshell, you start with natural uranium ore which is ninety-nine point three percent uranium 238 and only seven-tenths percent of uranium 235. For a weapon, you want uranium enriched to about ninety percent uranium 235. At Natanz, they use gas centrifuges which spin uranium molecules at a high speed. The heavier 238 molecules migrate to the outside of the centrifuge tubes and the lighter 235 molecules migrate toward the center of the tube. You then collect the separated molecules. The enriched 235 molecules are sent downstream and the depleted 238 molecules are sent back to repeat the process. Eventually the depleted uranium 238 is no longer needed and sent to storage in steel drums. This is the tail."

Aitan glanced at Zvi Avner. The defense minister very subtly rolled his finger, letting Aitan know to speed things up. Aitan returned to the immediate question. "With those assumptions, if the Iranians start with one hundred twenty kilograms of twenty percent enriched uranium, they can produce twenty kilograms of ninety percent uranium inside Fordow in less than a month." Yavi Aitan let that sink in for a moment. "If they can upgrade their centrifuges as they are trying hard to do – and we are trying hard to keep them from doing – the process inside Fordow would take under a week." The room was quiet, each man's thoughts lost in a different scenario. But each scenario had the same bad ending.

Aitan then added an exclamation point. "Keep in mind that it takes a lot more work to enrich raw uranium to twenty percent than to enrich from twenty to ninety percent. That is a simple mathematical consequence of how much uranium you are dealing with at each step in the process. I can illustrate this best by working backwards. You need about twenty kilograms of ninety percent U-235 for a warhead. To get that, you need to start with about one hundred twenty kilograms or so of twenty percent U-235. To get those one hundred twenty kilograms, you need to start with about four thousand kilograms of three point five percent U-235. And to get those four thousand kilograms, you need to start with at least twenty thousand and as much as twenty-six thousand kilograms of natural uranium, depending on the efficiency of your facility."

Aitan paused briefly, allowing time for everyone to run the math through their heads. Then he continued. "Once Iran starts to enrich to twenty percent, which I expect to occur in the near future, I become very worried about their ability to break-out from there. At twenty percent, they will have done the hardest part of the enrichment process."

Zvi Avner suppressed a smile. This was going better than he planned. "Thank you, Yavi. As usual, you have summarized the situation perfectly. We are indeed counting on the GBU-28, which I think everyone here knows has not yet been delivered to us." Avner had returned to the script that was running through his mind. "But even if we had it in our inventory, it's not capable of destroying Fordow. So when the Persians bring Fordow online in eighteen months or less, they are immune. We cannot destroy Fordow."

Avner paused for effect before continuing. "We have been working with the Americans and independently to enhance the penetrating power of the GBU-28 with the use of depleted uranium and an alloy in the head of the bomb. But it appears the best that we will do is add about five meters.

"However, there is a new weapon the Americans are working on. They call it the massive ordinance penetrator, or MOP. Officially it's the GBU-57 and it's a beast. It weighs almost fourteen thousand kilograms and will penetrate the Fordow facility without a problem. It was first tested two years ago. But there is a hitch. We don't have a bomber that can carry it. This …"

Cohen spoke up. "This is why the president politely refused to sell us this bomb. He said that since we don't have the airplane that can deliver it, he couldn't approve the sale to us." Cohen simply shook his head as he thought about it. "The only good news is that I did get him to agree to accelerate the delivery of GBU-28s to us. God willing, we will finally receive these bombs sometime this summer."

Avner was thinking of his next sentence when Cohen added another thought. "But I should be fair to the president. We discussed Fordow and he did agree to publicly reveal the site later this year if the next round of Geneva negotiations fail." There was brief laughter which Cohen couldn't ignore. "Hey, maybe we will get lucky and the president will be able to call me a putz."

Raibani could not restrain his sarcasm this time. "And maybe Ahmadinejad will convert to Judaism."

"Better chance of that, I think," replied Cohen.

"So let me summarize our situation," Zvi Avner continued. The pen in his hand slashed through the stale haze of the prime minister's Cohiba cigar. "We have four primary targets and another two dozen secondary targets. Three of the primary targets all have underground components. We are relying on a weapon we do not yet have for the underground targets and even if we had this weapon, it will only work for sure against one of the three targets on our list. We face an integrated air defense network that will need to be suppressed in the first wave. The combination of air defense suppression and the number of targets means we will need virtually all of our F-15 and F-16 aircraft for the first sortie. Even with this, as we sit here now, we do not have a way to destroy Fordow or the Isfahan tunnels. In fact, we cannot destroy Natanz today – not until we get the GBU-28s delivered from the United States.

"By the time our air force returns to its bases in Israel, there will be rockets landing all over the country, including Tel Aviv. The people will be screaming for action against Hezbollah and Hamas. The cry will be even louder than three years ago. And even if you assume that we can go back to Persia for another sortie, this impacts our planning considerably. We have the ability to shut down the Persian air defense network in a way that leaves me confident for the first sortie, especially if we achieve tactical surprise. But the turnaround time is at best five hours. In those five hours, the Persians will regroup. They will repair anything we have done to them that they can repair and they will have units on alert that were asleep during round one. This means that when we go back, I will have to dedicate more aircraft to air defense suppression than during the first wave. With the loss of tactical surprise, I will have a much wider set of targets to deal with that have nothing to do with their nuclear program. I am saying that in the second wave we will be focused on airfields and C-two nodes that we can ignore if we are only over Persia one time. This will be the entire effort. So two times means we have to go back more times. In fact, if the plan from the start is that we are going to Persia more than once, it changes what we will do on the first sortie. The first wave will have to overwhelmingly be geared to suppression and destruction of the defense network and C-two.

"As if that is not bad enough, I will point out the obvious if you are not already ahead of me. Every time we have to go back, we have to overfly at least two of our close Arab allies. How exactly do you think that will go over?" Avner answered his own question. "It is one thing for the Saudis to claim that they didn't pick us up on radar as we send four hundred planes over Persia, but I am quite sure that they will not be able to make that claim the second time around."

It was Raibani who finally jumped in. "Your point is well made, Zvi. I have to say that the last issue is absolutely right. Politically, the Jordanians and Saudis won't be able to make excuses for inaction more than once. And that assumes that the U.S. Air Force will be conveniently quiet as we fly – something that never concerned me until hearing today about the attitude of the new president."

Avner nodded his head. He knew from experience that if he had sold Benjamin Raibani, then the prime minister was sold. And if the prime minister was sold, then the rest of the Kitchen Cabinet would be on board. "The reality is that to obtain our strategic objective we need multiple sorties," Avner continued. "But we are clearly constrained to just one initial sortie."

"So what are you saying?" Eli Cohen asked.

"I am saying, Mister Prime Minister, that we cannot achieve our strategic objective without the United States Air Force."

3 – The Nuclear Option

"I can't accept this," said Mordechai Yaguda to the rest of the Kitchen Cabinet. Yaguda was a career politician, the scion of a famous politician from the founding of the country. At six-foot-three-inches, he was the tallest man in the room and carried himself in a manner that reflected his education at Cambridge and then Yale. The 59-year-old minister without a portfolio was a fixture in Israeli cabinets. His wife was 20 years his junior and a former model. The pair formed a power couple that spent as much time in the U.S. and Europe lobbying for Israel as they did in their home in Tel Aviv. He was the type of man everyone wanted to be friends with and he made a nice income serving on the boards of numerous public companies in the U.S. and Israel. His friends called him Mort. "Why are we limiting the first strike planning to only the IAF?" Yaguda asked. He looked around the room, eager for support.

"What do you mean?" asked Cohen.

"Can we airlift troops into Iran? Can't we take Fordow with troops and blow it up? Don't we need to get creative here?"

All eyes turned to the defense minister. "Well, Mort, this is something I have given a lot of thought to," Avner replied. "Let me hand out the current strike summary." Avner opened his manila folder and handed out six pieces of paper, each a copy of the summary page of the current state of planning for a strike on Iran's nuclear program. "This assumes that we have the GBU-28. But this still doesn't do anything with Fordow."

Raibani now offered his opinion. "It seems to me that we have two options. We can go now before they finish Fordow or we can put soldiers on the ground in Iran to seize Fordow and destroy it. There is a large salt lake just north of the site. I'm sure we could land C-130s there. We go in, blow it up and kill everyone we find. Then we get out. It's Entebbe on a larger scale."

"We have been racking our brains on this," Avner replied. "This is very high risk. We know the Persians have thought of this." In fact, Avner had been expecting this line of discussion and was prepared. "Yavi, please update everyone on the state of Persian ground defenses at Fordow."

"Sure." Yavi Aitan leaned forward in his chair as he gathered his thoughts. "Keep in mind that Fordow is an old military base and they have a small number of security troops based there. But that is changing rapidly. The Iranians have moved some command units and advance elements of the Mohammad Rasulollah Corps to Fordow. That is the premier Pasdarin unit, the Iranian Revolutionary Guards. It has the best equipment and training and is the largest of the thirty-two Pasdarin corps that are maintained. The Iranians are currently building housing and support facilities for a portion of this unit. The unit has a little over four thousand troops. We don't yet know how much of the unit will move to Fordow, but we expect at least a full battalion. We think they will keep at least half the unit in Tehran, including its headquarters. But that is just a guess at this point. The Rasulollah Corps also has indigenous armored units, including twenty-eight T-72 tanks and fifty-eight BMP ones and twos. The bad news is that we think all of their armor will be moved to Fordow.

"Also, within three hours' notice the Iranians can deploy a number of first-line Artesh units down from Tehran, including the 65th Airborne Special Forces Brigade. Artesh is regular army. In Qom, which is only an hour away, they have the Ali Ibn Abi Talib Corps, another premier Pasdarin unit, probably second only to the Rasulollah Corps. These units may not be on par with comparable IDF units head to head, but they are highly motivated fighters who will be defending their home turf. To underestimate any of these units would be a dangerous mistake."

Avner jumped in to hammer home the point. "You don't have to be a career officer to know that our troops would need to fight their way into Fordow and then fight their way back to any extraction point." Avner was looking at Avi Gresch and Mort Yaguda. "We would have to figure out how to give our soldiers close air support. My assessment is that, assuming we have tactical surprise, we will probably be able to fight our way in and we might even successfully blow the chamber. But we will never fight our way back out. In my professional opinion, this would be a suicide mission."

The room was quiet. Eli Cohen extinguished his cigar. This was the moment Avner had been waiting for. The defense minister cleared his throat. "There is a way to make this work," he said. Cohen knew what was coming next. A week earlier, he and Avner had a heated discussion in private about this issue. Ben Raibani had already guessed Avner's destination. But no one wanted to touch the topic, so Avner had free rein. "A low yield nuclear warhead could be attached to a GBU-28. We have been working on the design and I ..."

"Insanity." The voice was loud and powerful. Benjamin Raibani stood as he spoke the word. "The State of Israel would come to this? Becoming the first nation in sixty-five years to use a nuclear weapon in anger? If you think we are a pariah nation now, we will be absolutely alone."

Cohen pondered stepping in but Raibani was saying what needed to be heard. Raibani was exactly the right man to react to Avner's trial balloon. The Holocaust survivor – the only one in the room – continued. "I will not be party to such a decision. We will be viewed as the new Nazi state. This would galvanize the Arab world and we would lose even our hardcore Jewish support in America. We will have won the war and lost our souls in the process. And the future of Israel will be sealed." His lips were quivering. It was the level of rage he was known for while he was a general but that had softened in the intervening years.

Raibani started to sit down, confident he had correctly punctuated his points. Half way through the motion, he abruptly stood again and looked down at Cohen to his right. "If you go forward with this, Mister Prime Minister, you will have my resignation in the morning." He sat down in his chair.

At the far end of the table, Avi Gresch was emboldened by witnessing the side of Raibani he had never seen before. "And mine as well," he stated, looking at Avner not Cohen.

These types of threats were not unusual in politics and Cohen was not surprised. But he wanted to stop this thought process before emotion became the only deciding force in the room. As he had done earlier, he raised his left hand and motioned, palm down, for everyone to be calm. His voice was calm. "I appreciate your views, Ben. But I am not sure I agree with your conclusions. You are free to follow your conscience and I respect that. Of course, if you choose to resign, we will need to devise an appropriate cover story." The prime minister was calling Raibani's bluff. He knew the man and he knew that Benjamin Raibani had to be in this room and in the middle of this process while the State of Israel was discussing its very survival. As for Avi Gresch, Cohen didn't care what he did and never gave him a thought.

"But before any decision is made," Cohen continued, "what I want now is to have a rational discussion among this group of the pros and cons of this path. I will start. Ben, you have passionately stated the downside. I cannot deny that this would galvanize the Arab street and severely hurt us with our allies. But I make the following points in favor: First, we need to strike every target on that list and destroy each one, especially Isfahan, Natanz, Arak and Fordow. Second, we have a high chance of evading Iranian air defenses on the first strike, but every return visit will put us at higher risk and we will suffer ever greater losses. And that is not to mention the political issues of overflight." He gave a nod toward his defense minister. "Third, it appears to me that to destroy Natanz and Isfahan with its tunnel complex will require most, if not all, of our Ra'ams. So if we need to use GBU-28s elsewhere, it will be difficult. Fourth, we don't have a weapon to destroy Fordow. Even if we can get one or two of this new bomb – what was it, the mop?" Avner nodded. "We don't have a plane that can deliver it. Fifth, we could probably get troops into Fordow – I was thinking along the lines of a commando team infiltrated in – but I have to agree with Zvi. The odds of getting them home afterwards are very low. Sixth, when we go, we will face a massive barrage of rockets from Lebanon and from Gaza. So the army will need to be ready and it will need the IAF to support it. Seventh, the worst thing that can happen is to go and to fail to destroy their nuclear program. Eighth, using tactical nuclear weapons ensures that we will obliterate the primary targets. Ninth, we have the total support of every Arab leader other than Assad. Tenth, we will suffer losses in the retaliation. Our cities will be hit and our civilians will be killed. This will create sympathy. If we have a PR campaign ready to go, we will survive the initial onslaught of bad press."

Benjamin Raibani was not the only one in the room to cringe in reaction to Cohen's last point – it was simply too cold and calculating. But Raibani was the clear leader of the faction against this idea. He was now calm and ready to embrace this analytical challenge. "I can understand your point and I agree with the military issues. But when you suggest that a public relations campaign is all we need to overcome the fallout from this, then I tell you as my friend and my prime minister – with all due respect – that you are one hundred percent wrong. The moment the world hears that we have used a nuclear weapon for anything other than retaliation, we will be completely alone.

"I will make a prediction, the president will, if we give him time, come around to support us. Why? Not because he will become your friend. Not because of A-I-pac." Raibani was referring to the American Israel Public Affairs Committee, the strongest pro-Israel lobby in America. "Not because he will become buddies with Lieberman or Dershowitz or any other Jew. But because the majority of Americans are on our side. But I tell you that the day we initiate the use of nuclear weapons, regardless of the reason, is the day the vast majority of Americans turn against us. And that is the day we lose the support of the U.S. And when we lose the U.S., Israel is doomed."

Eli Cohen drank more water and let the wisdom of Raibani wash over him. His old friend was wise and he was persuasive. It was the reason Raibani was in the room. Cohen thought about the point Raibani could have made and didn't. The America that will react to Israel's first use of nuclear weapons will be led by the president he had been sitting with three days earlier.

Zvi Avner could see the tide turning in Cohen's mind. He added his voice. "Okay, now I will review some facts. Persia's program is massive. Once all of Natanz and Fordow is up and running, it is designed to create enough highly enriched uranium for up to ten warheads a year. They will soon have Arak online and producing plutonium. They are building ballistic missiles with greater range and greater accuracy. They are gearing up for a huge arsenal. And we all know that the Saudis will not stand by and watch this happen. They will start their own program. And we will re-start our warhead program. This is going to be a massive nuclear arms race in a part of the world that – let's be honest here – only pauses to catch its breath between wars.

"And there will only be one sure loser in this equation. Ben, you say we are doomed when we lose American opinion. Well I say we are doomed when Persia has a nuclear arsenal and the missiles to deliver them. For me, this is easy. Under your version of being doomed, we have to suffer the slings and arrows of nasty editorials – my apologies to Shakespeare. Under my version of being doomed, we will be nuked. I, for one, would rather deal with being a world pariah for a year or two than be the defense minister of Israel when Tel Aviv and Haifa are nuked into oblivion.

"And don't sit here and tell me about mutually assured destruction and deterrence. Yes, we can nuke all of Persia into fused silicate, but every man in this room understands who Ahmadinejad is. Everyone has read his profile. Mossad's conclusions are clear – and I agree with them. When that man has nuclear weapons, he will push to use them. Okay, maybe today Khamenei would stop him. But what about tomorrow? Everyone in this room should read about the Twelfth Imam believers. This guy is nuts and to sit here and let him get nuclear weapons when we can stop him is criminal." Avner stopped. The arguments had been well made by both sides.

Once again the prime minister filled the void. "Thank you, Zvi. I think there is a lot of passion on both sides of this argument and that is how it should be. Now I need to use the rest room. Let's take five minutes." Prime Minister Cohen stood and walked out of the room.

4 - Decisions

Exactly fourteen minutes later, Zvi Avner was the last man to return to the conference room. Cohen spoke up as he massaged a new cigar. "Are we all here now? Okay, we have more to cover today. Let me start by saying that this decision ultimately rests on my shoulders and I accept that. However, I want to have a consensus among this group. I don't expect that to happen today or tomorrow, but I would like to continue to have this option available in our planning."

Benjamin Raibani was thinking and close to speaking. Cohen read his mind and cut him off by continuing. "We need time. Time to plan. Time to obtain all the weapons we need. I think everyone here will agree that all covert efforts will be undertaken and accelerated to slow down their program."

Heads nodded in agreement. Danny Stein spoke up for the first time. "How do we gain time, if I may ask?" Stein, the 60-year-old minister of industry, trade and labor, was respected in the group. He had spent more than a decade in the military before a successful career as an executive of Israeli Military Industries. He was the rare person who moved comfortably through the halls of politics, the military and the private sector. He had been decorated for his command of an infantry company during fighting in the Golan Heights during the Yom Kippur War. His performance during that war had made his subsequent career, just as those men who faltered under combat were often ruined in Israel. He had been wounded by shrapnel from a mortar round, a wound that caused him to limp slightly the rest of life. The nation was in a perpetual state of war and relationships and respect were earned through blood on the battlefield.

"Ah, good question," Cohen answered. "Not everything went wrong with the president. We discussed Olympic Games. He gave it the green light to continue. We ..."

"Excuse me, Mister Prime Minister. What is Olympic Games?" asked Danny Stein.

"I'm sorry, Danny. Operation Olympic Games was begun about two years ago. I guess now is the time to talk about it. Only myself, Zvi, Ben and Yavi know about it. Yavi, you want to provide an overview?"

Yavi Aitan shifted forward in his seat. "Yes. Let me start by giving a little context. As was probably clear from our earlier discussion, there are a couple of key choke points in the Iranian program. The most important choke point is that they have to enrich uranium. There are a number of ways to do that, but Iran uses just one: gas centrifuges. These are not terribly complex devices, but they have to be built to fairly precise tolerances. The faster they spin, the more efficient they are. The rotor – the tube inside the centrifuge that is spinning – in a good modern centrifuge is made of carbon fiber. If, like Iran, you don't have access to the right quality of carbon fiber, you have use a metal like aluminum. But for reasons I am not going to get into now, aluminum tubes need internal support. The support comes in the forms of rings of an alloy known as maraging steel. This is what the Iranians are using in their IR-1s and what they will probably use in the next generation centrifuges they are working on. There is a lot we are doing to keep them from getting maraging steel. But that is another discussion."

Around the room, the three men who knew nothing about Operation Olympic Games were devoted to Aitan's words. The minister of intelligence and atomic affairs looked at his prime minister. Cohen could tell that Aitan was not comfortable expanding the group of people who knew about Olympic Games, known inside Israel under the codename Operation Myrtus, even when it was three of the most senior members of Israeli government. Cohen spoke to reassure his young minister. "Go ahead Yavi."

"About two years ago we were approached by the Americans," continued Aitan. "They had an idea that was, well, inspirational. They suggested a computer virus – a worm – that can secretly take control of the software that controls the centrifuges at Natanz. They agreed to fund the project if we accepted responsibility for getting the worm into the right computers in Iran. It took a while to research and design, but about eighteen months ago a team began writing code." He paused and exhaled noticeably. "How do I describe this? All centrifuges are controlled by computer. In the case of Iran, the controlling program is written by Siemens. The ..."

"Goddamn Germans," exclaimed Mort Yaguda involuntarily.

"Yes. Well, anyway, the Americans led the effort to write a new code for the Siemens controller. We led the effort to write the code necessary to inject the software into the Iranian network, look for the right computers, propagate and hide. The software is designed to cause early failure of their centrifuge rotors and related parts, such as the motor. At the same time, it sends signals to the monitor stations that tell them that everything is running fine. By the way, Mort, the Germans cooperated with the Americans on this project." Yaguda just shook his head.

Aitan continued. "The Americans tested the software inside the United States on exact replicas of the IR-1 centrifuge. The process creates extraordinary stress on the rotors and takes a couple of months, but I can tell you that it works. If the rotor cracks or the spinning motor on the IR-1 fails, the unit is trash and has to be replaced. Our job – that is the job of Mossad – is to introduce this virus into the right computers in Iran. Unit 8200 is responsible for the coding. This project is known as Operation Myrtus here. We have made some test runs on early versions, but the real worm was finished up this winter. We will start straight away now that we have a green light from the new president."

"Assuming we can get this virus onto the right computers, what do we expect to happen?" Avi Gresch asked.

"As of last week, there were three thousand nine hundred and thirty-six centrifuges operational inside Hall A at Natanz and another eight thousand under construction. We expect most of the centrifuges under construction to become operational by the end of summer. We hope that our worm will also be in place and fully operational by the end of summer. If all goes well, we will destroy every operational centrifuge before the end of the year. Ami Levy is very confident of the ability of Mossad to get this worm onto the right computers."

"How will we know if this worked?" asked Gresch.

"So far, the Iranians are allowing continued IAEA access to Natanz. But even if that changes, we have sources," Aitan responded.

"This seems like a long shot. What else are we doing?" The question came from Danny Stein this time.

"Let me tell you that this software virus is like nothing ever unleashed before. It is very sophisticated and it targets only the software that controls the Iranian centrifuges. So like Director Levy, I am also confident. As for other activities, we are active on many fronts. This includes an extensive program to cut off their access to maraging steel for new centrifuges, killing any scientist working on the program that we can get to, and good old-fashioned sabotage. We have a close relationship with the CIA and MI6 in these activities."

"How much time can we gain with all of this?" asked Stein.

Aitan exhaled loudly. "Impossible to tell, really. The most promising outcome is combining Myrtus with our activities to reduce their ability to build new centrifuges. Look, it isn't realistic that we will destroy all of their current centrifuges, but I think we have a real chance to destroy a third to half of them. If we do that over the next year and we can slow down their construction of new units, we can set them back a couple of years."

"That's best case scenario, right?"

"Well, best case may be longer, but I think that I am giving you an achievable scenario. We will know this year whether or not it has worked and to what extent."

There was a brief pause in the room which the prime minister decided to end. "Okay, gentlemen. I have meetings coming up and I would like to leave here with some consensus. We are, after all, here to make decisions." Cohen took time to drink some water. "I'll tell you what, I have a timing question of my own. What is the time it will take us to be in a position to go? To strike Iran." He pointed to his defense minister.

Zvi Avner drummed his pen on the manila folder still open in front of him. "Honestly, that's a tough question. We don't have a plan and we don't have the weapons we need. If the president comes through with delivery of the GBU-28s and we come up with a viable plan, we still need time to train and get our forces in position. If the plan is complex, we need more time, etcetera. I don't know."

Cohen was not happy with that non-response. "Off the record. Okay, Zvi? I want some type of timeline to work against. What is the fastest we could pull the trigger?"

Avner was not happy with being penned down. He was a career military man who had the necessary political instincts to rise to chief of staff of the IDF. His time in government since leaving that role had only sharpened his political skills. "If you are telling me this is guideline only and not for the record, I think we could be ready to go around year end if a plan is agreed to this summer and if the weapons we need are ready by the fall. I can also tell you that winter time is not when we will go, so the realistic answer is that the earliest we can go is next spring."

Cohen looked to his immediate left to get the opinion of the other ex-chief of staff of the IDF in the room. Ben Raibani was not as reticent. He did not worry about politics. "I think Zvi is in the right ballpark. I would only add that with the U.S. out of the equation, being ready by next spring is going to be a monumental task. This plan will require a lot of thought and then a lot more introspection. After that we will need to prepare and to train. After that we need to rehearse. And then rehearse more. I would say eighteen months, but that puts us back into the wrong season. I agree with Zvi. This is a spring or summer event."

Cohen just shook his head. "You guys sound like old men. Maybe we should look into testosterone pills. Maybe some Viagra." Eli Cohen wasn't happy and no one around the table was amused. The prime minister's reaction was knee-jerk. He rubbed his forehead as he looked down at the ashtray in front of him. Raibani recognized this body language as capitulation on the part of his boss. "Sorry guys. It's been a long few days and right now I am probably even a bigger son-of-a-bitch than usual.

"Okay, we need to take this a step at a time. Zvi, I would like for you to return here with the outlines of two plans. The key assumption for each plan is that we are alone. But one will assume we use only conventional weapons and the other will, as a contingency, assume we use nuclear weapons. When can you be ready?"

"No," uttered Ben Raibani as he shook his head, not allowing Avner time to respond.

"Ben, you do not agree?" asked the prime minister.

"No, I do not. I have been watching and participating in military and government planning in this country for too long. If we have a contingency plan, it means we will work to build this tactical nuclear device. Of course, we will do so just for the sake of contingency. But if we have the plan and the device, we will use it. I cannot support planning for something that we cannot and we must not do."

Eli Cohen had hoped to skip past Raibani's resistance, but had instead ignited a furious ten minute debate – really an argument – between two clear factions. The argument was ostensibly about the wisdom of creating a contingency plan, but that was a thin veil. Everyone knew exactly what the discussion was about. As before, Zvi Avner led the arguments in favor with support from his prime minister. Ben Raibani led the arguments against with support from Avi Gresch and an increasingly vocal Danny Stein. Everyone found themselves talking to Mort Yaguda, who was clearly undecided, as if he were the swing vote.

Finally Eli Cohen turned to Yavi Aitan, who had been silently absorbing each argument, his mind processing the issues a dozen steps into the future. "Yavi, you have kept quiet. What do you think?"

Aitan once again leaned forward in his chair. The youngest man in the room had just been vested by his prime minister with tremendous authority. "I think that Iran with nuclear weapons is catastrophic. I think that the State of Israel nuking them may be worse. Ben is right, if we use a nuclear weapon first, we will lose all support and our tiny country will stand utterly alone. I have come to learn and appreciate much in the seat that I currently have the honor to occupy. One thing I have learned is that the last thing I want to see happen is for us to lose the support of the American military and intelligence community." Aitan was looking directly at his boss. "I am sorry Mister Prime Minister, but I have been thinking through how using nukes would play out and, while the tactical advantage is obvious, I cannot come to a conclusion that is good for us in the long-run."

Eli Cohen threw his hands up in the air. "May I remind everyone in this room that we are deciding whether or not to allow Iran into the nuclear club." He looked around the room. "This cannot happen." He knew that every man in the room at least agreed with that statement. He suddenly relaxed and leaned back into his chair. "Okay, let's do this. Zvi, come back with the outline of a conventional plan. Let's go from there. All I ask each man here to do is to think about the alternative if we come to the conclusion that we have no viable conventional plan. Is that a fair request?" Each man in the room nodded in consent.

Raibani turned to his old colleague Avner. "But you have to give your planning group real support. You can't sabotage their planning or poison the well." Only he or Cohen could admonish Zvi Avner in this manner.

Cohen did not wait for Avner to reply. "That is a good point, Ben. Why don't you participate with Zvi and the planning group? Zvi, what do you think?"

Both Avner and Raibani were caught off guard. But Raibani liked the idea and his face showed it. Avner did not, but he recognized that the only way he could come back into this room with a plan that he had concluded was not viable and have it accepted as such was if Raibani had been involved in the process. As Avner's political mind came to this realization, he knew that the prime minister had just given him a great gift. "Yes," said the defense minister. "I welcome Ben's involvement."

5 – Home

Amit Margolis enjoyed the view north and west over Tel Aviv and its Mediterranean waterfront. The fortieth floor of the Neve Tzedek Tower was commanding. It was a little before 6 p.m. on December 31, 2009, and the last hints of sunlight were rapidly fading away on the western horizon. Amit tried in vain to pick out his apartment home in the Tel Baruch neighborhood five miles to the north. His eyes followed the traffic on Highway 20 north past Mossad's new office tower on the edge of Camp Rabin, the compound in Tel Aviv that houses the headquarters of the IDF, up toward his exit at Boulevard Keren Kayemet Le-Israel. But from there it was already too dark to pick out his street.

This was Amit's first visit to the apartment of his long-time friend Dov Hirsch. Like many of the katsa, the professional Mossad spies who find themselves on long-term assignments in foreign, sometimes hostile, lands under assumed identities, Amit spent his free time with his fellow Mossad brethren – or just alone. Dov had served with him in Mossad but had left the Institute four years before to join Rafael Advanced Defense Systems, Ltd., the large Israeli defense contractor. Now a Rafael sales professional, Dov had purchased this three bedroom apartment a year earlier.

Dov walked out of the living room and onto the balcony. He handed a beer to his friend. "Happy New Year," he said.

Amit raised the bottle to examine the label. "Dancing Camel? Where's the Goldstar?"

"Just try it," Dov replied as he smiled. "This beer is fantastic. My favorite now." Hirsch raised his own bottle of Dancing Camel in salute to Amit.

Margolis tried some. "Mmm. Not bad."

"You are getting shit-faced tonight, my friend." Dov Hirsch was known as a party boy while at Mossad and, as Amit suspected, being in the private sector did nothing to curb this aspect of his personality. "And you are definitely getting laid."

Amit laughed and turned his eyes toward the beach, which was only a quarter mile away. The white sand and breaking surf was clearly visible in the gathering night. "You haven't changed a bit. The view here is amazing. How long have you been here?"

"I gave Rachel her *get* about eighteen months ago." Hirsch was referring to the writ of divorce that had to be granted from husband to wife under Israeli law. "I bought this place in January. Got a great deal from some guy who had bought three units here on spec in 2007. He rented two of them for less than he expected and couldn't find a renter for this one. He was sucking wind on the mortgage payments."

"All right. Are you going to make me ask, asshole? How much?"

Hirsch smiled and looked at his old friend. "I offered him 1.2 million dollars and settled at 1.3 million. You believe that?"

"Sounds like a deal. But to be honest, I'm the last guy to ask about the real estate market here. How did you afford that? Rafael paying you that well?"

"Hell no. I mean, Rafael pays me okay, but … you know my background. My parents were helpful." Dov Hirsch was the scion of a family that had made a small fortune developing real estate in Tel Aviv and Haifa.

"Ah, yes. Maybe your dad can support me."

"Hey, I'm lucky. Someone has to be. You are working way too hard, Amit. Still going to Russia all the time?"

"You know I can't talk about that."

"I will take that as a definite yes."

"Come on," implored the active Mossad agent. He was suddenly uncomfortable. "How's Rachel and the kids?"

"Okay, okay. No talking about the Institute." Dov took a deep swig of his beer. "She's doing great. We had our bitter period. You know how that goes." He shrugged his shoulders. "I guess like everyone does. But we are on decent terms now. The kids are doing well – as well as can be expected."

"That's good to hear."

"She still lives in our old house in Tel Baruch, not far from you. You should call her, she always liked you."

"Ah, no. Not going there," Amit replied to his friend's suggestion. "What's the story tonight?"

"Tonight will be legendary my friend. Wait until you see my girlfriend." Dov made a face as if he were going to whistle, but no sound came out, only a long exhale. "She's a smokin' coosit. A fucking twenty-five year old sex machine."

Amit laughed. "You are totally out of control."

"She is bringing this one girlfriend of hers, Enya. Oh, man, you are a lucky son-of-a-bitch tonight." He slapped his friend on the back. "The body on this woman is just mind numbing. I can't sit here and think about it or I will have to go jackoff."

"Oh, boy," Amit said with a laugh, shaking his head from side to side. "You definitely make be forget about work."

"Hey, buddy, that's what it's all about." Dov turned and headed back into the living room. "I have the last couple Real Madrid games on DVR. Let's watch some football. The girls won't be here for a couple of hours." Hirsch stopped as he was passing through the open sliding door and turned. "In case you were wondering, I spoke to Dori Goldman yesterday. Enya is officially cleared. Oh yeah!" Dov pumped his fist in the air and went inside.

Margolis turned back to look over the city. Night was fully encompassing the skyline and artificial lights now danced through the arteries of Tel Aviv to the accompaniment of the occasional car horn and ambulance siren.

Mossad maintained a policy of reporting sexual liaisons, both on duty and off, to internal security. The intelligence agency was extremely paranoid about its agents falling victim to "honey traps" – the seduction of government employees and other useful targets by enemy agents. Dori Goldman was a senior internal security officer of Mossad and had only one job. His sole responsibility was to discretely check the names and background of sexual partners. For a single heterosexual man like Margolis, this was no problem, but the policy applied to everyone, including married employees having an affair or a one night stand or employees who attended a gay bar on a weekend night. The deal was simple: Dori Goldman's files were never opened other than by him unless espionage was suspected. No employee of Mossad had ever been black-mailed as a result of reporting the names of their sexual contacts, including the time when a young agent bedded the wife of the prime minister. But the Mossad employee who was caught having sex with anyone who had not been reported to Goldman within 48 hours of the act was assumed to have compromised Mossad and would be fired or worse. Dov Hirsch had cleared the way for his good friend – both personally and professionally.

6 – A New Year

With an hour to go until midnight, Amit Margolis was already feeling the effects of too much alcohol and not enough food. The girls were responsible for the latter but had yet to show up. Amit found his way to the bathroom. He stood over the toilet, voiding the byproduct of three beers. All he could think about at that moment was that he would turn thirty-five in 2010. He was about to start the downhill slide to forty. And forty was no longer young. He was single and committed to a career that offered no prospect of changing his marital status.

It wasn't supposed to be this way, he thought. He remembered his college girlfriend and his plans to marry and start a family. He would be a successful business executive and she a beautiful courtroom attorney, defending the wrongly accused. All she had to do was wait for him for two years while he attended the Fuqua School of Business at Duke University. It would pass so quickly, they told themselves. Their phone calls and emails were frantic and passionate at first, the ebbing not even noticed by Margolis as he struggled with school. He had his business classes and he grappled with the added burden of taking English courses during that first semester to gain mastery over a language that his father had taught him at home, but that had been buried beneath the onslaught of Hebrew in school.

The email he opened on the night of December 10, 2000, had come earlier that afternoon while he was in the library studying for an exam. It came from a close friend and he still remembered every word of it to this day. His soul mate, the woman he knew he would marry once he was settled back in Tel Aviv, was involved with another man – an older attorney. She was "in love," the email went on to say. Amit's friend could not stand the thought that Amit was in the dark when all in their circle of friends back home knew what was happening. Amit had called her four times that night, each call fueled by more alcohol. Each call reaching the voicemail of her cell phone. Each call growing angrier, the accusations of betrayal becoming harsher and cutting deeper.

He did not sleep that night and by the time an email arrived from her at 3 a.m. his time, all his senses were impaired. But he could read it well enough to know that his plans were in ruins. He drank until he passed out that night, missing his exam. It had taken all of his charm and a faked email to convince his professor that his grandmother had unexpectedly passed away that Sunday night. The ruse worked well enough for Amit to reschedule his accounting exam and continue his studies at Duke. But the wounds to his heart and his pride had never healed. And as a new year neared, he knew that he had to get his mind off the subject to avoid ripping the scabs open yet again.

Amit emerged from the restroom to sounds of laughter and the sight of two perfectly formed women, both in jeans and very tight tops. "There he is," exclaimed Dov, stretching his right arm out towards his friend as his left arm held tightly to his girlfriend. Amit walked over to be embraced into a huddle. "This is my best friend, Amit," he said enthusiastically to the two women. "This is Nava." Amit shook the hand of Dov's girlfriend, who looked every bit the sex machine that Dov had described earlier. "And this is the gorgeous Enya."

Amit extended his hand, but Enya stepped to him and hugged him. She had a big smile. "You are as handsome as Dov said."

Her auburn hair and blonde highlights combined with her green eyes made her beauty as exotic as it was instantly hypnotic to Amit. The Mossad agent was happy to have three beers under his belt. His natural reticence was on holiday. "Well I have to say Dov did a terrible job describing you. He said you were gorgeous, but anything short of beautiful and intoxicating is simply insufficient."

"See, I told you Enya," said Dov. "Watch out for this guy."

Fifty minutes of food, wine and a round of vodka shots followed. Amit Margolis soaked in this 26-year-old with a five-foot-seven-inch frame that carried 118 perfectly distributed pounds. But what surprised Amit was that the beautiful woman in front of him had a mind to match her looks.

As midnight approached, Amit was on the balcony with Enya as Dov and Nava came out, each holding two crystal champagne flutes with the contents of a newly opened bottle of Veuve Clicquot Brut. In the background, the television announced a countdown to midnight. Amit and Enya each took a glass of champagne in hand. "Five, four, three, two, one. Happy New Year!" Dov shouted, his judgment and volume filter now impaired significantly. "Shanah Tovah," replied Nava. All four took a sip of champagne and Dov and Nava immediately wrapped themselves in a passionate clinch.

Enya did not wait for Amit to make his move. Her two years of service in the IDF following high school had taught her more than just how to shoot and strip a M-16 rifle; it had given her self-confidence and the assertiveness that came with it. She brought her left hand up and wrapped her long fingers around the back of Amit's hair, pulling his head down to hers. The kiss was tender and, to the pleasant surprise of each of them, emotional. They lingered in the moment. As their lips parted, Enya smiled. "Very nice," she said softly.

In the city, a scattering of firecrackers could be heard. On the beach, a few parties were underway with sparklers and the occasional Roman candle or bottle rocket. No large fireworks display could be seen as would be happening in major cities all over the world that night. Israel did not formally recognize the Gregorian date of January 1 as a holiday. In the ongoing tension between secular Israel and observant Israel, this battle had been won early in the State's history. Only Rosh Hashanah, the new year for humans as determined according to the Torah, was officially recognized as a holiday. By the time Amit and Enya were able to think beyond the moment, they realized they were alone on the balcony. They sat down. Enya broke the silence. "You are not what I expected in a Mossad man."

Margolis looked at her. He was not happy. "Is that what Dov told you?"

"Oops, am I not supposed to know that?" She reached across and caressed his right forearm. "Does that mean you have to kill me now?"

"No, it means I have to kill Dov." Enya laughed openly, almost choking on a sip of champagne. Amit pulled out his wallet, retrieved a business card and handed it to her. "That's my business." He pointed to the name on the card. "I own a financial consulting company. Dov likes to bullshit. Still like me?"

Enya wasn't sure who was being honest. Her girlfriend had told her that both Dov and Amit were Mossad agents and that thought was exciting. But as she looked at Amit she concluded that it didn't matter at this moment. "Yes, very much."

Amit Margolis woke up at a little after 8 a.m. on Friday, January 1, 2010, with a dry mouth and a slight hangover. The room was not familiar to him, but he knew he was still in the apartment of Dov Hirsch. He turned on his right side, his body gliding easily under the single tan sheet. He reached across the short distance of space between him and the naked body next to him. Enya was lying on her right side and still asleep. He ran his hand gently through her long soft hair, down her shoulder, coming to rest on her hip. He knew from that simple act how dangerous this woman was. He was no stranger to waking up with a woman by his side, but his usual emotion was to get out or get her out. His emotional response this morning was the opposite. He had not felt that in a very long time.

Amit rolled back over to check his cell phone. He lifted his slacks off the floor, reached in the pocket and pulled out his phone. A red light flashed in the upper right hand corner. He pressed the power on button and pushed the icon for email messages. He had one email waiting. Amit touched the screen and the message opened.

Conference call with client anytime this morning. You set the time.

There was no day off for Amit, and his employer wanted him to stop by the office sometime this morning. He did not get this email too often and he did not want it now. But he had a job and that job had ruled his life since he returned to Israel from Durham, North Carolina and joined Mossad in September 2002.

7 – Back to Work

"You don't look too good, Amit." Shlomo Fiegelbaum was the no-nonsense director of the Collections Department of Mossad, the Israeli equivalent of the CIA's deputy director of operations. This was not the man who usually gave Amit Margolis his assignments, so Amit was more than curious as he sat down. "You need coffee?"

"No, sir. Just a late night. I'm fine."

"You weren't hanging out with Dov Hirsch last night?" The question from Fiegelbaum was rhetorical. "I miss Dov's, shall we say, 'liveliness'. His skills, however – I must admit – are perfectly suited for his role at Rafael." Fiegelbaum paused and sized up his underling. He felt a fatherly attachment to every man and woman he sent out on missions. "Enough about Dov. We have a new assignment for you."

"Sounds good."

Fiegelbaum shook his head. "I have always thought that to be an odd expression. You haven't heard what your assignment is yet." Margolis smiled and shrugged his shoulders. "You have done a great job in Russia. This has been noticed and appreciated. We need you to do something very important, but it might compromise your ability to return to Russia."

Margolis was excited. He was tired of being assigned to operations in Russia and ready to spend time back home. "It sounds important."

"It is. And you are the one who made it this important. The operation you handled a few years ago when you got the chips into the Iranian Tor systems was a huge success. Now we need you to keep the value of that mission intact.

"As I am sure you are aware, the Russians signed a contract in December 2007 to sell the S-300 anti-aircraft system to Iran. This was a billion dollar contract, enough to make the Russians eager to see the deal through. Since then there has been intense pressure on Russia from the USA, us and Europe to kill the deal. Unfortunately, the Russians have been using this deal as leverage and we are afraid that they are getting close to going ahead with delivery. We need to stop that from happening.

"Your assignment is to meet a Russian FSB operative named Dmitri Arkanov. You will be negotiating on behalf of Israel. We need to figure out what they will take in order to call off the deal permanently. You understand Russians and you understand business. You are the right man for this job." The FSB, or Federal Security Service, is the Russian descendant of the Soviet Union's KGB.

"Sounds exciting. I'm on board. Timing?"

"Here's the deal. We want the negotiation to be between us and Russia. No Americans. No Europeans. No one but you and Arkanov. You will need to be very discrete and very careful."

"Then I suggest that either I go to Moscow or he comes here. Since the headquarters of FSB are no secret, I should go there. If he doesn't have to travel, we cut out at least half of the traceable chain."

"Exactly my thoughts, except that I'm not sure about you going into the Lubyanka. The Americans watch that place closely and it wouldn't surprise me if the NSA can listen in on most of what goes on in there."

"I will have to think about that," replied Margolis. "To be honest, I would be happy to die without ever seeing the inside of the Lubyanka. There must be a million ghosts in that building. Makes me ill thinking about it." Both men thought about the bloody history of the building, which had housed Stalin's secret police, the NKVD, before being home to the KGB and now the FSB. This was the same building where Lavrentiy Beria in the late 1930s built a drainage area for the more efficient cleaning of blood from the execution of prisoners every night, typically dispatched with a bullet to the back of the head. The same place where Beria was himself executed shortly after Stalin's death.

Amit came back to the issues of the moment. "May I ask why me? You realize that once I show up in Moscow and make contact, I am blown for future operations there."

"First, this has been discussed. You have done your duty in Russia, Amit. It is time for you to change venues. As for why you were picked. That is easy. You speak fluent Russian. You know how Russians think. You clearly know how to negotiate. You are trusted and this is a critical mission. By the way, you will be alone. No team. No backup. If you have trouble, you will need to get to a friendly embassy on your own. Can you accept that risk?"

"When do you want me to go?"

"I have your tickets." Fiegelbaum opened a drawer in his desk and passed an envelope to Amit. "You fly out Monday to London. London to Moscow. The first passport is for here to London. The second passport will be your identity once in London. You will become a Brit named Roger Wilkinson. Your meet in Moscow is this Wednesday. The information you need to know is in there. It includes a couple of reports. One on the S-300. It is a world-class system. We do not want that system in Iran. The other is everything we know on Dmitri Arkanov. I would like to tell you we have leverage on him or that his grandmother is Jewish. But this guy is clean and as goy as it gets. Both of those reports are to be left here. Background only."

They spent another half hour discussing the mission, including the level of authorization Amit had and the methods of communication for Amit to use. Margolis was surprised at the amount of latitude he was being given. In the middle of the discussion, he realized that this mission would probably be the last time he could travel to Russia. By the time it was over, he was sure the FSB would have his fingerprints, his DNA, his voice print and many photographs.

Margolis started to stand as Fiegelbaum added one last statement. "By the way, bring in your Michael Jenkins passport and documents today. That alias is officially retired. We don't want the FSB tracing you back to prior operations. We will keep the business front in Toronto open for cover purposes, but you no longer travel under that alias."

8 - Contact

The McDonald's at 29 Bolshaya Bronnaya Street on Pushkinskaya Square in Moscow was first opened in 1990. It quickly became the highest volume McDonald's in the world. While customers no longer waited in line for hours, this restaurant was still one of the busiest in the world for the fast food chain. Amit Margolis ordered nine chicken McNuggets with sweet and sour sauce and a Coca-Cola. It was January 6 and Moscow had a fresh coating of several inches of snow from the prior night. As instructed, Amit sat next to the long stretch of windows facing the street. His training wanted him to turn his back to the window, but he was resigned to the fact that he was being photographed in detail. He continued to wear his leather gloves. He was determined that at least the FSB would not get his fingerprints. Per the agreed contact plan, he wore a red scarf and kept his long black winter coat on. His eyes scanned the restaurant and the street, trying to pick out the FSB team.

He was down to his last McNugget when a man who had been at a back table stood up and walked over. "May I join you?"

"Please do."

"Visiting Moscow?"

"Here on important business for a few days. You?"

"Not a visit for me. I live here."

"Perhaps you can show me around?"

"My pleasure." The man was much older than Amit. The Israeli would have put him in his sixties if he didn't know from the file that Dmitri Arkanov was fifty-seven. It struck Amit that most long-serving intelligence professionals he knew, like Arkanov and Fiegelbaum, tended to look older than they were.

Amit ate his last piece of chicken in one bite. "Well then, let's go." He stood and shook the man's hand. "I'm Lev." Amit wheeled a cheap black overnight suitcase behind him that he had purchased the prior afternoon.

"My name is Dmitri."

A half hour later, Amit opened the door to a randomly selected hotel room in a randomly selected hotel. The odd couple walked in and arranged the pair of chairs in the corner for an open discussion. Amit put the suitcase in the corner and removed his coat, the red scarf having been left in the trash at the McDonald's. He kept his gloves on. "Shall we begin?" Both men sat down.

"Of course, Mister ..?"

"Cohen."

"Mister Cohen. That is appropriate." Arkanov smiled at his counterpart. "I must say that your Russian is flawless. Did you grow up here?"

"Yes. Right here in Moscow as a matter of fact." The response was the opposite of the truth, but Amit was more than happy to send the Russians on a goose chase.

"I am guessing that Cohen is not your real name."

Amit smiled. "Well, I can't make it that easy for you. But I can assure you that I have the full authority and backing of my government."

"I have no doubt about that. And I can assure you of the same." Arkanov crossed his legs. His dark gray suit was much higher quality than what the old-time KGB used to wear, but was still short of the standards on Wall Street. "It seems that Israel has concerns about Iran."

Amit raised his right hand in the air, his palm facing the Russian. "Please, Dmitri. We have important matters to discuss. Let's not waste time discussing obvious issues. We want you to agree to permanently forego the sale of the S-300 system to Iran and you want something in return. I have no idea what this is, so please tell me what you want."

Arkanov cocked his head to the side and shook it slowly. "Your directness is refreshing. In my position politics has become too common and I am used to the dance. I will try to be more to the point." Arkanov reached into his breast pocket and pulled out a box of Winston cigarettes. He offered one to Amit. "Do you smoke?" Amit shook his head. "Mind if I do?"

"If you must."

Arkanov put a cigarette in his mouth and placed the box down on the table. He then pulled a lighter from the same pocket, lit the cigarette and placed the lighter on the table next to the box. "Thank you. I can't think right unless I have a smoke." He reached over to the far end of the table for the glass ashtray. "As you know, my government has a long history of supporting Iran. We feel it is appropriate and important for them to be able to defend their sovereign territory. We strive to achieve a fair balance in the region and your country, along with your allies, are in no danger of any military imbalance. Quite the contrary."

"What is it you want?" Amit's words were stern. He commanded a level of respect far beyond his years. At his request, his hair had been colored almost completely gray for this journey and the impact helped him with the older Russian.

"Your country maintains close relations with Georgia. Georgia is, to us, much as Iran is to you. In addition, we have ongoing concerns in Chechnya. Were you to provide certain support for us on both of these issues, my government is willing to seriously consider your concerns with respect to our dealings with Iran."

Amit Margolis had spent the last five years negotiating with Russians. There was a pattern of speech that every Russian over 50 years old was locked into. It was the art of subtle vagueness that had been so critical to longevity in the old Soviet Union. For the men who had come of age in the old system, the pattern was set in granite. The pattern held true today. "We certainly share much with regard to Chechnya and we certainly have had a relationship with the Georgians," Amit said. "How is it, specifically, that you think we can help you?"

"Since we share a common interest in Chechnya, we would like to have active cooperation between our intelligence agencies."

Amit broke the Russian's train of thought. "How?"

Arkanov was taken aback. He was used to complete deference from his subordinates. On the other hand, he thought to himself, Jews are notoriously pushy and rude. "We would like to have an active liaison. We want you to have a representative here in Moscow that interacts daily with the FSB."

"I am not sure that daily makes sense; however, we are willing to work with you to share intelligence on Chechnya."

"You understand that your objectives in Chechnya must be in line with ours," the Russian continued.

"And those objectives would be?"

"I will be very candid. Like you with Arab terrorists or America with al Qaeda, we actively seek to interdict Muslim Chechen terrorists. We wish to cooperate in the identification of appropriate targets." Like any good negotiator, Arkanov had sought agreement first on the easier issue.

"I think that you can correctly assume that we have common objectives in Chechnya. Now let's discuss Georgia," Amit responded.

"Georgia is of historical importance to my country. I will start with our objectives. We desire that they maintain an even hand in their relations with us. We are not seeking to annex Georgia, we only wish that they stay close to their historic roots. After all, the birthplace of Stalin should not become a playground of American imperialism." Arkanov smiled but got no response from the Israeli. "We wish for your active support in restraining American inroads into Georgia and we ask that you stop selling advanced weapons systems to Georgia."

"Israel is always happy to seek a level playing field in your backyard. Is this the key issue for you?"

"I welcome that response. But there is something more concrete we desire. You have provided command and control computers for the Georgian radar network. We would like to have access to what they see on those radars."

This was a direct request and Margolis knew exactly what the Russians wanted: the ability to take control of what the Georgians see on their radars in the event of a Russian attack. Amit thought about his response carefully. "I certainly believe that my country can refrain from selling weapons that are commensurate in quality with the S-300," he said. "And I am comfortable telling you that we will join you in urging restraint with our American ally. But I do not have authority to agree to what you want on their radar system, nor do I think such a plan would be acceptable to my government."

Arkanov took a last draw on his cigarette and buried the lit end into the glass ashtray. The cigarette had not been even half consumed. "That would be unfortunate. My government is under intense pressure to fulfill its contractual commitments to Iran. Perhaps you could discuss the matter with the appropriate authority."

"Yes, I am happy to discuss your proposal."

"How much time do you need?"

"Let's meet in the lobby tomorrow at thirteen hundred."

Dmitri Arkanov stood. "I will be there." He extended his hand and Amit stood and shook it.

Amit escorted the Russian out the door, glanced down the hallway, which was empty, and closed the door. He walked back to the table. The cigarette box and lighter were gone. The Israeli thought about that and recalled that the Russian had returned the cigarettes and lighter to his right pants pocket when he stood up to leave. Amit remembered that the FSB operative had earlier retrieved those same two items from his breast pocket. Amit went down onto one knee. He bent over at the waist and stuck his head under the bed. The lighter was there on the rug about two feet underneath the bed. Amit knew that it had to be a listening device.

He stood back up and headed for the door. Within a minute he was downstairs in the lobby, his eyes scanning for FSB men. It only took a few seconds to spot two men. Their strident attempts to avoid looking in his direction made them obvious. Amit headed back to his room.

Back in his room, Amit opened his cheap overnight case. Inside were a pair of sneakers, a hat and a blue Gore-Tex winter jacket. Amit took off his overcoat and suit jacket and hung both up in the closet. He put on the contents of the suitcase and then placed it in the small closet. He turned on the television and found a news channel. Next he went to the door of his room and opened it, stepped into the hall and closed the door. He stood in the hall for a minute and then opened and closed his door while he stayed in the hallway. Now he headed to the rear exit of the hotel, stopping to look out the window. He was on the second floor and he could see the alleyway below. There was no one visible. He entered the stairwell, walked down and exited into the alley. Within a few minutes he was several blocks away. He hailed a taxi and gave the driver directions in broken Russian to the hotel he had checked into the previous day, doing his best to sound and act like an American tourist.

Forty minutes later Margolis checked the telltale he had put on his door when he left earlier in the day along with a "Do Not Disturb" doorknob hanger. The clear piece of tape was along the top edge of the door and still bent outward toward the hallway just as he left it. He opened his door and entered the room, relieved to see that the bed was unmade and the dirty towel he had left on the floor by the door was undisturbed. He opened the closet and pulled out his real suitcase, supplied to him by Mossad. He opened it and removed a computer. The computer had only one purpose and he placed it on the room's utilitarian desk to put it to use.

Amit booted the computer up and it opened directly to a word processer. Amit typed in a review of the meeting and the questions that required answers from Jerusalem. Only the prime minister of Israel could approve Russia's request. When he was done he retrieved a cable from his suitcase along with his cell phone. He plugged one end of the cable into the USB port of the computer and the other into the micro USB port of his BlackBerry phone. He clicked an icon on the computer and the memo he had just typed was compressed, encrypted and downloaded onto his phone. The computer then erased the memo automatically from its random access memory and erased the one-time cipher key it had just used, rewriting a random sequence of digits over the prior disk drive space. The message written by Margolis had never been saved on any drive.

On the cell phone, an email message light appeared. Margolis unplugged the cable and opened his email. A photograph of Red Square appeared on his screen and he pushed a button to forward the photograph in a text message to a contact named "Mary." Along with the photo, Amit typed "Safe in Moscow. Miss you." and then hit the send button. Encoded and embedded within the photograph was the memo he had written on the computer. Once confirmation that the message had been sent was received, he relaxed, turned on the TV and lay down on the bed to wait.

Inside the Israeli embassy at 2 Palace Green in London, a resident Mossad communications officer received a text on his recently activated Virgin Mobile prepaid cell phone. The phone was one of several that sat on his desk mated to his computer. Each phone supported communications with a single katsa who was operating in the field. He transferred the texted photograph to his computer, which stripped the embedded text from the photograph, keeping it encoded in its original cipher. This raw ciphered message – a long string of binary digits – was itself mated to a routing code and the combination was encoded into the embassy code in use that day. This final encoded message was sent along with the day's traffic to Tel Aviv via satellite transmission.

This convoluted process had a purpose. Israel wanted to keep the NSA, the National Security Agency of the United States, from learning about these negotiations. The NSA would certainly pick up the text messages between Margolis and London, but they would be just a handful of messages out of tens of millions scooped up by the NSA that day alone. The first line of defense for the Israelis was to send messages that would not be flagged by NSA computers as worthy of more detailed scrutiny. The keys for this were the use of innocuous words and photographs; the use of phone numbers that would have no reason to be flagged; and the careful sizing of the photograph file so that it was within the expected range – a file that was too big would fall under suspicion. The only thing that worried the professionals in Unit 8200 who designed this system was the fact that the texts were routed through one of the cell towers located near Embassy Row in London. This could be a flag in and of itself. But even if the NSA picked these texts out, and even if, after they intercepted the satellite communications, they had broken the Israeli embassy code for the day, the critical message from Margolis used a one-time cipher that was theoretically impossible to break.

Two hours later a chime sounded and the message light on Amit's phone started blinking. Margolis retrieved the email and reversed the process to read the message from Israel.

> Cannot accept request to access radar system. Working on alternative ideas. Standby.

Amit Margolis deleted that message and started typing. He had spent the prior two hours thinking about what alternatives were possible if he received exactly this response.

We could offer access to real time data from UAV sale. All that is needed to provide are code keys. I believe this solution will be acceptable.

He texted this message, embedded in a photograph of the Bolshoi Theater, to "Mary". It took only thirty-five minutes for a response. The prime minister liked his idea. He had approval.

9 – Cutting Deals

Amit Margolis entered the lobby of the meeting hotel a few minutes after the noon hour. He had been dropped off by taxi a couple of blocks away and had walked in with his real suitcase in tow. He warmed up quickly, the glare of two FSB agents adding their own heat. Both men had been chewed out for losing track of Margolis the prior day. It was a mistake they wouldn't make twice, so Margolis was heading home after this meeting. The Mossad agent headed up to his room on the second floor.

Exactly an hour later, Dmitri Arkanov knocked on Amit's door. The Israeli turned off the TV and opened the door. "Welcome," he said. Both men sat in the same seats as the prior day. Amit wore the same gloves.

"It must be nice to be back home," said Arkanov.

"I am always happy to be in Moscow."

"Did you visit relatives last night?"

"No. I spent the night right here. Slept well. I appreciate your concern."

Arkanov did not like being ridiculed. But he had to admit that the man he knew only as Lev Cohen had won the prior day's exercise in spy craft. He moved on. "Have you had the opportunity to discuss our request with the right authority?"

"Yes, I have. Unfortunately your request is not acceptable, but I do have a suggestion that I think you may find to have equal or greater value to your country."

"I am listening."

"We have supplied Georgia with unmanned aerial vehicles."

"Yes. The Hermes UAV." Arkanov was interested.

"We can supply you with the communications codes. You will be able to see what they see in real time."

Arkanov had briefed the Russian President the prior evening and had a good idea as to what would please his boss. He knew his boss would be very pleased with this outcome. Whatever they got from this deal was pure gravy – they had already decided not to sell the S-300 to Iran as a result of intense pressure from the U.S. "I was fully prepared for a long afternoon. But I believe we have an agreement," he said. He reached over to shake the Israeli's hand.

"I believe we do."

The agreement would not appear on any treaty or paperwork, the word of these two men being the only formal recognition. Russia knew that if it broke its word, cooperation on Chechen terrorists would end and the codes being used by Georgia would be suddenly changed. Israel believed that if it failed to deliver then S-300 missile batteries would be shipped to Iran. Both sides had good and valuable consideration to maintain their obligations.

On Friday, January 8, 2010, Shlomo Fiegelbaum did something rare; he left the offices of Mossad to travel to Ben Gurion International Airport to meet a returning Mossad agent. As Amit Margolis exited the customs doors in Terminal 3, Shlomo stepped forward. "How about a ride?" he said as he extended his hand. "Welcome home. I'm very proud of you."

Only twenty feet away, two young Mossad agents with bulges in their jackets carefully watched over the aging deputy director. The two guards followed their charges outside to a waiting black GMC Suburban for the ride to the Kirya Tower in Tel Aviv. The armored Suburban was quickly onto Highway 1 headed into town. The dialogue between the two principal men in the car was not substantial, only the exchange of pleasantries.

A half hour later, Fiegelbaum led Amit Margolis towards a conference room on the 41st floor of the Kirya Tower adjacent to Camp Rabin, known within the IDF as HaKirya, or the Campus. He stopped for a second just after the pair passed through the lobby's security doors. "The prime minister wants to meet you," he said.

Margolis was surprised and not sure how to react. "Why?" It was the only response that came to him.

"You will soon learn. The director is in there as well."

"I hope I'm not in trouble."

"Don't worry."

Outside the conference room several of the prime minister's security detail were seated in the hallway. Fiegelbaum entered the room with Margolis following. Eli Cohen stood up and walked over to the young Mossad katsa before the director of collections could say anything. "Pleased to meet you, Mister Margolis." Cohen extended his hand.

"Mister Prime Minister." The pair shook hands vigorously. Margolis was self-conscious, feeling as if he was being treated like a war hero, which he was not.

"Please have a seat."

Before he sat down, Margolis walked over to the far side of the table where Ami Levy sat. Margolis shook his hand. "Director," he said.

Through the multiple layers of windows that were separated by vacuum, the view of Tel Aviv looking south towards Herzliya reminded Margolis of the views from Dov Hirsch's balcony and the beautiful woman he had not seen since Sunday afternoon. He had told her that he had a business trip to Canada and would be unable to communicate until he got back. He was eager to talk to her, but it had to wait for now.

"Welcome home, Amit. Have a seat." Levy pulled on the back of the chair next to him. Margolis sat down where told while the prime minister sat down at the head of the table. Fiegelbaum sat across from Amit.

"I knew your father well," Cohen said. "You know he prevented world war three."

Margolis first heard this tale from his mother. During his time at Mossad, his father was occasionally talked about, especially by the few old timers who were around. Amit never quite knew what to make of the stories. He heard different versions and they all seemed so improbable. He still remembered the visit to their home by Prime Minister Menachem Begin in the summer of 1983. What he didn't learn about that visit until he joined Mossad was that Begin had posthumously and secretly awarded his father the Israeli Medal of Valor, the highest decoration in Israel. The medal was now in Amit's possession, secured in a safe deposit box in Tel Aviv. But despite all of this, Amit had remained unsure. "Perhaps, Mister Prime Minister, you can tell me about it someday."

"When the day comes, Amit, it will be my honor." Cohen opened a bottle of water that had been sitting on the table. "Water?"

"No, thank you sir."

"Please tell us about your trip."

Margolis spent only a few minutes reviewing his two meetings with Arkanov. The next twenty minutes were taken up by a discussion on what was required for Israel to honor its side of the deal and the ramifications of the deal itself. During this time, the dialogue was almost entirely between Cohen and Margolis, with the prime minister quizzing the Mossad agent on his opinions and analysis. When they were done, Cohen asked Margolis to leave the room for a minute.

Four minutes later, Shlomo Fiegelbaum opened the conference room door. "Amit," he called out. Margolis stood and walked into the room. He returned to his same seat.

"We have a new assignment for you Amit," said the prime minister. "But unlike what you are used to, there will be no danger and not much travel. I want you to join a planning team that is based right here on the Campus. Before I tell you what it is for, is this something that would interest you?"

"Sir, I have taken an oath to serve Israel as my father did. That oath is in my heart and in my soul. I will serve in whatever capacity you ask of me."

"I can feel the emotion you have. I must say you inspire me, Amit. Consider yourself part of Yahalom Group. You will spend the next six months planning the attack on Iran's nuclear program."

Amit Margolis was shocked. This was not at all what he expected or even suspected. This was a military operation and the only military experience he had was his mandatory three years in the IDF. "I am confused. Why would you want me to do this?"

"Yes, I assumed you would react this way." Eli Cohen took a sip of water. "As you would assume, we have been planning for this on a contingency basis for some time. Last year our planning had to change a key assumption. We began planning for an operation alone without any active assistance from the United States."

Amit was surprised, he had assumed that Israel had always been planning for an operation without direct American involvement, at least as a contingency. Prime Minister Cohen continued. "Our problem is that we are, quite frankly, stuck in a rut. The Yahalom Group, the team charged with coming up with the plan, has existed for almost a year. It consists of half a dozen senior staff officers. One is from the navy, two are ground force officers and the remaining three are air force officers. All of them are colonels or generals. All of them are career officers. And all of them think conventionally."

This still did not answer Amit's question and his face showed it. Director Ami Levy jumped in. "You see, Amit, they keep going in circles and coming to the same conclusion. It is the conventional military conclusion …"

"And that is that this can't be done without the Americans," Margolis interjected.

"Exactly," replied Cohen. "These men are stuck in conventional dogma. We need someone to inject fresh thinking into this group."

"But I am not a military man."

"Again, exactly. Any military professional who joins that group will come to the same conclusions. It is the nature of the profession. I … no, we … no, Israel needs someone just like you to shake up this team. You have imagination and a deeply analytical mind. You need to get these men thinking outside the box."

"Easy. Use nuclear weapons."

Eli Cohen started laughing. It was genuine. "Have you been listening in on our cabinet meetings? No, no Amit. That contingency plan is easy enough. The point of your involvement is to come up with a non-nuclear plan that works. The Yahalom Group has one mandate: deliver a plan that destroys the Iranian program without the use of nuclear weapons and that everyone will look at and say 'yes, that will work'. Can you do this?"

"Sir, I have already committed. I will join this planning group as you desire. I just want to be sure that this is the right decision for you and Israel. None of these men will even respect me."

"Amit, that last comment is nonsense," Cohen responded. "You are how old? Thirty-five?"

"I turn thirty-five this year."

"Look around you. The prime minister and the two senior members of Mossad are sitting here begging you to undertake this assignment. Do you think this is from lack of respect? Quite the opposite. Look, let me tell you this story. I have known Ami and Shlomo for a very long time. These two men are the best judges of character I know. What it takes to gain their respect is really more than I can contemplate. I came to them two weeks ago to suggest a man for this assignment. Anyone from Mossad or Shabak or Aman or even the private sector. They came back with your name. The only thing I knew about you was your blood lines. But what they described was a man every bit the equal of his father. He would be very proud of you.

"As a last test, I wanted to see how you did in Russia handling the S-300 issue. Believe me, when you came back with the suggestion on the drones, I knew that Ami and Shlomo were absolutely right. You are the man for this. The man to bring a new perspective and shake these guys up. Time is running out, Amit. This is not a country club assignment. We need a working plan and we need it yesterday."

The room was quiet. The power of any prime minister or president is massive by virtue of the position. But Eli Cohen had the charisma and passion to cause men – and an entire nation –

to march to the gates of hell. Margolis had gone from skeptical to excited. "Okay. When do I start?"

"I know you are tired, but I want to introduce you to the group right now. They are across the street in the Matkal Tower."

"I'm ready."

10 – Myrtus

Eli Cohen entered the conference room late. He had just finished an interview with CBS News that was intended to air on *60 Minutes* within the next month or two. He was in a good mood. Not because the questions were easy – they were, in fact, openly hostile to the prime minister's belligerent attitude towards Iran – but because Eli Cohen felt he had proved his points with indisputable logic. Never mind if the *60* Minutes correspondent believed otherwise, it was the way Eli Cohen always felt. The prime minister was in such a good mood that he already had a cigar fired up and underway as he walked in.

"Gentlemen, please be seated," he began. The date was Tuesday, March 9, 2010. "We have a focused agenda today." The Kitchen Cabinet was formally in session in Jerusalem. Prime Minister Cohen sat in his chair at the head of the conference table. Ben Raibani stood up and walked to the wall to turn on the air filtration system – this role having been long established for him. "We are here to review the latest Esther planning," Cohen continued. "Esther" was the working codename for the various plans being formulated by the Yahalom Group. "I regret to inform everyone that Mort is still in the United States and can't join us today." Cohen had asked Mort Yaguda and his wife to spend the month of March in Washington making the rounds among the politically powerful and influential. It was what Yaguda did best and Cohen needed his skills to be fully employed. Israel was pushing hard to counter what the prime minister saw as the dangerous policies of appeasement being followed by the President of the United States.

Cohen continued. "First I want to update everyone with a critical change since we last met on this topic in December. As everyone here no doubt recalls, that was a lengthy and frustrating meeting. It was, in fact, essentially a repeat of the meetings we had in May and August. Since we have been spinning our wheels, I made the decision to add a new member to Yahalom Group. In early January, we added a young Mossad officer to the group. He is not a military man, but he is a very strong analytical thinker who is very creative." Cohen paused a moment to see if any questions were coming. Nothing. "The purpose of this meeting is to update everyone here on the state of Esther and to review any key issues affecting the Iranian situation. I believe that Yavi has some important updates, so I will turn it over to him."

Yavi Aitan looked older than in the prior May, much older. He was on the frontlines of the covert struggle to slow the Iranian nuclear program. The stress of the role he played was showing, and the impact was very clear. His hair, which was jet black at the May meeting, was already showing a salt and pepper look on the sides of his head. His eyes were bloodshot and dark rings now formed a forbidding foundation under them. But his habits were the same. He pulled his seat up and leaned forward against the table. "Thank you, Prime Minister. We have a number of items to review. The first thing I would like to cover is the latest intel we have on Myrtus. As you know, we were successful in injecting the worm into the centrifuge control systems at Natanz. The software worked the way it was designed. The bad news is that the damage so far has been less than we expected. So we did not destroy all of the IR-1 centrifuges in place in Natanz. We did, however, destroy over two thousand centrifuges based on our current best estimate. We …"

"How accurate is that estimate?" asked Minister of Defense Zvi Avner.

"I have a high degree of confidence. The sources for this are multiple and include humint." Human intelligence meant spies inside the Iranian nuclear program. Having responded, Aitan continued where he left off. "We have had Operation Lead Vault in action for almost a year now and we have committed a lot of resources to this in cooperation with allied intelligence agencies. Lead Vault is the ongoing program to deprive Iran of raw materials they need to build more centrifuges. We have particularly targeted their ability to make or import maraging steel, which is used for the bellows in both the IR-1 and their newer designs."

Ben Raibani started to ask a question. Aitan raised his hand to acknowledge his thoughts before he spoke. His tone suddenly changed from authoritative to that of a professor in front of a class. Aitan continued. "Rotor tubes inside a centrifuge are spinning at great speeds. The longer and wider the tubes, the more efficient is the centrifuge. But a long rotor tube is also subject to greater levels of vibration stress. So one way to reduce that stress load is to cut the tubes into shorter sections that are then connected together with joints that combine strength and resilience. These joints are known as bellows. The bellows in the IR-1 combine four aluminum tubes into a single rotor that is one point eight meters long.

"So bellows provide the critical internal structural support for the rotor tubes as they spin and incur vibrations. They allow for longer and larger rotor assemblies. Maraging steel is just a very strong alloy of steel that has a high degree of resistance to distortion. The Iranians use grade 300 maraging steel that has about eighteen percent nickel, nine percent cobalt and four and a half percent molybdenum.

"They have to import all of the maraging steel they use. This type of steel is controlled by the IAEA and is technically banned from Iran. But they use a number of front companies operating outside Iran that acquire controlled materials like maraging steel. They have purchased this steel from mills in Japan, China, Russia and North Korea. Fortunately, international pressure has gotten all but China and North Korea to stop selling. The large Chinese companies won't sell to Iran but some small steel mills will still do business with a wink and a nod assuming they get a nice profit in the process. We are working hard to end these sources. North Korea continues to supply some but their mills have spotty quality and we are usually able to interdict their shipments. The North Koreans have become leery as a result of our interdiction success. The bad news is that the Iranians are planning on building an indigenous capability. We are watching those developments very closely and will take action as necessary.

"The same analysis applies for carbon fiber, which can be used for rotors and bellows. The fact is that the most advanced centrifuges in the world are now made of carbon fiber. But fewer than a dozen countries in the world can manufacture quality carbon fiber and none of them will knowingly sell to Iran. Just like the situation with maraging steel, we have heard chatter that they are planning on building an indigenous factory. This is very early, so we will have to wait and see what they do."

Eli Cohen interrupted Aitan's review. "How did Myrtus work?"

"I'm sorry, sir, I thought I reviewed that at the beginning."

"No. I mean, how did the virus accomplish the destruction of two thousand centrifuges?"

"Oh. Well, the key, Mister Prime Minister, to understanding how Myrtus does what it does is to understand how a centrifuge works. It's a precision machine. The internal rotor is spinning at very high speeds, over one hundred thousand RPM in top quality machines. The faster it's traveling on the periphery, the more efficient the enrichment process will be. But to achieve higher rotational speeds means that the machine must be built to ever tighter tolerances. The slightest vibration at a speed of, say, sixty thousand RPMs, becomes a destructive vibration at seventy thousand RPMs. Plus, every rotor has certain frequencies at which there is a natural harmonic vibration, known as resonance. These types of vibrations place huge stress on the rotor and its components.

"The rotor assembly is the key and it has to be perfectly balanced and aligned. As a result, a great deal of effort is taken to balance the rotor for the design speed. The best analogy I can give you is when you have your car wheels aligned. They may be perfectly aligned at one hundred kilometers per hour but then you get a vibration at one hundred thirty or one forty. That vibration, if you continue to drive at that speed for too long, can damage the original alignment and create a vibration when you are back at one hundred.

"We created – I should be fair and say the Americans created – a program that changes the converter frequency, or the rotational speed, to induce a new vibration for a period of time. If you want the scientific detail, the Americans calculated the average flexural resonance frequencies of the rotor for the IR-1. Notice I used the plural. There are a number of harmonic resonance frequencies for the IR-1. The Iranians operate their centrifuges at a frequency that is just below the fourth resonance frequency. Myrtus increases the frequency to the point of the fourth harmonic. This induces what is called an s-form deformation in the rotor. This particular resonance puts significant stress on the rotor, the bellows, the bearings and even the motor.

"In non-scientific terms, any imperfection in the rotor assembly is magnified by the change in rotational speed. Myrtus does this briefly then returns the rotor to its design speed for four weeks. Then the program slows the rotor down to a very low speed. This does two things. First it induces more vibration imbalance by passing through the first three resonance frequencies, but second, it allows the uranium hexafluoride to condense inside the rotor. Hexafluoride gas is highly corrosive, so doing this can significantly accelerate the corrosive impact of the gas inside each affected centrifuge.

"But we have added a second piece of software to Myrtus. This we came up with ourselves. Not even the Americans are aware of it. The software very quietly adjusts control valves in the piping to allow for a small amount of oxygen to be introduced in each cascade."

Aitan looked at the blank stares and decided to provide more background. He thought for a moment how best to explain it. As he spoke, he was using his hands to illustrate. "Rotors are spinning at great speed. That speed generates tremendous friction with the air, producing drag, heat and stress just like the leading edge on the wing of a supersonic fighter. To eliminate this, the rotor is inside an airtight vacuum casing. Vacuum pumps in the piping and molecular pumps in each centrifuge run continuously to maintain the vacuum and remove any uranium gas that escapes from the rotor assembly into the vacuum of the outer casing.

"What we have done is to take control of the inlet valves into the vacuum system, which is a centrally managed network of piping for each cascade. We are not eliminating the vacuum completely, we are just making it a partial vacuum. This introduces friction which increases the stress on the rotors and their motors by a meaningful amount. Myrtus also takes control of the vacuum pressure warning systems and makes sure they register that a proper vacuum is being maintained.

"Over time, we expect that this will cut the life expectancy of each centrifuge by at least fifty percent. We think that Iran will have a hard time finding this second method of attack, even after they uncover the core software worm. This method hides elsewhere in a very clever location and the injection is done via an encrypted code that we don't think anyone is capable of breaking, maybe with the exception of the NSA – and I am sure they won't be helping Iran on this. We have actually been able to refine this attack on infected machines by using information sent to us over the internet and then modifying the code." Aitan looked around the room. He was very proud of what the team at Unit 8200 had accomplished, like a teacher whose student was accepted into a prestigious university. "Questions?"

"Yes," responded Ben Raibani. "Have the Iranians figured out what is happening with Myrtus yet?"

"Good question. We aren't completely sure, but it appears that they do not yet recognize that a worm is behind recent centrifuge failures. What we do know is that the IAEA, in its recent visits, has noted a large number of centrifuge failures at a rate much higher than at any time prior to the summer of 2009. Iran is trying to figure out why this is happening. They are methodically running through the most likely causes of the failures. Since the guys trying to figure this out are all engineers, they think like engineers. They are thinking in the physical realm and tackling the issue from that perspective. We can only hope they continue to think in a conventional manner."

Aitan thought for a moment and added an afterthought. "By the way, when the Iranians uncover the Myrtus software, which they will inevitably do, there are cruder ways to achieve the same impact on the IR-1 centrifuge. For instance, if we simply disrupt the power source, the centrifuge stops spinning and in the process passes through all of the resonance frequencies as it slows. Likewise, when they are restarted, they pass through the resonance stress points on the way back to the design rotation speed. Myrtus just does this surreptitiously. But my point is that we have, uh, what I will call 'conventional' ways of damaging their centrifuges."

"Even more conventional is to blow that damned site off the face of the earth," responded Zvi Avner, much to the satisfaction of Raibani.

Aitan wanted to discuss the latest worm that Unit 8200 had come up with and that was now being unleashed in Iran, Syria and other enemy targets by Mossad agents. It was designed to eavesdrop by turning each computer it infected into a big listening device, sending files, logging keystrokes, listening through the microphone and even quietly turning on any built-in video camera. It was so sophisticated that it secretly reprogrammed the wireless card on the computer to interrogate any nearby Bluetooth-enabled cellular phones and to inject any phone it found with a sub-virus, turning the targeted phone into a powerful mobile eavesdropping device for Israel. All of the data were being transmitted back to servers located around the world but controlled by Israel. It was proving so effective that the men and women working on the project had nicknamed it "Tunnel," since it created a virtual tunnel into the work and personal environment of its victims. The amount of data being generated was so significant that a separate unit of Aman was being created just to collect and analyze everything coming in. The Tunnel software had been written without American involvement, and Aitan wanted to brag about that fact to the other men in the room. But he had agreed with the prime minister to keep this new cyber weapon secret for the time being.

11 – Outside Influence

Prime Minister Cohen checked his watch. He was impatient by nature. "What is the next item on your list?"

Aitan was used to this. The only men in the room who could push back when the prime minister was ready to move on were Raibani and Defense Minister Avner. "The Iranians are continuing their initiator research inside Parchin," he explained. The Parchin military base, just outside of Tehran, was the center of Iran's effort to develop a functioning mechanism to create a reliable nuclear implosion. "This is not news, but what is interesting is that we have information that they have started working on an initiator design theory that originated in China."

Danny Stein had been listening intently to Aitan. He was an amateur physicist and understood nuclear weapon design better than any member of the Kitchen Cabinet with the exception of Yavi Aitan. He knew that a nuclear weapon, designed to be imploded into a critical mass, needed an initiator in the middle of that mass. The initiator starts the nuclear chain reaction by bombarding U-235 atoms with neutrons. The absorption of a neutron by a U-235 atom causes that atom to split, releasing energy in the form of heat, gamma radiation and an additional two or three of its neutrons, which in turn cause, on average, two other nearby U-235 atoms to split.

"What are you saying?" asked Stein. "The Chinese are running their program?"

"No, but they are playing an influential role as they did with the Pakistanis in the nineties."

"Wait. Are you telling us that the Chinese are helping the Iranians build a bomb?" The question came from Ben Raibani.

"Not directly, no. But Chinese physicists have been making trips to Tehran. They are lecturing at Tehran University and bringing weapons-related research that is still classified in the West."

Now the prime minister was compelled to grill his minister of intelligence and atomic affairs. "Yavi, neither you nor Levy have mentioned this to me." Cohen was agitated.

"I'm sorry, sir. This has only come to light in recent weeks. Two Chinese physicists have been lecturing in Tehran this winter. We only learned about these lectures recently. Mossad was able to record a lecture that was given to an invited group of graduate students, professors and scientists about two weeks ago. We also obtained a copy of the handouts. The lecture was on initiator designs and implosion lenses. We didn't get the handout materials out of Iran until this past weekend. Mossad has now dedicated resources to learn as much as possible about these continuing lectures."

Cohen leaned over to Raibani. "Remind me to yell at Ami." It was loud enough for everyone to hear. He was not happy with Amichai Levy, the Director of Mossad. He turned his attention back to Yavi Aitan. "You guys have to keep me better informed. The Americans have to come down on the Chinese for this. If they don't, we should leak this to the press." Cohen took a drink from his most recent water bottle. "Well, what is your assessment of all this?"

"In terms of?" asked Aitan.

"In terms of impact on their program. Is this useful information or are the Chinese giving them bullshit?"

"In my opinion, sir, this is a mixture. Some of this, like the Iranians pursuing uranium deuteride research, is probably a waste of their time and resources. But some of the information is useful, especially regarding warhead miniaturization. I think the Chinese are playing both sides here."

"What else is new? They must have invented the two-step." The prime minister was angry now.

"Exactly," Aitan continued. "If confronted, they can tell the Americans that they are sending the Iranians down a blind alley. But the Iranians have plenty of physicists who are smart enough to assess the value of what is being discussed. And some of this research is highly valuable for Iran. If we give the Americans the evidence, they can call China out on this issue."

"I want a full report on this later today from either you or Ami Levy."

Zvi Avner jumped into the discussion for the first time. "Can we add these two guys to Dead Lead?" The question was to the prime minister. Operation Dead Lead was the internal code name for the targeted assassinations of Iranian physicists and scientists deemed critical to their nuclear program.

"You mean the Chinese physicists?" Avner nodded once. Cohen started to shake his head. A smile formed. "Sometimes, Zvi, you make me feel like I'm a peace activist." The men in the room laughed and even the defense minister himself could not suppress a smile. "I don't think now is the time to pick a fight with China." The prime minister was going to stop his response there, but added a qualification. "If these two Chinese physicists were operating on a rogue basis, let's say they were now employed by Iran and living in Tehran full time, then I would absolutely consider it. That would put them in the same category as the supergun guy. Ah, what's his name?"

"Gerald Bull," responded Yavi Aitan. Bull, an engineer who was an expert at designing and building very long range artillery, had sold his services to Iraqi dictator Saddam Hussein. His work made him an enemy of the State of Israel. He was assassinated in Belgium by Mossad agents in 1990 with the consent of then Prime Minister Yitzhak Shamir.

"That's the guy. He went rogue. He certainly was not being sanctioned by the Canadians. He even had to live in Belgium when he wasn't in Baghdad. But I don't think these Chinese guys fall into that category." Cohen looked at Aitan. "Do they?"

"No, sir. That is part of my concern. They are in Tehran lecturing with the full knowledge and approval of Beijing. I would go so far as to say they are on official Chinese business."

Aitan continued. "We are also picking up early signs that Iran and China are discussing a closer relationship in the cyber technology side. Nothing concrete has happened yet that we know of, but discussions are underway. Some of this information we have gotten from the Americans."

"Stay on top of that, Yavi," replied Cohen. "What else?"

"That is the key point on China. The next issue on my list is …"

"I'm sorry," interrupted Avi Gresch. "Before we leave the subject of scientists and Operation Dead Lead, was the killing of Masoud Ali Mohammadi part of Dead Lead?" Dr. Mohammadi was a physicist at Tehran University who was killed on January 11, 2010, as he walked past a parked motorcycle laden with explosives.

Aitan started to respond, but the prime minister beat him to it. "No," said Cohen in an emphatic tone. "Unless Yavi is about to admit to something very serious, I never heard of this man until his name came up in the news."

"Nothing to admit to on this one," Aitan added. "The Iranians killed him. He was a vocal supporter of Mousavi who committed the crime of trying to organize other professors in Tehran to go on strike over the election results." The irony of Aitan's comment was lost on the prime minister. To Cohen the equation was simple. Israel was killing physicists out of legitimate self-defense. That Iran jailed and sometimes killed its dissidents were acts of an illegitimate regime.

Mir-Hossein Mousavi had been the reform candidate running against President Ahmadinejad during nationwide elections in Iran that previous summer. Independent observers – and Israeli intelligence – were convinced that Mousavi had actually won the election, but the official results declared that Ahmadinejad had won a decisive reelection. The meeting of the Kitchen Cabinet the prior August had largely focused on the election and its aftermath, when the people of Iran came as close to overthrowing their government as they had since the fall of the Shah in 1979. The consensus reached during that meeting was very strong and had not waivered since. The Israeli government could do very little to help the reform movement. Any action they took that was subsequently revealed to the people of Iran would only harm the movement. Despite the potential to dramatically affect Israel, Cohen and his administration were reduced to spectators.

But the analysis that led to the consensus opinion was the belief, held by every man in the room, that regardless of the nature of the regime that ruled Iran, the nuclear program had become a source of national pride and therefore would not be halted. Even if the mullahs were kicked out of power, as far as Cohen and Avner were concerned, Iran's nuclear program had only one point to it: the development of nuclear weapons. And that outcome was an existential threat to Israel even if Iran was a free democracy. There was no question that a free and secular Iran was less of a threat, but a nuclear armed Iran was a gun at Israel's head just waiting for the wrong leader to come along and pull the trigger. So the consensus had been established: better to let other countries do what they could to help Iran become more free. Israel had an existential threat to worry about.

"You had another issue?" The prime minister was ready to move along.

"Yes, sir," Aitan continued. "I want everyone to be aware of the latest with Hezbollah. The Syrians continue to deliver M-600 missiles to their control. The pattern of delivery is the same. The Syrian Shu'bat al-Mukhabarat takes control of the missiles and delivers them to one of two storage locations off of highway one near the Lebanese border." Aitan was referring to Syria's military intelligence agency, which works closely with Iran to maintain ties with Hezbollah. "Both locations are in Syria and are run jointly with Hezbollah. Handover occurs at these two spots. From there, once Hezbollah has found a location to base each missile, they move the missiles over highway one into the Bekaa Valley and on to each missile's new home.

"All of the M-600s are housed north of the Litani River using Hezbollah's pattern of placing their highest value assets in homes or other places that are going to cause us problems if we hit them. For instance, the town of Nabatieh has a very good hospital that is six stories tall. It was built with an underground garage in the basement. Hezbollah built new parking across the street and now stores six M-600 missiles and their launchers under the hospital.

"For my job, these missiles are very big and impossible for them to hide when they move them into and around Lebanon. We have been able to account for every missile inside Lebanon. Aman has done an incredible job with their Lebanon group."

"Yavi, this is interesting, but it is not new," Prime Minister Cohen said. "I assume you have a number to update us with?"

"The latest transfers put the number of M-600 missiles under Hezbollah control at two hundred thirty-four. That number is up by forty-eight since our last meeting. But that is not the part that concerns me. The last forty-eight missiles all have GPS guidance supplemented with an inertial navigation system. We expect them to be targeting military command and control and airbases."

Zvi Avner broke in to add key information. "They are looking to retrofit all of their M-600 missiles with GPS. We need to have a process in place with the Pentagon to scramble the GPS coding over the Middle East."

"Can they do that?" asked Avi Gresch.

Avner gave him a look that was not meant as a complement. "Really, Avi?"

"Is that a stupid question? Honestly, I don't know."

"Yes," Avner responded. Gresch was not sure if Avner was responding to his first question or his second. "GPS was created by the U.S. military for its own use. The Pentagon has control over the system. They can alter the signal globally or regionally on command. They will change it regionally for us."

"What about our units?" asked Gresch.

Avner glared at Gresch in disgust. As far as the defense minister was concerned, only military veterans should be in this room deciding matters of life and death for the nation of Israel. Avner worked hard to calm himself; he would have exploded years ago when he was in command of the IDF.

Prime Minister Cohen watched his old friend struggle with his emotions. He found the situation amusing. But he also knew that it was critical to maintain a working cohesion within this small group. He decided to salvage the situation before his defense minister lost his composure. "Avi, the signals from the satellites get scrambled. The Americans can do everything from making the signal unintelligible, to degrading the accuracy, to actually altering the reported position of any GPS receiver by a fixed amount if they want. But whatever they do, they will provide their own military and hopefully the IDF with the codes necessary to reverse the effect and have accurate coordinates. Make sense?"

Avi Gresch nodded his head. "Thank you, Mister Prime Minister. I apologize for my ignorance on this subject."

Yavi Aitan had been listening to this exchange, wondering to himself how far to let it go before jumping in. He thought through the situation and decided that it was too important to let misperceptions linger. "Actually, if you will excuse me, Mister Prime Minister, I think that Minister Gresch has in fact raised some important issues. There are some meaningful technical issues we have to deal with. First, it is important to understand how GPS works. The system broadcasts a civilian signal known as C/A, or the course acquisition signal. This is unencrypted and generally accurate to ten meters or so. They also broadcast a more accurate military signal that is encrypted. Of course, we have the codes for that signal.

"The signal that we are concerned with is the open civilian signal. The Americans have adopted an approach towards GPS over the last decade known at 'regional denial'. They can distort the accuracy of the civilian GPS signal on a regional basis that is remarkably precise. For instance, they reduce the accuracy of GPS broadcasts over Afghanistan. But keep in mind that what they have done to date – and this is the only thing they have ever shown a willingness to do – is reduce the accuracy. Technically speaking, they increase the circular error of probability. While theoretically they could alter the signals to literally read false positions, they have never done this in the past. But that is the just part of the issue." Aitan looked at his prime minister for approval to continue.

"We're listening," said Eli Cohen.

"The reasons they are unlikely to ever do anything with GPS other than reduce the accuracy from several meters to, say, a hundred meter circular error or so, are many. First, there are so many civilian uses, including aviation, that rely on GPS. Second, there are other systems now available, including the Russian Glonass and commercial systems like Galileo. Glonass is in poor shape right now, but the Russians have budgeted the funds to launch new satellites to return the system to a true global system. Even the Indians have a regional system under development. Just like we do, most modern military GPS receivers can use other networks to check and triangulate against the GPS signals."

In addition to the prime minister, General Avner was learning more about GPS than he had known. As minister of defense of Israel, he was embarrassed. "Where are the Iranians on this?" he asked.

"Unfortunately, General, they have already embraced this new technology, which is not very sophisticated. The signals are out there and if the receiver has a good internal clock, it is relatively easy to determine which signals are being intentionally degraded, especially if the receiver is moving slowly."

"What does 'moving slowly' mean?" Avner asked.

"In the world of three-dimensional global positioning, slow is an airplane or a bomb in its early phase of free-fall. But a ballistic missile is not slow and despite the existence of multiple space-based positioning signals, the speed of a ballistic missile works against accurate positioning and makes it more than worthwhile to ensure that the Americans degrade the GPS signal, which I am sure they will do when the time comes."

"Thank you, Yavi," the minister of defense replied.

"There is more that everyone here should understand," Aitan continued. "Differential equations can also go a long way to allowing a user to reverse the effects of GPS degradation and return to a high level of accuracy. This is as simple as having a signal being broadcast from a transmitter with a known location on earth. This transmitter is comparing what it is being told by the GPS signals it picks up to its known position and then broadcasting corrective information that is used by another mobile receiver. If you have several of these corrective transmitters broadcasting, you can achieve very high accuracy. We anticipate that Hezbollah and even the Iranians will attempt to use this enhancement if they launch GPS guided weapons at us."

"What are we doing to defeat this?" The question came from Cohen, who realized that Avner had the same question but was too embarrassed to ask. On his notepad, Zvi Avner made a note to himself to dig into this matter after the meeting.

"We have jamming and spoofing equipment along the Lebanese border and around every major target," Aitan answered. "More importantly, we will have an EC-130 airborne with high powered jamming and spoofing equipment as well as receivers designed to locate any differential beacons. The IAF would then attack the beacons. Now, if Hezbollah attacks us by surprise, these last couple of steps are tough to get into place quickly. But in the case of Esther, I am sure we will be prepared." Aitan relaxed and leaned back in his chair, yielding the floor.

Eli Cohen was willing to apologize to his minister of foreign affairs, even if Avner wasn't. Cohen looked at Avi Gresch. "It's okay, Avi. This isn't common knowledge." Cohen looked at Avner and gave him the type of scolding look that a parent gives to a teenager who is too opinionated at the dinner table. "Zvi, will you take care of establishing the right communication channels with the Americans please. Obviously we need to be sure all of this is properly coordinated for Esther." Zvi Avner nodded and wrote down a reminder on the notepad in front of him. Cohen turned to Aitan. "Have you covered what you need?" Cohen laughed. "Maybe I should phrase it 'what we need'."

"Yes, sir."

"Good. Zvi, since you were finally getting animated, please continue."

"Thank you, Prime Minister." Avner was eager to get back to a topic over which he had mastery. "I have a couple of things to review before we discuss the primary issue for us today. The first item is related to our last discussion on the M-600, as well as all of the other missiles we are facing these days. We are moving towards operational deployment of Iron Dome. During January we successfully tested the system against multiple targets simultaneously. It intercepted three inbound rockets as designed and we now have a unit fully trained for initial deployment. I expect to be operational by year end.

"Rafael is already gearing up missile production and we are lobbying the Americans for emergency funding for more batteries. Each battery will have three twenty tube launchers and initially two reloads on hand for each launcher. So we will have one hundred eighty missiles available for each battery. If we get the funding from the U.S., I expect that we will field five batteries per year in 2011 and 2012.

"Iron Dome is our tactical or point defense system. Arrow 2 is our strategic anti-ballistic missile system and continues to undergo improvements and upgrades. But I am not satisfied with the current range of Arrow 2, so we are working on a longer range intercept missile. We are working with Boeing to develop Arrow 3, which will give us much higher effective altitude capability, including the ability to kill low earth orbit satellites. That said, I have a high degree of confidence that the latest Arrow 2 block 3 version will be capable of intercepting any Persian Shahab-3 missiles fired at us. And of course we have the six Patriot missile batteries in place. All of the Patriots are now upgraded to GEM-T standards and we have a total of 384 missiles on hand. Discussions are underway to bring more Patriot batteries into the country. We also continue development of David's Sling, which will far exceed the Patriot in range. Although for this group only, some of the recent testing has shown us that issues exist."

"Give me an honest timetable." Cohen requested.

Zvi Avner did not to be on the record regarding this matter. Sophisticated systems which are highly dependent on software development are never glitch free and never come in on time – and Avner felt that everyone else in this room should understand the same thing. "If you are pressing me for a guess, I think the missile is a year behind schedule. I don't think we can count on deployment before late 2011."

"We will already have dealt with Iran by then," Cohen responded.

"We have Arrow 2 in position to handle the primary Persian threats. If you want we can negotiate to obtain Patriot Pac-3 batteries until David's Sling is ready."

"Maybe we should ask the Americans to bring in some Pac-3 batteries while we finish development." It was not a question by the prime minister. He was instructing his defense minister.

"Yes, sir. We will pursue those discussions."

Now Ben Raibani added commentary. "I hope the Patriot actually works when we need it to this time." The Patriot missile had undergone its baptism of fire during the first Gulf War in 1991 and there was still anger among many IDF senior officers at its lack of ability to destroy the missiles fired at Israel by Saddam Hussein.

Avner had been in this same discussion a hundred times in the two decades since that war. Both he and Raibani knew that detailed analysis by the IDF had shown that the Scud missiles being fired by Iraq were breaking apart during reentry into the atmosphere above Tel Aviv and Haifa. The result was that the Patriot radar at the time could not distinguish between the inbound warhead and the other various pieces of broken up missile. The Patriots were hitting pieces of missile, just not the warheads. When the Patriot missile was intercepting the inbound warhead, subsequent analysis had shown that the closing speed between the two was much higher than the Patriot's programming anticipated. Simple software programming revisions after the war had corrected that problem and new seeker systems had been developed since then at great expense to allow the missile to better distinguish its desired target.

Avner gave Raibani the type of look he had given Gresch earlier. "Ben, you know what happened. For God's sake, we have almost twenty years of development since then." He stared at the old general, imploring him to stick to asking good questions. "Can I move on?" Raibani simply nodded as he turned his head and glanced at Cohen, wondering if he had also irritated his prime minister. Cohen never returned the gaze.

Avner calmed down and now started waving his pen around. All the men present knew this meant that he was focused and ready to get back on message. He continued. "We now have three Arrow 2 batteries deployed. One battery protects Tel Aviv, one battery protects Haifa, and we have completed operational deployment of a battery protecting Dimona. The last deployment is the direct result of intelligence developed by Mossad and Aman over the past couple of years regarding Persian targeting. We are working to fund another battery for deployment outside Jerusalem. The first two batteries now have a full complement of eight six-tube launchers. The newly deployed Dimona battery has four launchers. That leaves us with a total of one hundred twenty missiles currently available.

"We are systematically upgrading older missiles to block 3 status. We are also working jointly with the U.S. to network all of our batteries and add the American X-band radar system into the network. That radar gives us an added four to six minutes of warning time on anything headed our way from Persia."

Ben Raibani shook his head. "The Americans installed that radar in the Negev two years ago. I thought we have been networked with them since then. What am I missing?"

"Well, Ben, we have been networked in the sense that we have direct communication between the American operators and Air Defense Command in Tel Aviv. But we have yet to create a directly linked network."

"May I ask why?"

Once again the prime minister felt compelled to come to the aid of Avner. Only this time the reason was that the answer involved politics, not military realities. "The answer, Ben," said Cohen, "is the same as why the Americans are operating the radar without any Israeli personnel on site. They are using the radar for a lot more than just giving us early warning capability. They don't want us to know exactly what that system is picking up."

"What are they doing, spying on us?" Raibani assumed a tone of surprise.

Cohen laughed. "Please, Ben. You are way too old and wise to act like that. Who knows what they are doing? Frankly, I don't care. I am happy to have that system here and have American soldiers on our soil as a tripwire."

Raibani was not satisfied. "I don't think having an American listening post on our soil spying on us, not too far from Dimona I might add, makes a lot of sense."

Cohen was exasperated. This decision was argued over long ago and the issue was moot. Yavi Aitan stepped in now to support his prime minister. "General Raibani, I have to say that while this radar is very powerful, the fact is that there is nothing I can think of that the Americans can use it for relative to Israel that they don't already have the capability to do and have had for a long time. There is an American Aegis class cruiser or destroyer on station in the Mediterranean within two hundred kilometers of our coast every hour of every day. There are American AWACS planes over Turkey, Iraq or Saudi Arabia all the time. They have satellites in stationary and low earth orbit that scoop up everything going on in Israel and the rest of the Middle East. This radar station is just another redundant system added on top of a long list of redundancy. And if you want to talk about spying on us, I can assure you that there's just about no communications that take place in Israel that travel over the airwaves or over the internet that aren't picked up by the NSA. So with all due respect, it is silly to point to this one radar system as a problem."

Raibani leaned back in his chair, his body visibly deflating. For the first time in one of these meetings he felt like the old dinosaur being made a fool by the young whiz kid.

Aitan continued. "The reason for the delay in integrating directly into our Arrow network is twofold. First, they have been working on software that will send us what we want and need, which is early warning of missile launches, without sending us whatever it is they don't want us to see – which could be as simple as them not wanting us to see what their aircraft are doing over Iraq or the Persian Gulf. But the second reason is on us. As General Avner knows, we have not yet networked our Arrow batteries. The Americans have used that as an excuse, but we should be successfully networked soon."

Aitan paused for a second and had a new thought. "I want everyone to understand that if you are assuming that we can somehow launch aircraft on a long-range mission and do that without the Americans knowing almost immediately, you are making a bad assumption. We cannot attack Iran without U.S. involvement at least on a passive basis. American fighter planes are all over the airspace between here and there. I don't think I can imagine a worse scenario than IAF planes and U.S. planes getting into a mistaken dogfight over Iraq or Kuwait or the Gulf. So when we do pull the trigger, it will have to start with a phone call to U.S. Central Command in Qatar." The officers in the room understood this. Raibani took this as a further rebuke, but in his dejected mood he held his fire.

Danny Stein, the minister of industry, trade and labor, had been increasingly asserting his intellect as these Kitchen Cabinet meetings progressed. He was about to earn more respect. "Excuse me General Avner." Stein was not yet comfortable addressing the three senior members of this group by their first name. "I am having a hard time with the economics of our missile defense systems. By our own estimate, Hezbollah has over forty-five thousand missiles and Hamas has thousands of missiles in Gaza. Almost all of these missiles are relatively inexpensive, ranging from homemade Qassams to old Katyusha rockets, which I understand can be purchased on the arms markets for only a few hundred dollars each. Against this, we have deployed a small number of Arrow missiles, which cost about eleven million shekels per missile, and by the end of next year we will have, let's call it, one thousand Iron Dome missiles. I know these will cost about two hundred thousand shekels per missile. These numbers make no sense to me. We will either go bankrupt building missiles or we will simply be overwhelmed. If I were the head of Hezbollah, I would simply launch thousands of Katyushas until Israel has used up its defensive missiles. Am I wrong about this?"

"No, I can't question your basic mathematics," Avner replied. "We have been thinking through exactly the scenario you describe. I will say that first and foremost, the Arrow is specifically set up to intercept ballistic missiles from Persia. So this system will not be used against adjacent threats. As for Iron Dome, there is a concerted effort to develop the command software so that it discriminates between different levels of missile threat.

"Stated more directly, the software for Iron Dome, once it goes operational, will discriminate between a Katyusha and a M-600 or a Scud. This is accomplished three ways. First, the radar cross-section helps to differentiate given that the bigger the missile, the greater the threat. Second is the trajectory of the inbound target. The system quickly estimates the general impact area of an incoming missile. We also know, for instance, that Hezbollah will launch their big missiles from north of the Litani. Obviously these types of calculation will give you the range of the missile. Longer range missiles are greater threats. Finally, the speed and projected maximum altitude is critical to differentiating between missile types."

"Ah, I see. Thank you."

"But it is clear that we need to get Iron Dome operational as quickly as possible and we need more of these missiles sooner rather than later. Finally, we will need to integrate the Patriots, Iron Dome and the Arrows onto a network. This program is our highest priority right now."

Cohen took a deep gulp of water and put his bottle back down. "What is your second point, Zvi?"

"Yes, yes. It is my great pleasure to report that the day after our last meeting, two U.S. Air Force C-17s landed at Hatzerim Airbase and unloaded fifty-five GBU-28s." This was news to only Avi Gresch and Danny Stein. It would be news to Mort Yaguda at the next Kitchen Cabinet meeting.

Gresch clapped his hands. "Well, at least we are a step closer."

"Yes, it's about time," Avner continued. "We are working to get the remaining forty-five bombs in our original deal, but I do not have a timeline on that yet."

12 – Block G

"Okay," Cohen interrupted. He was ready to get to the point of this meeting. The reason had been established two nights earlier when Zvi Avner came to the prime minister's home for dinner. Avner was excited and couldn't wait to share news with his commander-in-chief. Finally a concept existed which gave Israel a real plan to destroy the Iranian program, and the man who had been the most pessimistic was now enthusiastic for the first time. "Let's talk about why I called this meeting," Cohen said. "I will start by reminding you all about Amit Margolis, the Mossad agent who was added to the Yahalom Group in January. I hoped at the time that he would bring some creativity to the very conventional planning that had occurred up to then. And, Ben, I think you will agree that as of year-end, despite over a year of planning, there was yet to emerge anything that seemed plausible that did not involve the U.S. Air Force." Cohen looked at Raibani. He wanted acknowledgement that 2009 had been a fruitless exercise in conventional planning. "Ben, you agree?"

"Yes. No question. I have to admit that we do not yet have a workable solution to this challenge. Not last year or this year for that matter. But I still have not changed my mind on the nuclear option even one bit."

"Good, because I am hoping that after this meeting, the nuclear option will be permanently off the table." That comment was more than enough to get everyone in the room excited. "Zvi, please continue."

Avner gathered his thoughts, drumming his pen on the notepad. "Last week I received a request from Amit Margolis, the man that the prime minister just mentioned. He wanted to meet me one-on-one and run an idea past me. He called it 'Esther's Sling.' He had not previously mentioned this concept to anyone in Yahalom Group or anywhere else. We met in my office at the Campus. I planned for only a few minutes, but we talked for almost two hours. The prime minister and I met for dinner Sunday night and reviewed the concept.

"The whole point of this plan addresses the core tactical issue we face: Our Air Force is simply not large enough to achieve the strategic goal in one sortie. And yet, for all the reasons we have discussed ad nauseam, we have to find a way to get the job done in one sortie. We have been racking our brains to think of a force multiplier other than nuclear weapons. Well, I think Margolis dreamed up a conventional force multiplier. The concept of Esther's Sling starts with …"

Zvi Avner spent the next twenty minutes explaining to the Kitchen Cabinet of Israel the plan's conception of operations. As he spoke, expressions of surprise gave way to smiles. By the time he was done, the atmosphere in the conference room that was surrounded by reinforced concrete was electric. Cohen could not remember another meeting like this. In a room where the problems facing the State of Israel were laid out in bare detail, the feeling was that of a birthday celebration among old friends.

Ben Raibani was excited as he asked several clarifying questions. When Avner was finished, Raibani had a smile. The aging ex-chief of staff of the IDF added a simple comment. "This is brilliant. I want to meet this guy."

"You will," replied Cohen.

"You should put this guy under armed guard. He is the most valuable man in Israel right now." Raibani looked at Cohen. "My apologies, Eli, but I am serious."

"No need to apologize. I don't disagree with you. I hadn't thought about it, but I think you are exactly right. Zvi, can you make arrangements?"

"Certainly. I will take care of it."

Discussions broke out among the five men around the table other than the prime minister. The excitement was igniting the thought processes of each man. Cohen's goal of having Amit Margolis get the Yahalom Group officers to think outside the box had not worked with that group, but was doing wonders with the Kitchen Cabinet. Eli Cohen retrieved a fresh cigar from his humidor. As he prepared it for lighting, he gazed at Yavi Aitan. The prime minister needed to know what Aitan thought. Eli Cohen realized at that moment just how much he had grown to respect the mathematician turned intelligence czar.

Cohen took several puffs and then loudly interrupted everyone's discussions. "Yavi, we have yet to hear your reaction." The room grew quiet. Cohen realized that even the old warrior Raibani wanted to know what Aitan thought. "Please share it with us."

Yavi Aitan pulled his seat closer to the table and leaned forward. "Well, Mister Prime Minister, I have just been thinking it through."

"And?"

"And after thinking it through, I can see many challenges in actually pulling it off, but I have to say – and I will use General Raibani's word – it's simply brilliant. If we can get all of these pieces in place, I think it will work. Secrecy is paramount. If this slips out in even the smallest detail or hint, it will fail. This cannot be shared outside this room. Not with spouses or parents or even your rabbi. I am guessing this takes at least a year to prepare and the circle of people who will need to know some piece of the puzzle will grow during that year. To me, that is the challenge. Keep it secret and we achieve our strategic objective in a way that will stun the world. If the secret gets out, we will preside over one of the colossal disasters this nation has ever had to endure. In the former scenario, we are heroes and the U.S. will never be overtly involved. In the latter scenario, we will go begging to the Americans hat in hand to bail us out of disaster. I feel so strongly about secrecy that I even have my doubts about informing Director Levy."

Cohen smiled broadly as he enjoyed his cigar, the first puffs always being the most satisfying. "We will have to see, but I appreciate your point. Secrecy is everything and it will be difficult to maintain. I want the commitment from everyone here to not discuss this outside of this room or the Yahalom Group." Cohen went around the room and looked each man in the eye as they committed to him personally. "Thank you all."

Zvi Avner now added his thoughts. "I have been thinking about Yahalom Group since my discussion with Margolis last week. I don't like the dynamics on the team. The six members other than Margolis are all career staff officers. They don't respect ... ah, that's not the right word. They don't accept Margolis in the team. He is the newcomer and the outsider. He's not a military man. It says a lot to me that he was not willing to disclose or discuss his concept with any of the other men he's supposedly been working with for the past ten weeks. That bothered me as I thought about it over the weekend but now I'm glad he hasn't said a word to them. I want to shake up the team. I have a man in mind to come in and I think Margolis should be the co-head of Yahalom Group along with this new officer."

"Who?" Cohen asked.

"David Schechter." General David Schechter was the Head of Operations of the Israeli Air Force. He had earned his reputation as one of the IAF's first F-15C fighter pilots and earned respect as the first commander of 69 Squadron, the 'Hammers' – the IAF's sole wing of F-15I Ra'am fighter-bombers that would lead any attack on Iran. He had become an ace over Lebanon and Syria during June 1982 by shooting down three MIG-21s and two MIG-23s over a 72 hour period. He was only 25 years old at the time.

Cohen turned to Raibani. "Ben, you know General Schechter well."

"Yes, I do. He is a first rate commander. He is a leader. He is fearless in combat. If we are talking about the man to take this from planning to operation, then I agree with Zvi. Great choice."

"If Ben likes him that much, then I have no objection," said Cohen. "Who else do you want to add?"

Avner thought for a moment. "I have some thoughts, but the right answer is that we get David and Amit Margolis together to bond first and then let David decide who he wants to bring onto the team with Amit's involvement ... and my oversight, of course."

"Of course," replied Cohen with a smile. "When can you meet with General Schechter?"

"Whenever you have the time to come to Tel Aviv. I think you should be with me."

"Okay, we can check my calendar after the meeting."

Aitan interrupted. "I think we need a new codename now that this is moving towards an operational phase."

Cohen exhaled a plume of cigar smoke. "What's wrong, you don't like Esther?"

"No sir. I think the name is too obvious and suggestive."

Cohen started to bob his head up and down. "Okay, I can see that. Have something in mind?"

"Yes sir. Something innocuous. Project Block G."

"What the hell does that mean?"

"That's the point, sir. We should use a codename that has no tie to Iran. Project Block G simply sounds like we are talking about another weapon upgrade cycle." Aitan looked at Avner. "I suggest you decide who will be part of the new Yahalom Group. Obviously Amit Margolis, hopefully General Schechter. Whoever else you and they agree on. The new team will use

Project Block G going forward and tell the guys who don't continue on that the Esther project is dead for now."

Cohen took a puff on his cigar and looked to Avner, who returned his gaze. Avner nodded his head. Cohen then looked at Raibani. Raibani nodded his head. "Done," said the prime minister. "God be with Project Block G."

13 – Lunch with Friends

Almost a month had passed since Project Block G became official at a Kitchen Cabinet meeting in Jerusalem. General David Schechter had enthusiastically accepted his new assignment as the head of Yahalom Group. More importantly to Cohen and Avner, Schechter had reacted to Esther's Sling the same way that every member of the Kitchen Cabinet had done. He was on board, but the wheels of IDF bureaucracy turned slowly – even when the grease was being applied by the prime minister himself. Schechter had only met with Amit Margolis twice and the agenda for each of those meetings had been to decide upon the new members of the planning team now charged with developing the concept of Esther's Sling into a real battle plan.

David Schechter had done something to endear himself to Amit Margolis. As his first official act as head of the Yahalom Group, he cancelled the pair of bodyguards that had been assigned to watch over Margolis. Both men agreed that the presence of two bodyguards simply turned Amit Margolis from an anonymous Israeli citizen into a target. When Margolis asked the general if countermanding the bodyguard orders, which had come from Zvi Avner, would create problems, the simple answer was "Let me worry about that." This single action created instant respect by Amit for David Schechter.

General Schechter was a career fighter pilot who discovered only later that he also possessed the skills to plan, organize and lead a professional fighting force. He had a style, and that style was a unique blend of the traits that made him a great fighter ace as well as a career Israeli officer. He was a great judge of character and a quick thinker. He wanted to know the people he was commanding on a personal level. He wanted to understand their strengths and their weaknesses and their motivations.

The edge that made him a ruthless fighter pilot in his youth had admittedly dulled a little, the result, he told himself, of marriage and fatherhood. He had enjoyed his twenties, a period of time occupied by a long list of women when he wasn't flying F-15s. Life had been simple and he used his hero status to full advantage in the bars and discos of Tel Aviv. Change for him came in the most unlikely manner. When he was 29, like many young IAF pilots, he went to see *Top Gun* when it was released in Israel. He identified immediately with Tom Cruise's character, not only because of occupation, but also because Schechter looked a lot like Cruise. When his friends started calling him 'Maverick', he realized that he was uncomfortably close to a character that, to Schechter, had as many flaws as attributes. The movie made him see a reflection that he was not satisfied with. He matured quickly over the next few years, a process that was capped when he married at the age of 33. Marriage, in turn, helped his career migrate from legendary fighter pilot to professional commander – a man that other men wanted to follow into combat.

Now twenty years later, David Schechter had four children along with his wife. At home in Raanana he led a suburban life that would fit perfectly into any bedroom community found anywhere in the world. In the office, he oversaw the operations of an air force that had to be ready to fight every moment of every day – a perfectly tuned instrument that was the guarantor of Israel's survival. Every senior military commander in the world knew that as long as the IAF remained unchallenged in the Middle East, Israel would prevail over its enemies. Lose that edge and the death of the state would follow. For David Schechter, this knowledge informed his every working day. On his shoulders rested the fate of a nation. The only threat to that strategic reality was – God forbid – the use of nuclear weapons against Israel. And now, Schechter was given the responsibility to ensure that such a possibility would not come about. For him, it was business as usual.

On this night, however, the weight of that responsibility would take a back seat to getting to know Amit Margolis, a man nineteen years his junior who would now be his partner in the single most important endeavor in either man's life.

Orah Schechter opened the front door to her home on Etsyon Street. The wife of General David Schechter was eight years younger than her husband but now looked a little older. She was a full time housekeeper and mother, the role leaving too little time for exercise and too much time for eating. Like many married women in their forties, Orah's weight swung in a range that reflected, on a good day, the success of recent dieting will power or, on a bad day, the frustration of having succumbed too easily to the temptations of a full refrigerator. Tonight, like most nights, her weight was somewhere in the middle. "Shalom. You must be Amit." Her smile was still as beautiful as the day it caught the eye of a 31-year-old IAF fighter pilot.

Amit Margolis smiled as he shook Orah's hand. "Shalom, Mrs. Schechter."

"Please call me Orah."

"Shalom, Orah. This is my girlfriend, Enya."

Orah Schechter looked up to the stunning model, fighting to control her feminine instincts. She immediately noticed that Enya was wearing a pair of Gianni Bini brown wedge shoes paired with a Dolce & Gabbana peach colored mid length dress. Enya's shoes added two inches to her already formidable five-foot-seven-inch frame. Orah smiled and extended her hand. She couldn't help but think that she was welcoming her daughter to dinner. Enya smiled back, which did nothing to help the hostess feel more at ease. "It's a pleasure to meet you."

"I'm going to have to hide you from my teenage son," said Orah, not sure what possessed her to make the comment.

Enya laughed nervously. The young couple followed Orah into the home, walking down a hall and into the kitchen. The hostess offered wine. "My husband will be home soon. He took our two youngest kids to a friend's home." Amit Margolis smiled. He couldn't come to grips with the air force general he had now been in meetings with twice also being a suburban father chauffeuring kids around town.

Thirty-five minutes later, all four adults were seated at a small rectangular table in the walled backyard of the Schechter home. The weather on this early spring day just north of Tel

Aviv was perfect. The late afternoon temperature was now 76 degrees and the sky was cloudless. Everyone had finished a cucumber and tomato salad and Orah had just placed grilled lamb on the table to complement the vegetables and couscous. "Please help yourselves," she added. She returned to the kitchen to open another bottle of wine.

As his wife walked away, Schechter added an instruction. "Open a bottle of the Joseph Phelps Insignia, honey. Make sure it's 2007." Orah did not respond as she headed inside, but she heard every word and would be sure to comply.

"I think we all share something in common. All of our parents immigrated here," said Schechter, wanting to learn more about Amit.

Margolis spoke up first. "My father was American but his parents had emigrated from Russia. My mother came here from Russia after a brief time in the U.S."

"That certainly explains why you speak Russian like a Russian," observed the general.

"Da," smiled the young Mossad katsa. "Same with Enya."

Enya had been somewhat reticent. She was not at all sure if she was up to a dinner at the home of an Israeli general. Her Saturday nights were usually spent with friends at a party or a dance club. "Yes, my parents came here from the Soviet Union in 1983," she said. "My mother was three months pregnant with me when she arrived. How about you, General?"

"Please call me David. You make me feel too old." Schechter smiled at the beautiful woman seated to his left and took a sip of wine. "I … am not Russian. My parents came to Israel from France. They were fortunate enough to live in Aix-en-Provence. My grandfather owned a vineyard that had been in the family for generations and my father started running it just before the war. They somehow survived the Vichy period and the denaturalization laws. My mom always told me it was because my father was very popular in town. Of course she also told me that he was smart enough to give away cases of his vintage reserve wines to the right people, including the chief of police." Schechter laughed at the thought, his outward expression masking the anger that he harbored inside. He had spent his youth daydreaming about being a vineyard owner in southern France. "Even after the Nazi occupation, they were able to survive for over a year. Finally the Germans started sending SS units across the countryside to round up remaining Jews. The property had a series of caves in the hillsides where wine was aged. My parents spent almost a year living in a hidden part of the caves with a small number of local Jews. They were supported by some of their workers who brought them food and never revealed the secret. But my grandfather, who was in his 70s, I think, stayed in the house and gave the SS a story about how his son and daughter-in-law had escaped to Spain by boat. He died on a train headed east towards a concentration camp."

"I'm so sorry," said Enya, unable to bring herself to call him David.

Schechter regretted going into that detail. He did not want to create a somber mood. Margolis could sense this. Amit spoke up to bail out his new partner. "I am guessing that French is your, eh, first language? 'Ex' – that's how you pronounce that? It's spelled a-i-x, right?"

"Oui. *Ex-on-provence*. That is how a Frenchman in the south of France says it."

"I have always wondered about that." Margolis looked at his girlfriend. "I always like to learn something new."

The general smiled as his wife returned from the kitchen, an open bottle of one of the world's best cabernet sauvignons in her hands. "Who would like some red wine with their lamb," she said as she approached the table.

"Please," came the response from Margolis.

The general liked that his new partner had recognized the situation and intentionally sought to lighten the mood. "You are right, Amit. French is what I grew up with at home." As many men knew, the language of romance was one of the most powerful aphrodisiacs, especially when used by a fighter ace in Tel Aviv in the '80s. But with his wife back at the table, that was a memory that would not be shared at the moment.

Enya Govenin filled her plate with vegetables and couscous. She passed on the cabernet, instead continuing to enjoy her chardonnay. Orah was not as perceptive as her husband. "You should try the lamb. It's delicious," the lady of the house said.

Amit looked at his girlfriend. She was embarrassed and not sure how to respond. He interjected to help her out. "Thank you, Orah. The lamb is really delicious. But Enya is a vegetarian."

"Oh," responded Mrs. Schechter. "I'm so sorry."

"Nothing to be sorry about," said Enya. "I have not eaten meat in a long time now." Enya ate a bite of food as the hostess sat down, having filled three of four wine glasses. "I wanted to thank you for having us over. Your home is beautiful." Enya smiled at Orah and then turned to the general. She was curious and the time had come to quench that desire. "I'm sorry, how do you and Amit know each other again?"

"Ah, I can understand your curiosity." Schechter put his fork down and reached for the wine glass. "Amit is helping the air force with our budgeting. It is the age old problem, you know. We have a lot we want to do and unfortunately limited funds to do it with. Amit helps us project out our expenses and look for savings." He took a sip of wine and shrugged his shoulders. "Not very exciting, but a reality of life." He smiled at his young guest. Across from him, Orah noted the flirtatious tone in her husband's voice, something she had not heard in years.

"Didn't I read that you were recently appointed as the special military advisor to Prime Minister Cohen?" Enya asked. Amit had pulled up the article from Haaretz on his computer earlier that day, asking her to learn a little about their host for the evening.

Schechter was surprised, immediately wondering if he had been underestimating the auburn haired beauty in front of him. The story had been given to the press to cover Schechter's removal from his operational duties in order to head up Yahalom Group. "I'm glad to see that our youth are keeping up with current events. I thought that no one cared about the news anymore," Schechter said. He smiled at Enya. "Yes, I was recently asked by the prime minister to act as his personal advisor on military matters and serve as a liaison between the IDF and the Americans. It's an important role and I am honored to serve the prime minister."

"I think Amit is somehow related to this," Enya pressed, her tone slightly accusatorial.

"Well, you are not supposed to know this, but Amit will be consulting with me on budget priorities for the entire IDF." Schechter looked at Margolis and reached over with his right hand to clasp Amit's left shoulder. He looked back at Enya. "You have a very important man here, Enya. Please take care of him. I will need his budget advice over the coming months." Schechter squeezed Amit's shoulder and abruptly released his grasp.

"Oh, don't you worry," Enya said, and she looked into Amit's eyes. "I will take care of him and make sure he is very happy."

"Hey, hey," joked the general. "Now don't wear him out. I need him to be focused in the office." Schechter laughed and brought his wine glass up to his mouth. Across the table, his wife rolled her eyes.

"Amit tells me you are a war hero," Enya stated in a voice that Schechter interpreted as seductive.

David Schechter returned his wine glass to the table, its contents a little lighter. He suddenly longed to be a single man, if only for an evening. "Is that so?"

"The general is one of our leading aces," Margolis added, clearly feeling honored to be at David's table.

"I got lucky a couple of times," Schechter said finally. He was thinking more of the many women he had bedded than the unlucky Syrian pilots who were his victims.

"Lucky?" Margolis blurted out, looking at his girlfriend. "This man shot down eight Syrian fighters."

Schechter smiled and started to shake his head. "No, no. One of those was a Hezbollah UAV. That definitely doesn't count." He laughed the laugh of false modesty.

"Wow. I am eating with a war hero," Enya cooed.

Orah was not happy as she watched the smile on her husband's face. It was a smile she recognized. It was her husband on the hunt. This visitor to her right was making her feel like an old woman.

"Do you still fly?" Enya asked.

"Yes, but not on combat missions anymore. I fly to maintain my rating and be ready in the event of … well, let's just say that if the country needed me at this point, we would be in a serious situation."

Amit Margolis found the banter amusing but kept an eye on Orah Schechter. On the one hand, he assumed this dinner would be a one-off event. On the other hand, he figured that there was never a reason to have an enemy on the home front. He turned to his hostess. "I must compliment your cooking. Everything has been wonderful."

Enya, to her credit, was quick to add her voice. "Yes, Orah, I loved the salad. You have to give me the recipe." She had spoken only out of a sense of politeness. She was oblivious to Orah's growing feelings of inferiority because she had no attraction to the general. To her, he held only the fascination of an accomplished fatherly figure.

The next fifteen minutes was a discussion of cooking and children that centered on Orah. David Schechter observed Margolis the entire time, impressed with the young man's ability to change his wife's mood.

14 – To the Drawing Room

Another quarter hour later and the men had retired to the general's office, which was swept periodically for listening devices by IDF internal security. The room was in the center of the home and had no windows. The walls and ceiling were made of reinforced concrete poured just over a foot think. This room had a triple role. It was the home's shelter in the event of war, a building code requirement born of unfortunate necessity in Israel. It was also a safe room for the general and his family in the event that he was targeted by any of the country's many mortal enemies. A gun safe in the corner held a small arsenal, enough firepower to arm every member of the family. Back in the kitchen, the women engaged in conversation with the Schechter's 16-year-old son, who blushed whenever Enya spoke to him.

In the office, David Schechter walked over to a cabinet, opened it and pulled out a bottle of Fonseca Porto 10-year-old tawny port wine and two dessert wine glasses. "You will love this port. Perfect complement to any grilled meat."

Amit Margolis sat down on a leather sofa against one wall. David turned to deliver a small crystal glass to the Mossad agent. "You know your girlfriend is a real knockout." Amit nodded and smiled as he took the glass of port wine. "Reminds me of the fun days of my youth. Enjoy these years, Amit. Before you know it, you have a family and a mortgage and you are spending every weekend driving your children to football matches."

"Doesn't sound so bad," replied Margolis, raising his glass in a toast to his new partner. "L'chaim."

"L'chaim," replied Schechter. "To a successful operation."

Margolis took a sip. "Mmm. Excellent. Your knowledge of wines is impressive, General."

"Okay, let's get over the first important hurdle right now. There is a tradition in the IDF. Peers call each other by their first names. You may not accept it yet, but as far as I am concerned, we are peers. I have already developed a real respect for your mind, Amit. And I already like you a lot. Okay?"

"Okay, David."

"Better. Now you call me David in every setting. Especially when we are in meetings with the Yahalom Group or at the Campus or any IDF facility. I want everyone to know that we are peers. We are partners in this endeavor. If this ever goes operational, you will be at my side. This is going to be our baby and we will either succeed or go down together." Schechter extended his right hand to Amit.

Amit shifted his glass to his left hand and reached out to Schechter with his right. They shook hands firmly. "Agreed."

"So be it, Amit. So be it." Schechter sat down on a chair that was perpendicular to the sofa, a small coffee table now the resting place for the open bottle of Fonseca. Around the walls were photos of Schechter in front of various aircraft, mostly F-15s, or standing next to each prime minister of Israel since the early 1980s. Margolis was struck by the fact that in each photo, the prime minister was the more excited of the pair. On the desk were a number of photos of Schechter's kids and a handful of Orah Schechter. Margolis noticed that there were two photos of Orah alone and both were probably a decade old, when the woman was at least thirty pounds lighter.

"You and Enya seem to be in love. Are there wedding plans in the future?"

Amit was shocked back into the moment. Neither he nor Enya had yet said those fateful three words to each other. But it hit him at that instant that he was falling in love with her. He had been ignoring the feelings and she had been doing the same. But she had recently started joking with him about what she would do when her lease expired in the summer – joking about moving in with Amit. As the man that was quickly becoming famous for his analytical abilities sat and pondered his personal life, he realized that he had simply been denying what was happening between him and Enya. "Oh, no. We have only been dating a few months now. We met on New Year's Eve – Gregorian new year, not Rosh Hashanah."

"Well I have to say that watching you two together, I don't know." David shook his head and then took a sip of port wine. "You are a lucky man. I wouldn't let her go if I were you."

"So far, so good." Amit raised his glass in salute to the thought and then took another sip.

"Are you religious?" the general asked. "I have always heard that Mossad is a great bastion of secularism. I am guessing that the secular thinking goes out the window about the same time it does for fighter pilots – when the shadow of death is stalking your aircraft."

"I suppose Mossad is similar to that. Not too many men seem to be torn between attending rabbinical school and joining Mossad. But if we are being honest, then the fact is that we all turn religious when, as you put it, death is stalking. But do I regularly attend synagogue? No. If that is the measure of my faith, then I guess I am a secular Jew. But in my heart I do believe in my faith even if I am not strictly observant."

"I think we are very similar, Amit. I always think of the term 'silent majority', which was a hot phrase when I was in college. We are they." David Schechter had attended Ben Gurion University of the Negev, starting there in 1975 as he went through the IAF two-year pilot training program. He had been recruited while in high school to attend the *gibush*, a weeklong selection to pick the smartest and most physically appropriate Israeli males to receive flight training upon entering the IDF at the age of 18. Because he chose one of the hardest degrees offered, mechanical engineering, he continued his studies even after being assigned to an active fighter squadron. He had finally earned his BS degree in 1981.

"You are not driven by religion," Schechter continued. His statement was an observation. "So what motivates you? Why join Mossad?"

Amit slowly sipped his port wine, taking the time to think about a response. He suddenly felt as if he was in a job interview. The last time he had been asked questions like these was when he being interviewed for Mossad. It dawned on him how similar were the personalities and traits of those who joined Mossad and those who became pilots for the IAF. "Probably no different than you, just a later realization. I attended business school in the States at Duke ..."

"So did I," said Schechter, smiling.

"Oh, yeah? Duke?"

"The IDF sent me to Harvard, the Executive MBA Program. I spent a year working on it with very little flying. Not sure what it did for me, but looks good on the resume. When I got back, the 69 Squadron was reactivated with F-15I fighter-bombers. I was named the commander and kept going up the chain from there."

"Very nice." Both Amit and David forgot the question that had led to this mutual revelation of business school experiences. But now each man realized the many things they had in common. For Schechter in particular, this was unexpected. The thought entered David's mind that Amit was exactly what he hoped his sons would grow up to become. The connection was set. The bond was real.

15 - Olympus

Spring months quickly merged into the Israeli summer of 2010, hotter and drier than average. General David Schechter restructured the Yahalom Group. Only the navy officer and one of the two ground force officers were retained. All three IAF officers were dismissed from the group, replaced by General Schechter and two combat veterans. The new officers represented all of the areas of expertise necessary to make Esther's Sling a real operational battle plan. One of the new air force officers was considered the top logistics expert in the IDF, having previously commanded the airlift and aerial refueling assets of the IAF. The other new air force officer was a man Schechter had worked with over the years. He was a helicopter pilot who earned his reputation under fire in Lebanon and had since become known for his ability to turn a conceptual plan into the actual steps necessary to make that plan a successful reality. Finally, on the suggestion of Amit Margolis, the dismissed ground forces officer was replaced by a special operations veteran and senior officer, a legendary commander in the IDF who knew and understood intimately the capabilities of all of the IDF's growing special operations groups.

Yahalom Group moved shortly thereafter to an underground bunker beneath the Campus in downtown Tel Aviv. Its computers were joined into a small network but cut off from the outside world. Two separate computers were set up for any internet research activity, their search activities routed through a series of servers outside of Israel that were maintained by Unit 8200 and that made the searches impossible to trace back to Israel. These two computers had no USB ports or ability to connect to the computers used for detailed operational planning. They contained no microphones and no video cameras. No one could use them to quietly eavesdrop on the activities in that room as Israel and the U.S were doing in Iran at that very moment. Any virus that made it through the various firewalls maintained by Unit 8200 would end on those two computers. Signs maintained on the wall behind the two computers warned any user to never, ever conduct any personal activity on the computers. No checking on email accounts. No banking. No visits to a personal Facebook account. All of these instructions were to ensure that no user of these two computers could be identified by any outside intelligence agency that somehow defeated the firewall and routing safeguards set up by Unit 8200.

Only the seven members of the group had access into the bunker room where maps and grease boards soon occupied all available space on the walls. Each man in the group knew he had two leaders. As Eli Cohen had predicted and David Schechter had ensured, Amit Margolis, the youngest member of the group, was respected by each of the six career military officers, both for his brain power and as the clear co-leader. Schechter reinforced this by having Amit lead morning status meetings. The thoughts and ideas were materializing into a methodical plan that, step by step, would culminate into what the politicians like to call an actionable operation.

On Tuesday, September 7, 2010, a meeting was held in a conference room on the Campus. Nine months had passed since Prime Minister Cohen had invited Amit Margolis to join the Yahalom Group at the start of the year. The outlook for Esther had evolved from a frustrated stalemate into a plan that now excited everyone in the small circle privy to it.

Outside, the gathering morning light struggled to pierce through low hanging clouds over Tel Aviv. Inside, the most powerful group in Israel assembled to make a fateful decision. General David Schechter wanted sign-off and authorization to move forward with Project Block G as an operational plan. He wanted it in writing and signed by the prime minister, the defense minister and the chief of staff of the Israeli Defense Forces. He needed a working budget and real funds to begin acquiring all of the required assets and pay for the training and preparation to enact the plan. And he explicitly wanted the concept of Esther's Sling to be authorized – he would not be the scapegoat if something went wrong with a concept that would, after it was used, alter international relations.

Amit Margolis and General Schechter entered the conference room a little before 10 a.m. as requested. As they walked in, they realized that a meeting had been underway between Prime Minister Cohen, Defense Minister Avner, Chief of Staff Natan Fishel, Yavi Aitan and Danny Stein. Eli Cohen was in a side conversation with Danny Stein, who had been tasked by his prime minister with finding the funds to pay for Project Block G. Stein, the minister of industry, trade and labor, would act as the negotiator and intermediary with the Ministry of Finance. An elaborate cover story had been constructed to justify the request for up to $300 million, a sizable amount in the tiny nation, to pay for items that could not show up on the IDF budget.

Eli Cohen noticed the pair walking in and broke off his conversation with Danny Stein. The prime minister stood up and walked toward Margolis. "Amit, how are you?" Cohen was excited to see the two men who now formed the most important team in Israel as far as he was concerned.

"Very good, sir." The two men shook hands. Cohen then turned to Schechter and repeated the process.

Cohen next introduced each of the men first to Yavi Aitan and then to Danny Stein. Next at the table was Lieutenant General Natan Fishel, Chief of the General Staff of the Israeli Defense Force. Amit Margolis had never met the career infantry officer. Fishel, like the eighteen men who preceded him in the position, was now one of the highest profile persons in Israel. The job thrust the holder from professional obscurity into the limelight as the commander-in-chief of a military machine widely viewed to be the best in the world man for man. In the era of 24 hour news coverage, the position tested the political skills of the man in the seat, a fact that affected the decision by Avner and Cohen on whom to nominate. General Fishel was widely respected for his planning and leadership talents, but he was every bit as comfortable at a party full of Knesset members as he was in a command bunker.

Cohen introduced Margolis. "Amit, this is General Fishel."

Amit Margolis shook hands with Natan Fishel. "It's an honor to meet you."

"I have heard much about you, Mister Margolis." Fishel did not finish the narrative, leaving Margolis in suspense as to whether the general was favorably impressed or not.

Fishel turned his attention to Schechter. "David, how are you this morning?"

The men shook hands. "Very good, Natan. It is good to see you here." Schechter was not being truthful with his boss. The air force officer was wondering if he would still be in command of Project Block G at the end of this meeting.

Each man next shook hands with Defense Minister Avner and took his seat to the right of Prime Minister Cohen, who sat at the head of the table. Schechter immediately spoke up, not waiting for anyone else to take the lead. "I want to thank Defense Minister Avner for arranging this meeting. I am very pleased to report to all of you that the Yahalom Group has unanimously and enthusiastically agreed to a plan for Project Block G. The purpose of our meeting today is to obtain your authorization to go operational." Schechter lifted up a Redwell expanding file from the side of his chair and placed it on the table. He pulled out seven printed and bound PowerPoint presentations and passed six of them out to the men around the table. Each presentation had a cover sheet with the simple title "Esther" and the classification "Top Secret – Limited Violet" written on it in English and Hebrew. Nowhere in the document did the phase "Project Block G" occur – either you knew what that phrase referred to or you didn't; there would be no written reference. The presentation was just short of one hundred pages, the planning having been developed down to tactical detail at the unit level.

Schechter and Margolis spent the next three hours reviewing all of the detailed information of Project Block G. For General Fishel, this was the first time he had heard the concept of Esther's Sling. When asked by Cohen what he thought after hearing it, he had smiled and simply given the table a thumbs up sign, the gesture saying more than any words could. But the most heated exchanges had come from Cohen and Avner's questioning of the timing necessary to implement the plan. Schechter and Margolis were adamant that Israel could not be ready to launch Project Block G prior to the fall of 2011. The prime minister did not like this timing at all, wanting the plan to be ready to go by the coming spring. Only a detailed review by Margolis of the steps necessary to prepare Esther's Sling convinced Cohen of the necessity of waiting. The long list of munitions still needed by the IAF only reinforced the timetable. Reluctantly, Cohen and Avner conceded the point, surrendering implementation of the plan to the men who had conceived it.

As the review of the presentation finished, Schechter summoned the courage to ask the question that had been in his head since he entered the room. He looked directly at General Fishel. "Who will be in operational command?"

Fishel did not hesitate. He had never questioned the appointment of Schechter, even though it had been made without his input. "That question was settled months ago, David. This is primarily an air force operation. Don't let your nation down."

Schechter relaxed for the first time since entering the room. "Thank you, sir."

Natan Fishel sensed the right timing and looked at Margolis. "Mister Margolis, I have to admit that I was very skeptical when Zvi told me about your role. But listening to you has alleviated my concerns. I officially endorse your appointment as co-head of this operation."

Margolis had not been pondering the general's reaction to him, so the statement caught him off guard. But it was welcome nonetheless. "Thank you, sir. I hope to live up to the trust you have all placed in me."

Fishel continued. "All IDF forces utilized for Project Block G will come under the command of General Schechter when we launch. Mister Margolis, you will be in command of all aspects of Esther's Sling."

16 – Olympic Games

Once all of the questions on the operational plan had been satisfied, Cohen turned to the man who had become his second favorite advisor next to his long-time partner Avner. "Yavi," the prime minister said, "since we need at least a year to prepare, please update everyone on operations to slow down the Iranian program."

Yavi Aitan shifted his seat and leaned forward, the area between his chest and stomach pressing into the edge of the conference table. "Yes, sir. Perhaps the most successful campaign underway the last couple years has been Myrtus." For Schechter and Margolis, this was their first official briefing on the cyber warfare underway against Iran that the Americans referred to as Olympic Games. For this reason, Aitan gave a brief history that only took a couple of minutes. Natan Fishel had previously been briefed in a separate meeting.

Once the quick background had been provided, Aitan began to review current events. "Anyone who has been watching the news is, unfortunately, aware that since June, our primary Myrtus worm is being dissected by private anti-virus companies. Obviously, the world now knows it as Stuxnet. The identification of the worm by Iran was a setback for us. It came as a fluke. An Iranian engineer at Natanz had problems with his computer crashing and the Iranians contacted a small firm they use in Belarus. Their lead guy found Myrtus. Then he blogged about it on the tight network of software pros who work in these anti-virus firms. It quickly exploded into the news."

Eli Cohen interrupted. "What caused the engineer's computer to crash? Was it Myrtus?"

"We don't know for sure. It is possible that it was Myrtus or Tunnel or one of our other worms. We aren't sure yet which computer had the problem, so we aren't sure if this resulted from a recent revision."

"I don't understand," Cohen complained, echoing the thoughts of everyone else in the room.

"Sorry. Let me back up a little. Myrtus and our other worms are communicating back to us when they can. This gives us a wealth of information about what the Iranians are doing and about their entire network. Myrtus was designed so that we can update the software based on what we learn. We have established a joint center in the U.S. with the Americans to share everything learned, scope out and design changes and updates, assign coding responsibilities and, finally, to certify new updates."

"Where is this happening? Langley?" asked Cohen out of curiosity.

"No, sir. The center is at Fort Gordon in Augusta, Georgia."

"Augusta?" responded Zvi Avner. "You mean where the Masters is played?"

"Yes."

"Why in God's name there?"

"The NSA is building a large data and operations center there. The Americans wanted a spot outside of the Washington area where our guys could come and go away from all of the prying eyes."

Avner, an avid golfer, chuckled at the thought. "I didn't realize there was anything in that town other than Augusta National."

Aitan was impatient to get back on the topic. "Anyway, the bad news for us is that the Iranians have finally figured out what has been causing so much unexpected damage to their centrifuges. They will clean the worst of Myrtus off their network in time."

"What's the good news?" asked Prime Minister Cohen.

"The good news is that there is a lot more to Myrtus and our other worms," Aitan continued. "The Iranians are focused on what the world calls Stuxnet, but we have much more underway. Despite the fact that Myrtus was discovered in early June, we still have contact with their network and we still have a lot of activity, much of it destructive. Our software is embedded in parts of their network in a way that is probably impossible to eradicate without tossing out one hundred percent of their hardware, including computers, servers, printers, routers, firewalls and even cell phones. They would have to throw out all of that on one day and start over the next day with brand new hardware that is clean. And in my opinion, they cannot buy hardware, other than isolated equipment, without us getting to it and corrupting it first in our favor."

"What does this virus mean now that it is out of Iran and out in the world?" The question came from Amit Margolis. His mind was thinking about the future, thinking about the counter attack sure to come some day.

"That is a good question, Mister Margolis," responded Aitan. "This technology is like any other. Once mankind has understood something and developed it, it is impossible to keep a monopoly on it – not that we had a monopoly anyway. Russia, China, Japan, Korea, Germany, the U.K., all of these nations could produce what we have done and probably have. But your point is right, all of the analysis and publication of research on Stuxnet will help the second tier countries come up the curve. That includes Iran and every other Muslim nation for that matter.

"As for Myrtus itself, we have programmed safeguards into the worm. First, it targets very specific industrial controllers, namely the type and configuration that is, to my understanding, unique to Natanz. The Americans, in particular, were very sensitive to the worm migrating into the U.S. or another western nation. So, for example, Myrtus targets centrifuges operating at 1,064 hertz. Only the Iranians and Pakistanis operate their centrifuges at this frequency cycle. The Americans also insisted on a drop dead date for the worm. The current date is June 24, 2012, although we can extend that through updates if needed. And as the prime minister and defense minister know, we have some of the more exotic aspects of the worm encrypted in a very strong cipher that we don't think anyone can crack.

"But none of that means that the Iranians and everyone else won't learn from the code that is being discussed and analyzed publicly at the moment. There is nothing we can do about that."

Aitan paused briefly to await a follow-up question. None came. "Mister Prime Minister," he continued, "I can report that the revelation of Myrtus has led the Chinese to enter into serious negotiations with Tehran to bring in Chinese computer technicians to help defend their networks."

Eli Cohen already was fully aware of this developing aspect of the Iranian problem. He had been updated daily over the phone by Mossad Director Levy and occasionally by Aitan. But the minister of intelligence and atomic affairs had made the statement to inform the other men in the room. Zvi Avner had not been previously informed. "How serious?" Avner asked.

"Mossad believes that a group of a dozen or more Chinese computer technicians will fly into Tehran in October. We think they will set up shop in the basement of a classroom building at Tehran University."

"To hell with these Chinese bastards," exclaimed the defense minister. "They are getting in bed with Persian devils. They will get what they deserve."

Prime Minister Cohen had earlier been dismissive of his old partner's histrionics regarding China, but he was beginning to think of China as an active enemy. It was one thing to supply weapons, it was another to supply warriors – and Cohen had come to think of cutting-edge computer hackers and programmers as combat soldiers. Worse for Cohen was the knowledge of the many years of cooperation between Mossad and the Chinese intelligence agency, the Ministry of State Security, or MSS. Director Levy had asked him the week before if he wanted Mossad to reduce or end cooperation with the MSS. Cohen had told him to make no changes.

"This is becoming too serious to ignore," Cohen said. He looked at Schechter and Margolis to his right. "Can you add this Chinese cyber center in Tehran to your target list?"

"Yes, sir," Schechter responded.

"Mister Prime Minister," interjected Chief of Staff Fishel, "I would strongly advise against targeting the Chinese. I don't think we want to pick a fight with them."

"Exactly my words earlier this year when the first reports of discussions came in." Cohen stopped and looked down at the Esther presentation. He wanted a cigar but had not brought one with him this morning. But he had his water. He took a sip. "Thank you, Natan. I know you are giving me sound advice." He turned back to Schechter. "Can we make contingency plans on this? We have a year to see what develops."

"Yes, Mister Prime Minister. We will do that." Schechter had no issue with striking the Chinese or anyone else threatening his country. "You know, sir, the Americans hit the Chinese embassy in Belgrade in '99, if my memory serves me. They begged forgiveness claiming an accident, but I have my doubts."

"It was no accident," Aitan added. He and Levy had discussed the American attack over the prior few weeks, holding the lessons learned in reserve in the event that the prime minister hardened his stance as he just had. "The CIA had good intelligence that the Chinese were acquiring parts of the F-117 stealth fighter shot down over Yugoslavia in late March. All of these parts were being collected at the embassy. On May 7, 1999, the Americans put five satellite guided bombs into the embassy building. President Clinton profusely apologized and blamed the attack on faulty maps. There were demonstrations in China and relations hit a low, but all things were patched up with time."

"Mister Prime Minister," said Fishel, "we are not the United States."

"And of course, Natan," Cohen responded, "we are not talking about attacking the Chinese embassy. This is a secret operation by the Chinese. As far as they know, we have no knowledge of it. If we hit them tomorrow as part of a broad strike, I bet they would not ever say a word."

"You are absolutely right." The support came from Avner, who was very much in line with Schechter's approach. "They will keep their damn mouths shut out of embarrassment, but they will know Goddamn well that we targeted them intentionally. Fuck them."

"Okay, gentlemen," said Cohen. "I know where everyone stands. We have a year. Let's do some contingency planning and keep our eyes on how this develops. Yavi, what else?"

"Lead Vault continues to develop and gain momentum." Aitan spent more than ten minutes updating Fishel, Schechter and Margolis on the operation that was systematically depriving Iran of the raw material needed to build centrifuges and other nuclear program components. More than a dozen intelligence agencies were actively involved, led by Mossad and the CIA, but actively utilizing MI6 and the intelligence agencies of Saudi Arabia, Egypt, Jordan, Turkey, Japan, Korea, Germany, France and others. When he was done, everyone in the room was satisfied that more was being done to starve the Iranian program than they could think of short of a military strike.

Yavi Aitan concluded his review and Eli Cohen asked if anyone had any other topics.

"Of course this is your prerogative, Mister Prime Minister," said Schechter, his lead-in hinting at a controversial request, "but I strongly recommend that only General Fishel and Defense Minister Avner leave with this presentation." Schechter held up his copy of the Esther presentation.

Cohen looked at Avner, the man whose opinion always mattered to him. Avner nodded. "Agreed," the prime minister responded.

"How are we getting the money for this?" Schechter asked as suddenly as the thought entered his head.

"Danny is taking care of that," responded Cohen, looking at the minister for industry, trade and labor.

Danny Stein cleared his throat. "Yes, I am dealing with the Ministry of Finance to fund the cost of Esther's Sling and supporting black operations. I think I will have 1.1 billion shekels funded within the next few months, with the initial funding of 300 million shekels in the bank within two weeks. This is the money we will use for all of the black assets and operations for Block G."

"Who will control the account?" asked Amit Margolis.

"I will," Stein said. "We have already created the entity, which is a subsidiary of El Al."

"Why an El Al sub?"

"Oh, sorry. The cover for the funds is that El Al is in need of new security equipment to meet a specific security threat that is classified. We need to fund it off the books to avoid the publicity and negative impact to their passenger traffic. I am the Managing Director of the new entity, which also has two El Al board members. But I will have complete control over the funds."

"Okay," said Amit. "But what about the two El Al board members? They don't know anything about this, do they?"

Prime Minister Cohen responded. "No, Amit. They won't ask any questions and you won't have to worry about any Board meetings. Trust me." Cohen was smiling. The two men from El Al were old friends of Eli Cohen and knew when they were being asked to do a favor for their nation.

"Everyone realizes that the cost of this operation, above and beyond the off-budget items that Minister Stein is handling, will be in the billions of shekels. Many billions." The comment came from General Schechter. He paused for a moment to look around the conference table. "And that is assuming we don't lose any of our aircraft. That is not realistic. Realistically, I estimate ten percent loses among our aircraft."

"What about aircrews?" asked Zvi Avner.

"We have that covered in the plans you have. We have three ways to extricate downed crewmen. First, we will have two Super Stallion and four Blackhawks of the Flying Cats in Kuwait at Ali Al Salem Air Base." Schechter was referring the IAF's highly trained Airborne Rescue and Evacuation Unit 669, an elite unit established to save downed airmen in hostile territory.

"The Americans will allow that?" responded Avner.

"As is clear in the planning, we have assumed American knowledge and support for Block G, even though they will not know about Esther's Sling. We need their support. Otherwise the risks in this plan are too great. They have to know when we go. We can't cover the distance from here to there without their knowledge and we will need IFF codes on the way."

Avner nodded in agreement and then a question occurred to him. "What if the Americans get angry in reaction to Esther's Sling? What if they back out and retract their IFF codes?"

"We have discussed that as a group," replied Schechter. "The best answer is in the timing of Esther's Sling. By the time anyone figures out what it is we did, IAF strike units will have made it to their targets. At the time of the initial attacks, our strike aircraft will be over American controlled airspace and it will be too late for them to back out even if they fully understood Esther's Sling. But the simple fact is that it will take them hours to figure out what we did in Esther's Sling."

Avner nodded as he thought through the scenario. "Yes, I see what you are saying. Amit, you agree with the theory, right?"

Margolis was fast with his response. "Yes, sir. Completely."

Schechter continued. "The second way to retrieve downed crew will be having Flying Cat units in Azerbaijan. This also supports Operation Northwind, which we will talk about next.

"The third and perhaps the most probable route to success is the use of the Iranian network run by Mossad. We know from prior planning that Mossad has a network in Iran they are comfortable with. Many of the people in this underground railroad are Kurds and other oppressed minorities and most of the targets are in the right areas for these people. We still have to work out contact information and, of course, the crews who go down first have to escape and evade before they can attempt contact. Some crews will bail out over cities like Tehran. For them, capture is almost certain. So, Mister Prime Minister, we ask that you consider what you are willing to do for those men who are captured."

"By 'to do' you mean what am I willing to trade?" Cohen asked.

"Yes, sir, that is what I mean."

"A lot." Cohen pondered the scenario for a moment. He had not previously thought about it. "The bastards will want money." His mind ran off in a maze of possibilities.

"Not something we need an answer to now, sir," Schechter said.

Cohen looked at his old friend, Defense Minister Avner. "Zvi, what do you think of the ten percent estimate?"

Avner cocked his head to the side. "We are going into well defended airspace that is a long way from home. The Persians will throw everything they have into the air while we are overhead. Ten percent is high, but possible. Just at the high end."

"What is your guess then?" probed the prime minister.

"I certainly hope it will not be that high. But for purposes of planning, I think General Schechter is making the right type of assumption."

Eli Cohen turned and looked at an empty white grease board, his eyes focusing on nothing. Perhaps for the first time his mind contemplated the costs and the possibility of true disaster.

"Does Director Levy know about Esther's Sling?" asked Margolis, his question directed to the prime minister.

Cohen snapped out of his thoughts. "Levy? Not unless you have told him."

"No, Mister Prime Minister. The only people I have ever discussed Esther's Sling with are in this room or the other members of Yahalom Group."

"Good. Keep it that way. I have decided … no, let me rephrase that." The prime minister gathered his thoughts for a moment. "The Kitchen Cabinet has unanimously decided that Director Levy does not have a need to know about Esther's Sling. Of course, he will be in the loop about the general airstrike and timing. Esther's Sling, however, must stay outside of Mossad. The organization has too many contacts, too much wheeling and dealing. I want Esther's Sling to be run by the military – by you guys. Understand?"

"I understand, sir," replied Margolis. "Of course I am not military."

"Yes, yes." Cohen waved his hand through the air. "You know what I mean."

Margolis nodded his assent.

"General," the voice was that of Zvi Avner, "what is Northwind?" He was talking to Schechter.

"Ah, yes. Operation Northwind is a deception plan. This we think Mossad can be very involved in. The one unit … um … Amit, what is it called?"

"LAP," Cohen responded before Margolis could speak. LAP is the disinformation and psychological warfare group within Mossad.

"Yes, that's it," Schechter continued. "The goal of the operation is to get the Iranians thinking that we will use airbases in Azerbaijan to launch the attack."

"Azerbaijan?" exclaimed Avner. "That makes no sense at all. The Russians would know everything we did. Hell, they would call the Persians with details of our strike packages an hour before we crossed into Persian airspace."

"Militarily, no, it makes no sense. But the more we can get the Iranians nervous about it, the better. Any air defense unit transferred to the border with Azerbaijan is a positive for us. The added benefit is pulling Azerbaijan and Iran apart and even getting the Russians to chase their tails in Azerbaijan."

Cohen looked at Avner, who nodded his head. Cohen spoke. "Okay, give the plan to Director Levy and let Mossad handle that. I like it. What else?"

General Schechter opened a manila folder and pulled out two original and identical letters, each two pages in length. "I have taken the liberty, Mister Prime Minister, to draw up a letter of authorization for Project Block G. I have two originals here. They are and will remain, of course, under the highest classification."

"Let me see that," said Cohen as Avner also reached out with his hand. Schechter gave one copy to each man.

Avner grew mad as he read the letter. "Who authorized this?"

Prime Minister Cohen reached out with his left hand and touched the right forearm of the defense minister. "Calm down, Zvi. Just read it."

A couple of minutes later Cohen continued. "I understand this. I would prepare the same thing in your shoes. Where were you intending to keep these letters?"

"I assume, sir, that you will take one and I will retain one on behalf of Yahalom Group."

"And you will keep this letter where?"

"In a safety deposit box here in Tel Aviv."

"You know we have been working on this with such a small team and for so long now that I had not thought of the legal process of making this operational," said Cohen. "We are clearly outside of the normal chain for military operations and we have to stay that way as long as we can. I think what you have drafted here is entirely appropriate. We will sign this and you will keep your copy. If this works, we are all heroes and you can sell your copy some day at Christie's in New York. If we fail, there is not a man in this room who will survive the fallout." Cohen paused for effect. "These are the stakes, gentlemen. If you want out, now is the time."

General Fishel spoke up. "Can I at least read the letter?" The request was light-hearted.

Cohen laughed. "Yes, Natan. Read it and then sign it. Who has a pen?"

Cohen, Avner and Fishel signed each letter where indicated. Israel had committed itself to a course of action.

Defense Minister Avner spoke next. "Yahalom Group has done its job. The planning is done and the group is officially dissolved. I want to relocate the team to a hidden bunker complex at Sde Dov Airport. You will now be referred to as Olympus and your new location will be known as Mount Olympus." Sde Dov was right on the Mediterranean and just north of Tel Aviv. It was convenient for all of the men who would now form a growing combat command to be known as Olympus. The bunker complex had been secretly constructed between 2002 and 2005, one of many built around the country in reaction to the growing vulnerability of Israel to massive attack. It had been designed as an emergency command post in the event of the destruction of the Campus and it had all of the communications necessary to exercise operational command of Project Block G.

"Is that it for this morning?" asked Cohen. No one offered any dissenting opinion. "If I don't see you, I wish each of you Shanah Tovah." Rosh Hashanah was two nights away.

17 – Business Matters

On November 8, 2010, a Russian businessman walked out of the Dubai offices of the prestigious law firm of Heinrik, Waddington & Smythe LLP in the Dubai International Financial Centre. The man's name was Gennady Masrov and his navy pin-striped double-breasted Savile Row suit was hand tailored by Gieves & Hawkes at a cost of £4,750. The business card that he left behind had a London address, a serviced rent-an-office building in the upscale business neighborhood of Belgravia. He opened the rear door of his hired black Mercedes S600 sedan and was quickly driven away to the Armani Hotel. The middle-aged man carried himself with all of the confidence and arrogance of his role in life. As the trusted confidante of one of Russia's billionaire tycoons, Masrov lived the lifestyle of modern royalty, confident in the knowledge that as long as his patron stayed on good terms with Vladimir Putin, the money would roll in as if on an endless conveyor belt.

The meeting was to finalize the terms and corporate governance structure of a new entity to be created by the lawyers. Its name would be "Swiss-Arab Air Cargo FZE" and it would be established in the Ras Al-Khaimah Free Trade Zone in and around the Ras Al-Khaimah International Airport. The new entity would be a wholly-owned subsidiary of a Swiss company named SAC Holdings AG. SAC Holdings was, in turn, owned by Gennady Masrov. But he had very intentionally and repeatedly dropped the name of his very wealthy patron, making it clear to the two attorneys in the meeting exactly who it was who would be the real capital behind Swiss-Arab Air Cargo.

One week later, Masrov returned to Dubai on a direct flight from London's Heathrow Airport and checked back into the Armani Hotel, occupying a Signature Suite as he had the week before. The next day Masrov strolled into the lobby of the HSBC Middle East Bank. He asked for Branch Manager Mukhtar Al-Zubaidy. Within moments an excited banker emerged from his office, eager to meet the client that had been referred to him by the attorneys at Heinrik Waddington.

"Welcome to Dubai, Mister Masrov." Al-Zubaidy extended his hand and quickly ushered the Russian into his office. Tea was prepared and waiting, the banker offering to pour Masrov a cup. The Russian accepted and several minutes of introductory conversation over tea followed. The men spoke in English, the accepted language of business in the Middle East. The banker's English was perfect. He had been educated in England at the University of East London.

As Masrov finished his tea, he was ready for business. "Thank you for tea. Now, let's get this done. Do you have the account paperwork ready?"

"Yes, sir," Al-Zubaidy responded. "I was instructed to prepare for two accounts. Is this correct?"

"Yes. A checking account for the business and a sweep account." The latter account would automatically sweep all funds in the checking account greater than $50,000 into a money market account.

"Exactly. I regret that rates are so low." Al-Zubaidy looked at Masrov as he opened a file folder in front of the Russian. "Just to confirm, this is to be a dollar denominated account, correct?"

"Yes." Masrov started to review the documents. The corporate resolutions had been prepared by Heinrik Waddington and were more thorough than the standard pre-printed form typically provided by the bank. "When will the accounts be open?" he asked. Masrov simultaneously pulled a fat roll of money from his pocket. He removed ten crisp new $100 notes. As he folded the roll back up, the banker noticed that Masrov had at least another twenty or so $100 notes wrapped by larger £100 notes, the entire wad forming a stack a couple of inches thick when folded over. This was not uncommon for the types of customers that Al-Zubaidy took care of every day.

Masrov placed $1,000 on the desk. "Please open the accounts with this."

"Your accounts will be in our system tomorrow."

"Okay, I will wire fifty million dollars into the account tomorrow from Union Bank Switzerland."

Al-Zubaidy's eyes opened wider. The reaction was involuntarily. "Yes, sir." He put all his effort into maintaining a professional demeanor. "Please have the wire instructions list our street address and me as your contact."

"Excellent."

Masrov spent the next five minutes signing his name as the banker indicated what each form was for and where to sign. As soon as he was done, Masrov stood and thanked his host. He had an appointment to get to.

Thirty-five minutes later Masrov was in the lobby of the Fortune Tower on Sheikh Zayed Road waiting to meet a real estate agent who was running late. After five minutes, Kara Livingston, a stunning British expatriate, walked into the lobby. She spotted Masrov instantly. She strode across the lobby effortlessly, her business attire and four inch pumps appearing completely out of place among the Muslim ethics of the United Arab Emirates. Masrov had been referred to her by Al-Zubaidy, being told that she was the top commercial real estate broker in Dubai.

As she walked up, Masrov realized she was looking at him eye to eye, matching his 5-foot 11-inch height. She was breaking every norm expected by the conservative Arab businessmen in the city. But her niche was finding office space and apartment rentals for the plethora of European, Asian and North American business people setting up shop in Dubai as their Middle East headquarters.

"Mister Masrov," Livingston extended her hand. "What a pleasure to meet you." If she was self-conscious about being late, she showed no sign.

The Russian was pleasantly surprised, his eye quickly scanning her left hand and seeing no ring on her finger. "Miss Livingston. The pleasure is mine." The pair shook hands.

"Please call me Kara. Shall we head on up?"

"Of course." Masrov said, smiling. He stepped to the side and swung his arm out. "After you."

The elevator ride to the 32nd floor took only seconds. Livingston bantered with her new client, not quite sure whether the discussion had passed over into flirtation. Walking off the elevator, she turned to her left and used a white scanner card to pass through the glass doors and into an unoccupied lobby that featured Persian rugs and a granite and mahogany reception desk.

"As you can see, everything in this building is one hundred percent first class, on par with the finest office buildings in London, New York or Moscow." She added the last city in deference to her client. "You have 3,130 square feet in the northeast corner. The views are phenomenal." She walked through a lobby door and down a short hallway. "Let me show you your new office." She opened a three inch thick mahogany door hung on four gold-plated hinges. "Viola," she said as she stepped in and out of the way of Masrov's view.

The Russian stepped in and stopped. "Wow." The corner office had floor to ceiling glass windows that formed an arced flowing corner. Outside, the many office and residential towers of the Jumeirah Lake area of Dubai formed the rapidly growing skyline of the most modern city in the Middle East. In the distance, the blue waters of the Persian Gulf shimmered in the afternoon sun.

"Fantastic isn't it? You can see the Palm Jumeirah and the marina. This is the hottest area in Dubai."

"What are the asking terms?"

"Eighty-eight dirhams per foot, escalating at four percent per year for five years. In dollars that's about twenty-four dollars a foot to start."

The Russian laughed. "The owners must think we are still in 2005. If they want to have a tenant in here then they better get real." Masrov thought about the asking price, doing some math in his head. "If you can get me eighteen dollars U.S. per foot, I will take the space. And I want the first six months free."

"I will take that to the landlord and see what they say."

"Like I said, if they aren't interested, I will see if I can get lucky with some of the other millions of square feet of empty office space in Dubai."

The Russian started to walk out but stopped and looked at Livingston. "Are you are free this evening?"

Livingston laughed. "Um, right then ... that was an abrupt change of topic."

"I am Russian. This is the way we think."

"Oh. What is it you are thinking?"

Now Masrov laughed. "Perhaps we should share that over some champagne. I am sure you can recommend an appropriate location."

"You are being very presumptive, Mister Masrov."

"You are not saying no, Miss Livingston."

Kara Livingston blushed slightly and turned her eyes toward the view of the Gulf. "Touché."

"Seven o'clock? I will pick you up."

"Seven-thirty. I will meet you at Vu's. Your driver will know where it is."

The real estate agent turned to walk out of the office and back down the hall. "Did you want to see the rest of the space?"

"I have a good feel for what I am getting," he replied.

"Now it is my turn to ask you something. How is it your English is so good?"

"Many years in London now."

"But your accent is American."

Masrov laughed. "Touché." He was following her toward the elevator, enjoying the way she filled out her tight skirt. "I attended business school in America."

"I see." She turned right and passed through the glass doors dividing the lobby from the elevator landing. She held the door for her client.

"I am betting that you would not have guessed that," Masrov responded.

Livingston nodded her head as she pressed the elevator call button. Her hair was shoulder length and had been dyed a sandy blonde, no doubt, thought Masrov, to cover any gray hairs that were always an unwelcome visitor. He judged her to be somewhere around 40, give or take a couple of years.

She stepped to the side, waiting for the elevator to arrive. She looked at the Russian. "Are you married? I won't go out with married men."

Masrov raised his left hand. There was no ring and no white line from a recently removed ring. "Are we going out, then?"

She looked him in the eye. "I need to hear you say it."

"I am not married. I can assure you of that."

She smiled as the bell rang, indicating the arrival of their carriage. "Neither am I. Please call me Kara."

18 – The View

Masrov arrived at Vu's Bar on the 51st floor of the Emirates Hotel Tower at 6:45 p.m. He told his driver that he would be anywhere from two to three hours. His late afternoon had been spent in another meeting, this time with an aviation attorney at the same firm of Heinrik Waddington. It was this specialty and this attorney that had caused Masrov to hire the firm in the first place. Forming companies was a commodity service, done online in the U.S. or Europe for about $100. But navigating the ins and outs of obtaining civil aviation authority was a specialty, one in which experience and connections were invaluable. Abraham Sanjoors was considered the best in the Gulf Region and Masrov was more than happy to pay his senior partner rate of $450 per hour for his advice. The meeting earlier in the day had been introductory, each man learning about the other. Sanjoors wanted to understand the goals and timing of Swiss-Arab Air Cargo and he wanted to set the Russian's expectation on the amount of time and money required to obtain an Air Operator Certificate from the General Civil Aviation Authority of the government of the United Arab Emirates.

The Russian had reacted to the projected twelve- to eighteen-month timeline with anger, insisting that in Russia, any attorney worth his money knew how to bring about an expedited review. Sanjoors was offended by the suggestion, threatening to quit. Masrov was about to walk out in disgust when the junior attorney in the room, the associate who worked for Sanjoors, suggested another way to get the desired outcome. The firm was representing a small air cargo company that he thought would entertain an offer from Swiss-Arab Air Cargo. They owned two small turbo-prop Antonov AN-32 transport aircraft and barely broke even. He suggested that Abraham Sanjoors call the owner the next day. Masrov asked the obvious question: Can the authority be transferred? Sanjoors answered that it couldn't be transferred, but if Swiss-Arab purchased the stock of the company, it would control the authority and could change the name of the company.

The meeting ended on that upbeat note, with Masrov already impatient to hear. He extracted a promise from Sanjoors to call him as soon as the discussion with the owner had occurred.

But now the Russian's mind was occupied with other pursuits. The bartender at Vu's brought him a bowl of mixed snacks along with his Crown and seven. Masrov took a sip, trying to figure out why sesame sticks were always mixed in with the peanuts in every bar. He motioned the bartender back to him. When the young Emirati came over, Masrov extended a folded $100 bill pressed between the forefinger and second finger of his right hand. The bartender smiled broadly.

"Yes, sir. What can I do for you?" His English was quite good. It was the language most widely used at Vu's – even more than Arabic.

"I am going to move to this table right here." Masrov pointed to a table just a few feet away. "I have a friend joining me and I want you to be very attentive."

"Yes. Of course."

"Excellent. Now I want you to get a bottle of Cristal Brut and keep it on ice behind the bar." The Russian handed over the American banknote with Ben Franklin's portrait on it.

"Yes, sir. It will be ready when you let me know."

Masrov nodded his head. "Very good." He stood up, lifting his glass and his small snack bowl to walk a few steps over to the table.

It was almost an hour before Kara Livingston walked up to the table. "You look lonely," she said as she pulled out the chair to the left of Masrov. "Mind if I join you?"

He cocked his head to his right and waved his left hand toward the chair. "My pleasure." He looked her over as she sat. She had changed from earlier in the afternoon and had correctly guessed that Masrov had not. She was now wearing a black cocktail dress. Masrov couldn't quite decide if she looked better now or before, but he knew that either way, she was still very attractive to him.

"Can I get something for you?" he asked.

"Yes. My favorite drink here is called the Hibiscus."

Masrov turned and signaled to the bartender with his right hand. The young Arab came over from behind the bar and the Russian ordered the drink, a specialty of the house. He turned back to her. "You look very beautiful."

"Thank you. Mukhtar told me you are here to form a new airline."

Masrov looked puzzled.

"Your new banker," she said to prompt his memory.

"Ah, yes. Of course." Masrov took a sip from his Crown and seven. "No, not an airline. An air cargo carrier."

"Is that any different?"

"Yes, of course. We won't carry any passengers, just cargo."

"I understand that. I meant from a regulatory perspective."

Masrov looked at her, mentally noting that she was more inquisitive than he expected. "So you're an airline attorney now?"

Kara shifted uncomfortably, not wanting to come across as too probing. She always wanted to make the right initial impression. "Well I'm a businesswoman. I find this stuff to be fascinating."

The bartender walked up to the table with a glass filled to just under the rim with a reddish mix of tequila, hibiscus syrup, agave syrup and lime. Vu's was known for not scrimping on the alcohol, very unlike most Dubai bars. But with a well-compensated bartender, nothing would be spared. "Our world-famous Hibiscus for the lady."

"Thank you," said Kara. She took the glass and immediately raised it in salute to her date for the night. "Cheers."

"Cheers," replied Gennady. The pair clinked their glasses.

Kara took a sip. "Wow. That's strong."

"This is the first time I have had a drink in Dubai. I thought alcohol would be banned here."

"Many people think that. But the Emiratis are really quite liberal and tolerant as Muslim nations go. As long as you don't flaunt it. Alcohol is limited to bars like this that are associated with a hotel. Just don't go out in public drunk and absolutely don't drive – even after a single drink."

"That's more like what I thought."

"Still, it is completely different than being in the Kingdom." She was referring to Saudi Arabia.

"Aren't there any extreme preachers here?"

"You mean Imams? There are certainly conservative Imams here, but really not much in the way of extremism. This is a wealthy country as you can see."

"So is Saudi Arabia. But that is where bin Laden is from, along with most of al Qaeda."

"Yes, but the Saudis let Wahhabi clerics preach freely before nine-eleven. They made a mistake."

"A mistake that they aren't making here?"

"That's right."

Masrov took a short sip before continuing. "How have they avoided it?"

"The Sheikh has spent freely."

"Ah, but now you are in a circular argument." Masrov smiled the type of smile that a chess master gives to a beaten opponent.

Livingston took a big gulp and swallowed. She leaned forward toward her date. "Is this how you do it in Russia?"

Masrov could not deny his Russian heritage. He slammed back the balance of his Crown and seven. "Nyet. That is how we do it in Moskva."

Kara smiled and lowered her voice. "Okay, I will admit what you want to hear. The police are active here. The clerics who stray too far across the line get arrested. Keep pushing it and you will get deported."

The Russian leaned forward, their heads now only a foot apart. "As a Russian, I understand the necessity of harsh measures." He softly ran his left forefinger along Kara's exposed right forearm. "Now we enjoy what we came here for." He abruptly leaned back in his chair and turned toward his new friend behind the bar. The young man came over quickly and Masrov ordered his champagne. He turned back to the British expatriate and smiled.

"So how does a Russian wind up in Dubai starting an airline?" Livingston asked.

"I go where my employer tells me."

"And your employer is?"

"I never mention who my employer is. He does not like when the people who work for him talk about him." Gennady shrugged his shoulders. "But I am always happy to admit that I am a big fan of the Chelsea Football Club."

"You work for Roman Abramovich?" Her voice was excited.

"No, I did not say that. I just said I am a fan of Chelsea. I like Didier Drogba." Masrov gave his date a sly smile, making sure she understood his point.

Kara leaned back in her chair as the bartender approached the table. "In that case," she said with a smile, "we are done. My side is Liverpool." She laughed at her own joke.

"Excuse me, sir," said the bartender as he presented the cold bottle of Cristal to Masrov. The Russian nodded his approval. The bartender opened the bottle, filled two crystal flutes and left with the bottle. He returned in seconds with a silver champagne bucket full of ice and the bottle of Cristal inside of it. "Anything else I can get for you, sir?"

"No." Masrov raised his crystal flute and the pair clinked the flutes together, the sound created being the perfect ping that only fine crystal produces. "To new and lasting friendships."

"Indeed," responded Kara. She sipped the champagne.

The couple spent the next hour getting to know each other. During this time they added an appetizer of fried calamari to complement the bottle of Cristal. Masrov learned that Kara Livingston had moved to Dubai seven years earlier when her American husband, an investment banker she met and married in London, accepted a job to open a Dubai office for his firm. She loved life in Dubai, choosing to stay even after her husband left her for his young Indonesian secretary. Divorced for four years now, she had found her calling as a powerful businesswoman in a country in which the official ethics called for women to stay in the home. She relished the dichotomy. Every day that she closed another deal was another chance to flip her middle finger at the male dominated society she opted to live in – and at the man who left her for a 28-year-old. Now she had risen to the pinnacle of the real estate brokerage business in Dubai. She was earning a lot of money and depended on no man.

Gennady Masrov poured out the last few drops into Kara's flute. "You are a fascinating woman, Kara. Not at all what I expected to meet in the Middle East."

"What did you expect?"

"Women in burkas riding around on camels."

Kara laughed out loud. "You are funny. Are all Russians like you?"

"No. Most are lousy lovers."

Kara stopped in the middle of a sip of champagne and lowered her flute. She looked at Gennady and shook her head. "You are trouble."

"I try."

"Let's go to Boudoir."

"Boudoir? What's that?"

"It's the hottest club in town. Do you dance?"

"I am flying out very early tomorrow morning. How about we go to Boudoir the next time I am back."

Kara frowned with a pouty face, the alcohol in her system exaggerating her mood. "Oh, come on. You can give me an hour."

Masrov knew exactly how the evening would end – if he wanted it to end that way. "I will take a rain check. But I promise you that we will have a great night next time."

"Well, when is next time?"

"Not positive. Probably next week. But let me drop you off at home."

"You didn't drive, did you?"

"No, Kara. I have the same driver I have had all day. The same car you saw when we left the office tower."

Kara Livingston was drunk and now felt the regret of a silly alcohol induced mistake. "Oh, yeah. Of course. I remember." She attempted a sip of champagne from her flute that only produced a solitary drop. She put the flute on the table for the final time. "I am honored to go home in your company."

Forty minutes later the Mercedes S600 pulled up in front of a garden home on Al Bumaan Street. This street formed a leaf of the famous Palm Jumeirah, the man-made palm-shaped island just off the coastline of Dubai. Masrov walked Kara to the door.

"Very nice home," Gennady observed.

"Thank you. I brought it last year after renting it for a couple of years. Great price. The only problem is that most of the homes here are vacant." She put her key in the door and unlocked the deadbolt. "You should come in and see the beach. It's right behind the house."

Gennady Masrov reached across her front, firmly grasped her left arm above the elbow and spun her toward him. He leaned his head forward and softly kissed her. The pair lingered on the kiss, enjoying the feel of each other's lips. Gennady pulled back after some seconds had passed. "Good night, Kara. I look forward to our next evening together."

"Good night, Gennady. I am glad I met you."

19 – Investing

Danny Stein stepped out of his office at 5 Bank of Israel Street in Jerusalem, turned left and walked across the building to the temporary office of Marc Leizman. Leizman had been recommended by the CEO of El Al after being asked by the prime minister for the name of a man with exceptional mechanical knowledgeable, great resourcefulness and enduring patriotism. Leizman had retired from El Al about a year earlier at the age of 62. After learning to be an aircraft mechanic in the IAF, he had spent 28 years at the airline, rising to head up all aircraft maintenance. It was said that there was not a plane that he couldn't take apart and reassemble better than it was before.

Leizman's office was protected by a locked door that only Stein and the retired mechanic could open. Stein knocked first and then used his key to enter. "Good morning, Marc."

Leizman was happy to have company. He was a mechanic by profession and even when he was part of the senior team at El Al he would relieve the stress of management by going to one of the hangers at Ben Gurion Airport and assisting a crew working on one of the many Boeing aircraft used by the airline. But in the two weeks since being called out of retirement by his prime minister, he had been doing nothing other than some online research and negotiating to buy a couple of planes. He knew he was on an important mission that was not to be discussed, but he did not know what it was – and he could not figure out why he was stuck in an office in Jerusalem in the building that housed the Ministry of Industry, Trade and Labor.

He had been set up in this office with two computers and two phones. He was instructed that one computer was for his internet searches and emails related to buying planes and engines. This computer was networked to the El Al system and his email address had been set up on the El Al exchange server. The other computer was for taking notes and any planning or analysis. Likewise, one of the phones in his offices, which was clearly marked with red tape on the receiver, was a Voice over Internet Protocol, or VoIP, phone that was connected to El Al's telephony network and used a number that came from El Al's library of assigned phone numbers. Anyone tracking Leizman's activities would find that all roads led to the El Al network. The other phone was an internal Ministry of Industry phone that had one purpose: allowing him to talk to Danny Stein when he needed to.

Leizman was told to restrict all personal calls to his cell phone. But there were not a lot of personal calls for Leizman. His wife had died of lung cancer half a decade earlier and his daughter, his only child, had moved to New York after marrying an American. Marc Leizman's life had been taking care of the El Al fleet and retirement had not turned out the way he expected. He had been spending all his days in his apartment in Rishon LeZiyyon just watching TV and sinking slowly and inexorably into a morose attitude that threatened to migrate into a full blown depression. His dreams of world travel had degenerated into a single trip to New York to spend a week with his daughter, son-in-law and his two grandchildren. But it was clear to him that he was not a welcome guest, his son-in-law being too busy and stressed to be able to handle another distraction.

He had been sinking lower when Danny Stein called him out of the blue a month earlier. Leizman was shocked when a member of the Kitchen Cabinet of Israel drove to Rishon to have lunch with a retired man who lived alone and no longer seemed to matter to anybody. But Leizman immediately felt the excitement of being important again, the rush of having a purpose in life. Whatever it was that Stein wanted, Marc Leizman was fully on board.

"Morning." Leizman motioned for Stein to take a seat.

"How's the progress?" Stein asked. He continued to stand.

"Good. I should finalize a deal for the second plane today. This one is located in Kazakhstan."

"How much?"

"A little more than the first. This one will cost eight point three five million dollars."

The higher price got Danny Stein excited. "PS-90 engines?"

"No, unfortunately. I still can't find any 76s with the 90 engines. All of the ones with the 90s are just not for sale. Period."

"Damn it." Stein was deflated. The first assignment of Marc Leizman had been simple. He was to find two Ilyushin 76 cargo planes for sale and negotiate their purchase on behalf of a newly formed subsidiary of El Al with the name of Sun d'Or II, Ltd. The four engine Ilyushin 76 cargo plane had been introduced into the Soviet Air Force during the 1970s. The huge cargo plane had been designed to carry large military loads into and out of rough unimproved runways of questionable length. Over the decades, almost a thousand had been built and the plane was now being operated by militaries and civilian cargo airlines the world over. Many knew the plane by its NATO-given codename: the "Candid". Finding planes for sale had been easy – as long as you were satisfied with the older engines that were not Chapter III compliant, meaning that they violated the noise abatement requirements of most of the world's biggest commercial airports.

Leizman was looking for the Il-76TD model, the most widely used civilian version – and the most widely offered for sale. But all of the planes for sale had D-30Kp engines, which were older technology engines. They were louder, generated less thrust and were less fuel efficient than modern jet engines. He had been hoping to find Il-76TDs with the new high-bypass technology turbofan engines made in Russia but utilizing many components from the West, known as the PS-90A2 engine.

"How do we get delivery?" asked Danny Stein.

"They will fly the planes here if we pay for airfares to return the crews."

"Where is the first plane coming from?"

"Ukraine. Kiev to be exact."

"No problem. When?" Danny Stein was inpatient. The money he needed to fund these purchases had taken much too long to obtain from the Ministry of Finance – the bureaucracy of the State of Israel being as frustrating as most governments.

"We close on the first plane tomorrow and they can fly the plane to Ben Gurion in a couple of days. If I get this deal finalized today, we should close next week and have the plane shortly after that."

"Great job. Happy with the planes?"

"Very much so, other than the engines. Both planes still have about a third of the lifetime design hours left on the airframes. We got these planes at a decent price because we accepted obsolete engines."

"You did great, Marc. How do we get the engines we need?"

"I talked to Aviadvigatel, the manufacturer. They are backordered for at least eighteen months. So I have been working some industry contacts I have." Leizman paused and offered the hint of a smile. "I have a possible deal but it will cost us. A friend of mine owns a company in India that supplies the Indian Air Force with many of its engines, including retrofitting their engines. We used to trade parts all the time." Leizman was giving Stein some "inside baseball" knowledge that left the minister uncomfortable. "The Indian Air Force is the largest buyer of PS-90 engines. I called him and got lucky. He is the next delivery from Aviadvigatel for sixteen PS-90A2 engines." Leizman was very satisfied with his skills and his contacts.

"And? Can we get eight engines?"

"Yes, but we are going to fund his retirement in the process."

"How much?"

"Maybe you want to sit down."

"That bad?"

Leizman nodded. "Five point two-five million dollars per engine."

"How much is the engine direct from the manufacturer?"

"For him, about four million per."

"This guy is robbing us."

"No, this guy is setting the price he needs to disappoint his biggest client, the Indian Air Force. My guess is that he will have to spread some of his profit around to his Air Force contacts to keep everyone contented."

"We spent how much? Under seventeen million U.S. for the two planes, and for eight engines we will have to spend over forty million dollars?"

"Or I can keep looking. Or we can place an order and wait. Or I can look for refurbished engines. But if we want the A2 engines, they are just too young to be available other than new from the factory. You tell me what you want."

Stein exhaled. "We need the engines. Go ahead."

"It could be worse. If we were buying new GE or Pratt & Whitney engines, they cost more."

"Well, that raises another question. Are these engines good? Should we buy American engines or Rolls Royce engines?"

"These engines are very good. They are modern and the critical components come from the U.S. and Germany. More importantly, the conversion kits to mount these engines on the 76 are established and widely available. As far as I know, nobody has put American engines on the 76 yet."

"Okay. When can we get them?"

"He is taking delivery in New Delhi early next month. I want to have both of our 747-400 freighters waiting there when the engines are delivered. I don't want the engines to sit around while my guy ponders everything."

"I agree. That makes sense." Stein thought for a moment and then continued. "We still need to train some crews. How do we do that?"

"The fastest way is to put an ad out and hire pilots and flight engineers with ratings and histories on the Il-76."

"Not an option. We will use Israeli crews that need to be trained."

"All right. I can arrange the training. With experienced pilots and engineers, it won't take long."

"Can we train them in India?" Stein asked.

"Yes, absolutely. Is that what you want?"

"Yes." Stein thought for a moment. "How long to put the new engines on?"

"With my best crew from El Al, I could swap out the engines and make all related modifications in a week to ten days."

"That timing is fine." Stein looked at a calendar on the wall. It was November 17, 2010.

20 – The Boneyard

On the same day, 7,500 miles away, the weather was sunny, what Americans like to call "Chamber of Commerce" weather. The temperature just before noon was 73 degrees Fahrenheit and the high for the day would get only a few degrees warmer. Located on a high plain of the Sonoran desert and surrounded by mountains, Tucson, Arizona, has an average annual humidity under 40%, one of the lowest in the United States. The heavy rain that falls every year in July and August evaporates so rapidly that little trace is left of its brief passage through time.

In a command building located on the corner of Miami Street and Wickenburg Avenue, an email arrived from the new civilian director of the 309th Maintenance Wing of the United States Air Force based at Hill Air Force Base in Utah. The email was opened by the civilian deputy director of the 309th Aerospace Maintenance and Regeneration Group, known as AMARG. The email contained orders to activate fifteen KC-135 Stratotankers for return to the fleet. An estimate of the time required to meet this command was due back to Hill AFB by the next day.

AMARG runs a unique facility on the grounds of Davis Monthan Air Force Base, which is located on the southern edge of Tucson. The facility, known as the "Boneyard", is home to more than 4,000 mothballed aircraft of the U.S. government, an air armada that would be the second largest air force in the world if all of the aircraft were in flight condition. Many of the aircraft are in various states of dismantling, their carcasses being permanently disabled to comply with arms limitations treaties. For these aircraft, which had served their country proudly, the future held only a slow dismemberment, their various parts now being scavenged to extend the life of other aircraft. But most of the planes parked on the desert floor, which has a layer of clay under the topsoil that is as hard as cement and known as caliche, are in short-term or long-term hibernation, remaining available for call-up to active duty – no different than the aging reservists who await recall to every major army on the planet in the event of crisis.

On the day of this request from higher command, 60 KC-135s were parked on the desert floor, aligned neatly in seven rows in a triangular portion of the AMARG facility. With more than 800 Stratotankers delivered to the USAF between 1957 and 1965, the four engine variant of the Boeing 707 remains the backbone of the USAF's global aerial refueling capacity to this day.

The deputy director picked up his phone and dialed the three digit code to reach Eduardo Suarez. Suarez, the senior mechanic on the many multi-engine Boeing aircraft residing on the facility, had joined AMARG after a two-decade career with Continental Airlines. Like most of the employees of AMARG, he was a civilian contract worker. He picked up after a single ring. The men exchanged pleasantries before the deputy director got to the point.

"We need to activate fifteen of the KC-135s as soon as possible."

"Which tail numbers?"

"It's at our discretion. They want the fifteen best planes we have that can be quickly operational."

"Hmm. That's unusual. But, hey, no problem. Let me review the files and I will let you know which ones I like."

"Can you let me know timing, please?"

"To flight worthiness certification?"

"Yes."

"Can do."

"Thank you, Eduardo."

"No problem."

Three and half hours later Suarez called the deputy director back. He was in a good mood. "I have the tail numbers. I will email them to you after the call."

"Timing?"

"Good news there. All of the 135s are here on 'Flying Hold.' They are all in pretty good shape and we have twenty-six that are within two thousand flight hours of their PDM." Suarez was referring to the program depot maintenance overhaul that is scheduled for aircraft that have 15,000 hours of flight time on the airframe. He meant that these particular planes had already undergone their PDM and their airframes should be in very good condition. "I picked fifteen from that group. I think we can have the first FCF for all of these aircraft within two weeks." FCF is the acronym for a functional check flight, during which the systems of a plane are checked out and reviewed in flight. "We will trouble shoot and have the second FCF for all aircraft within another week. Give me a week of slack and I will commit to one month from now."

"That works."

"Okay. I will have crews out tomorrow removing the spraylat." Spraylat is a product that is used by AMARG to seal aircraft going into storage. The first layers used are a black rubbery substance. The final layers are a white insulation that helps moderate the inside temperature of each stored airplane. "We should be able to start towing planes to the flight line tomorrow afternoon."

"Great. You're the best Eduardo."

"Talk to you soon."

On December 20, 2010, the first of fifteen KC-135 Stratotankers lifted off from runway 30 at Davis Monthan AFB in Tucson. After 93 minutes of flying almost due north, the 52-year-old plane landed at Hill AFB in Ogden, Utah, 30 miles north of Salt Lake City. Over the next several days the remaining fourteen planes made the same flight, all being lined up on the apron to await the arrival of USAF crews.

On the same day that the first KC-135 arrived in Utah, in a room that occupied less than 200 square feet of the 3.7 million available inside the Pentagon building, paperwork was signed by the deputy general counsel of international affairs, representing the Air Force Material Command. The document transferred ownership of all fifteen KC-135 Stratotankers from the U.S. government to a company named Rhinestone Leasing, Inc., a Delaware corporation. The Treasurer of Rhinestone executed the transfer documentation along with a number of other documents that made clear that the transfer was pursuant to a military aid program administered by the Pentagon that had been established under the authorization of the State Department and funded by Section F of the Fiscal Year 2010 Consolidated Appropriations Act passed by Congress and signed into law a year earlier. The next document executed by the men in that office was an agreement by the USAF to deliver the planes, at U.S. taxpayer expense, to Incirlik Air Base in Turkey. The final document signed was a lease and operating agreement that allowed the USAF to lease back and operate the aircraft at the direction of Rhinestone. Six sets of originals had been signed.

When the half hour process was finished, the Pentagon attorney kept three original sets. The Treasurer of Rhinestone took the other three and exited room 4C756. He walked the long distance to exit into the south parking lot. After getting into his government-issue car, he made a fourteen minute drive to the west until he passed a sign that read "George Bush Center for Intelligence CIA FHWA Next Exit".

Back in his office in McLean, Virginia, in an unincorporated area known as Langley, the man who was Treasurer of Rhinestone Leasing now signed documents that transferred ownership of the fifteen KC-135 tankers from Rhinestone to a company called AS-3 Air Lease Limited, an Isle of Man registered company. AS-3 was, in turn, owned by a bearer share corporation registered in the British Virgin Islands. The same man served as Corporate Treasurer for each entity. Anyone attempting to find the real owner of these airplanes would run into roadblocks and frustration – and anyone looking for the Corporate Treasurer of Rhinestone Leasing or AS-3 Air Lease Limited would come to the conclusion that the man just didn't exist.

21 – Special Delivery

On December 25, 2010, a crew of four Israelis, consisting of a pilot, co-pilot, flight engineer and navigator, boarded an Il-76TD90 with the new tail number 4X-CGE. The plane was pulled from the hanger by a tug. It was only the third time it had been pulled out of the hanger since it arrived at Ben Gurion International Airport on November 22. The prior two times had been to test its newly installed PS-90A2 high-bypass turbofan jet engines. This time, the newest certified member of the El Al cargo fleet taxied to take off on runway 30 on its first flight under its new Sun d'Or II Air Operator's Certificate. The empty plane reached its rotation speed of 130 mph using only 1,740 feet of runway and was airborne another 165 feet further on, barely utilizing the more than 10,000 feet of available runway. The local time at takeoff was 10:07 p.m.

The plane continued west, climbing rapidly into the pitch black sky over the Mediterranean Sea. The scheduled flight plan called for the plane to land in Palermo, Italy, to pick up cargo after three hours of flight time. Once the plane, now at its designated cruising altitude of 36,000 feet, had flown some 320 miles and was in a radar and Air Traffic Control gap, an Israeli Air Force KC-707 that had been orbiting in the vicinity made contact with the crew of the Ilyushin. The big cargo plane maneuvered to come in behind the KC-707, an airborne gas station that could refuel the plane in a matter of minutes. However, there was a problem – the Ilyushin was not equipped with either a refueling probe or receptacle and there was no way to transfer fuel from the KC-707 to the Ilyushin. But anyone listening in on the radio communications between the two planes would have had no way to know that.

After several minutes of maneuvering to bring the big Ilyushin behind and slightly below the IAF refueling tanker and another couple of minutes of formation flying, the two planes bid each other farewell over the radio, marking an end to their wireless communications. The KC-707 turned east to return to its home field at Nevatim Air Base in the Negev desert ten miles to the east of Be'er Shiva. The Ilyushin 76 dropped back slightly and then turned off its transponder and its nighttime navigation lights. The crew of the big cargo plane put a small infrared strobe light on the cockpit window, its suction cups sticking to the cold glass in the same way as a highway toll transponder. The big plane then maintained its position behind and slightly below the KC-707, following the air tanker home to Israel and a landing at Nevatim a few minutes after midnight – the timing having been determined to avoid the prying gaze of all scheduled overhead reconnaissance satellites. The Ilyushin landed on runway 07, turned right after deceleration and taxied 3,350 feet to enter one of two large hanger buildings on the southern edge of the airfield. The KC-707 airborne refueler they had been following had pulled up at the last minute, circled the airfield and came in for a landing a few minutes after the big Ilyushin.

The Il-76 crew shut down all four engines as a tug hooked onto the large four wheel nose gear assembly and pulled the plane forward the final one hundred meters. The crew deplaned as the hanger doors were quickly closed behind them. As they walked down the port side exit just aft of the cockpit area, they were greeted by Amit Margolis, the man who had briefed them earlier in the day after they had returned from India. They had undergone an intense month-long training program for the Ilyushin 76 that El Al had paid a steep price to fund. Margolis' briefing had been the first indication that they were learning to fly the cargo plane for a purpose other than routine cargo flying for El Al. The men had all been recruited from El Al and all had previously been distinguished pilots or flight engineers in the IAF.

The entire team would return by helicopter the next day to Ben Gurion Airport where the men would be free to return home for a week of rest. Margolis told them that they would repeat this same process with the other Ilyushin 76 about ten days later. When the men asked for some reason as to why they had just conducted this unusual secret mission, Margolis told them that the two Ilyushin's were being converted at Nevatim Air Base into aerial refueling aircraft. He then admonished them to never discuss what they had just done and what was happening at Nevatim.

Amit Margolis pulled onto Highway 20 and headed south toward Tel Aviv. The time was 8:45 a.m. and the worst of morning rush hour was easing rapidly. But the co-head of Olympus kept going past the Campus and continued onto Highway 1 headed toward Ben Gurion Airport. Minutes later, he turned into the Industrial Zone of Yehud, just on the north edge of Ben Gurion Airport.

Margolis parked in one of the guest parking spots near the entrance of the headquarters of Israel Aerospace Industries Ltd, or IAI, in Yehud. He walked into the lobby and asked for Hillel Meir. Mr. Meir was Vice President of Aerospace Systems and was expecting Margolis. Within ten minutes Margolis had a guest pass and had been escorted into the Vice President's office. As a government-owned defense contractor, the offices of IAI reflected the Spartan utilitarianism of their parent. Amit looked around and thought that the furniture, such as it was, had to be left over from the days of British rule over then Palestine.

The pair shook hands. They had spoken on the phone a number of times, but this was their first face to face meeting. The date was January 12, 2011. After several minutes of introduction, Margolis focused on the topic that brought him here.

"What do you think? Can we get this conversion done?" he asked.

"You know, when I was called into the CEO's office in early December and walked in and found Defense Minister Avner sitting there, I was very nervous. The defense minister asked if I was willing to put my career on hold for the sake of Israel, swore me to secrecy and then described what the project was that he wanted me to get done. When he had finished, he asked how long I thought it would take. I said at least one year. He told me I had to get it done in six months. You are my boss on this project and I want to be honest with you. This will take longer than six months from today."

"First let me hear whether or not we can actually do it."

"We can do it."

"Okay. Now give me your honest opinion about how long."

Meir looked down at his desk top, which was covered in notes and printed reports. Margolis followed Meir's eyes and noticed a set of drawings of the Ilyushin 76. The engineer exhaled and pursed his lips. "This is tough. I have to work with this guy from El Al."

"You mean Marc Leizman?"

"Yes. I don't know him. I hear good things, but I don't know him."

"Assume he is as good as we have both been told."

Meir looked at Margolis. "If I can add a few more key people to my team, I think we test fly sometime this summer."

"When this summer?"

"Oh boy. You know engineers are conservative by nature, right?" His entreaty to Margolis went unanswered. "If you put a gun to my head, I will say mid-July."

"Do your best to shave a month off of that. This conversion needs to be operational by the fall."

"The one thing I can promise you is that you will have one hundred percent of the effort of me and the team. The commitment will not waiver." Suddenly a question popped into Meir's conscious. "What is the status on getting hold of a simulator?"

"Marc Leizman is working on that now. The Indian Air Force can supply us with one."

"No. I know what they have. I talked to one of the El Al pilots that went through the training. Those are Level A simulators. They are glorified computer games. They are fine for getting an experienced crew up the learning curve quickly on a new plane, but I need a Level D full flight simulator. I don't even know if they exist for the seventy-six."

Margolis looked concerned and somewhat confused. He was not a pilot. This was the first he had heard of the need for a Level D simulator and he had never thought of the difference in simulator types. He had not even heard the terms before. He quietly cursed the IAF officers that had helped him plan all of this out, but he realized that they were not engineers.

Meir could see the confusion on the face of his new leader. "A Level D simulator has all of the mechanical flight systems that are found in a real cockpit. The seventy-six has the added complication of having the separate navigator station in the nose. But a well-built Level D simulator by a company like CAE has about a year's worth of programming that ties the mechanical systems to the simulator. I need that programming. Without it, this is much more difficult to pull off."

Amit Margolis processed this new information and began to analyze options as he always did in times of stress. "What if there are no Level D simulators for the Ilyushin seventy-six?"

"That is not good. I will need more resources and more time."

"What type of resources and how much time?"

"More software programmers. If I have the Level D software as I assumed, then we can leverage that software. Without it, we start from scratch. As for time, I am guessing at least another six months."

Margolis did not want to hear that answer. "There are hundreds of these planes in service around the world. There has to be someone who has a Level D simulator. We will find out soon enough."

"I hope so."

Amit realized that nothing more could be decided until this problem was fully explored by Leizman. He decided to change the subject. "You do know that you and your team will need to set up inside Nevatim?"

"Yes. My wife is not happy that I am relocating for a while."

"I understand. You can come home on weekends."

"At least my children are grown up and out of the house. I can't say that for some of the team."

"Hillel, what you are working on is the most important thing Israel has done militarily since the opening moments of the Six Day War. Every member of the team should understand that and embrace that. Anyone who hesitates in his commitment is not suited to participate."

Hillel Meir's face turned angry. "You know, you are twenty years my junior. I fought in the Sinai during the Yom Kippur War. I have this to remind me." Meir lifted up his right hand and pulled his collar away from his neck, leaning his head to the right. On the side of his neck, the normal line of the trapezius muscle was interrupted by a gouge about an inch wide and half an inch deep. Scar tissue surrounded the gouge. "This, Mister Margolis, is the reminder I carry every day of my life. It reminds me of the comrades who died in the Sinai by my side. It reminds me of the price I have paid personally for the country I love. I have spent my life working and sacrificing for Israel. The people who will work on this project are the same. We don't need you to lecture us about commitment."

Margolis looked Meir in the eye. His mind could think of two ways to proceed. One was to apologize and the other was to appreciate. He choose the latter. "How did you get that?"

The question was natural but caught Meir by surprise. "I was in the armored 401 Brigade. But I arrived early in the Sinai before our tanks were there. I was thrown in against the Egyptian 19th Division as infantry. We were west of the Mitla Pass along the Bir Gafafa Road. We arrived around noon on October ninth and dug in. The Egyptians hit us late in the day. I defended a foxhole with two other men. We held off an Egyptian squad as the sun set. I got hit by an AK-47 round and the guy on my right was killed. We would have been overrun and killed but, thank God, a couple of A-4 Skyhawks showed up and dropped napalm a hundred meters in front of us. I don't think they knew we were there, but they had the Egyptian units spotted. I can still feel the heat and smell that aroma of petrol and burning flesh." Meir was reliving the moment again – telling the story for only the third time since the war ended. "A little while after that I passed out from blood loss. I was evacuated out that night and spent the next couple of months getting patched up."

Both men sat silently for a moment, the time ticking slowly. Margolis finally spoke. "I am honored to be working with you on this project."

Meir shifted his gaze out the window of his office. "I apologize." The words were directed to Amit but were spoken into the stagnant air as if Meir were apologizing to the men who died in the Sinai 38 years before. Meir turned back to face Margolis. "You have my commitment and my loyalty, Mister Margolis."

"Please call me Amit."

22 – No Debt Financing Required

Gennady Masrov arrived in Dubai for the fourth time on January 31, 2011. The manager of the Armani Hotel, as he did with all of his VIP guests, came out of his office to welcome Masrov, bypassing check-in to escort the Russian directly to his suite. Masrov did not let Kara Livingston know he was coming to Dubai this time. He had too much work to accomplish.

His last visit had been in the first week of January and he had been true to his word. He had taken the British expat real estate broker to Boudoir. They had a fun evening, but Masrov had been preoccupied most of the night and Kara could sense it. They had spent the car ride to her house kissing in the back seat. Their Emirati driver was catching an occasional glimpse in the rear view mirror, enjoying the show and realizing why it was that he liked to chauffeur Westerners around. This time Masrov had gone in to Kara's home to share a final nightcap. But when the moment came, the Russian had stopped the British expat, insisting that the pair go slow and prompting an interrogation from Kara as to the status of Masrov's personal life. She did not sleep with many men, but when she wanted to, men never refused her. This was something new and she did not like it. It made her feel old, even though the looks she received from men every day told her otherwise.

But Masrov had left her that night and she remained to contemplate the sexual rejection. He had a lot to do on the trip and his mind was focused on the following day when he would meet with the controlling Arab owner of a failing air cargo company. The meeting occurred over lunch at the Exchange Grill and the two men hit it off, the Arab's English proving to be quite good. By the time they parted ways, the terms for an acquisition of the Arab man's company by Swiss-Arab Air Cargo FZE had been agreed upon. A firm hand shake sealed the commitment on each side.

Now, almost a month following that lunch, Masrov was driven the short distance to the law offices of Heinrik Waddington. The Russian exited the elevator on the 4th floor of Exchange Building No. 5 in the Dubai International Financial Center. Masrov introduced himself to the attractive young Emirati woman behind the reception desk and was directed to a large corner conference room. He entered and was met by the associate who had first suggested that Masrov's company purchase an existing air cargo carrier.

"Good morning, Stephen. Are we all ready?"

Stephen Hughes was a 27-year-old associate in his second year with the firm. He was learning aviation law from Abraham Sanjoors but his real interest was merger and acquisition law. His skills had come in handy for this small deal. He quickly rose to his feet. "Morning, Mister Masrov." He extended his hand. The six foot four inch associate towered over the Russian.

"You look like hell. Did you sleep last night?" Masrov asked.

"A couple of hours." It was the young associate's duty to proofread all of the closing documents that were now spread out on the table in small neatly aligned piles a few inches apart from each other. In front of each of the 49 piles, a small yellow sticky note with the associate's handwriting gave a brief description of each stack of paper. The stacks that required Masrov's signature – which accounted for most of them – were noted with a hand-drawn star on the sticky note.

"I passed a lot of police on the streets coming over this morning. What is going on?"

Stephen Hughes grew tense immediately. "The Arab Spring." The associate lifted up the front page of the morning's issue of the *Financial Times*. It featured a photograph of Tahrir Square in Cairo with tens of thousands of people demanding the resignation of Hosni Mubarak underneath a headline that read "Countdown to Departure". "The Sheik is nervous," Hughes explained.

"Here in Dubai? That's crazy."

"I hope you're right. But this is spreading through the Middle East like wildfire."

Masrov waved his hand through the air in a dismissive gesture. "Ack. Not here my friend. Not here." The Russian looked down at all the paperwork spread across the long conference table. "Where is Abraham?"

"He will stop by soon." Closing the acquisition of one company by another involved a small forest worth of paperwork and was the province of young associates like Hughes, not partners like Sanjoors.

"You sure you know what you are doing?"

"Yes, sir. Abraham has reviewed all of the documents. We are set. If you are ready, I can walk you through everything."

"I read through the full set of documents you sent me last week. Anything change?"

"Yes." Hughes went through the handful of final changes that had been negotiated between Abraham Sanjoors and the attorney representing the seller, who had hired another law firm. All of the changes were for minor legal or regulatory matters or were for the benefit of Masrov's company. Sanjoors had recognized early on that the seller was desperate to close the sale – his business had been deteriorating rapidly as the Dubai economy fell on hard times. Sanjoors had even called Masrov two weeks earlier to tell him that he could re-negotiate and get a better price, but the Russian insisted that a deal was a deal and told his attorney to get the acquisition closed.

"All of this makes sense," responded the Russian after he had heard the explanation of the handful of changes. "Let's start signing."

Signing the documentation took more than an hour. Eight original signature pages had to be signed for each document, which included 37 documents for the acquisition and another 12 documents that would be filed the next day with the Dubai Civil Aviation Authority and the International Civil Aviation Authority. Somewhere else in Dubai in a similar conference room, the seller was signing exact replicas of the same signature pages.

Masrov was down to his last handful of signature pages when Abraham Sanjoors walked into the conference room. "How are you, Gennady?"

"Well, it's about time." Masrov placed his pen down on the table and stood to shake hands with the senior attorney.

Sanjoors smiled broadly as he shook hands with his Russian client. "I left you in good hands."

"That you did. That you did." Masrov looked at Hughes and winked.

"Almost done?"

"I hope so. My hand is cramping up."

"Yeah, I know it's bad. I'm sorry that we need so much documentation. But look on the bright side, this deal is all equity financed. If we had a bank involved or a mezzanine lender, the documentation would be double or triple and this whole process would have taken another two or three months."

Masrov shook his head. "It's easier in Russia."

Sanjoors did not respond. Instead he pulled a piece of paper from his pocket and sat down in front of a telephone that was on top of a side table. "Did you have any questions for me?"

"No. Stephen was able to answer all my questions."

The partner turned to his associate. "We all done?"

Stephen Hughes paused for a moment as he watched Masrov sign the final page, which was the last of eight pages of a Resolution of the single owner of Swiss-Arab Air Cargo FZE authorizing the acquisition of all outstanding shares of the target company. Gennady Masrov finally signed his name for the last time that morning. Hughes looked at his boss and nodded.

Sanjoors dialed nine and then the number on the paper. He waited as the phone on the other end rang several times. "Hello" came the response as the phone was picked up. Abraham Sanjoors spoke briefly with the attorney for the selling company. Each man confirmed that all of the required documentation had been signed by their clients and agreed to scan and email the signature pages of a few key documents to each other. Sanjoors then confirmed the amount of money to be wired from the bank account of Swiss-Arab Air Cargo FZE to the bank accounts of the four individuals who had owned the shares of the target company before this morning. The proceeds were not being divided equally. The man that Masrov had negotiated with in early January owned 78.6% of the outstanding shares. The rest was split approximately equally between three other owners. All of the selling shareholders were Emiratis.

A half hour later, as Masrov was finishing a cup of tea, Sanjoors walked back into the conference room. "Okay. We are ready to finish this. I have been talking to Mukhtar Al-Zubaidy at HSBC and they have all of the wire instructions and required documentation. All that is needed is a call from you to authorize." The partner was talking to Masrov. "Last chance to back out. You ready to wire seven point eight five million dollars?"

"Yes, Abraham. Hand me the phone. Let's finish this."

Two hours later, a black Mercedes S600 pulled up to the door of one of the smaller hanger buildings at Ras Al-Khaimah International Airport. Calling it an "International Airport" was far more ambitious than the facility was able to live up to. It features a single runway of 12,300 feet that runs from the northwest to the southeast. The lone runway doubles as a taxiway. The tarmac, at only 2,000 feet long by 750 feet wide, is tiny by the standards of a major airport. Along the eastern edge of the tarmac is a small passenger terminal building and a series of hangers used by various aviation companies. As of this day, the newest user was Swiss-Arab Air Cargo, FZE through its brand new wholly-owned subsidiary.

Over the next three hours Masrov was introduced as the new owner to the employees who were present. The company had a payroll with only five pilots, three mechanics and another fourteen employees. Masrov was introduced by the prior owner, who said his farewell to each employee, promised to be available if anyone needed him and quickly drove off in the back of a green Land Rover.

Masrov told the assembled group the most important thing they wanted to hear: their jobs were safe. He went on to tell them of his plans to grow the company and told them that the days of being starved for cash were over. They would be very well capitalized. He introduced them to their new name and showed them the new company logo and the plans for a significant Internet presence. He spoke of the many connections he had in Russia and the expectation that the company would see a meaningful share of the growing cargo traffic between Russia and the Middle East.

Finally, he told them that in order to support their expected growth, they would be adding planes, starting with two Ilyushin Il-76 cargo jets. If things went well and everyone worked hard, he assured them, there would be more Il-76 cargo planes added to the company's fleet. Masrov shared his dream of operating the largest fleet of Il-76 aircraft outside of Russia and its former Republics. To properly manage the new growth and new planes they would be adding, he told them, a new Russian operations manager would soon be introduced to oversee all operations. He immediately reassured the current managers that this new employee would be an addition to the team, not a substitute for one of them. What Gennady Masrov did not share was that he expected to bring in many new employees who were trained professionals and could properly maintain and fly the growing fleet of Ilyushins.

When he was done, the employees, who had been demoralized by the slow drip of failure under the prior ownership, were excited about the future for the first time in a very long time. The senior operations manager, a former East German who had been bouncing around the Middle East since the collapse of communism, walked up and shook his hand. The man spoke little English, but his Russian was quite good. He hoped that his language skills would endear him to his new boss. "On behalf of the entire team," the East German expatriate said in Russian, "I welcome you as our new leader. We are very happy you are here." Masrov received a standing ovation from the team.

23 - Simulations

On the same day that Gennady Masrov met his new employees in the UAE, Marc Leizman hanged up the phone in the small cubicle that was now his office. He had a feeling of great satisfaction. He was spending all of his time now living and working on Nevatim Air Base in the Negev, his home a room on the base that he shared with Hillel Meir during the week and had to himself during the weekends. His small cubicle was located inside one of the two hanger buildings that each housed one Ilyushin 76. The desktop was covered in manuals and work records and the walls were dirty, the grease and grime of an active hanger being impossible to clean. As per the standards established while he was in Jerusalem, Leizman had a secure phone and a secure computer that each connected to the outside world through the El Al network.

Leizman reached into his pocket and pulled out a key chain. He flipped through a half a dozen keys and wrapped his fingers around a security key that he used to open a box on his desk. The open box revealed a telephone that looked like a typical full function office phone. He lifted the handset. The encrypted telephone connected over the dedicated IDF intranet only to one place: Mount Olympus. He entered a six digit code that turned the unit on and a phone immediately rang at the operational headquarters of Project Block G. After a two minute wait, General David Schechter was handed the phone on the receiving end.

"Shalom, Mister Leizman," answered the general.

"General?"

"Yes, it's me."

"Couldn't recognize your voice, sorry."

"It's the encryption. Do you have an update for me?"

"Yes sir. I have made a deal to buy the simulator." Leizman had been given the task to find and acquire a level D simulator for the Ilyushin to provide to the growing team of Israel Aerospace Industries engineers and software developers working at Nevatim. The search had been challenging.

"Where did you find it?"

"Azerbaijan Airlines commissioned one for their training center. It includes pilot, co-pilot and flight engineer stations, the main cockpit. But there is no navigator section."

"What does Meir say about that?"

"He wishes we had it, but he is still very happy that we were able to find what we did. He will work around it."

"When do we get it?"

"I am arranging for FedEx Cargo to deliver it to Ben Gurion. Just about any cargo plane can fly it down from there. But first we need to sign a contract and wire two million dollars. It should be ready to pick-up in two weeks after they get the money."

"Two weeks?"

"The simulator is in operation. This is a full flight simulator. It is mounted on hydraulic pistons and fully articulated."

"How long to get the papers signed?"

"Minister Stein is already working on it. I don't know the timing."

"I will talk to him." The cost of acquiring the simulator finally hit Schechter. "Two million dollars for a simulator? That's expensive."

"No sir. That would be reasonable. We will have to wire another two million dollars before they will let FedEx take it. It will take them six to twelve months to get this replaced. We had to pay up to compensate for the lost revenue."

"Are you saying four million U.S. dollars?"

"Yes sir."

There was silence for a few moments. The general silently smiled, grateful that none of this was coming out of his pocket. "Just get the simulator here as soon as you can."

"Yes sir. Will do."

"How is the rest of the project?"

"The internal mechanical work is on schedule. I'm not in the loop regarding everything IAI is working on with the avionics and electronics. You will need to talk to Hillel on that."

"Okay. Shalom."

"Shalom."

24 – Levy Comes Calling

On Saturday morning, February 12, 2011, a black SUV pulled up in front of the apartment building of Amit Margolis in Tel Baruch. Ami Levy, the director of Mossad, stepped out of the back seat after telling his bodyguards to wait in the vehicle. The 63-year-old master spy headed into the building and quickly found the elevator to the third floor. After an elevator ride that seemed painfully slow, he exited and walked down the outdoor hallway to find apartment 34. His steps were labored. Levy's body reflected a life of service to his country, including combat in two wars and a decade of infiltrating Arab held lands to terminate enemies of the state. It had now been more than two decades since he last fired a weapon in anger and arthritis was exacting a revenge on his body that his enemies had failed to achieve.

Levy knocked on the door. The time was 8:12 a.m. After a moment, the door opened and a beautiful young woman confronted the aging director, her breasts perfectly outlined by a tight fitting t-shirt. "May I help you?"

Director Levy knew all about Enya Govenin, who occupied a growing percentage of Margolis' Mossad file. Still, he was caught off guard by the beauty of the woman, who was completely unconcerned that her perfect body was on full display for this stranger at her door. The 5-foot 7-inch director was facing her eye to eye, trying unsuccessfully to maintain eye contact. "Shabbat shalom. I am looking for Amit Margolis. Is he in?"

"And who are you?"

"Forgive me. Tell him that Shlomo Fiegelbaum is here. I will wait." Levy used the name of the director of collections because it was not widely known in the Israeli press, but would cause the correct response from Margolis.

Enya was not sure if she should leave the man in the hall. But something about him seemed familiar to her. He reminded her of the photos of her grandfather, who she had never met. She pulled the door into a fully open position. "Come in," she said.

Levy entered the modest apartment and closed the door behind him as Enya walked down the hall. He could not help but notice that she was effectively nude underneath her tight t-shirt, which stretched down to her thighs. He could make out the faint lines of a G-string as his eyes focused on her rear end. He scolded himself for his lack of self-control.

Levy was standing just inside the door when Amit Margolis turned the corner wearing a polo shirt and a pair of shorts. He was moving quickly to meet the senior Mossad officer he expected. It took his mind a second or two to realize that it was Director Levy standing in his apartment.

"Shabbat shalom, Amit," said Levy as he extended his hand.

Margolis did everything possible to control his surprise. He shook hands. "Good morning, Director. Is there something wrong?"

"Not at all. I was hoping you could walk with me a while."

"Of course, sir." Margolis looked down at his bare feet. "I need, um, I need sandals." He lifted his right hand and raised his forefinger. "One second."

"Take your time." Levy looked past Margolis and smiled at Enya as she stood about ten feet behind her man. The director tipped his head slightly as Amit slipped past Enya and went back into his bedroom in search of a pair of sandals. He re-emerged within seconds and paused next to Enya, kissing her forehead softly. "I will be only a few minutes, honey."

"Amit, what is going on? Who is this man?"

Amit fumbled with his words. "Ah … just part of this project I am doing for the IDF. Sometimes they need to discuss important matters." He looked at her and shrugged his shoulders. Amit turned to walk to Levy, who had already stepped back out into the hall.

Levy looked at Enya. "Pleasure meeting you. Shalom." He turned and started walking back toward the elevator, confident that Margolis would quickly catch up. As Margolis reached his side, he spoke. "You have a basement shelter here, no?"

"Yes, sir. Of course."

"And we can get in?"

"Yes, my apartment key works."

"Have your key?"

"No." Margolis turned and ran the short distance back to his apartment, his speed limited by the flopping action of his sandals. He ran in, grabbed his keys, and was back with his director by the time the elevator door opened.

A couple of minutes later Amit unlocked the shelter door and turned on the lights. Inside was a barren room with a wash basin in the far corner and a stack of folding chairs leaning against the wall. Margolis unfolded two chairs and put them on the concrete floor.

"I don't think this is up to code," Levy joked as he sat down.

"Sorry, sir. Are you sure you want to talk here?"

"This is perfect, Amit." Levy looked around the poured concrete walls. "No one is listening." He smiled.

"Is something wrong, sir? It makes me nervous that you came here."

"Nothing's wrong. You know, next to the prime minister, I think you are the only person I have travelled to see in Israel."

"What brings you here?"

"Sometimes Mohammed must go to the mountain." Levy reached down and rubbed his left knee. "I'm afraid that age is taking a toll on me." He looked at Amit. "Arthritis."

"Sorry to hear that."

"Enjoy your youth, Amit." Levy continued to rub and then chuckled. "Listen to me. After seeing your girlfriend, you are the one to teach me about enjoying your youth. Her name is Enya Govenin, yes?"

"Yes, sir."

"That is quite a coincidence. It must be God's plan." Like most humans, Levy's faith had strengthened as he aged. He would not have given this a second thought a couple of decades earlier, but was now mindful of giving up his Sabbath to come visit Margolis. But it was the only day that he could hide a stop like this from his official calendar.

Margolis looked confused. "What is a coincidence?"

"You and Enya Govenin meeting and becoming a couple."

"I ... I don't understand. What are you saying?"

Director Levy stopped rubbing his knee. "You don't know who she is? You don't know about her grandfather?"

"I'm not sure what you mean. I know her grandfather came here from Russia in the early eighties. He was a famous Soviet dissident."

"And a famous physicist. Like Sakharov."

"Yes. I knew that."

"That is all you know?"

"Yes. What else is there?"

Levy smiled and exhaled. "A lot, Amit. A lot." Levy began to rub his right knee now. "I worked closely with your father, you know."

"Yes, sir."

"How much do you know about his story?"

"My mother told me he was a hero. People like you and the prime minister tell me the same, but I don't know much detail."

"Well let me fill in some of the detail for you." Levy paused for a moment to collect his thoughts. "Your father asked the Americans to help arrange the emigration of a Russian family in exchange for a couple of Soviet spies who had been caught. This was routine back in those days. It was the Cold War. But for men like me and your father, it was all too often very hot indeed.

"The family belonged to a Russian who had immigrated to Israel a little earlier. That man had information that could endanger a coup plot that was underway in the Soviet Union and he was killed for that. He was killed, Amit, right here in Tel Aviv.

"That man's death led to your father going into the Soviet Union to find out why he had been killed. What he found out and unmasked was a coup plot by some of the most powerful generals in the Soviet Army, the men who controlled all of the first line fighting power of the Red Army based in East Germany and the rest of Eastern Europe. These men were intent on invading Western Europe. World war three, Amit. That is what we are talking about. Your father foiled that plot. He paid for it with his life. In my opinion, your father saved the world from world war three."

This was more detail than Amit had ever heard before. His mother did not know the full story, only telling him that his father had died fighting evil men inside the Soviet Union. But as Amit soaked in this new information, his mind stuck on a more immediate detail. "I still do not understand the coincidence with Enya. You mean because she is Russian?"

"No, Amit." Levy paused briefly. "The man that was killed in Tel Aviv, the immigrant, he was a dissident." Levy suppressed a smile, wondering if the famously analytical mind of Margolis would put the pieces together. "He was a physicist." Levy watched as Margolis' mouth started to unconsciously fall open, his eyes widening. "His name was Alexander Govenin. He was …"

"Enya's grandfather." Margolis finished the sentence.

"Yes. Her parents came here because of the work of your father. Her grandfather's death directly led to your father's death. By my book, this is divine."

Amit just sat and thought for a moment, not quite ready to accept an explanation of divine intervention. His mind began to think about Enya. "You said that Alexander Govenin was killed here by the KGB?"

"I did not say the KGB, but, yes, he was killed here by a Russian team, a very good one. Whether they were KGB or army, I don't know to this day."

"Was my father responsible for his security?"

Levy paused. He had not expected this question and had never really thought of this issue. He was unsure how to respond. "I am not sure." His response was a lie. "This was an elite team that got to Govenin. No one expected it."

"You are telling me that my father was responsible."

"I don't know for sure. But I am sure your father felt responsible."

Margolis wondered how Enya might react to the knowledge. He shook his head, telling himself that he could not think through all the permutations at this moment with the director of Mossad sitting next to him. "You came here to tell me this?"

"No, Amit. I came to pay my respects to you and the job you are doing at Olympus."

Amit stiffened imperceptibly. He possessed knowledge that Ami Levy did not and he had been ordered by his supreme commander, the prime minister, to not enlighten Levy. Margolis waited for what was coming.

The director, for all his ability to read others, did not recognize that Margolis was already a couple of steps ahead of him. "But you know that you are still Mossad. You are still part of this brotherhood we have." Levy looked Margolis in the eye, the compassion of only moments ago now gone and replaced with steely resolve. "And I am still the head of Mossad."

"Yes, sir. I understand and respect that. I respect you."

"Thank you. But you have to admit Amit that you are doing things that I need to be aware of. It is not good that I am in the dark. You are using Mossad resources and even recruiting people that we need for important operations."

"Sir, you know what I am working on and you know that I am working directly under the command of the prime minister. I think it best that you and he discuss these issues. I am merely a servant of the state."

"Don't fuck with me, Amit." Levy's voice was raised, his notorious temper emerging for the first time this morning. "I do not want you to jeopardize any of the Olympus activities and planning. You know that I support this effort. I just want to know about certain activities so that we are not bumping into each other. Do you think it is smart if you are out doing something in the Middle East and someone else in Mossad comes across this activity? If we don't know what is going on, then all of the sudden I am spending resources chasing your operations. We could wind up blowing each other's operations accidently. This is why we coordinate."

Margolis had to admit to himself that what Levy was saying made some sense. He could not know all of the resources that Mossad had in the region. "Go on."

"For instance, a Russian oligarch shows up in Dubai and starts buying an airline. Now, do you think that is not going to come to the attention of Mossad? Then I have to send a man to the Emirates and investigate. Imagine my surprise when he returns with a photograph of a gray-haired Amit Margolis driving around the countryside in the back of a Mercedes. How do you think I should react to this revelation? I need every resource I have to be used efficiently. I can't have assets chasing you around the Middle East." Levy stopped to catch his breath. "So tell me what is going on."

"I think you know it all at this point."

"No. All I know is that you are posing as a Russian named Gennady Masrov and you purchased an airline. The point is why?"

"Obviously this is related to the Olympus planning." Amit hesitated.

"You are about to make me lose my patience. This is not a good outcome."

Amit thought through the situation as best he could given the burning fuse in front of him. He needed to mollify Ami Levy or the ramifications would be very negative to Project Block G. "I will fill you in on the key pieces of the plan. But I need to know that you will keep this to yourself. Every additional person who knows about what we are doing puts our plans at greater risk."

"You don't think I understand this? You are telling me because I have a need to know this. We need to keep our activities coordinated."

"All right. We are creating a small fleet of aerial tankers that will operate out of Dubai. You are more than smart enough to figure out how this will work. We need refueling capacity and this is how we will do it."

Levy reached out with his left hand and patted Margolis on his right shoulder. It was at the same time paternal and condescending. "Now I understand. That is what I needed to know. Thank you." He retrieved his arm and leaned back in his cheap folding chair. "How does El Al fit in with this?"

"We are using them as well to buy Ilyushin 76 cargo planes. We are converting them to fuel tankers."

"How many will you have in the end?"

"I don't know yet. That depends on a lot of things: money, timing, our ability to acquire without raising suspicion."

"Okay. Okay" Levy raised up his right hand, its fingers extended and palm down. He motioned his hand in a way that indicated to Margolis that he should stop. "This is good. I can call off my men. Are you buying more companies?"

"No. I am done with the private company side of this. I have what I need in place now."

"Okay. What about funding? I know you have a source. Is it enough?"

"Is any amount of money ever enough?"

"Look, Amit. I don't need to know how you are being funded, but I offer this sincerely: If you need some funds, I have access to accounts that are hidden away in Swiss and Russian banks. I can help." Levy felt better. What Amit told him made sense and he knew from years of experience that when the pieces fit together in a way that created a logical story, then the truth had been revealed.

"I appreciate that, sir. As you hinted at earlier, though, what I really need are some qualified people to assist in key operations. I now have a cargo carrier to run."

"Yes you do." Levy was happy again. He smiled and then suddenly snapped his finger. "Oh, I almost forgot. Your lady friend in Dubai ... what's her name?"

"Kara Livingston."

"Yes, that's it. She works for Emirati intelligence."

Amit lowered his head and laughed. It was a mask. He was very angry with himself. "Thank you for the notification."

"Emirati Intelligence is not happy with us right now. You need to be very careful."

"Tell me about it. The assassination of the Hamas guy is still a hot topic there. I have had to spend half my time cursing the Jews while I am there." Amit smiled.

Director Levy did not smile. This was a very raw issue for him. The assassination of Mahmoud Al-Mabhouh in Dubai on January 19, 2010, by a Mossad kidon team had succeeded, but became an international embarrassment for Israel when the local police were able to use hotel videotape to trace the assassination team members. Their use of fake British, Irish, French and Australian passports had enraged each country. For Amichai Levy, the result had been a trip to Jerusalem to be chewed out by the prime minister for half an hour. Levy's pride was still wounded a year later.

"How is your cover?" Levy was concerned that anyone, especially UAE intelligence agents, checking on the background of Gennady Masrov would learn enough to believe the man was for real.

"I had the full legend put in place. I am not concerned."

"It must be working since you haven't been arrested yet. If the Emiratis even suspect you are Mossad, they will arrest you, rough you up and then publicly deport you. They are itching for a public win over us."

"I understand that. I think we always face that risk."

"True enough. If you need anything to support your cover, let me know. It will happen."

"Thank you."

"Like I have been saying, we are both better off if we communicate."

Amit's thoughts returned to the attractive British expatriate. "She is a direct agent?"

"The Livingston woman? No. No. She just feeds information to them. That's all. My point is that you ... uh, maybe I should say Mister Masrov ... you need to realize that your activities are on their radar."

"I had assumed as much, but I must admit I did not suspect Kara."

"Never forget, Amit – women. Women are our Achilles' heel. It will always be so. Now, you promise to keep me informed of key developments I need to know?"

"Yes, I will keep you informed. Key things only. Is that fair?"

"Nothing is fair, Amit. But I can work with what you propose. Now, we have to discuss current events and how they might affect Olympus."

"Current events?"

"The Arab Spring. Mubarak was ousted yesterday."

Margolis contemplated what he just heard. He had spent the day on airplanes, first from Dubai to Zurich and then Zurich to Tel Aviv. He had been exhausted and slept most of the time. When he got home late the prior night, Enya was waiting. What was on her mind had nothing to do with the news. She had a bottle of wine waiting and was wearing a very sexy dress with nothing else. She could not wait to get Amit into bed. "Mubarak has left Egypt?"

"No, but he was effectively removed from office yesterday. I have barely slept this week."

"Tunisian revolution. Now Egypt. Where does this end?" Amit pondered.

"Exactly the right question. I told the prime minister that I think Syria, Jordan and Saudi Arabia are at risk. This needs to be in the contingency planning for Olympus."

"Yes. I agree. What about UAE?"

"I am not worried about UAE or the other Gulf States. Of course, rioting has been underway in Yemen, but that pseudo-country is in a tug of war for its soul."

"God help us if Saudi Arabia falls. Who will run Egypt now?"

"Our analysis is that the Muslim Brotherhood is the only institution ready to govern other than the military. Maybe we get lucky and the military just takes over, but I have doubts about that. Imagine, the head of Mossad rooting for the Egyptian military." Levy shook his head. "Funny."

"This could make it impossible to launch the attack depending on what happens in Syria, Jordan and Saudi Arabia."

"I understand. Here is the deal. You will keep me informed of the key Olympus plans and I will keep you informed with the best intel on the Arab Spring."

"What about Iran? Any chance of revolt?"

"Always a chance. And we will be glad to help, but I am not optimistic. Vevak is too proactive at eliminating the smartest opposition leaders. After the demise of Mubarak, I doubt that the Iranian Regime will be caught off guard."

"The UAE?"

Levy was going to give a dismissive response because Amit had just asked about the country, but he understood the obsession. "Possible but very unlikely. We know the Iranians are agitating Shiites in Bahrain, Qatar and the UAE. But if you had to pick one of the Gulf States that will survive this, the UAE is it. I think you chose wisely on location."

"Not that I foresaw any of this happening."

"I will deny what I am about to say, but the fact is none of us saw this happening, certainly not with this speed." Levy stood up. "Don't lose sleep over Saudi Arabia or Syria. The Saudis have spread the wealth effectively and the Alawites in Syria have an iron grip just like the Mullahs in Iran." The director started to walk toward the door, his mind now on the future. "Still, it would be nice to see the Iranians lose their client state."

Margolis stood and followed the head of Mossad toward the door. He was quiet.

Levy started to open the heavy blast door of the basement shelter and paused briefly. He turned and shook Amit's hand. "I am proud of you Amit. You come see me once a month and we will catch up with each other."

Margolis knew an order when he heard it. "I appreciate your support, sir."

Levy walked into the hall to take the elevator up, deciding against using the stairwell in front of him. His knees were not cooperating with him on this Saturday morning.

After the one floor ride up, Levy stepped out of the elevator and Amit started to follow, but the director stopped him. "I have taken you away from your woman too long already. Enjoy the rest of this beautiful day with her. Shabbat shalom." Levy walked down the hall to his waiting SUV.

Amit continued up to his floor and walked quickly to his apartment. He found Enya on the computer. She had Google images open and on the screen Amit could see about 15 photographs, most of which were of Amichai Levy. As he walked up behind her, she turned to look at him.

"Why is the director of Mossad visiting you on a Saturday morning?"

"Enya, please." Margolis thought about possible eavesdropping. He reached underneath her right armpit and raised her off her seat. "Come on." He led her into the bathroom attached to his bedroom. It had no windows, which Enya hated. He turned on the water and a small radio he kept on the vanity. "You figured out who just visited me, please don't ever discuss his name or that he was here. Not to anyone. Understand?"

"No, I don't understand. We have dinner with a senior general, you travel all the time. This man," she stabbed her hand into the air, "comes to visit you. Do you think I'm that stupid? You are Mossad, just as Nava told me you were when we first met."

"Please, honey. You can't say these things. This is dangerous. You don't understand." Margolis paused to catch his breath. "Is it not enough to know that I am advising the state? Is it not enough to accept what General Schechter told you?" His eyes were imploring the woman he loved. "Is it not enough that I am in love with you?" The words were coming out of Amit's mouth for the first time. His timing was not good.

"Don't change the subject, Amit. I don't know who are. You have been lying to me."

"Honey. Please understand me. I work on behalf of our nation. What I do is very sensitive. I can't …"

"Stop lying to me," Enya shouted.

Margolis raised his hands and gestured with his palms down, the motion urging her to calm down. "Shhhh. Shhhh."

"Don't treat me like a child."

Margolis knew this point would come. He pondered for an instant why he faced having to reveal secrets to two people in the span of a few minutes. *Have I angered God somehow?* "Okay. Calm down. What do you want to know?" He thought to himself that he should feel relief, but he only felt defeated at the moment. It was the same feeling he always had when he lost control.

"Are you Mossad?"

Amit looked at her and slowly nodded his head up and down. "Now, we can never discuss this again, okay?"

"Why didn't you tell me this? We have been together for over a year now."

"Please, honey. Don't do this. This is dangerous. You should not know this. It just puts you in danger. I could lose my job because you know."

"Well, blame that old man. He is the one who came here. I'm sure he violated all the rules doing that, didn't he? And his eyes almost popped out of his head looking at my body."

Margolis laughed. He didn't want to, but he couldn't help himself. "You can't blame him for that."

Enya Govenin rested her head against Amit's left breast. "I just wish you had told me and that I didn't have to figure it out." Suddenly she snapped her head back and looked at Amit. "Just how long were you going to wait?"

"I don't know honey. It is not good that you know. There are plenty of people who would kill me and harm you just because of what I do. Now you have to promise me that you will never, ever discuss this with anyone. I mean no one, Enya. Just stick with what you thought I was."

"Do you kill people?"

"Honey, seriously? We can't have this discussion."

"We are having this discussion, Amit. Do you kill people for a living?"

"I cannot discuss what I do. But know that I don't kill people. Before you ask, I have never killed anyone. This is not like the movies. I am not Daniel Craig."

"Who?"

Amit immediately regretted throwing out the name. "You know, the new James Bond."

"Oh." Enya smiled. "You are as hot as he is." She rubbed her hands across his chest and down his stomach. "Well, almost."

"You are too much sometimes." Amit grabbed her hands as they were making their way below his waist. He pulled them up to his mouth and kissed the top of each hand. "I can accept being almost as hot as Daniel Craig." He chuckled. "But you must promise me, Enya. This is deadly serious. This is life and death and it could be my life if you are not careful. You understand what I am saying?"

"I do. Talk to no one. Ever."

"Keep in mind that everything you do over a phone or on the Internet – and I mean everything – can be monitored and is probably being monitored now."

"What? Why? How?"

"Because you are my girlfriend."

"I don't understand. If no one knows you are Mossad, what does me being your girlfriend have to do with anything?"

"Because, honey, I can guarantee that the Americans know who I am. That means they know who you are. That means they monitor you for information about me."

"Wait. You are talking crazy talk. The Americans have a spy following me?"

"No. They …" He thought about the right way to proceed. "Do you know what the National Security Agency is?"

She just looked at him and shook her head.

"It is a huge American intelligence agency. They can intercept everything on the planet that goes over the Internet or travels through the airwaves. Your cell phone. Your texts. Your email. Your Google searches. Your phone calls. Facebook. Everything."

"How do they pick me out of all the stuff everywhere?"

"They have the most computing power in the world by a wide margin. Everything passes through their computers. If they know what they are looking for, they sift all of it, the millions and millions of calls and texts and emails every hour of every day. They can search for known phone numbers or email addresses or Twitter accounts or even names or words in a phone call. I can assure you that my name is in their database. Just like Prime Minister Cohen or Director Levy. Or Osama bin Laden. If you are on the list, anything that has your name or address in it is flagged and reviewed."

"That is scary, Amit."

"I am only telling you so you realize what is at stake … what reality is. You have to accept that you can't discuss me with anyone or over any medium."

"But the Americans are our friends."

"That's not the point, honey. That's just an example. There are plenty of people out there that aren't our friends and nobody has a monopoly on technology."

Enya realized what Amit was saying, the realization making her face relax involuntarily. "I understand." She hugged her man. "Did you just say that you love me?"

Amit felt like his heart stopped beating. "Yes. I love you Enya Govenin."

"I love you, Amit Margolis." She put her arms around his neck. They kissed.

"Has it been a year?" he asked.

"You have been traveling most of the time. I hope you can stay home more."

"I will try." Margolis paused and a strange look came over him.

"What is wrong?"

"There is something else I need to tell you about." Now Enya assumed the strange look Amit just had. "It is … I don't know how to describe it."

"Tell me what is wrong."

"It's not that something is wrong. It is just a remarkable coincidence. The director came to tell me something about my personal life that I didn't know." He hesitated, gathering his thoughts. "It's just that … I don't know. It's crazy really."

"Amit," the tone was pleading. "Just tell me what it is."

"My father was in Mossad as well."

Enya was not sure how to respond or where Amit was going with this. "Is this why you are now in Mossad?"

"No. No. It's something different." She simply gave him a puzzled look. Amit continued. "My father is the man who arranged for your parents to get out of the Soviet Union. He brought them here."

Enya stepped back one small step. "No. This is too freaky."

"It is a crazy coincidence. I don't know what to think about this."

"What are the odds that we would meet and fall in love? Maybe this was meant to be."

"There is more, though. Do you know about your grandfather?"

"My grandfather? He was a Soviet physicist. A dissident."

"Do you know about his death?"

"All I know is that he was the victim of PLO terrorists."

"They were definitely terrorists. But not the PLO. The PLO was a cover story." Amit gathered his emotions, scared to death about where the next few sentences would lead. "He was murdered by a Soviet kill team."

"Here in Israel?"

"Yes. I don't know the whole story but apparently he knew about a coup plot in the Soviet Union. They came after him for that."

"How does your father fit into that?"

"My father went into the Soviet Union based on the information he learned from your grandfather. He – my father – was killed inside the Soviet Union. But apparently he uncovered this coup and foiled it before he was killed."

Enya exhaled loudly and covered her mouth with her left hand. "Oh my God, Amit. Your father died because of my grandfather?"

The statement caught Margolis off guard. It was the opposite of the way he had been thinking and it was not the message he was trying to convey. "No, honey. My father died for his country, for what he believed in. There is another aspect." Amit looked down, unable to make eye contact. "He was responsible for protecting your grandfather while he was here."

"So?"

"So? Don't you see? He failed. That failure cost your grandfather's life."

"Amit, really? You just said my grandfather was killed by the KGB … or whoever." She raised her hands up and cupped Amit's jaw in her palms. She brought his face to hers. "I don't know everything like you, but I am smart enough to know that if the KGB wants to kill someone, they will probably succeed." She kissed him softly. "I never even knew him. The way it sounds to me is that your father died for him, and for you, and for me. That is what I call a hero. And you, Amit Margolis, you are my hero."

25 – Into Baghdad

Ibrahim Hajjar sat in the over-wing exit row of the Emirates Airbus A330 as it corkscrewed down to its final glide path into Baghdad International Airport. The plane's steep left hand turn leveled out only a mile off the end of runway 15 Right. Just seconds later the rear tires of the plane scorched the concrete runway. Only three minutes later the plane was at the gate, its passengers eager to deplane. Another hour long journey through customs awaited, but at least the venue would be the relative safety of the terminal building. Beyond that awaited the eight-mile taxi ride into the International Zone – the chosen Iraqi name for the area of downtown Baghdad defined by a sweeping bend in the Tigris river and known to the world as the Green Zone – where foreigners could find comparative normalcy and a decent hotel. At least, thought Hajjar, the route from the airport into the city, which had been dubbed "Route Irish" by the American military during the dark days following the fall of the country in 2003, was now fairly safe. The experienced taxi drivers kept a healthy distance from any American convoys – both to minimize the chance of being caught in an ambush and to keep any trigger happy GIs from unloading a machine gun in their direction.

Hajjar checked into the Al Rasheed Hotel a little after 6 p.m. on February 17, 2011, hungry and tired from the travel. The flight from Kuwait City had been short, but the added stress of flying into Baghdad made every traveler weary. The next day he would meet a man named Joseph Calantro in the lobby of the unmarked Iraq Civil Aviation Authority building on Nasir Street. Mr. Calantro, he was told, would be the "grease" he needed to accomplish his job over the next few days in Iraq. But right now, he just wanted some food and a good night's sleep.

Ibrahim Hajjar awoke the next morning to a cold cloudy day. Odds were high that rain would fall on any given winter day in Baghdad and as Hajjar looked out the window of his room he was thankful that he had planned appropriately. After a surprisingly good breakfast of omelet and fresh melons, he retrieved a backpack from his room and a large aluminum-sided case on wheels. In the backpack, Hajjar had packed enough clothing and basic supplies to last him for several nights. In the aluminum case, he had the instruments of his profession: a Radiodetection RD-1000 ground penetrating radar, a GPS mapping device, an 18-volt cordless drill with a series of bits, and a set of batteries and charging adapters to ensure power for each instrument. He had a contract to perform engineering services, and he was prepared for the most hostile environment short of combat.

A taxi dropped him off at 8:47 a.m., Hajjar tipping the driver well to compensate for the short drive from the hotel. He quickly gathered his items and walked into the lobby. Inside, two Iraqi policeman checked his ID and confirmed that he was an invited guest. Before he was allowed into the reception area, he was frisked and his backpack and aluminum case were searched. He was made to explain what the lawnmower-shaped device was in his case. The ground penetrating radar was portable and not particularly powerful, but to the trained eye it could reveal the geological properties of the first 20 feet or so of earth underneath it when run along the ground.

Finally Hajjar was issued a pass and allowed into the reception room. Inside, a shorter man wearing a long sleeve button down cotton dress shirt and dark slacks immediately stood and walked toward the engineer. "Ibrahim Hajjar?" came the challenge.

"Yes. Mister Calantro?" The men exchanged smiles.

"Salam alaykum," said Joseph Calantro to his guest. "Welcome to Baghdad."

The men exchanged a firm handshake. "Wa alaykum salam." Hajjar put his hand to his left breast.

"Please follow me."

Over the next hour in the office of Deputy Director Walid Hafeez al-Salih, Calantro and Hajjar discussed the Kuwaiti's contract with the Iraq Civil Aviation Authority. The common language spoken was English. Hafeez's English was nearly fluent, a skill that had been useful in keeping him gainfully employed since the American invasion. Hajjar did not speak fluent English. He described his knowledge as "conversational", but it was clear to all in the room that he was quite rusty. Deputy Director Hafeez would occasionally speed the process along by explaining technical matters in Arabic. But by the end of the meeting, all three men understood the project clearly: Hajjar would be assessing the status of a small number of abandoned Iraqi airfields. His job was to deliver a report with a detailed assessment of the condition of each of five airfields located in the western region of Iraq known as Anbar Province. Two main airfields, called H2 and H3, originally had been built by the British in the 1930s to protect and service pumping stations along a pipeline built to bring oil from Kirkuk in Iraq to Haifa, now Israel's third city.

The Iraqi Air Force had expanded H3 and added two small single runway airfields during the 1970s to create a grouping of bases for the defense of Iraq, each theoretically supporting the other. The network of airbases had been abandoned since the opening weeks of the 2003 invasion, when British and Australian special forces, supported by larger elements of the U.S. Army, seized control of the airfields. The objective was to keep Iraq from launching Scud missiles at Israel and to seize expected caches of chemical and biological weapons thought to be stored in the area. Both objectives failed.

Joseph Calantro played the same role he usually did. As one of the many State Department employees based in Baghdad, he functioned as a facilitator for the huge number of vendors from around the world who flew to the Iraqi capital in a quest to win contracts for the reconstruction of Iraq. It was the modern day equivalent of the California gold rush. The fact that U.S. taxpayers were footing much of the bill gave the State Department significant power in the process. Men like Calantro were invaluable, with the ability to draw on the resources of the U.S.

military on the one hand and adroitly navigate the landmines of Iraqi politics on the other. In this case, he had arranged for the U.S. Army to act as escort service for Hajjar.

Two hours later, following a short lunch in the building's small cafeteria, the quality of which was the opposite of Hajjar's breakfast, Calantro received a call on his cell phone. He spoke for only a few seconds and hung up. "They will be outside in a few minutes. You ready?"

"Yes."

26 – West to Anbar

A convoy of three up-armored Humvees headed west out of Baghdad on the Abu Ghraib Expressway, which conveniently bypassed the towns of Falluja and Ramadi. The modern multi-lane highway, which paralleled the historic route of combined Highway 10 and 11 towards Jordan and Syria, was a public works triumph of Saddam Hussein, a road to rival any highway in Europe or the U.S. This small group of American military vehicles was heading into the heart of Anbar Province, the center of much of the hardest combat between Sunni insurgents and the U.S. Army until just a few years earlier.

Ibrahim Hajjar was well aware of the history and was obviously nervous as he sat in the rear seat behind the driver of the third Humvee. Next to him was a 23-year-old sergeant named Jose Gutierrez, but everyone called him Rican. He had been born in Puerto Rico and grew up in Brooklyn and was equally proud of either geography. Rican had been given a simple order from the lieutenant who rode in the first Humvee: make sure nothing happens to their guest.

Rican was not used to being a host, but smiled as he looked over to his nervous Arab charge. "Ever been to Iraq before?"

"No."

"Well, look. Don't worry. The roads here are safe. We can patrol the streets of Fallujah now and the kids swarm us. Not like it was four, five years ago. Plus it's Friday. Less traffic."

Hajjar smiled back at the sergeant. His poor English combined with Rican's accent and fast rate of speech left him understanding only a fraction of what was being communicated. But the Kuwaiti could tell from the American's tone that he was calm and attempting to reassure.

The trip into the western desert took six hours, the heavily armored Humvees struggling to maintain a speed of 45 mph despite the perfect condition of the highway. Sedans and trucks occasionally whizzed past the small convoy, each driver accelerating as fast as he could to get past the menacing 50-caliber machine gun mounted on the top of the second Humvee.

Finally the group passed just to the north of Ar Rutbah, a town of almost 59,000 that had grown up to support the nearby oil pipeline and the H3 and H2 pumping stations and airbases. Twenty miles further down the road, the convoy pulled off and turned into Camp Korean Village, a military outpost built a few hundred feet north of Highways 10 and 11 by the Americans shortly after the invasion. Now the camp had been turned over to the Iraqi National Army and was manned by elements of the 7th Iraqi Army Division.

After settling down into a hut that featured cots that were surprisingly comfortable, Rican was surprised when his guest, who had been taciturn during most of the drive out, became very outgoing and chatty with the small number of Iraqi officers at the base. Rican had no idea what they were talking about, but he was struck by how intently the engineer was listening to whichever Iraqi opened up to him. Wherever Hajjar went, Rican followed. He had assumed the role of the Kuwaiti's personal bodyguard, not that it was necessary.

The next morning, just as the sun appeared on the eastern horizon, the convoy of three Humvees pulled onto the eastern end of runway 29, the primary runway at the main airfield known as H3. Two decades earlier, during the war with Iran that many of the Iraqi military now looked back on with fond nostalgia, this had been known as Walid Air Base and H2, only 57 miles to the northeast, had been known as Saad Air Base. The town of Rutbah was situated about 32 miles to the east of H3, the town and the two airbases forming a right triangle on the map. The temperature outside was only a handful of degrees above freezing. As they had the prior day, Ibrahim Hajjar sat in the back seat of the third Humvee with Rican next to him. Rican leaned in toward Hajjar. "Okay, sir, we are here. Tell us where you want to go."

The young sergeant was already a veteran of this war and was now on his third tour in Iraq. He had seen occasional combat, usually only a brief firefight with insurgents or just pissed off locals who were brave enough to fire a round or two in the direction of passing Americans, the mere act a sign of courage and resistance for many in Iraq. On his second tour he had been wounded by an improvised explosive device, an IED. He had been in a Bradley fighting vehicle reinforced with reactive armor when an IED with an explosively formed penetrator, the handiwork of the Iranians, pierced the engine compartment. The copper penetrator caused an explosion that was largely contained by an intervening bulkhead, but that still sent pieces of aluminum shrapnel into the crew compartment, wounding four men, including Rican. His thigh had been penetrated, but not too deeply, the wound being treated with a thorough cleaning and four stainless steel staples to close it shut. He had been sent home after that, but his recovery was not difficult. He knew that in a major war he would have spent a couple days in hospital before being sent back to the front. But in this conflict, the Army took a different path.

Hajjar lifted himself up in his seat, leaning to his right to look past the driver, supporting his weight by grabbing the back of the driver's seat with his left hand. He simply pointed straight ahead to a confluence of two runways more than a mile away.

The convoy drove for almost 8,000 feet, passing old trucks and an obsolete MiG-21 fighter without an engine, all placed strategically on the runway to keep planes from landing. "Here?" asked Rican.

Ibrahim Hajjar just nodded his head. He looked out the front windshield. "There," he said as he pointed again to a spot a few hundred yards away. "Good." He gave Rican a thumbs up sign.

"You got it," responded the sergeant, telling his driver to head for the approximate location. For the next four hours Hajjar had them stop near each end and in the middle of all three runways, the main taxiway and at two spots in the main tarmac comprising this airfield. At each stop he followed the same routine. First he set a waypoint in his GPS device. Then he placed his ground radar device, which looked just like a lawnmower complete with wheels at all four corners, on the ground about half way between the center line and the edge of the runway, walking up the runway about two hundred yards before turning and crossing the center line to walk back half way between the center line and the opposite side. A computer mounted on the handlebars recorded all of the readings picked up by the device.

Finally he would take out his cordless drill and attach a foot-long coring bit. He would drill into the runway. After penetrating the maximum length of the bit, he would withdraw it and use another device to remove the coring sample and place it in a plastic tube sized perfectly for the core. He then noted the GPS coordinates, temperature, humidity and time of day on the plastic tube.

It took about fifteen minutes at each stop to complete the process and another few minutes to pack up and move to the next stop. At the stops that were near the end of the runways, Hajjar took photographs from several different perspectives. His camera recorded the time, GPS coordinates and compass direction on each photo taken.

The two other Humvees took up covering positions. All of the men were bored, correctly guessing that the chance of enemy action was about equivalent to the chance that Meghan Fox would suddenly land in an airplane for their entertainment.

After the last stop, Hajjar climbed into the back of his Humvee. "Thank you," he said to Rican.

"Just doing my job. This is about as interesting as most of what I do in country."

The convoy moved quickly to cover the 21 mile driving distance to the next airfield, known as H3 Southwest. It had a single runway running and taxiway. A small apron was located near the southeastern terminus of the airfield. This time the Humvee carrying Hajjar drove to the runway/taxiway junction and stopped, the driver not needing to ask the Kuwaiti where to go. The engineer exited and retrieved his gear. The process began at the right junction, moved up the runway and came back down the taxi. Only a single core was drilled on the apron. The time on the base was a little over two hours, each man except for Hajjar able to enjoy an MRE for lunch.

The three Humvees headed out to the final airfield of the day, the second of the two dispersal fields established to support the main H3 airfield, this one known H3 Northwest. The drive took about fifty minutes, the Kuwaiti engineer able to eat some lunch on the way. The established process began again. Hajjar was tired as he worked. He was still in his 30s, but was clearly not in the same physical condition as his American military hosts. But despite this, the small base with a single taxiway and small tarmac took less than three hours to complete.

The convoy was back at Camp Korean Village as nightfall began to make Rican nervous about being outside the camp's protection. The process of the prior night repeated, with the Kuwaiti talking endlessly with every willing Iraqi, this time adding a couple of enlisted men in his discussions.

At 0630 hours the next day, the convoy set out again, this time not expecting to return. The lieutenant went out of his way to find the commanding officer of the base and shake his hand, thanking him for the hospitality. One hour later, the convoy pulled on to the southern tip of runway 34 at H2 airfield. This field had two long runways, two long taxiways and two tarmac areas. Every 700 feet or so, a large rectangular pile of sandbags blocked the runways and the taxiways. But Hajjar followed the same procedure he had the prior day, except for one change in the routine. On this day Rican asked to operate the cordless drill after the first stop, taking over the drilling function at each remaining stop and speeding up the process. It gave Rican something to do and made the lieutenant happy since they had a long drive to reach the last of the five airfields they would visit on this trip.

The convoy loaded up and moved out from H2 around noon. To the north, dark clouds heavily laden with moisture were headed their way. Distant thunder rolled along the sandy earth, heightening the desire of everyone to outrun the storm. That goal was successfully achieved. The convoy drove back east 84 miles to the intersection with Highway 21 and turned south for another 55 miles before turning right onto an unmarked road for the last 11 miles of their journey.

The road they were on terminated at an isolated air base known as Mudaysis Airfield. Mudaysis had a single 9,800 foot runway with an equally long parallel taxiway and a single rectangular tarmac that was adjacent to the taxiway and measured 1,325 feet by 380 feet. As the convoy pulled onto the tarmac at 1532 hours, lightning struck the southern end of the runway only a quarter mile from the Humvees. As if under the direction of the lightning bolt, rain suddenly hit the convoy hard. All three Humvees buttoning up as tight as they could. The convoy simply sat in position, hoping the rain would soon pass.

After almost an hour of heavy rain, a small amount of fading sunlight broke through the clouds as the raindrops slowed to a trickle. The lieutenant walked up to Hajjar's Humvee and opened his door. "What would you like to do?" asked the young officer.

Hajjar got out onto the tarmac, stepping into a pool of water about three inches deep. He looked around the barren airfield. Other than some earth-covered aircraft bunkers and a handful of roofless buildings that looked like they had been deserted and decaying for decades, there was nothing to see but desert flatness that was now covered in most spots by a layer of water. "Too wet," said the Kuwaiti. "Radar not good now."

"That's what I figured," responded the lieutenant. "We will spend the night right here and start at first light."

Hajjar got back into the Humvee, and the officer informed the soldiers in the vehicle of the situation. The lieutenant then closed Hajjar's door and walked to the other Humvee to inform them before walking back to his vehicle. Inside the lieutenant's Humvee, a communication specialist radioed the home base outside of Baghdad. The radio call was relayed by an unmanned aerial vehicle orbiting at 62,000 feet over central Iraq to facilitate U.S. military transmissions. It took less than a minute to report their location and status. They were warned that aerial support was not close if they got into trouble.

The vehicles started up and drove over to the one aircraft bunker that appeared to be in the best condition. The lieutenant got out and investigated before ordering the two Humvees without a mounted gun to back in while the Humvee with the 50 caliber machine gun backed in last, its nose just inside the roof of the bunker. The steel doors which used to close up the opening to protect the airplane once housed here were long gone. But now, anyone who approached the opening to the bunker would be met by half inch diameter machine gun rounds, more than enough to deter any but the suicidal.

Rican hopped out. The ground was wet. He looked up at the sky through a three foot wide circular opening in the roof with rusting rebar pointing downward into the hanger area. The hole was the only remaining evidence of the weapon that had destroyed whatever airplane had been unlucky enough to be parked here when the U.S. Air Force came calling. He walked around and found an area where they could set up a couple of tents that had been brought along for this contingency. The sergeant yelled at several privates to get them going on their new task, exercising the prerogative that dictated life in every military throughout time. He returned to his Humvee and climbed into the rear seat. "Fun night tonight," he said. "Already feels like forty degrees out."

Ibrahim Hajjar was excited, feeling like he was kid at a scouting event. He looked at Rican. "This is very far from people," he said, his English having improved slightly as a result of three days of constant usage. "Anyone here ever?" he asked.

"No, sir. I asked the Iraqis that question this morning at Camp KV. They said they come out here once or twice a month. The guy I talked to has been at KV for nine months and has never seen a soul here. He couldn't remember any stories of people here neither. If you ask me, this is the last place the Iraqis want to build. This place is fit only for Bedouin. Even the Iraqis want nothing to do with it. There ain't even no villages within miles. Plus, it's a hell hole in the summer time."

"How far is town?"

"You mean the nearest village? Shit, gotta be at least twenty klicks from here." Rican leaned forward, talking to the soldier in the front passenger seat. "Hey, Chris, check the map for the nearest village."

Christian Watson, a 21-year-old specialist from Iowa, had been navigating. He looked down and, cupping the back of the map with his left hand, raised it up and pointed at a dot on the detailed map. The town of Al Kasrah was indicated to be 13 kilometers from this airfield as the crow flies. However, to get there would require driving back up the road connecting this airbase to Highway 21 and then turning south, a total of 22 kilometers of driving. Watson also pointed out another small village called Al Habariyah that was even further south along Highway 21. It was 29 kilometers, or 18 miles, from where they were now parked.

Hajjar slept only sporadically that night. Somewhere in the middle of the night, with the temperature close to freezing, the Kuwaiti engineer got out of his sleeping bag, rolled it up and walked over to his Humvee. He spent the rest of the night trying to stay warm in his seat, the sleeping bag now acting as a blanket. Thankfully, the sun finally began to illuminate a sky that had more blue than gray for the first time in days. Hajjar was eager to get to work but took the time to drink two cups of coffee one of the men had brewed up and eat a MRE, picking the vegetable lasagna when offered the choice between that and chicken and dumplings.

At 0716, with the power of the sun quickly dulling the coldest edges of the wind, the convoy drove off. Hajjar's Humvee headed to the southeastern end of the single runway, which ran from the southeast to the northwest. He began the process that was now well rehearsed. Rican took over the coring duties as he had the prior day. The other two Humvee's assumed covering positions, one on the tarmac and the other, the one with the 50 caliber machine gun, by the only road leading into the airfield. Unlike the larger H2 and H3 airfields, where cars occasionally passed by on the nearby roads, there was no sign of any life or movement around this airfield.

The Kuwaiti could not help but think that Mudaysis Airfield reminded him of the western ghost towns in the movies he used to watch as a kid, only minus the tumbleweed. He took numerous photographs of the airfield, noting that, unlike the first four airfields, no major obstacles existed on the runway or its adjacent parallel taxiway. During 2008, U.S. Marines of Wing Support Squadron 374 of the 3rd Marine Aircraft Wing had occupied Mudaysis to create a forward refueling base in support of U.S. military activities in Anbar Province. The Iraq "surge" was in full bloom. As part of that operation, the obstacles on the runway and taxiway had been removed. After the operations had ended, the airfield quickly reverted to its abandoned state. Since then, the entire airfield seemed to be forgotten by the Iraqi government, the Iraqi Army and the local populous.

The engineer, along with every soldier in the convoy, was happy to find that all of the water of the prior evening was completely gone, leaving behind no hint that this land was anything other than an arid desert. As they worked their way to the northwest up the long runway, Rican realized that Hajjar had decided to stop at five points to take samples and make radar readings instead of the three per runway on the previous days. They repeated the same five stops coming back down the adjacent taxiway. Finally, Hajjar took samples and readings at three spots on the tarmac.

At 1300 hours, with the men of the convoy now thoroughly bored with this assignment and eager to head back to Camp Victory, their home base outside Baghdad, Hajjar approached the lieutenant. "Okay, thank you and the men."

"We are here to help Iraq," replied the lieutenant. "Ready to return to Baghdad?"

"Yes. I have question, ah … what is word?"

The lieutenant was not sure what Hajjar meant. "Question?" Then it hit him. "Oh, you mean a request?"

"Yes, that is the word. Request."

"Okay."

"Please we go south on road two-one. I need to see towns."

The lieutenant could not understand why this engineer would want to go by the local villages, but walked over to Hajjar's Humvee. "Watson, let me see the map."

Chris Watson stepped out and spread his map out on the hood of the Humvee, holding down the edges with his hands as the officer reviewed distances. The lieutenant guessed that returning the way Hajjar wanted would add a couple of hours to the trip home, but he was under orders to accommodate the engineer's needs.

The lieutenant walked back to the engineer. "Is this really important?"

"Yes. Part of my job to get done."

"Okay, we will head south on Highway 21. That will take us through Kasrah, Habariyah and Nukhaib at the junction with Highway 22. Does that work for you?"

"Yes. Thank you." Hajjar offered his hand in gratitude and the lieutenant shook it firmly.

The convoy set out on its new route back to Baghdad that took them south for 35 miles before turning to the northeast on Highway 22. From there, they passed through Karbala and Iskandariyah on the 180 mile journey back to Baghdad.

Ibrahim Hajjar, whose real name was Yosef Sayegh, had everything he needed to create a report for his employer, Mossad. As a Syrian born Mizrahi Jew, Yosef had grown up in Damascus and then moved with his parents to Amman, Jordan, when he was 12. After two years in Jordan, his parents immigrated for the last time to Jerusalem to become Israeli citizens under the Law of Return. Yosef Sayegh had been spotted early by Mossad recruiters and had become a much in demand katsa for Mossad, intimately familiar with Arabic and Islamic customs and very much at ease portraying a Muslim professional. The contract from the Iraq Civil Aviation Authority was real and he would deliver a full report to them – one that would be essentially the same as that delivered to Mossad. But the CIA officer who had skillfully maneuvered to deliver the funding to the ICAA from the State Department for this study had also assured his contacts at Mossad that, as with most government funded studies, nothing would ever come of it.

27 – Outback Games

Exercise Talisman Sabre 2011 commenced on July 11, 2011. The biennial exercise has become a major war gaming operation to test the planning and operational integration of U.S. and Australian military forces – a continuation of the military alliance between the two nations that dates back over 100 years and spans both world wars, Korea, Vietnam and the first and second Persian Gulf wars. Hundreds of millions of dollars would be spent by the Pentagon to deploy American naval, ground and air forces into Australia for the exercise. The rise of Chinese military and economic power had provided renewed impetus behind the historic American-Australian ties. The result was that Talisman Sabre, along with other exercises with codenames like Tandem Thrust and Green Lightning, was growing accordingly. This year's exercise was slated to last two and a half weeks.

On July 12, a flight of four F-15E Strike Eagles landed in quick succession on the main 9,000 foot runway of Tindal Air Base, a major facility of the Royal Australian Air Force located just to the southeast of the city of Katherine in the Northern Territory. The American planes proudly displayed their tail code of "MO" in large black letters. They were from the 389th Fighter Squadron based permanently at Mountain Home Air Force Base, 40 miles southeast of Boise, Idaho. But they had flown in from Guam where they were in the middle of a four month rotation. They would spend the next two weeks practicing their skills on the nearby Delamere Air Weapons Station, a bombing range operated by the RAAF that had previously been a large cattle ranch in the heart of Australia's rugged Outback.

The eight men who flew in joined a larger group to complete the complement of 24 American aviators now at Tindal. They would take turns flying the same four aircraft, making the logistics of the exercise a little more economical and easier on the host Australians. At precisely 4 p.m. that afternoon, all of the men were called into a closed-door briefing session. As the men took their seats, their commanding officer walked up to the dais with the base commander behind him.

"Welcome to Australia," said the American colonel. He went on to spend the next fifteen minutes reviewing the standard rules for this exercise. There would be a hard floor of flight level 140, or 14,000 feet, except while on bombing runs over Delamere. They would be taking off to the southeast, into the prevailing winter winds. There was a steep landing approach corridor from the north to reduce time and noise over the township of Katherine. All of the rules were of the type that these men were well accustomed to – intended to keep the local civilian population happy, or at least to minimize their agitation.

Next, the RAAF base commander stood to introduce himself. "G'day gentlemen," said Group Captain Peter Wells. He thanked his American counterpart and added some information about local navigation beacons, communication frequencies and call signs. He reminded the men that Tindal has civilian aviation as well as military and that contact with Tindal air traffic control and strict use of established military corridors was critical to avoid mishaps. All of the men kept notes.

Finally he turned to a matter that was anything but routine for the aviators in this briefing. "I have another topic to cover today. Every man in this room is an officer and has classified clearance. I remind you of that fact because you will be flying alongside some other guests of Australia. Tonight five Israeli Strike Eagles will land here. Tomorrow another forty Israeli aviators and twenty-seven mechanics and technicians will arrive on a transport flight. I tell you this because you will certainly run into these men during your time here. But this information is strictly classified. From an official point of view, no Israeli aircraft or crewmen are in Australia or participating in Talisman Sabre in any way. You are not to refer to or mention this information to anyone. Is that clear?" The men all nodded in agreement.

Their commanding officer stood up. "I have forms that must be signed by everyone here," he said. His job was to drive home the seriousness of this situation. "As Group Captain Wells said, this information has been classified Top Secret. If any man reveals what you have just learned or anything that you see or learn regarding this matter, you will be violating Article 104 of the Code and you will be prosecuted under the Code. The form I am passing out is your acknowledgement of the situation. I do not want anyone here to have any misunderstandings." The two senior officers had discussed the best way to handle having Israelis secretly operating side by side with them and concluded that this up-front acknowledgement was the best way to stop rumors and speculation from starting on the base and spreading from there.

28 - Tindal

Slightly after midnight that night, five IAF F-15I Ra'am fighter bombers landed at Tindal. All five aircraft had been painted gunship grey, the same color as the American F-15s at the base. No national insignia could be found on any of the F-15Is, leaving any observer to assume naturally that these were American aircraft. Only the mechanics who daily worked on the F-15E could pick up on the subtle external differences between the F-15E and the F-15I. Likewise, the Israeli pilots, mechanics, technicians and officers who were arriving on base all wore American flight or duty suits, just without any national flag or squadron patches. There would be no display of unit pride that was ordinarily a central practice for military aviators the world over.

Early the next morning, two USAF C-17 Globemasters touched down about five minutes apart. Each of the big cargo aircraft taxied to the military apron. Through the forward port-side passenger door of the first plane, 77 of the most highly trained assets of the nation of Israel exited, joining the 10 men already on the base. Another ten Israelis exited the plane. They would form the security detail to protect the airplanes, pilots, mechanics, technicians and specialists. From the rear cargo doors of the second plane, crewmen of the USAF's 437th Airlift Wing unloaded two large crates, each containing a Pratt & Whitney F100-PW-229 jet engine, and another eight pallets of tools, instruments and spare parts – all of the items necessary to support five F-15Is for two weeks.

But the cargo that was the reason these precious assets of the IAF had travelled more than 7,000 miles would not arrive until later that day. At 5:17 p.m. on July 13, 2011, a C-17 touched down at Tindal. The flight originated from Elgin Air Force Base in Florida 36 hours before. It flew to Seattle to pick up its human cargo and some related equipment. After a 14-hour layover, it flew from Seattle to Tindal non-stop, being refueled three times over the Pacific. The last leg had taken 16 hours. On board, in addition to the crew, were half a dozen USAF officers and technicians along with four engineers from the Boeing Corporation. Also on board were two live BLU-121B bombs. Each bomb was just over 12 feet long and weighed 2,015 pounds. They were designed and built to penetrate thick steel doors and surrounding earth in order to detonate at precisely the right moment inside a tunnel or bunker complex. They had been designed by Boeing and developed by the USAF over the prior eight years to be dropped from a plane travelling at high speed and very low altitude. With the proper training and the assist of targeting computers and laser designators, a good pilot could launch the bomb horizontally into the entrances of underground tunnel complexes.

The two live bombs were for one test run that would be the culmination of the training to take place over the next two weeks – the Israeli pilots would be in competition to determine who got to fly the live bombing mission. But live BLU-121 bombs were too expensive to use for basic training. So the C-17 also carried twenty-five inert bombs identical to the live bombs on the outside but with their weight coming from concrete instead of the thick Elgin steel alloy shell of the real bombs. In addition, 225 lighter practice units were on board. These inert bombs were the same length as the live bombs but only weighed 378 pounds each. To maintain the same flight characteristics of the live units when released, these practice units were narrower in diameter, the reduced surfaced area calculated to offset the impact that any crosswind would have on the unit due to its reduced mass. Every plane that flew with these inexpensive practice bombs would also be fitted with a centerline mounted shroud that mimicked the aerodynamic drag of the real bomb and added 1,600 pounds of weight to ensure that the pilot felt all of the impact of having a live unit mounted underneath his airplane.

Work began that night with a briefing session starting at 9. Almost the entire Israeli contingent of 97 was in attendance, excepting only three men who were on the tarmac watching the five F-15I aircraft. Three IAF officers sat up front, the commander of 69 Squadron and two junior officers whose job, along with the commander, would be to review and rate the performance of each aircrew over the training period. Unknown to anyone outside the group of Israelis, the two senior "technicians" present were actually two of the senior IAF officers comprising the Olympus planning team. It would be their job to understand exactly what the BLU-121 would be capable of in the hands of the IAF and to plan its usage in Project Block G accordingly.

A Boeing engineer started with a general overview of the BLU-121 bomb and its classified capabilities. The first discussion was meant as introduction to the system and lasted about 40 minutes. The next speaker was a USAF officer and F-15E pilot who spent the next half hour discussing his experiences with the system and introducing the Israeli pilots to the flight patterns they would be using during the next couple of weeks.

Finally, another Boeing engineer stood to review a system called Tunnel Defeat, which was the most sensitive and secret aspect of the BLU-121 program. Israel would be the only nation outside of the U.S. to receive the Tunnel Defeat system. The engineer reviewed the concept first. The system integrated up to six BLU-121 bombs dropped by six different aircraft so that the weapons all detonated simultaneously with a timing error of no more than a quarter second. The system was designed for tunnel complexes with multiple entrances. A BLU-121 could be launched from separate aircraft simultaneously so that each bomb penetrated a different tunnel entrance at the same time and detonated at the same moment, creating converging shockwaves that destroyed everything between the blast points not protected by large enough blast doors. The engineer then went into some level of technical detail about how the system worked and the necessity for the planes involved in a coordinated attack to maintain line of sight between each other. The system depended upon each plane's onboard targeting and release computers being able to communicate via a coded millimeter wave radio mounted into each plane.

Over the next two weeks, the fifty pilots, taking turns in the five available F-15Is, would learn the optimal approach, release point and egress pattern to ensure that they could place a

BLU-121 directly onto a point on a mountainside with a circular probability of error of no greater than one meter. That target point could be the entrance to a tunnel or simply a patch of earth through which the bomb could penetrate to reach an underground tunnel or chamber. They would learn the flight characteristics of the bomb and the impact that target altitude, wind speed and direction, air temperature and relative humidity had on the weapon. They would study the physics of the bomb's penetrating capabilities. They would become masters of the system's targeting and weapon release computer, the avionics of which would be installed the next day in the Israeli F-15s by Boeing engineers.

During the same period, thirty-two mechanics, technicians and weapons specialists would have to become experts at mounting and un-mounting the bomb and its practice variants, and at running diagnostics for the bomb itself as well as the onboard computer and support systems. Most importantly, they would have to become absolutely perfect at ensuring that the entire system was properly synchronized, knowing that even the slightest error could result in a bomb missing its target, making it nothing but an expensive piece of harmless metal. Between classes, the group would have to service the five F-15Is that would be flying constant sorties. This would not be a vacation for anyone involved.

29 – Delamere

On July 15, following a day of orientation flying, the first bomb runs over Delamere by the IAF took place. The Delamere bomb range measures 30 miles wide along its northern edge by 40 miles tall with a shape reminiscent of the state of Iowa. The range is mostly flat topographically, but the northeast corner of the range is undulating with a number of small hills. On a couple of these hills the RAAF had constructed faux tunnel entrances covered by plywood doors. Importantly, the RAAF mounted high resolution cameras overseeing each target, allowing the Israelis to record the impact spot of every practice bomb used. Since the IAF had brought 25 aircrews, each F-15I would fly five sorties on this day, giving each aircrew the opportunity to make three passes at their target, dropping the single lightweight practice bomb on the final pass. Since Tindal was only 80 miles from the target area inside Delamere, each sortie took less than 50 minutes, with a plane departing Tindal every 20 minutes.

Over the target zone, a single RAAF CH-47 Chinook helicopter hovered as each plane made its passes. On board were the IAF commanding officer and the two junior officers. They operated a stabilized camera and instruments that could read and record all of the flight control settings on each plane as it made its pass, marrying the readings with the video in real time. The Chinook kept its rear ramp down and its nose pointed away from the target zone. The three Israeli officers sat in chairs bolted to two pallets that also had the camera and instruments bolted down. In turn, the pallets were secured in place on the helicopter floor. Between sorties, the helicopter landed to preserve fuel.

By the afternoon of that first day of bomb runs, all of the flight crews were in a conference room watching video on a large screen. The video accurately recorded every crew's two practice passes and single bomb drop. One of the junior officers, a respected IAF pilot who had contracted diabetes and lost his flying certification, commented on each pass, having each two-man crew stand as its performance was critiqued. The actual bomb runs had all been done without the use of the laser designator from the F-15I's LANTIRN laser pod. This was the condition set by the squadron commander and would hold until later in the training process. These pilots had to be able to "fly" their bombs onto the target and the only acceptable performance was perfection. Without the use of laser designators, the definition of success was a hit anywhere in the 20 square meter surface area of the plywood doors.

The review had covered the performance of twenty-four crews when the squadron commander stopped the video and interrupted the junior officer. He stood up; his voice was part anger and part disappointment. "Today was pitiful," he said, his right hand trembling the way it always did when his blood pressure was elevated. "Thank God the Americans weren't watching this performance. If this crap continues, I am going to leave you guys here and take the American pilots back to Israel with me.

"Now, look. We had only one hit today. One!" The commander lowered his head and swung it from side to side in disgust. He raised his head back up, every pilot in the room certain that he was staring at them. "One out of twenty-five. What's that? Four percent? That's a hell of a long way from one hundred percent. And we will be at one hundred percent or I will make you bastards hitchhike back to Israel." He paused and scanned the room, his stare being the scourge of any pilot who failed to perform up to his standards.

"Gadget, where are you? Stand up."

In the fourth row to the right of the squadron commander, 27-year-old Gil Bar-Kokhba stood. The F-15 pilot was viewed as the best in this group of elite IAF pilots. His nickname, Gadget, had come from his off-duty passion of building radio-controlled planes and boats. The unmarried pilot was handsome, but unlike so many IAF pilots such as General Schechter, he was not interested in chasing girls in Tel Aviv whenever he was on leave. Instead, he was happy to be in a long-term relationship, even though they all seemed to end somewhere around the second anniversary. He felt that long-term relationships cleared his mind for flying – the opposite belief of many of his compatriots.

"You too, Pacer," added the squadron commander.

Ronen Isser, Gadget's 31-year-old backseat weapons systems officer, stood up next to his partner. Pacer had earned his nickname from his love of triathlons and his mistake of telling his fellow pilots that he had to pace himself to win.

"Congratulations. You were the one and only hit today. You two can fly home. As for the rest of you guys, time will tell." The commander sat down as the junior officer reviewed the videotape showing the performance of Gadget and Pacer. More than a half hour was spent reviewing the flight control settings and angle of attack chosen by Gadget. The men were learning from success.

Two more days of the same routine followed, with direct hits rising to six on day two and seven on day three. Day four was a day of rest for the pilots and maintenance for the F-15Is. The mechanics made a decision to swap out one of the two engines in F-15 airframe number 261 for one of the spares that had been brought from Israel. The plane's Digital Electronic Engine Control software indicated that the third stage variable stators on the high pressure compressor turbine were failing to adjust to the commanded angle of attack. The engine still operated, but the mechanics were nervous and there was no reason to risk an engine – and perhaps an airframe – on any scenario that was not fully controlled.

Day five started with a review of the video from day three. At the end of the review the squadron commander stood. "The bullshit ends today. Everyone here should know how to put that weapon on target. We have more advanced work to do and a limited number of bombs to work with. Get your heads out of your asses and get the job done today."

The pilots had indeed learned and the day off allowed everyone to shake off the lingering effects of jetlag. The results showed. Sixteen of twenty-five bombs dropped were direct hits. Of the remaining nine, four were near misses, just outside the plywood doors.

On day six, each crew flew one sortie with one pass over the target. This time, however, the sorties were flown at night, the crews using night vision and forward looking infrared to see the terrain and their targets, which had been moved to a new hill during the day. The results were encouraging, with eighteen direct hits and four near misses. As during the day, video had been taken, this time with a night vision lens attached to the same camera. The video was reviewed the next morning.

The training intensity was accelerated during days seven through nine. The poorest performing aircrew – the only one without a direct hit – was excused from further participation, leaving twenty-four aircrews. The remaining aircrews started simultaneous attacks, first with two aircraft during the day, then with three, this time using laser designators on the targets.

On day nine, the crews began using the Tunnel Defeat system, with three aircraft at a time targeting three plywood doors in a single hillside. During the day, each set of three planes made three practice runs without dropping any bombs. The exercise was intended to get the aircrews used to the close flight coordination necessary to successfully use Tunnel Defeat. If the planes were not properly coordinated, the onboard computers would not allow them to release their weapons. By the final pass, all of the groups successfully coordinated their timing. Following a late afternoon review, the crews prepared for nighttime sorties.

The results were good. All eight groups were able to drop their bombs, with 22 of 24 bombs hitting their targets.

Day ten started with a review of the prior night's mission. What had each crew done right and wrong? All of the 48 airmen in the room were asked for their opinions. Finally, the men were briefed on the next assignment, a repeat of the prior night's mission. To raise the pressure, the squadron commander made an announcement at the end of the briefing: Any group that failed to drop its bombs on the first pass would be dismissed from further training. The men were given the afternoon off.

That night all eight groups flew and all eight groups succeeded in ordering the release of their bombs. However, one bomb failed to release, the error being quickly traced to a short in the centerline pylon circuitry that was repaired within a half hour of the plane's return. Of the 23 bombs actually released, 22 hit the plywood doors as intended. None of the aircrews were dismissed.

Day eleven was a day off for the crews, with movies and beer being delivered to the briefing room. The day passed quickly.

Day twelve was a daytime attack in coordinated groups of four. The smaller practice bombs were now used up and each plane was armed with a full sized practice bomb. The RAAF, at the request of the commanding Israeli officer, had built four plywood doors along a distance of 850 feet on the east face of Delamere's longest hill structure. To increase the difficulty of attack,

one of the tunnel entrances was placed on a north-facing segment of the ridge. The men were briefed on their assignments during the morning. Sorties would begin at noon.

The first of six groups of four aircraft took off in quick succession just minutes after the noon hour. Gadget flew in the second group and assumed the role of the northern plane. His plane had to break away from the other three, wheel to the north and turn back to the south to make the run at its designated target. The timing of this plane was critical, so the best pilot was picked for this maneuver.

In the rear seat, Pacer counted the time to begin their turn to the north. "Initial point at three, two, one, bank," said Pacer into the intercom system. Gadget initiated his turn at precisely the right point. He pushed his two throttles forward through full military power to apply his afterburners for the calculated amount of time, quickly accelerating the F-15I to 521 knots. After twenty-two seconds of flight, he had created 1.7 miles of lateral distance between his plane and the nearest in his group.

"Turn in," said Pacer. Gadget began to bank slowly back to his left. In the rear seat, Pacer tracked the plane's position on a navigation map versus the known GPS coordinates of their target. He called out corrections to his pilot in a code the two men had worked out over several years of partnership. "One right," said Pacer, indicating to Gadget that the correct vector was one degree further right, meaning that the plane was banking too hard to the left.

The plane continued on its arc, its speed being critical to arriving at the right release point at precisely the right time. The onboard targeting and release computer was communicating with the three other aircraft, continuously calculating all four relative positions as well as the position of all four aircraft relative to each plane's designated target. The computer gave important feedback to Pacer.

"Minus ten," said the weapons officer, indicating to Gadget that they needed to decrease their airspeed by ten knots. Gadget eased his power just slightly, an amount that would be imperceptible to an outside observer.

"Speed good. One left." Gadget increased his angle of bank just slightly. The plane was now on the right vector and flying at the right speed. The plane continued its arc, coming around to a heading of 185 degrees. Inside his DASH helmet-mounted display, the onboard flight computer, synched into the targeting and release computer by the Boeing engineers, projected a red triangle over the precise spot that was being targeted. Gadget leveled the wings. "Zero final," came the comment from Pacer, indicating they were properly on their planned attack bearing. "Zero speed." The plane's speed was exactly correct.

"Fuze hot," said Pacer, indicating that the bomb's fuze had been armed by the targeting computer. "Weapon lock," came the final comment from Pacer. They were properly synched with the other aircraft and on the precise approach for attack. On a video screen on the right of the cluster of instruments in front of Pacer, the target tunnel entrance was clearly visible and in the middle of the crosshairs on his screen. Pacer squeezed the trigger on his targeting joystick to lock his laser designator on the target and send a beam of light from the LANTIRN pod onto the center of the plywood doors.

In Gadget's ear, a tone sounded. It was an electronic beep of the type and tone heard on the BBC when counting down to the hour. Gadget knew it was the first of four tones and that the computer would release his bomb at precisely the instant the fourth tone sounded. He also knew the cadence of the tones, having heard them now many times. As the third tone sounded in his ear, just like he had done on every previous bomb run, he pulled his short joystick back just slightly, the pressure and distance being determined not by a computer but simply by his experience and gut feel. The nose of the F-15I rose a few degrees and the inert BLU-121 released from the centerline pylon precisely at the instant the fourth tone sounded in Gadget's ear. He immediately swiveled the joystick to his right to begin a five G turn. He added power to compensate for the forward momentum being robbed by the turning action of the plane. At the low altitude they were flying at, there was no margin of error.

In the backseat, Pacer kept the target firmly in the crosshairs of the laser designator. Each man voluntarily tightened his abdominal and core muscles and began short shallow breathes, a process called the anti-G straining maneuver. At the same time their G suits inflated to compensate against the force of acceleration, which was attempting to pull all of their blood from their heads to their feet. Defeating inertial acceleration meant living to fly and fight another day. If they lost the battle, Gadget would black out within a second or two, the F-15 flying into the earth that rapidly passed by only 150 feet underneath the right wing tip.

All four inert BLU-121s hit their targets within the span of a tenth of a second. Had they been live bombs, they would have all detonated at the same instant about 20 feet past the doors they had just penetrated.

Gadget and Pacer were the top scorers during this training exercise and were easy picks to be one of two aircraft to make a simultaneous run on day thirteen to cap off the IAF's time in Australia. The squadron commander made the decision to launch a night attack shortly after sunset on July 27, 2011. He had all of his pilots ferried to a clearing about one mile north of the target hill, along with several cases of beer. His Australian hosts supplied two Weber grills and a cooler full of steaks. His men were in place and well fed as night descended on the Delamere range. In the crowd of men, all in a celebratory mood, were the two senior officers of Olympus. The availability of this weapon system had already influenced their planning and they were eager to return to Tel Aviv to make alterations.

At exactly 7:00 p.m., two F-15I Ra'am fighter bombers streaked out of the east, the two planes only a hundred yards apart and flying at an altitude of 175 feet above the earth. To increase the show for his men, the squadron commander had the fusing on each bomb set to detonate only five feet after penetrating the plywood doors. The pass was perfect and each bomb struck its target at the same instant, their warheads of 355 pounds of AFX-757 explosive detonating only one millisecond apart. The thermobaric explosions lit up the night sky for just an instant. The booms of the two explosions hit the assembled Israeli airmen with just a split moment's difference, but still enough to clearly discern two distinct blasts. Men were high fiving each other and offering toasts with half empty beer bottles.

This group of flyers was ready to go operational. They would begin their long journey home the next morning.

30 – The Team at Ras-Al-Khaimah

On September 12, 2011, Gennady Masrov showed up at the offices of Swiss-Arab Air Cargo unannounced. Much had changed since the speech he gave to introduce himself to his new team at the start of February more than seven months earlier. The small cargo airline was growing rapidly under the day-to-day leadership of the Russian manager who had been brought in by Masrov in the middle of March.

The company had purchased two Ilyushin-76TD cargo planes. Unfortunately, the planes came with D-30Kp-2 engines, not the new high-bypass turbofan engines that Masrov wanted. But they were still impressive aircraft. Each plane could carry a payload of up to 110,000 pounds and with a typical payload of about 50,000 pounds could fly 4,500 miles without refueling. They were proven airframes – the jet age version of the DC-3 of World War II era.

The company had also purchased two CASA C-212 turboprop cargo aircraft. They were tiny compared to the Ilyushins, but they were economical to operate and perfect for the growing trade and mail volume across the Saudi peninsula. Even more exciting, rumors circulated through the company that they were looking to purchase two or three Ilyushin 78 'Midas' aerial refueling tankers. The Midas was a variant of the Il-76 modified to carry a little over 34,000 gallons of fuel that could be transferred to three aircraft at a time using drogues trailing from each wingtip and from the fuselage. It was said that the growing military air forces of the region, especially the Royal Saudi Air Force and the Indian Air Force, were willing to pay attractive rates to private companies that could provide reliable airborne refueling capacity.

With these aircraft added to the legacy fleet, the company had hired pilots in large numbers. The Ilyushin 76 Candid required a crew of seven: two pilots, a flight engineer, navigator, radio operator and two cargo masters. The company now had twenty-six employees just to crew the two Ilyushins. Ads were running online to recruit more experienced air crewmen and mechanics.

But of all the new employees for the Il-76s, the two senior Ilyushin pilots stood out. One was a Russian named Oleg Kolikov, in his fifties. Oleg was handsome and had the personality of a man with the world at his fingertips. Better yet for Swiss-Arab Air Cargo, he had almost 10,000 hours of flight time piloting the Il-76, having first earned his wings flying the big plane into and out of Afghanistan for the Soviet armed forces during the 1980s. There was hardly a rivet on the plane that he didn't know.

He had become famous in the Soviet Union by successfully landing an Il-76 that had been hit by an American-made Singer antiaircraft missile fired by the Mujahedeen. The missile's warhead had exploded just under the plane's right wing, its course having been diverted ever so slightly as it tracked a red hot flare fired defensively by the big plane's recently installed flare dispenser. The course deflection was just enough to keep the plane from losing its wing and plummeting to earth from 12,000 feet. But the explosion had sent shrapnel upward that penetrated each of the two starboard engines, their delicate turbines being damaged enough that both engines disintegrated in fiery displays. A piece of shrapnel punched through the cockpit wall and lodged itself in the right leg of the co-pilot, effectively putting the man out of action. In the cargo hold, 94 Soviet soldiers suddenly converted from atheists to true believers, each man praying for his life.

Kolikov kept his cool throughout, ordering his flight engineer to cut the fuel to each starboard engine, thereby allowing the wind to smother the flames. He turned the plane around and headed back to the big airfield at Bagram on just his two remaining engines. He had to fight the tremendous yaw force being put on the airplane by the two port side engines – the nose of the plane wanting to rotate to the right on its axis – threatening to deprive the wings of lift in the process. Thinking quickly, Kolikov had gone to full power on engine two, the inboard port side engine, and minimal power on engine one, the outboard port side engine. With his feet, he maintained almost full left rudder, keeping the big plane's nose pointed forward. Thankfully, his landing gear deployed and he evacuated his plane with no loss of life. The Soviet military at the time was desperate for heroes and the state media had their man. The press rightly called it a miraculous display of flying. Kolikov was awarded the medal for Distinction in Military Service, First Class.

The other senior pilot was an American named James Miller, but everyone called him Captain Jim. Jim was 62 and had impulsively accepted an early retirement offer two and a half years earlier, shortly after his 60th birthday. His career as a captain flying 747 jetliners for United Airlines had voluntarily come to an end when he convinced himself that the airline was only weeks from another bankruptcy filing. Accepting the early retirement buyout, his advisors assured him, would protect his pension.

When Jim Miller returned to his home in the Chicago suburb of Arlington Heights the day of his retirement party, he spent the afternoon tending to his garden and drinking beer. Two weeks later, when he realized that he had accomplished everything in his garden that he wanted and was now left with simply drinking beer, he realized he had made a mistake. He went online and it took him less than an hour to make contact with an air cargo carrier based in Moscow that had a single 747-400F cargo freighter in its inventory and needed an experienced pilot. Within a week he was on his way to Russia and a new career.

Moving had been easy for him. He had no family. Jim Miller was a gay man. He had briefly married at the age of 29 during the final year of his short tenure as a C-141 pilot in the USAF. After leaving the air force, an offer to join United Airlines was eagerly given and eagerly accepted. But the marriage ended two years later when his wife ran off with the man she was sleeping with. He was grateful at the time that he had no children, but had often regretted it since.

Miller came out of the closet a few years after his divorce in a time when the budding gay rights movement was colliding with the growing backlash of the straight world's reaction to

AIDS. Like all gay men of the era, he was at first appalled and then increasingly angered at the anti-gay hysteria characterized by the "Gay Plague" headlines of the day. The loss of friends to the disease did nothing to lessen the anger. But the fear of catching the disease was especially frightening to a pilot. By 1986, FAA licensed physicians were beginning to test pilots for the recently discovered virus, HIV, and this fact created a new fear for Miller. A positive test meant a death sentence of another kind, the immediate revocation of your pilot's license.

Captain Jim went through his period of sexual profligacy, always careful to practice safe sex in the process, but eventually fell in love at the age of 42 and lived with his partner for the next sixteen years, until the day his partner died in a motorcycle accident. Since then, Jim lived only to fly. He was very good at it, and by relocating to Russia he was able to continue his life doing what he did best.

Jim Miller realized quickly that standards maintained in a small Russian cargo carrier were something less than what he had experienced at United. When he found out that the company had decided to sell the 747 he was flying only five months after he arrived in Moscow, he thought hard about whether or not to return to the States. But weighing against his concerns and his homesickness, Miller was widely respected in the company for his skill as a pilot. The company no longer had a 747, but it had half a dozen Ilyushin 76 aircraft, and the owner offered to pay Miller to learn to fly the old Soviet-era workhorse. He accepted the proposal and was elevated into the captain's seat after six months flying as co-pilot. To his surprise, he found that he enjoyed flying the older plane. It made him feel like it was his skill that made all the difference, not a computer making decisions as was all too often the case in a modern plane.

Miller's Jewish ancestry never came up in any of his cockpit discussions or nights spent at restaurants in cities across the Middle East and Asia. No one ever asked him because no one cared. It reflected the overwhelmingly agnostic or atheistic views of the Russian flying community. Nor did anyone ask him about his sexuality. Miller realized that the latter fact was, unfortunately, a reflection of his age. The American's hair had gone completely gray and had thinned significantly over the prior 15 years. The fact was that he had been essentially asexual since the death of his partner. Neither his religion nor his sexuality were reflected in his personnel file. Miller often thought that business practices in Russia had to be similar to what things were like in the United States during the growth years after World War II, before regulations and litigation had turned every single process into a pre-defined set of forms to be followed to the letter.

Miller spent the next year flying as the chief pilot of whichever Ilyushin 76 required his skills. He was satisfied and being well paid – nothing like what he made in his final years at United, but enough to make him feel good. He didn't need the money anyway; it was the flying that mattered to him.

But change often comes in the strangest form and at the most unexpected times. Captain Jim was enjoying a beer in a Moscow bar that catered to English speaking expatriates. The crowd this particular evening consisted of a group of Indians, three Brits, two Canadians and Jim Miller, who sat alone, one ear listening to the Canadians and the other listening to the Brits. A man came in and sat down two seats over from the pilot, ordering a draft Spaten pilsner, German beers being a popular drink in Moscow. After a couple of sips, the man struck up a conversation with the American. The man spoke English, though not particularly well. After some discussion about nothing important, the man asked Miller if he ever attended synagogue. The question was in Hebrew. Jim Miller had not spoken the language since his Bar Mitzvah and had forgotten most of what little he knew.

The simple question opened the door for Jim Miller to make a meaningful turn in his life. The man who asked the question was officially an Israeli embassy employee. In reality, the man was a recruiter for Mossad. The question led to a meeting in Miller's small Moscow apartment, and that led to a long discussion on life, religion and the state of world affairs. After two more meetings, the offer was made: If Jim Miller was interested, there was a job waiting for him in the United Arab Emirates doing what he loved. The pay would be a little better and Dubai would be a lot warmer, but the real reason to make the change was that Captain Jim would have the opportunity to serve the state of Israel. Jim Miller accepted. He was in the UAE three weeks later.

Now on this late summer day, with the temperature outside well into triple digits, Masrov surveyed his gathered team with great satisfaction. So many pieces had been put in place. Swiss-Arab Air Cargo was doing business in countries all across the region, its success in gaining business driven by very aggressive pricing. The profit and loss statements were a disaster as the company added expenses with seemingly careless abandon, but it was growth and market penetration that Gennady Masrov cared about. The accounting department, which worked in downtown Dubai in the office space leased by Masrov, kept the books faithfully. The company controller, a young Emirati with a recent MBA from the University of Michigan, kept warning his boss about the growing rate of losses, but no one was concerned about their jobs. When cash in the bank fell below $3 million, a wire transfer from Switzerland for $15 million showed up in the account. The money appeared to be endless.

Masrov had the team assembled in its new hanger building. Negotiations were already underway to lease yet another hanger at the airport. The Russian owner called everyone to order and praised their growth and success in winning business since his prior visit earlier in the summer. He had a projector set up on a folding table and turned the floor over to a young Emirati who had been leading the effort to build their new website. The meeting was to introduce the website to the team. It had been promoted from their development server to the live Internet the night before. After a twenty minute presentation of the site and what it could do for customers and employees alike, the audience applauded as it had the first time Masrov was onsite. The team was highly motivated.

That night, Gennady Masrov took his a small group of managers and senior pilots out to dinner in Dubai. Everyone in attendance was a new employee added since the acquisition. He raised a toast to his team. "I am very proud of all of you," said the Russian in English for the benefit of Jim Miller. "Once we acquire some Midas aircraft, we will be where we need to realize our vision." Glasses were clinked all around.

31 – Election Time

"Gentlemen, please be seated." Prime Minister Eli Cohen was once again calling a meeting of the Kitchen Cabinet to order. The date was Tuesday, January 31, 2012. "I want to thank everyone for coming in on this cold, rainy day, especially our guests in from Tel Aviv." Cohen nodded towards the other end of the conference table. "Everyone of course knows General Fishel and General Schechter." At the far end, General Natan Fishel, chief of staff of the Israeli Defense Force, and General David Schechter, the operational commander of Project Block G, nodded slightly in acknowledgement. "I don't think that all of you have yet met Amit Margolis." Margolis raised his right hand off the table and smiled faintly to the six members of the Kitchen Cabinet who were present.

"I hope everyone," continued Cohen, "is keeping Ben Raibani in your prayers. My wife visited him yesterday at Hadassah at Ein Kerem." Raibani had suffered a mild stroke a week earlier. "He is doing as well as could be expected."

Cohen continued. "I am happy that Reuben has agreed to join the Kitchen Cabinet in General Raibani's unfortunate absence." Seated to the prime minister's right was Minister of Finance Reuben Herzog. He looked down at the table as the prime minister introduced him. "Of course, everyone here knows Reuben, except I am not sure if you have met Mister Margolis or General Schechter?" The question was directed to Minister Herzog.

Reuben Herzog looked up and to his right. "No, I have not." He stood and offered his hand to Amit Margolis, who was seated about ten feet away, and then to David Schechter. The three men exchanged greetings.

"Reuben is a wizard with numbers," added Prime Minister Cohen. He had a habit of treating the much younger minister of finance more as his son than as a peer.

Once Herzog sat back down, the prime minister turned to the issues at hand. "Well, let's get to the business of the day. We have two and a half hours until we will expand this into a full Security Cabinet meeting. I have asked Natan, David and Amit here today to review the state of readiness of Block G. My goal today is simple. I want consensus on the plan from this group and then final clearance from the Security Cabinet to green light the operation based on conditions. I yield the floor to Chief of Staff Fishel,"

"Thank you, Mister Prime Minister," responded Natan Fishel. "I think everyone here knows that this show belongs to the two men sitting to my left, so I am not going to steal their thunder. All I will say is that I am here on behalf of the entire general staff of the IDF to tell you that the IDF is fully behind this plan. General Schechter has the full support of the each branch of the IDF and he has my full backing. With that, I turn the floor over to General Schechter."

"Thank you, General." Schechter stood and walked to a large flat panel TV mounted on the side wall of the conference room. The TV displayed the computer screen in front of Amit Margolis. The IAF general spent the next hour walking through the plans for Project Block G, starting with the preliminary operations that would lay the groundwork for the main IAF action. After that review, the general detailed the IAF attack on the identified targets encompassing the Iranian nuclear program. The assault involved 206 aircraft of the IAF in a single coordinated sortie over Iran, plus dozens of other aircraft in support roles. Everything had been planned in extreme detail, including the assignment of specific flight crews to specific targets. The timetable had been calculated down to exact takeoff times for each aircraft involved. Even the loss of aircraft – whether that loss was the result of mechanical failure, crash or hostile action – was planned for, with redundancy taken into account by the separation of key assets into varied sorties.

When Schechter was finished, Amit Margolis stood and switched places with the general, who took over operation of the computer. Amit presented the non-conventional portion of Project Block G to the Kitchen Cabinet, the portion known as Esther's Sling. The Mossad agent presented the same level of detail on the attack portion of his plan as Schechter had on the IAF portion. But he left out any discussion of some of the private companies he had established to support his plan. For Reuben Herzog, this was the first time he had heard anything about Esther's Sling, including the codename. He was completely focused on every word spoken by the Mossad agent turned operational co-commander.

When Margolis was finished, Eli Cohen looked at Reuben Herzog. "What do you think?"

Minister of Finance Herzog had the hint of a smile on his face. "Can we do that?"

Cohen laughed. "That's exactly what I thought the first time I heard it. We can do it and we will."

Margolis stepped to his side and switched places with Schechter once again. The general started to speak as he walked the few steps to the spot in the room that had become the invisible podium. "Before we move on, let me bring up a serious issue that we face. A few days ago an Eitan UAV crashed while testing was underway with under-wing weapons."

Everyone in the room was fully aware of the news. The Eitan had been introduced into active service for the IDF in late 2010 and was one of the most sophisticated weapons systems in the Israeli arsenal, the latest and greatest example of the growing prowess of Israeli technology in unmanned aerial vehicles, or UAVs. The Eitan was very large by UAV standards, measuring over 80 feet in length. It had been designed and built by Israeli Aircraft Industries initially to fly at high altitude for an extended period of time over long distances conducting surveillance and electronic eavesdropping. But it had always been in the plan among IAF officers to put weapons onboard the Eitan, creating a rival to the success of America's Predator drones. Indeed, the Eitan had succeeded in launching Hellfire missiles. The latest testing was to add 500 pound laser-guided bombs and other sophisticated weapons under the wings.

"What do we know about this, Zvi?" Cohen asked. He did not want General Schechter to explain what happened; he wanted to hold his defense minister accountable.

Zvi Avner responded. "It is still early in the investigation, but it appears that the wing snapped while at altitude."

Cohen snapped his finger. "Snapped. Just like that?"

"We don't know for sure yet, but that's the way it looks. The load on the wings may have been too great."

"What are we doing on this?"

"This is a top priority. We have grounded the Eitan fleet until we finish the investigation and then we can look at alternatives or place restrictions on the airframe."

General Schechter jumped back in. "As you all saw from my presentation, the Eitan has been incorporated into our planning and has become important. This is not on my next slide, which reviews which weapons we still need, but it should be. We will have to change some of our planning without the Eitan."

"I am sure the review will be handled quickly. Hopefully this won't be much more than a few weeks," said Cohen. "Please continue."

The TV now contained a bullet point slide of the list of items still required for Block G. A small number of weapons had yet to be obtained and estimates were provided by Schechter for when they would be ready. Finally, Amit hit the computer's down arrow and the last slide came up. This slide had a bullet point list of the operational conditions necessary to launch Block G and the timetable from initiation to the IAF attack.

Schechter ran through the slide. "Here are the keys," he said. "We need to launch the IAF strike at night within two nights on either side of the night of a new moon. My strong preference is the night of the new moon or the night immediately before or after. We need good weather. There can be no rain clouds and ideally, no cloud cover at all. We need the best possible GPS reception and communications. Hopefully we will have low solar flare activity since solar activity can interfere with GPS signals and our communications, but this is only predictable about eighteen hours in advance. So, large solar flare activity could cause us to delay the attack date within our lunar window. I am a little concerned because this year we are entering a period of maximum solar activity." Schechter paused for a moment to elicit questions. None came.

Schechter continued. "We want relatively cold air at ground level. Cold air is denser and provides more lift. As I reviewed earlier, we will have aircraft taking off near their maximum takeoff weight. We are setting our limits based on the shortest runway we have to operate from." The general then pointed to a highlighted number on the screen that read "38.5°C." The temperature was equivalent to 87 degrees Fahrenheit. "That is the maximum safe takeoff temperature for the weapon load configurations in the plan. If we have to go in warmer weather, we will have to alter the plan, which, practically speaking, means we would have to reduce the number of targets we hit. That means the summer months are a problem. The winter months are a problem because that is the rainy season. If you factor in typical weather patterns along with the temperature issue, the months for us to go are – in order from best to worst – October, May, April, November, and December. We have an outside opportunity to go in January, February or March if we get lucky with an extended period of good weather that we can forecast.

"The next bullet point lays out the minimum cooperation we need from the American military. We have requested the expansion of area GPS denial to all of Iran, Iraq, Jordan, Lebanon, Syria and Israel. I am sure the Americans will want to degrade the entire Middle East. The Americans have agreed to this. They have plenty of bases that are potential targets, so regardless of what they think about our attack, we are confident they will do this."

"What about our use of GPS?" Eli Cohen asked.

"We will have the codes necessary to use the military Y channel, in addition to what I reviewed earlier with our augmentation plans. The one thing I am sure of is that if and when we do launch, even the President of the United States wants us to succeed in destroying as much of the program as we can.

"Of course, everyone needs to understand that Iran uses GPS redundantly," Schechter continued. "In other words, their GPS guidance systems receive the American civilian GPS signal and Russian Glonass. They then use algorithms and inertial guidance to compare positions and correct for degraded or scrambled signals. We will be jamming Glonass and even GPS the same as they do, but the best we can do is reduce their accuracy. So if the Iranians or Hezbollah launch missiles at us, they should not be accurate enough to hit a specific building, but they will fall within our cities or on our bases."

General Fishel interjected. "Thank you, General. You have more than enough to worry about. The home front defense is being handled."

"Understood. Let me return to Block G. The next thing we need from the Americans will be the current IFF codes over the region. They change their codes every twelve hours, so we will likely need two codes over the course of the operation. I do not expect an issue here, but this is the one area where the American administration could stop us cold. I cannot, in good conscience, issue the go order if we do not have the IFF codes."

Yavi Aitan, the minister of intelligence and atomic affairs, spoke first. "Are you suggesting the Americans would attack our aircraft?" He had said what was on the mind of every member of the Kitchen Cabinet.

"The odds are low, but I can't put them at zero. If they refuse to issue the IFF codes to us, then that refusal is, to me, an implied threat that they might attack. The U.S. Air Force and Navy presence along our attack and egress routes is extensive. The Americans are planning to deploy a squadron of F-22 Raptors to the UAE. But that is just a small aspect of the threat we would face. The amount of American SAM capability in and around the Gulf is formidable. We will be egressing from Iran. Their entire defensive posture is oriented toward aircraft coming from Iran being hostile. Without the IFF codes, the potential for disaster is very real even if it's unintentional."

Zvi Avner turned to his prime minister. "I had never even considered this. Would the president refuse us?"

Eli Cohen took a long drink. "I would not have thought it possible before this president, but it is a possibility now. He doesn't want us to attack Iran this year, or at least not before the election. That much is clear. If he thinks we won't attack without the IFF codes, he may withhold them for that reason."

Avner's face started to turn red. "Just who the hell is our enemy here?"

"Calm down, Zvi," Cohen responded. "He is not our enemy. He is just not our close friend."

"Of course, he might not be re-elected," Mort Yaguda interjected. The minister without portfolio had spent much of his time over the prior two years in the United States lobbying on behalf of Israel "My friends in Washington and New York think the odds are against him. He's definitely not getting the money he did four years ago."

"We should be so lucky," said Avner.

"The polls have him in front of all of the Republicans," Cohen commented.

"But they are a long way from determining who their candidate will be," stated Yaguda. "I met with some of the most respected pollsters in the U.S. while I was there last month. They all said the same thing. The president is polling under fifty percent. The history of American elections is that if the sitting president polls under fifty percent, then the undecided voters break to the challenger late in the process."

"All that is good," said Cohen. His voice had a different tone. He was ready to move on. "We will see what happens. But right now I want to look at our options. Zvi and Natan, you guys are talking to your counterparts regularly. What is the sense that we would be denied what we need?"

"I have had nothing but support from my counterparts," said General Fishel. "They would love to join us. At least they are assisting our plans to take action. But as for this key issue, there is only one way to know. We will have to ask directly."

Cohen looked directly at Natan Fishel. "This week, Natan. I want you to meet with your counterpart this week and directly ask about each item that we need."

General Fishel nodded his agreement.

Cohen turned back to General Schechter. "I think we have gotten too far off track. Please continue. I see some more points on your screen there."

Schechter continued. "The next issue to discuss involves the Saudis. We need their early warning radar systems to be down when we go. General Aitan, I think you are leading this effort."

Yavi Aitan leaned into the table. "Well, I am certainly more confident about that than we seem to be about the president and his intentions." He cleared his throat. "Yes, the Saudis have no ambiguities. They will support us every way possible that is not overt. We have already had one test run."

"Out of curiosity," asked Cohen, "did you have IFF codes from the Americans?"

"Yes, absolutely. We have never been denied the codes upon request. But when we go for real, the Americans will know we are going and why we want the codes."

General Schechter added an important point. "On the test run, our EC-707 was contacted by an American AWACS orbiting over Saudi Arabia almost immediately after entering Saudi airspace. I point this out as just another data point as we think about attempting to launch Block G without the IFF codes. Of course, the Americans have an X-band radar in the Negev as well."

Avner decided this was the time to make the counter-point. "Which means that there is no way the Americans could claim that they accidently attacked our aircraft. They will be tracking our aircraft from the moment they take off. So if that man doesn't want to give us the codes, the hell with him. We will attack Persia regardless. We will do it on our timetable, not his." The defense minister was an infantry man by experience and training.

The prime minister started to respond as he usually was forced to do when Avner's emotions were driving his talking points, but Schechter spoke first. "You make a good point, General Avner. No doubt that the Americans will track us all the way from take-off to our targets over Iran and back. I completely agree that the reality is that they would not have an excuse to claim mistaken identity. However, I will simply point out two facts that I must consider as the air force commander responsible for this operation. First, just because they know who we are doesn't leave me sleeping any better. A political decision to interrupt the attack could be made in Washington.

"Second, I worry less about an attack by American fighters, which, in my opinion, would only come about as a result of intentional orders from Washington, than I do about being attacked by surface to air missiles. These systems are often on a hair trigger and when a mass of targets comes onto a radar screen that has the profile of a large coordinated attack and none of the planes in that mass are squawking a friendly code, bad things can happen. Either one of these is a risk that I will not accept without direct orders, given the political implications to Israel."

Minister of Defense Avner weighed in. "There is just no way that the U.S. will intentionally attack us."

"I have to agree with that," added Mort Yaguda.

"Gentlemen, I am responsible for this operation," responded Schechter. "The impact of this issue, if you are – with all due respect – wrong, is catastrophic. The lack of IFF codes opens the door to a political decision to attack us and claim it was a mistake after the fact. I will remind everyone in this room that it was Israel that intentionally attacked the USS Liberty for political reasons in 1967 and then claimed afterward that it was mistaken identity."

Avner erupted. "How can you say that, David? That is bullshit. That was absolutely not an intentional attack." Avner's volume was uncontrolled, as was his temper.

Prime Minister Cohen raised his left hand in a signal for his minister of defense to calm down, but he was looking at General Schechter, his eyes furious. When he spoke, however, his tone was that of a statesman. "General, I am not quite sure how you came to this assumption, but I can assure you that you are wrong. The attack on that American ship was a case of mistaken identity. The evidence behind this conclusion is comprehensive."

At the other end of the table, Natan Fishel sat quietly. A smirk appeared on his face. He guessed at the tactics being used by the younger air force officer standing across the table from him.

David Schechter smiled broadly. He had engineered the response he was seeking. "Forgive me General Avner." He looked at Cohen. "Mister Prime Minister." He bowed his head slightly to his commander-in-chief. "I was making a point. Even forty-five years later, after thorough review by commissions in both Israel and the United States, it is still a source of contention as to whether or not we attacked the Liberty accidentally or intentionally. Israelis are, of course, completely accepting of the fact that the attack was an accident. But many Americans to this day, including many of the survivors of the crew, believe that the attack was intentional." Schechter paused. Both Avner and Cohen slowly sank back into their chairs, their thoughts racing. The fact that Schechter actually believed the attack on the Liberty had been deliberate was an opinion that every Israeli officer who shared it had learned to keep buried. Any public airing of such a thought was career ending.

"My point," Schechter continued, "is that without the IFF codes, much can happen, be it accidental or otherwise. The Liberty incident is a footnote in history. Block G will be the front page of history. If the worst occurs, the conspiracy theorists in both countries will spend the next century debating what happened and why, and the damage done between us and our most important ally will be irreparable and lasting. That is not to mention that any attack by the Americans on our strike force, regardless of the reason or cause, could destroy our chances of success."

Prime Minister Cohen clapped slowly three times. "You are damn good, General. Damn good." Cohen looked to Avner, who was rapidly calming.

Chief of Staff Fishel's smirk turned into a smile. He was proud of the man who was under his command. "I think you have made your point, David. Now let's move on."

"Yes, sir." Schechter turned to look at the TV.

Rueben Herzog interrupted. "Before we leave the topic of radar, I don't recall Jordan being discussed. You reviewed the plans for Syria and Iraq, but did you mention Jordan? Don't they have long-range radar?"

Yavi Aitan beat Schechter to the response. "Allow me to address that, General." Aitan glanced at Schechter who nodded his head in consent. "You are correct, Mister Herzog, there was no mention of Jordan. They do have a handful of early warning radar sets, including an American L-band radar and a refurbished Russian VHF Spoon Rest radar. Both units are located around Amman. We are not concerned about these units."

"Why not?" asked Herzog.

Aitan remained silent and offered only a forced smile in return. "I think it is enough to tell you that neither General Schechter nor General Fishel are concerned."

"Okay, okay." Herzog was annoyed that despite being elevated to the Kitchen Cabinet he was still not to be privy to the most sensitive secrets. But he knew that pushing his desire to gain knowledge too far would result in his demotion back to the Security Cabinet, a position he held as a matter of Israeli law.

In this case, Aitan was not willing to discuss the back door access that Israel maintained into the central command and control computers that received the data picked up by these two radar sets. This gave them the ability, if used wisely and rarely, to make their planes invisible on the Jordanian radar, or to make a large flight of planes look like a single aircraft on a routine mission. It was a state of affairs that the Jordanians knew existed and had long decided – a decision made by the king himself – to ignore. It made their life much easier.

Schechter decided to move on. He had finished up the last slide, but was not yet finished with the issues to be discussed. He spoke to all the members of the Kitchen Cabinet. "The last issue for the Olympus team is simple. We need to finalize the strike targets. The ones in question require the approval of this body." Schechter paused and looked at Margolis, who handed over a folder with a number of handouts. The general took the folder and handed out a single page print out to each man.

"The target package I am handing out is almost complete. We have planned for and are prepared to attack every target on the list. However, we need the final decision from this group regarding the targets highlighted in blue. There is a political element to each of these targets."

Schechter waited for everyone to look at the handout they had just received. The next few minutes were spent discussing the issue of striking the political leaders of Iran. The debate was lively and the opinions divergent. Finally, the prime minister turned to Amit Margolis. "Mister Margolis, I am interested in your analysis."

Amit Margolis straightened his back, immediately conscious of his tendency to slouch. "Thank you, Mister Prime Minister. In my humble opinion, I would strongly argue against striking their political leadership. Their military leadership is, of course, fair game and they are on the target list as everyone can see. But with regards to Khamenei and Ahmadinejad and any political leader, I think we guarantee a reaction from the resulting leadership that is vengeful in nature against us. They will launch everything they can against Israel and seek revenge for years to come against you sir" – Margolis was looking at the prime minister – "or your successor. If we leave them in power, then they have to live with and explain to their people how they allowed the Great Satan to come into Iran and destroy their supposedly impregnable nuclear program that they have spent so much time and money building. Plus I think they will have to consider long and hard just how many countries other than Israel they will want to bring into this conflict. And, yes, I am particularly referring to America."

Cohen nodded his head slowly and turned his gaze to Yavi Aitan. "Yavi?"

"I think Mister Margolis just expressed my views perfectly – probably better than I could."

"Okay then, the political leadership is off the list," commanded Cohen. "Okay. What's the next category on your list?"

General Schechter looked down at the sheet of paper on the table. "Ah … the next issue is China. We have identified two targets. The first is the cyber warfare center at Tehran University that is now staffed with over twenty-five Chinese nationals and growing."

"Yavi, what are they doing at this location?" asked Cohen.

"In a concise answer, everything. The center grew up to help the Iranians defend their networks but has expanded over the last year. They are now launching attacks on Israel from this center ranging from denial of service attacks to attempts to hack into the defense network and most of our largest corporations and financial institutions. It seems the Chinese feel emboldened operating out of Tehran versus the already aggressive activities they conduct from Shanghai. I honestly think that they don't realize that we know they are there."

"Thank you, Yavi." Cohen looked back at Schechter. "I see you have the Chinese embassy listed on here. You actually mean the real Chinese embassy?"

"Yes sir."

"Why?"

Schechter turned to Amit Margolis. "Amit, this is Mossad intelligence."

Margolis looked at Yavi Aitan. Aitan lifted his left hand with the palm up and nodded toward Margolis, indicating to him to respond. Margolis went ahead. "The Chinese are playing a dangerous game. Much of the support for the Iranian program is coming from North Korea. The Chinese, who publicly profess an anti-proliferation stance, are privately aiding and abetting this trade with the Koreans. This is coordinated inside the embassy, including running front companies in countries around the world."

"Don't the North Koreans have an embassy in Tehran?" asked Zvi Avner.

"Yes, but the nuclear program activity is being run through the Chinese embassy."

"Are you sure?" Cohen asked.

"I asked that question to Director Levy. His answer to me was that he was absolutely positive."

"Why? I don't understand."

Margolis thought for a moment. "I'm not sure I'm qualified to answer. I think you should talk to Director Levy on this. But my understanding is that the Chinese wanted to control this activity between a historic client state, North Korea, and a state that they increasingly view as a client state, Iran."

Cohen looked at Danny Stein. "Danny, your thoughts on this?"

"I fully support striking the cyber center. It is easy to claim ignorance if the Chinese protest about killing their people, although I expect that they will keep quiet about it and, in fact, deny that they had any personnel there. But the embassy? I can't support that. If it was the North Korean embassy, I might think differently."

This view was in synch with the opinion of the prime minister. Cohen bypassed Mort Yaguda and Reuben Herzog, both of whom he knew would go along with the consensus. He turned to Avner. "Zvi, your thoughts?"

Avner surprised the group. "I agree with Danny. Attacking the Chinese embassy would bring too many negative repercussions."

"Okay, I think we have consensus on this. We attack the cyber center. We pass on the Chinese embassy."

Schechter nodded and bent over to take notes on his printout. He straightened back up. "The next issue is hitting the homes of leading scientists. I know the scientists are legitimate targets, but we want approval to incur collateral damage. We didn't put in on here, but the same question applies to military commanders."

Yavi Aitan hated that obtuse phrasing. "You mean, General, a green light to kill the families of these scientists and generals?"

"If you want to phrase it that way, then yes."

"I prefer stating things directly and openly." Aitan adjusted his seat. "I hate to see families killed, but this is an opportunity to drive home Dead Lead and from a military perspective, we can't let it pass. I say yes." Aitan was referring to Operation Dead Lead, the ongoing assassination of Iranian physicists and scientists who worked on their nuclear program. "The same, of course, applies to the military commanders on the list."

Cohen was growing impatient with the meeting. He was always eager to move on to the next meeting, the next speech, the next challenge at hand. "I approve these targets unless anyone objects." He looked at Stein and Yaguda, knowing that Avner would not object. Yaguda nodded his consent. Stein never looked up and never objected. He then looked to his right at Herzog.

"Yes, hit them," responded the minister of finance.

"It is a consensus then. Targets approved. What else?"

General Schechter turned and looked at the television screen. On the slide there was a single remaining bullet point at the bottom. It had only one word: "Bushehr." "Finally, there is the issue of Bushehr. This nuclear reactor has always been on our target list and will be attacked via cruise missile from a Dolphin submarine. But …"

"But the calculus has changed," Eli Cohen interjected, eager to get to the point. "Yavi, please update everyone on what is happening at Bushehr."

"Yes," responded Yavi Aitan, "after decades of stops and starts, Bushehr is actually being commissioned. Over the next several months Iran will begin to power up the reactor, running a series of tests culminating in full power certification. At this point, any destruction of Bushehr will release radioactivity into the air and likely cause a core meltdown. Unfortunately, we have waited too long. Our destruction of the Iraqi and Syrian nuclear reactors were both accomplished while the reactor buildings were still under construction and before nuclear fuel rods had been placed in the reactor core."

"What kind of contamination are we talking about?" asked Avner.

"If we attacked today, very little," responded Aitan. "But every month that goes by, the Iranians will be loading more fuel rods into the reactor core at Bushehr. By the fall, this process will be complete if they keep to their timetable. At that point, we will be highly likely to trigger a core meltdown if we hit the reactor containment building. In a full meltdown, the radiation release will be quite bad. Prevailing winds come consistently out of the northwest year round and will send contamination to the southeast toward the Emirates. Much of the contamination, especially the heavy particles, will settle into the Persian Gulf or areas along the Iranian coastline that are sparsely inhabited. Most of the airborne contamination, given the weather profile of our planned attack and assuming we hit Bushehr the same day as the rest of Block G, will be carried aloft to be picked up by upper altitude winds that will carry the radiation out over the Arabian

Sea and toward India. Mid-level fall-out will endanger two cities in particular, Abu Dhabi and Dubai, even though they are each about six hundred kilometers away."

"Okay, what are we willing to do here?" asked Cohen. The question resulted in fifteen minutes of discussion before Cohen conducted a verbal poll of where everyone in the room stood, including Fishel, Schechter and Margolis.

After the opinions had been stated, Cohen continued. "I think the concepts just laid out by Mister Margolis make a lot of sense and are obviously supported by Yavi." He looked at Schechter and Margolis. "Please revise your planning accordingly and proceed on that basis."

"We will," replied General Schechter.

"Anything else?" asked Cohen.

Danny Stein had a thought. "Do we have the same issue at Arak?" He was asking about the heavy water reactor designed to produce plutonium and under construction in the middle of the country.

"No," responded Aitan. "They continue to slowly build the reactor facility. This is one area where delay is our friend. The further they get before we bomb the facility, the better – so long as they have not fueled the reactor. As of today, I think that is at least a year or more off."

"Okay, so that's a positive," said Cohen. "Now, is that all? Anything more?"

Schechter looked at Margolis, who shook his head. "No, sir." Cohen waived his hand, indicating to Schechter for him to wrap up. "In that case, thank you, gentlemen. That is it for the presentation and issues around Block G."

"Thank you General, Amit, Natan." The prime minister proceeded with the next issue on his agenda. "I want a voice vote for the record. I vote to approve Operation Block G as presented. The timing of the operation will be made by the Olympus command team in consultation with Minister Avner and myself."

One by one, the members of the Kitchen Cabinet verbally approved the operation as presented.

Part II

"Okay, we go."

32 – The Archer Draws his Bow

The President of the United States won re-election. The second term president was now focused on domestic issues, happy to relegate the painful experiences of the Middle East to the backseat. A trip to Israel, his first since becoming president, resulted in a renewed relationship with Prime Minister Cohen. Most of the frustration of the prior four years evaporated on the foundation of a new level of agreement over Iran. The two men came to an understanding and Cohen knew that when the time came, American support would be unequivocal – just not overt.

But the president still wanted time. Time to try diplomacy again. Time for the latest round of sanctions to bite. In return, a hard deadline was agreed upon for the first time.

Amit Margolis was ushered into the office of Mossad Director Amichai Levy late in the afternoon of Friday, August 2. "Amit, I did not expect a visit from you today," said the director as he motioned Margolis toward a seat in front of his desk. "This must be important."

"It is. I have just come from Jerusalem." Margolis did not sit down. "I met with Cohen this morning. We are going next month."

"Going?"

"Block G."

Ami Levy did not smile or get excited. He simply looked at Amit. "I see."

"You don't seem too happy."

Levy turned and looked out his window at the skyline of Tel Aviv. "I believe in your plan, Amit," Levy said, even though he still did not know all of the aspects of Esther's Sling. "I also know the Iranian response. I dread what is coming."

Margolis started to go into the same debate that had raged in Israel for years, but he checked himself. The time for debate was over. Decisions now superseded. "Operation Arrow is authorized."

"Timing?"

"September fifteenth, give or take forty-eight hours."

Director Levy spun back around and looked at Amit. He smiled. "Now that's my type of operation." He stood and shook the hand of the co-commander of Block G. "Okay, we go."

Amichai Levy had been wrong earlier when he provided the prime minister with Mossad's official opinion on the uprising in Syria. Of course, the prime minister knew full well that there was no separation between the official opinion of Mossad and the personal opinion of its director. Ami Levy was far too strong-willed to state any viewpoint that wasn't his at its core. But Bashar al-Assad had failed to crush the Syrian rebellion in its infancy and the result had been a slowly brewing insurgency that erupted into full-fledged civil war in the summer of 2012.

At the root of the rebellion was the age old strife between Shia and Sunni Islam. The Assad family, members of the Alawite Sect of Shia Islam, had ruled Syria since 1971. While originally the Ba'athist Party of the Assad family was defined by pan-Arab nationalism and cultural awakening, the decades and emergence of religious fundamentalism had seen the family become increasingly aligned with the Shiites of Iran. This evolution had fed the traditional schism between the majority Sunnis in Syria and the minority Shiites, who dominated the power nodes of government. Now, the civil war had created clear demarcation lines. Fighting to keep their power under the banner of Bashar al-Assad were the Alawites and their internal Shia allies, supported externally by Iran and its allies Russia and China. Fighting to overthrow the historic regime were the Sunnis and their allies in most of the Arab world supported by the Western powers.

But among the Sunni fighters, most of them just simple farmers and shopkeepers yearning for nothing more than basic human freedom, was a mix of Sunni fundamentalists who fought for a different cause: the creation of a greater Islamic caliphate under Sharia law. And the most feared of this group of Sunni fighters were those affiliated with al Qaeda. Since the early days of the Syrian revolution in the spring of 2011, al Qaeda had been infiltrating the country, recruiting religious Sunnis and plotting to exert influence on the future Syria.

The growing al Qaeda cadre included a rising star within the organization named Abu Muhjid. Muhjid was a 33-year-old Palestinian Arab who had volunteered for the al-Aqsa Martyrs Brigades at the age of 21 over the objections of his father, who dreamed of his only son becoming a professional. But Abu was full of a hatred that his father could not control or contain and the Martyrs Brigades were on the front line in the death struggle against Israel. They were always on the lookout for young jihadists willing to die for Allah. However, Muhjid's intelligence and outgoing personality made him stand out from the sullen group of recruits that would show up at the homes of recruiters scattered around the West Bank. He was soon earmarked as a gunman for the Brigades and found himself at a training base in the Bekaa valley in Lebanon.

He led a successful attack into the heart of the occupied capital of Palestine in January 2004. But luck did not accompany him the entire trip. He was stopped by Shin Bet agents as he tried to slip back into the West Bank. What followed for Muhjid was weeks of on-again, off-again interrogation inside Ktzi'ot Prison, some of it following days of sleep deprivation. He was then tried in a civilian court by Israelis. He stayed silent through the proceedings, even as he received nine life sentences from the judge. His hatred for Israel at that moment was complete. He was transferred to Ofer Prison in the West Bank to spend out the remainder of his natural life.

Like the many Palestinians inside Ofer, Muhjid was caught by surprise when the tensions between Fatah, the traditional political party of Yasser Arafat and generally secular in nature, and Hamas, the more Islamist party of the Palestinian people, erupted into open violence late in 2006. The tension inside the prison increased as battles between Palestinians grew on the outside. Men discussed politics and the role of Islam even more than they had before and the Israeli jailers were increasingly concerned about the possibility of major violence within the prison. But Muhjid stayed out of the politics of the prison. He was too busy taking advantage of the classes available inside the prison that were run by highly educated men. For the young Martyrs Brigades veteran, this included courses in English, mathematics and, of course, the Koran.

Abu Muhjid was happy to let the outside world determine its own course. His world was now confined by tall concrete walls topped with barbed wire and defined by a tempo set by Jewish masters. He did what he could to define his own world within this prison, certain that he would be locked inside Ofer until the day the Jewish state was toppled.

But news came one day that obliterated the world he had created. His 47-year-old father, a Fatah policeman, had been killed by Hamas gunmen in Nablus in January 2007. Abu's parents had been very young when they married and he was born when his mother was only 16 years old. Now his mother was a widow at the age of 42 and this was not a good situation. Abu could not support her from prison, despite sending her most of the modest "salary" he received from Fatah as a jailed fighter. His younger sister had married a drunkard who could not keep a job. As a widow, his mother would also receive a small pension from Fatah, but the financial footing of the Palestinian Authority was precarious at best.

Abu Muhjid had one other major concern for his mother – one that was serious before but could potentially kill her now. She suffered from a rare condition known as Chronic Granulomatous Disease, or GCD, an immune system disorder. To survive, she needed a constant supply of low-dose antibiotics and anti-fungal drugs. His father's income combined with his Martyrs Brigades salary and the charity of Western aid agencies had been barely sufficient to pay the bills. But now Abu knew she would start to face the choice between her drug therapy and eating enough to stay healthy. Cutting back on either would weaken her immune system and leave her open to fatal infection. Suddenly Abu Muhjid was eager to get out of prison, a complete change in his prior indifference to his fate.

Muhjid now began to write to charities like Médicins sans Frontiéres to plead for help for his mother. Of course, his letters were read by his Israeli jailers, a fact which he had no choice but to accept. The letters had continued for several months when Muhjid was informed that he was being relocated to a different prison, this one inside Israel. The tensions between Hamas and Fatah, he was told, made him a marked man and his life was in danger at Ofer. In early May 2007, Abu gathered what little he possessed and was processed out of Ofer prison, being remanded into the authority of the transport division of the Israeli Prison Service.

Muhjid was shackled and placed in a windowless van. After an hour and a half the van came to a stop and the back door was opened. He was helped out and his shackles were replaced with a simple pair of handcuffs. He was in an enclosed courtyard but this was unlike any place he had been as a prisoner. His gut told him that this was not a prison. He was escorted into a room that was neither a cell nor an interrogation chamber. It felt to Abu like the waiting lobby for a doctor's office. He sat down. A man entered and sat down across from him. The man was wearing a hat, sunglasses and what was obviously a false beard and mustache.

The next two hours of discussion were the most surreal in the short life of Abu Muhjid. The man across from him spoke perfect Arabic with an educated Saudi accent. The discussion started with current events and the state of disharmony between the two main factions of the Palestinian people. The topic migrated to Muhjid's family and the precarious position that his mother and sister found themselves in. Finally the man revealed his real intentions. He had a proposition for the convicted Palestinian terrorist. If Abu Muhjid would work for Mossad, then Israel would arrange for his mother and sister to relocate to France where they would receive a lifetime pension that included all of the free medical care his mother would need to live a long life.

The initial reaction of Abu Muhjid was negative, but he had yet to hear the best part of the deal. Mossad would make sure he was released from prison and they wanted him to continue in his struggle on behalf of the Islamic people. They wanted him to volunteer for al Qaeda and they wanted him to wage jihad. All they asked was that he communicate with them regularly. When Abu Muhjid asked how he could possibly communicate successfully with Mossad over a long period of time, the men from Mossad who were filming this encounter in the adjacent room knew that they had hooked their man.

At that moment, the career of Mossad's most valuable asset began. His codename inside Mossad became "Archer", or "ramy alsham" in Arabic. The existence and activities of Archer were known only to a very small group within Mossad and they reported directly to Director Levy. The only person outside of Mossad who was aware of Archer was the prime minister.

Abu Muhjid received several weeks of training and was transferred to Ktzi'ot Prison where he continued his correspondence with aid agencies on behalf of his mother. As instructed by his new Mossad handlers, he immersed himself in Islamic studies, introducing himself to the most fervent Islamic jihadists being held at Ktzi'ot. In September he received a reply from Médicins sans Frontiéres informing him that they had agreed to take up the cause of his mother. They believed that they would be able to arrange for her to emigrate from Palestine to France where she would be able to receive the medical care she required. His sister and her husband would be allowed to emigrate as well. The process would take time, they told him, but in the meantime they would ensure that his mother received adequate medical supplies.

In March 2008, Muhjid received a letter from his mother. She was on her way to France and expected to leave from Amman, Jordan, by the end of April. Her visa had arrived and they were only awaiting a visa for his sister and her husband. In late April he received a postcard with the Eiffel Tower on the front. His mother, sister and her husband were living in a flat on the outskirts of Paris paid by the generosity of a French charity. His mother had already seen a leading French medical specialist on GCD.

On August 25, 2008, Israel released 198 Palestinian prisoners as a gesture of goodwill and support for Palestinian leader Mahmoud Abbas. Among the prisoners released was Abu Muhjid. Within six months, Muhjid was at a training camp in the Waziristan region of Pakistan. When Israel asked the CIA to refrain from any Predator strikes against that specific training camp for a two month period, the CIA was happy to comply as long as they were told why. Mossad was happy to inform them that a unit of Sayeret Matkal was conducting an intelligence gathering operation around the camp and that anything of value would be shared with the Americans. The CIA analysts were highly impressed that they could find no trace of the Sayeret Matkal operatives in Pakistan – the legend of Israeli special operations growing on the basis of sleight of hand.

Five months later, Abu Muhjid was operating inside the Anbar Province of Iraq and making a name for himself as a planner of effective operations against the American occupation forces. When the pressure became too great, he would slip into Syria, where he found a safe haven and developed contacts. The value of Archer to Mossad was growing by the month.

33 – Ready, Aim

Syria has been a client state for Russia, and the Soviet Union before it, for fifty years. The value of that relationship to the Russians has waned and waxed over the decades. But the one constant for Russia has been that Syria has remained a counterbalance to the main client state of the USA in the region: Israel. That counterbalance comes from proximity. Syria shares fifty miles of disputed border with Israel. With proximity comes the ability to observe. To take advantage of this ability, Russia has supplied, built and partially manned a series of radar complexes and listening posts around Syria.

This network of radar sites had grown to 24 sites supporting 137 active Surface to Air Missile, or SAM, sites in 2007 when the IAF launched Operation Orchard on September 6, 2007. This mission resulted in the destruction of a secret nuclear reactor being constructed in the desolate desert region of northeastern Syria. The fact that fourteen Israeli warplanes flew so deep into Syrian airspace, destroyed their target and returned to Israel unscathed, created a serious rift in Russian-Syrian relations. The Russians had promised upgrades to counter the effectiveness of IAF electronic jamming. The Syrians played their cards as best they could, demanding and accepting every enhancement to their air defense network that Moscow was willing to provide. Quietly, the Syrians turned to China to ask for the latest in Chinese radar technology – not to replace the Russian equipment but to supplement it. The result was the delivery to Syria of two Chinese built JY-27 anti-stealth radar systems with a range of up to 500 kilometers.

At the same time, the Iranians were placing equal pressure on Russia to upgrade the Syrian radar network so that the Syrians could provide early warning to Iran of any departure of a large number of IAF aircraft headed east towards Iran. The pressure worked, and during 2009 and 2010 Russia delivered a range of upgrades even as the Chinese delivered their long-wavelength anti-stealth radar systems. Some of the upgrades required the active assistance of Russian technicians, who started manning radar installations and command posts in greater numbers. When the Syrians protested as a matter of pride, the Iranians intervened to insist on full access for the Russians, reminding the Syrians of the fiasco of Operation Orchard.

For the IAF officers planning Project Block G, this expanded radar network presented challenges. Russian technicians using Russian radar were able to look deep into Israeli airspace. The two Chinese JY-27 radars were both located in the desert east of Damascus and could see deep into both Jordan and the western region of Iraq. The Israelis had been routinely jamming these radar systems over the years leading up to Block G – a process which resulted in a tit for tat electronics war between Israel and the Syrians/Russians/Chinese. When the day came to launch Block G, the jamming that would take place needed to be a routine event.

But at Mount Olympus, simply jamming the early warning radar systems inside Syria was not enough. A greater margin of safety needed to be attained. The result was the first active operation for Block G: Operation Arrow.

On September 2, General David Schechter gathered the senior staff of the Olympus planning team inside the main conference room in the hidden bunker complex adjacent to Sde Dov airport. The bunker looked from the outside like one of the many mid-rise apartment buildings in the area, but inside, a full communications, encryption and supporting technology suite was now in constant use. The team had grown significantly over the prior two years and Schechter knew it would grow even more in the days to come. He called the meeting to order and started with a review of preparations and the state of readiness of the IAF. When this had been completed, he asked Amit Margolis to stand and address the group of 27 men and women.

"Thank you, General," said Margolis as he stood. He cleared his throat. "This group was officially formed over three years ago to plan and execute the most important military mission since our fathers and grandfathers won our independence. For the last year and a half we have been ready to go and waiting for the right conditions both politically and militarily." This was a speech that had not been heard before in the group, and Margolis could sense the excitement level building. He tried to remain calm, certain that everyone in the room could tell that he was anything but. "It is my honor to report that the time has come. We are going live."

A murmur broke out throughout the room. Somewhere in the back an officer whistled. Suddenly another officer starting clapping, and that emotion swept the room in an instant. Everyone was applauding. Amit joined in. General Schechter applauded as well, unable to fight off the emotion. It was a collective release of tension built over years of pressure. Schechter stood back up and walked a few feet over to his left to shake Margolis' hand. The action brought everyone to their feet. Schechter motioned for everyone to calm down and return to their seats.

"Okay. Okay," said Schechter loudly. "Calm down. We have a lot do to. Perhaps we should hold off on the celebrations until the day after the strike is done." He paused for a moment to allow the group to sit back down and focus once again on the enormous work to be done. "We have a new moon on Friday, October 4, and the forecast looks perfect. All leaves are canceled. I will have a work schedule posted on the break room wall later today to let everyone plan the coming weeks. When you are off, you can go home and stay home. No travel, no parties, no drinking. If you are called to return here, I expect you back here within thirty minutes. As always, everyone is welcome to use the dorm rooms for the duration. However, when you are off, you need to rest. There will be plenty of lost sleep over the next four weeks so it is critical that you rest and sleep when you can. Keep in mind that this event can be postponed up to twenty-four hours prior to takeoff. At this point, weather will be the deciding factor. The forecast looks perfect, but only God knows what will happen. So pray that the weather holds, but never forget that if it doesn't, we will be back on a one month hold. Any questions?" There were none. "Okay, IAF team stay here for full sequencing run-through and notification plan review. Sling team, please join Amit in the small conference room next door. If you are on the operator team," Schechter was referring to the officers who had been planning the special operations missions that were integral to the Block G, "we will meet here in two hours."

Amit Margolis left the large conference room to walk next door to a smaller conference room. He convened his team of five. Even within the Olympus planning team, a group that currently held the highest security classifications in Israel outside of the country's nuclear weapons program, the information about Esther's Sling was known only to the five in the room plus General Schechter. His team went through the status of all of the assets, both human and mechanical, that were necessary to make the plan work. But in the back of his mind, Amit was already inpatient to hear that the Archer had struck. Operation Arrow was the first part of Project Block G to go into action and no one inside this bunker complex knew about it except for Amit Margolis – not even General Schechter. It was a Mossad operation and it involved the single greatest asset of the state of Israel – Archer. If it worked, a special operations mission into Syria that had been planned for over a year could be canceled.

34 – Bullseye

Operation Arrow began preliminary operations months earlier when Abu Muhjid, inside his safe house in Ramadi, Iraq, logged onto an Arab dating website named muslima.com. He went to his "Favorites" list and, as he had been trained, pulled up the profiles on several women, aimlessly browsing through photographs. After a minute or two of that, he clicked onto the profile of a young Jordanian woman living in Amman. It was the profile he always returned to. Among her photographs was a newly posted photo of her in the Jordanian countryside with her uncle at a restaurant along Route 10 about six kilometers southeast of the town of al Mafraq. The date on the photo was April 20 of the previous year. The photo was a code for Muhjid, telling him when and where to meet his Mossad handler. He had a week until April 20 and he needed to be at the restaurant in the photo at 2 p.m. local time on that date.

A week later, the Archer was eating a meal of hummus and kubbeh at the appropriate time when he noticed a man walk out of the restroom. He didn't recognize the man, but he recognized the old home jersey for Manchester United that the man was wearing. On the back it had the number 7 and the name "Ronaldo," a relic of days past for the English football club. The man returned to his table and ordered a cup of tea. Muhjid continued to finish his meal, taking another ten minutes to eat and pay his bill. He stood and went to the restroom. After relieving himself, he washed his hands in a basin. Behind him, the man in the football jersey walked into the restroom and paused to make sure they were alone. The Archer turned toward the man, who handed him an envelope. Muhjid quickly stuffed the envelope into his pants and exited the restroom.

Muhjid headed back toward Iraq but pulled off the highway after a hundred kilometers of driving to find a spot in the desert where he could spend the night and read the contents of his package from Tel Aviv. What he saw when he opened the envelope got him both excited and scared. If he was able to pull off the attack outlined, he would gain fame inside al Qaeda. He stopped to think about why Israel would want him to attack an airbase inside Syria, but he couldn't come up with any logical reason other than that the Israelis and the Syrians seemed destined to an eternal death match. But it didn't matter to the Archer. He liked the assignment and, in his judgment, it would renown to the glory of al Qaeda, his new family. When he was recruited, Mossad told him that if they gave him an assignment, he would like it. They had been true to their word.

The final page of his instructions, which were always careful to look as if they had come from within al Qaeda, told him to be ready to go operational by the first of September. The other item in the envelope was a small stack of American $100 notes, one hundred of them. The money was better than gold in this part of the world. The Archer had work to do.

The Archer was ready to go on the morning of September 14, three days after receiving the green light via code in a photo posted on muslima.com. His target was the Palmyra Air Base in Syria, a military airfield located forty miles east of Tiyas Air Base, the main airfield of the Syrian Air Force. Tiyas was, in turn, about ninety miles to the northeast of Damascus.

Palmyra Air Base was just south of the M20 highway and adjacent to a town called Tadmur. The base had only a single landing strip with a shorter parallel taxiway. Both ran east to west. Sixteen earth-covered concrete revetments housed a half dozen MiG-23BN Flogger ground attack aircraft. But it was not the aircraft that Muhjid was tasked with destroying, it was a single building that had been constructed during 2011 on the northern edge of the base.

The building was not huge, encompassing 11,465 square feet, but its importance was enormous. It was funded by Iran and built by the Russians to serve as the central command, communication and analysis center for all of the early warning radar inside Syria. Inside the building, eight Iranian Air Force and Revolutionary Guard liaisons, twenty-one Syrian Air Force personnel and fourteen Russian technicians operated 24 hours per day, 365 days a year to collect and analyze all of the data that showed up on the various radar and monitoring units that were being fed into the building via hard wire from a microwave communication tower located on top of the town hospital. This tower communicated with a microwave tower on top of the 6,043 foot ridge of Jabal ash Shamail, located to the north of Damascus. The building was connected to the headquarters of the Iranian Revolutionary Guard Corp in Tehran via telephone and the Internet. If an Israeli action was detected, Tehran would know about it even before the Syrian air defense network was put on alert.

Archer was given intelligence on his secondary targets as well. The men who occupied the target building all lived in housing just to the northwest of the base. The Russians had insisted, against the advice of the Syrian security service, on constructing a road that connected the building with the small community of homes in the town of Tadmur where the Russian advisors lived, some with their families. The connecting road was only one mile long. Mossad not only wanted Archer to destroy the building, but also to kill all the Russians who were not on duty at the time. They had given him a map that showed the homes of Russians. He also had high resolution satellite photos of the base and the housing area.

Finally, Mossad gave him two tertiary targets. About ¾ of a mile to the east of the target building was a Russian P-14 Tall King radar with a range of up to 400 kilometers. Another third of a mile to the southeast of that was one of two Chinese JY-27 radar units now based in Syria.

The original package delivered to Archer had all of the information that he needed to plan his attack. He was feeling very confident, since the Syrians had done little to guard the Palmyra Air Base. It was far to the east of the population belt of Syria that ran north to south within 70 miles of the coast line – and that meant that it had so far escaped the worst of the civil war now raging. But Archer had to change his plans when he was called into Jordan again in early August to receive the latest intelligence. In the chaos of war, events occur beyond the ability of even the brightest minds to predict or control. Mossad analysts had come to realize that the information they gave to Archer on the defense of the base was outdated. IAF reconnaissance flights over the eastern deserts of Syria, combined with the intelligence gathering of Unit 8200, had shown that far more Syrian troops had been deployed to protect Palmyra in recent months. Instead of a simple guardhouse with one or two soldiers, a Syrian army company was now stationed on the base. A squad had set up a Russian DShK heavy machine gun to protect the entrance to the connecting road.

But the new package given to Archer also included a nugget that Abu Muhjid knew how to take full advantage of. Somehow Mossad had obtained a list of the men in the Syrian army unit now tasked with defending Palmyra Air Base. Beside each name was their religious affiliation – Sunni or Shia. Since this duty was not considered front line work, most of the men in this unit were Sunni Muslims. Next to some of these men was an asterisk. A note on the bottom of the page indicated that the asterisk meant that these men were known to harbor fundamentalist beliefs.

The sun on the morning of Saturday, September 14 rose unencumbered by any cloud formations. The day promised to be a gorgeous fall offering. Muhjid thought it a perfect day for combat. *Combat.* That is what Abu Muhjid thought of his actions, regardless of whether the targets were soldiers or civilians. Everyone was a combatant in his mind. He had spent the night in As Sukhnah, a small Sunni village only forty miles further to the east of Palmyra along the M20 highway. Muhjid was the honored guest of the local imam, a man who dreamed of the end of the secular decadence of the Assad family. Just about the entire village of As Sukhnah was of a like mind to the imam. The one family known to spy for the regime had been threatened enough to stay inside and mind their own business.

At 0629 hours, following morning prayers, Muhjid met with two men. The first was a comrade in al Qaeda who had fought by Muhjid's side during the past eighteen months inside Iraq and Syria. The other was a middle-aged man who Muhjid knew only as Mohammed. Archer did not want to know anything more about the man. Experience had taught him that it was easier that way. The three men reviewed the plan. All was ready. Archer turned to Mohammed.

"I envy you. Soon you will know Allah."

The man smiled. He was as calm and happy as if he was about to embark on vacation. "Allahu Akbar," he replied.

"Allah guide you this morning."

The two men embraced and kissed each other on the cheeks.

Abu Muhjid got into the passenger seat of a small four-door sedan. He held a two-way radio. Between his legs an AK-47 rested with its muzzle on the floor and the pistol grip handle on his lap. Its wire frame butt was folded over and out of the way, allowing him to pull the weapon into a firing position easily. In the small glove compartment he placed a can of bright orange spray paint. He turned to the driver, a young man with a beard who was a local Syrian fundamentalist who had been on a previous operation conducted in Syria under Muhjid's command. This one was much bigger and bolder than anything the al Qaeda commander had planned before. Muhjid told the man to head out. They had a fifty-minute drive to Palmyra, but they rarely said a word to each other. This sedan was leading a small convoy and Muhjid's primary job on the drive was to spot any police or army units on the way. If any hint of a roadblock was detected, they would abort the mission and return to As Sukhnah.

Allah was with them this morning. The highway was empty except for an occasional truck that passed by or was passed. They drove at exactly 100 kph, below the posted speed limit of 110 kph. The reason was not to avoid a ticket, it was to set a known pace that everyone who followed could maintain. The timing of the plan was laid out clearly. The shift change at the target building occurred every morning at 0800 hours and the plan was coordinated around that event. The second vehicle in the convoy left As Sukhnah exactly at 0700 hours, twenty-five minutes after Muhjid's sedan.

At 0727 hours, the sedan passed by the northern edge of Palmyra Air Base as it headed west into Tadmur. A minute later it came to a small roundabout as the two men entered the town. The car wheeled around the roundabout 270 degrees and exited onto the road that led to the base and the target building. But after a short distance, the car turned left onto a side road. They were now in the middle of the housing neighborhood that included eight homes occupied by Russian technicians. Four of the homes were on this street, conveniently located next door to each other.

"Slow down," Muhjid commanded. He looked at a map he pulled from his pocket. Homes of Russians were highlighted in yellow and their addresses were written on the map. "Here. Right here," said the al Qaeda commander as he pointed to a home to the right of the car. The driver pulled over and stopped. Muhjid grabbed the can of spray paint and removed the top, shaking the can violently for a few seconds. He opened his door and sprayed an 'X' on the sidewalk in front of the home's entrance gate. All of the homes on the street had an eight foot high concrete block wall around their property. The wall formed a long barrier adjacent to the sidewalk.

"Go to the next," Muhjid commanded. The process was repeated – and again two more times in quick succession. Archer looked down at his map. "Now go down and turn right." The remaining four homes were scattered throughout the small housing section. It took the men another ten minutes to finish the job of marking the homes. These were not scarlet letters – they were much worse. These marks were a death sentence for the occupants of each home. After the last home was marked the car pulled over and waited for a few minutes. The time seemed to Muhjid to take hours.

At 0755 hours, the car pulled back onto the road leading to the radar network building. Muhjid turned to his driver. "Now we learn if Allah blesses us."

The car drove slowly toward the target building. Almost immediately after it left the residential neighborhood, it approached the edge of Palmyra Air Base. Ahead, a guardhouse was built into the middle of the road. The car stopped about ten feet short of the guardhouse. "If I die, grab the gun and kill as many as you can. Allahu Akbar." Muhjid stepped out of the car, leaving his AK-47 still resting with its muzzle on the floor board of the passenger seat.

Abu Muhjid approached the guardhouse. To his right and a little further on he could see an emplacement lined with sandbags. Inside the emplacement, a large machine gun pointed at him. His fate would be known in the coming seconds. He figured that if he died, he would never know it until he awoke in heaven. A young Syrian soldier stepped out of the guardhouse and held up his left arm, motioning for Muhjid to stop.

"I am looking for Faraj." Muhjid could feel his heart beating at a furious pace. He prayed that the guard in front of him did not pick up on it.

The guard had been told by Faraj, a young corporal respected in the squad for his devout beliefs, that a man would show up this morning asking for him. Faraj had spent the last number of weeks quietly preparing his squad for this moment. "Faraj," the guard yelled in the direction of the machine gun nest.

A young soldier came running out toward Muhjid. He had been wondering for weeks if his recruitment by al Qaeda was real or was some trick being played by Syrian intelligence to test his loyalty. He knew at this moment that it was real. "Allahu Akbar," yelled Faraj as he approached Muhjid. The yell was a signal to six of the nine men in and around the machine gun nest. They turned their AK-47 assault rifles on the other three men, who were Shiites, and commanded them to raise their arms. Faraj reached Muhjid, grabbed his left hand and raised it to his mouth to kiss it.

"Allahu Akbar," said Abu Muhjid as he hugged Faraj. They kissed each other on the cheeks. The two men in the guardhouse were with Faraj. "Tell your men to take cover after the truck passes. The fireworks will begin shortly after. And cover your ears."

"Yes, sir." Faraj turned to his men and issued orders. The three Shiites were ordered to lie down inside the emplacement. Guns were trained on them to ensure compliance.

Muhjid removed the small radio transmitter tucked into his pocket. He lifted it to his mouth and pressed the transmit button. "We are good to go. Allah be with you." He turned to get back into the four-door sedan. He paused at the door. "Are you coming?" he asked Faraj.

Faraj ran to get in the back seat behind the driver. The car accelerated down the mile long road to the target building. The road headed due east, roughly paralleling the M20 highway about a half mile to the north. After they were half way down the road, the driver noticed a white van behind them and mentioned it. Faraj turned around. "That is the next shift."

"Good," replied Muhjid.

The sedan continued down the road, which curved to the south for the last hundred meters to the target building. The car slowed and continued past the side of the building, continuing south for another two hundred meters onto the empty tarmac of Palmyra Air Base. They reached the taxiway and turned left to head east, toward the radars. Abu Muhjid looked back over his left shoulder toward the guardhouse that was now over a mile away. He saw the headlights of a truck coming in their direction on the road leading to the building. The truck was just passing the guardhouse. "Speed up," ordered Muhjid to the driver. He knew how much explosive the truck carried.

The driver understood as well and was soon racing along the taxiway at 120 kph, about as fast as its four cylinder engine could get it to.

In the residential neighborhood a van had stopped to let five men out at the first of the four side-by-side homes that were marked with an orange 'X'. All of the men were armed with AK-47s and wore combat vests with eight additional 30 round magazines and two grenades. One man held a forty pound steel battering ram. They stopped at the first gate as the van drove off. The man with the battering ram, the largest man on the team, swung the ram against the gate handle. The gate gave way. He and two other men ran into the small courtyard and up to the front door. The same man smashed in the door and the other two men ran inside. The man with the battering ram ran back out the gate and over to the next home to repeat the process. All of the men wore the uniforms of the Syrian army – each man wearing the same uniform he had been wearing the day he defected during the prior year.

Inside the first home, a central hallway ran from the front sitting room past a kitchen and dining room toward two bedrooms – what residents in New Orleans refer to as a "shotgun" layout. The two gunmen moved quickly, glancing to their right and left as they headed towards the rear bedrooms. A bedroom door opened and a man in shorts stepped into the hallway. "What the hell are you doing?" the homeowner yelled.

The lead man froze, raising his AK-47. Then the words he had just heard penetrated his conscious. They had been spoken in Arabic, an Arabic that was in perfect alignment with the local dialect. The man was not Russian. "Where are the Russians?" screamed the lead intruder.

The homeowner saw the uniforms and, more importantly, the AK-47 leveled at his belly. He raised his arms in the air. "There are no Russians here."

The second invader walked around the first and told the homeowner to back up. He looked into both bedrooms, which were across the hall from each other. The homeowner's bedroom had only a very frightened Arab woman. The other bedroom had two small children. "Where do the Russians live?"

"I don't know. There are some in this neighborhood, but I don't know where."

The first intruder spoke. "Forgive us, we are in the wrong home. Who lives next door?" He pointed in the direction of the next home that had been marked.

"My cousin lives there. There are no Russians."

"Go back to bed." The two intruders turned to head out the front door.

At the same moment, Mohammed was maintaining an even speed on the mile long drive to the building. He slowed for the right hand turn to the south. The 2005 Mitsubishi Fuso box van had only two axles, but could still carry up to 4,000 pounds of cargo. This morning, however, it held only 1,400 pounds of RDX explosive along with three 130 millimeter M-46 artillery rounds, all courtesy of a pilfered Syrian army warehouse. As he straightened the wheel, he saw the shuttle van in front of him, with its shift change cargo still exiting. Several people were waiting to board the van. One or two looked up and noticed a small truck heading in their direction. One man in line thought it odd that the truck seemed to be accelerating. He wondered if the driver was experiencing a problem with his gas pedal.

In the cab, Mohammed reached over and grabbed a push button detonator that was taped to the left side of the vacant passenger's seat. At the same time his right foot pressed down on the pedal. He lifted the detonation trigger in his right hand, moving his thumb onto the plunger.

"Allahu Akbar," shouted Mohammed as the truck passed just in front of the van. Several of the men waiting to board the van were now running for their lives. They could not run far enough to save themselves.

The explosion created a shock wave that travelled outward in all directions. Windows were broken in one-quarter of the homes in the town of Tadmur. Almost a mile away, the sedan had come to a stop in front of its first target. Inside the small four-door, Muhjid, his new comrade Faraj and their driver shuttered. The sound hurt the ears of each man and the concussion forced each of them to catch his breath.

"Allahu Akbar." The phrase was repeated frequently by both Faraj and the driver. Faraj prayed silently to God, thanking him for allowing his humble servant to become a holy warrior – allowing him to feel, in that instant, that his life had purpose for the first time.

Muhjid looked back at the rising cloud of grayish-black smoke and dust. Where the building had been, nothing remained. Debris began to fall around the bomb site. Some things landed around the sedan, Muhjid not sure if they were pieces of wood, metal, dirt or human body parts. He shook his head to gather his wits. There was more work to do. He looked out the front window. A Chinese-built JY-27 radar loomed only twenty meters in front of them. Muhjid noticed that two men had run out of a radar control vehicle that was parked off to the right. They were in shock, watching the same growing column of rising smoke as Muhjid. The al Qaeda commander got out of the car and walked toward them. This time he held his AK-47 in his right hand, the muzzle pointing loosely at the ground as he walked.

The man closest to Muhjid turned to him. "What just happened?" the man asked.

They were his last words. Abu Muhjid raised his weapon to his hip and fired a three round burst, the first two rounds hitting the man in the chest. He died instantly. Behind him the other man began to run. Muhjid raised his weapon to align the sites on his target and squeezed the trigger. The man had made the mistake of running directly away from the Archer in a straight line. He was hard to miss. His body dropped to the earth like the sack of deadweight it had become.

Muhjid turned back to the car. The driver had stepped out. "Get the bag," he yelled, and then quickly turned to run toward the radar control vehicle that the two now dead men had just exited. He reached the doorway in seconds and jumped up the stairs, his weapon leading the way. He reached the floor of the vehicle's enclosed control area. No one was inside. He walked up to two large built-in flat panel displays. He fired bursts into each screen and then a burst into the area that looked to him like the main computers controlling the radar. He turned and exited.

As Muhjid stepped back onto the hard desert sand, he noticed that the driver was now holding an olive drab canvas bag in his hand that he had retrieved from the trunk of the sedan. He was already heading towards the radar. Muhjid yelled to Faraj, who was following the driver, to stand watch as they planted C-4 explosives to the base of the radar. It took a few minutes to get the explosives in place. Muhjid set a delay fuse as the driver and Faraj headed back to the car. After starting the timing device, Muhjid ran to the car and jumped into the passenger seat. "Go, go, go!" he commanded.

Back in the residential neighborhood, the first two home invaders were almost to the front door when the windows shattered. The home shook as if an earthquake had just hit. But instead of sustained shaking, the impact was sudden and sharp, like being in an auto accident. The sound was louder than anything either man had heard before. Each man said a silent prayer in praise of Allah. The two men could hear screaming and crying from the rear of the house as they exited into the front courtyard and out through the wall to the sidewalk, turning right to see what had happened at the house next door. They stopped at the breached gate and looked into the courtyard to see one of their comrades coming down the front steps. The gunman exiting the house looked at his friends and yelled out, "There are no Russians here." He was clearly shaken.

"Where's Abdul?" asked the first of the two men.

"He's coming." The man was white.

"What's wrong?"

"Abdul killed a child."

"What?"

"It was dark." The man just shook his head from side to side.

A moment later, Abdul came running out of the home. "Let's go," he screamed. The group went on to the next two homes. There were no Russians living in any of the four houses.

When the explosion occurred, the van from As Sukhnah, which had been carrying nine armed men when it pulled onto the M20 highway an hour earlier, had just finished dropping off the last two gunmen in front of a marked home. The two gunmen paused for a moment to recuperate from the concussion of the explosion and then used a battering ram to break open the gate to the wall. As they stepped through the opening into the courtyard, a European man was walking out of the front door of the home. The European froze when he saw the two Syrian army soldiers in front of him.

The lead gunman raised his AK-47 to his shoulder and fired a single round, hitting the foreigner in the right side of his chest. The victim's legs buckled and he fell to the ground in a seated lotus position. His eyes contained only fear and astonishment, his mind unable to comprehend the event. The trailing gunman walked around his partner, passed behind the man now seated on the walkway, and bounded up the front steps of the home. The first gunman calmly walked up the man on the ground and raised his weapon, the muzzle only a few feet from the head of his target. He fired a single round and the man's head exploded, the corpse now falling backwards onto the sandy earth that would shortly be soaked in blood. Clumps of skull with hair tissue still attached were scattered in the sand.

Inside the home, which had the same floor plan as the other homes in the neighborhood, the second gunman headed down the hall. A woman came out of one of the bedrooms. She was middle-aged with light brown hair. She had thrown on a bathrobe to go investigate what had happened outside, her imagination assuming something bad but falling well short of reality.

"Stop," yelled the gunman as he leveled his weapon at her. "Russian?"

The woman froze in fear, unable to speak.

"Russian?" shouted the gunman. He was stationary, his weapon at his shoulder and pointed at the woman.

A loud and sharp sound startled the gunman – the noise of a rifle round being fired. The woman was hit in the head, the round killing her instantly. The bullet had been fired by the first gunman, who had entered the home after he killed the man outside. He stepped around his partner and walked down the hall. He kicked open the bedroom door opposite the woman's bedroom and looked in. He flipped the selector on his weapon upward one notch with his thumb, enabling full automatic fire. He squeezed the trigger. Twelve rounds were fired before he stopped. A teenage Russian boy now lay dead.

The gunman turned and walked out. As he passed by his partner, he simply said, "I hate Russians. Filthy atheists."

The other three homes were all entered. They were empty.

The sedan carrying Abu Muhjid, Faraj and the driver turned back around to head back to the northwest toward the Russian Tall King radar set. As they drove, Muhjid heard metallic pinging. He started to wonder if there was something wrong with the engine of their car. "What is that sound?" he asked to no one in particular. As the last word left his mouth, a round came through the rear window. Muhjid ducked instinctively, his mind suddenly realizing that the sounds he had been hearing were bullets hitting the car. "Floor it," he yelled to his driver. "Where is that coming from?"

As the last word came from his mouth, a loud explosion pierced the air a couple of hundred meters behind the car. The C-4 had detonated, its chemically induced force instantly cutting through the steel pedestal that supported the large Chinese radar array. The radar toppled to the ground, its delicate framework unable to support its own weight. The array twisted and warped as it collapsed. No one would be repairing this particular radar.

Even better, thought the Archer, whoever was shooting at their car had stopped. Muhjid did not need to tell the driver to take full advantage of the lull. He thought about the situation and came to the conclusion that the last remaining target, the Russian Tall King radar, would have to wait for another day. It was getting too dangerous on the base and their sedan had been identified. "Head for the exit corner." Muhjid pointed off to his right.

The driver continued to accelerate, only now turning the car to the right, heading northeast toward a corner of the base. If they could make it, they would be half a mile south of the M20 highway. The base had a sand berm around the perimeter and the car would not be able to drive over it, but the sooner they reached a far corner of the base, the further they could run before soldiers arrived. The car traveled across the hard desert sand without problem, covering the last half mile to the northeast corner in under a minute.

The car came to stop just inside the corner of the berm. Muhjid told each man to get out and start toward the highway. He removed a block of the remaining C-4 explosive from the bag and placed a delay fuse into it, setting the timer for the maximum delay of two minutes. He placed the block back into the bag and placed the bag of explosives on the driver's side floor. He got out, taking his weapon with him. As he stood up straight, he looked back toward the interior of the base and smiled – no one was following them. He turned and scurried over the berm. When he reached the other side he began a fast jog toward the highway. In the distance, from the direction of the town, he could hear sirens. On the base itself, sporadic gunfire could be heard.

As he neared the highway, he saw what he had been praying for: a blue Nissan pickup truck was parked on the edge of the road. It had been the last vehicle in the morning convoy to leave As Sukhnah. He finally reached the truck and got in. The driver of the sedan was in the middle of the front bench seat. "Where's Faraj?"

The driver looked at him. "With Allah," he said. Faraj had been hit in the head and killed by the round that came through the window of the sedan. It was his fate. In the excitement of the moment Muhjid had never noticed.

"Let's go," said Muhjid. He shook his head and then said a silent prayer to thank God for watching over him this day.

The pickup truck headed toward As Sukhnah. It was not limited to 100 kph. Somewhere behind them, the van had picked up all nine of the gunmen and was heading toward a spot in the desert where the men had parked their cars. They would abandon the van there and return to their families. They had succeeded in killing three Russians, only one of whom was a legitimate target. They had also killed a young Arab child who was completely innocent. But in the blast that destroyed the building, most of the men of two shifts had been caught on site. Five Iranians, twelve Syrians and, most importantly, nine Russians had died in an instant. The timing of the explosion could not have been better. Such was the randomness of warfare.

A communiqué from the Islamic State in Iraq and the Levant was posted to several Islamic websites. It read:

> In obedience to the command of Allah, and in support of His religion, and to defend and avenge the oppressed in the Levant, the soldiers of the Islamic State of Iraq, in cooperation with our Islamic brothers in arms in the Levant, carried out an attack today. The action was conducted at an air base in the eastern region of the Homs Governate and operations of the infidel government in Moscow were targeted. All of the targets of the operation were completely destroyed. The representatives of the infidel government who support the criminal regime in Damascus, are warned to leave the Levant and all Islamic lands. This operation was conducted on the morning of 14 September.

The international press quickly picked up the story. There was no doubt that the claim by the political wing of the Islamic State in Iraq and the Levant was genuine, the first sentence of the communiqué had been posted ninety minutes before the attack occurred. An update added the detail after the fact.

35 – The Armenian Trucker

The temperature hovered in the low 60s Fahrenheit as the tractor-trailer rig crossed the Aras River from Agarak, Armenia, into Nordouz, Iran. Just over 100 meters past the bridge, the truck slowed and turned right into the dirt parking lot of the Iranian customs center. The time in Iran was 10:02 in the morning, exactly 30 minutes earlier than the time would be if the truck was still on the other side of the river in Armenia. Hamak Arsadian knew from years of experience that this was the optimal time to show up. A customs officer would get to him within an hour and that meant that he would want to wrap up quickly so that he could break for lunch and Dhuhr prayers at noon. For Arsadian that meant getting back on the road by noon so that he could make it through Tabriz before the start of rush hour.

On this morning, twelve trucks were parked as bored Iranian customs agents checked paperwork and inspected the cargo area of the trucks, always being more thorough for those drivers who were disliked or, more importantly, were too poor or naive to have placed two crisp new 100,000 Iranian rial notes on the inside of their passport. The banknotes were only worth about $10, but for the customs agents who worked the Nordouz crossing, the weekly distribution of pooled "gratuities" were handed out based on a strict seniority system, doubling the pay of rookie officers and tripling the pay of senior officers. Of course, 25% of the take had to be forwarded on to regional headquarters in Tabriz, which, in turn, sent 25% of their take on to Tehran. Everybody participated – and therefore everybody was happy.

Arsadian knew the routine from almost 20 years of delivering goods to the cities of Iran. The businessmen of the Islamic Republic had faced many hurdles since the Revolution, including boycotts, sanctions and the bad publicity that many western companies faced if caught doing business with Iran. One result was the evolution of trade with Armenian front companies that purchased goods in the west – often via an intermediary Russian company – and delivered them to the eager consumers of Iran via a network of trucks that plied the roadways between the warehouses of Yerevan and the major, and minor, cities of Iran. Muslim Azerbaijan's close relations with Israel over recent years had only added fuel to the growth of this trade network between Iran and the overwhelmingly Christian nation of Armenia.

Like his father before him, Hamak Arsadian made a decent living driving this route on a weekly basis, a history that had allowed him to build a wide network of Armenian and Iranian business associates. Arsadian had made his name by being on time and avoiding the inventory "shrinkage" that was so prevalent among many drivers. As a result, he was one of the preferred drivers for high-value items and his rates reflected this standing. The route through Nordouz meant driving along a poorly maintained secondary road that wound its way for almost 70 miles through the mountains until reaching Road 32, a four lane divided highway running into Tabriz. But the pay for making the trip was well worth the effort.

Just under an hour had passed when an Iranian customs officer approached. "Ah, Hamak," smiled the aging officer. "As-salamu alayka." The officer's teeth were rotting and his breath reflected it. Hamak involuntarily recoiled from his window and cursed his luck at drawing Abdul Hamid Sherazi.

"Wa' alayka s-salam, Abdul Hamid." The Armenian's Farsi had become quite fluent over the years of travelling the roads of Iran and engaging in the constant negotiating that was the foundation of Persian commerce. Arsadian passed his clipboard through the window and down to the officer, who began to scan the attached passport, manifest, bill of lading, invoice, certificate of origin, proof of insurance and TIR carnet. The motion of his right hand from the opened passport to his pocket was so routine that the officer did not need to think about it.

The customs officer stepped back a few feet, his head following his eyes as he scanned along the driver side of the tractor-trailer rig. He then took a couple of steps to his left and looked at the front of the tractor. "Is this a new truck?"

"New for me, but, no, not a new truck. I purchased it this week. It's a 2009 MAN GTX. What do you think?"

"You must be doing well, Hamak. Allah has smiled upon you."

"Praise be to him," replied the driver. Arsadian was raised a Christian and still attended church on major holidays, but he had long learned the wisdom of adopting a Muslim attitude once he crossed the border. "My old tractor was costing me too much money in repairs, so I had no choice. At least that is what I tell my wife." Arsadian chuckled.

The guard smiled broadly. "I am impressed." He looked at the 13.6 meter Montracon box van trailer, which lacked side doors. "A new trailer too?"

Arsadian felt his stomach muscles tighten. He had rehearsed this moment a hundred times in his head. *Just respond as you have practiced.* "Yes, it was a deal. The prior owner immigrated to the United States. To New York City I believe."

"Ah, lucky bastard," responded the officer. It was a spontaneous utterance that was not in keeping with the official position of Iran. As soon as the words left his mouth, he became self-conscious for the first time in many weeks. Fortunately for him, members of VEVAK, the Iranian secret police, were not particularly prevalent in this remote border crossing.

The truck driver picked up on the officer's emotion. It made him relax. "Not so much," joked Arsadian. "He's driving a taxi."

The customs officer thought about how he would gladly accept such a job for a chance to live in America, but he kept his thoughts to himself. "Hmmm," was all that came out. He returned his mind to his work. "I see you went with a hard side." Most of the trailers in this region had one or two canvas sides to reduce weight and make loading and unloading easier. Many trailers were open and the load simply covered in a large canvas that was tied down. This type of closed box van was rare.

"This is what he had." Arsadian shrugged his shoulders. "Besides, this lets me sleep easier while I'm delivering a load ... and no leaks."

Sherazi nodded his head slowly in agreement as he raised the clipboard up. He began to scour the manifest. "Where are you headed this trip?"

"I am delivering toilet paper to Ahvaz."

Sherazi looked up from the manifest, which clearly listed 450 cartons of toilet paper. "Toilet paper?" His right eyebrow was raised and his right palm was turned upward in wonderment.

Arsadian smiled. "Charmin." This was a true luxury in Iran.

"Ah, Charmin!" The customs officer was excited. Unlike the usual load of large appliances or automotive spare parts, this was something he could take home to his wife and kids. "Let's take a look," the officer said as he walked to the back door, not caring about Arsadian's response. The driver quickly exited his cab and hurried to the back of the truck, always mindful of the power that Abdul Hamid Sherazi could bring to bear if made unhappy. He reached the rear doors of the trailer before the overweight officer, who had no need to ever move quickly. The Armenian lifted the right side handle from its cradle and rotated it out and to the left effortlessly. An experienced observer could tell a veteran truck driver simply by how smooth his motion was when opening the back doors. After opening the right side, he just as easily opened the left.

The cartons were stacked right to the door and came within a few inches of the ceiling. Sherazi was excited; he had never before seen a shipment of Charmin. The printing on the cartons was clearly genuine – crisp, clear and straight from the Procter and Gamble plant in Mehoopany, Pennsylvania. Even though the same product could be purchased for less under the brand name Cushelle, wealthy Iranians wanted Charmin in their bathrooms and would pay for it.

Arsadian smiled and asked a simple question, "Ultra soft or ultra strong?"

Sherazi scratched his chin. "Soft. Soft. My wife loves it."

Arsadian raised his left foot up and placed it onto the square steel tube that doubled as both a bumper and a step. He pivoted his weight and swung his right foot onto eight inches of the now exposed flooring of the trailer. The Iranian was impressed at the agility of the five foot eight inch Armenian, who, he thought, couldn't be much younger than he. Reaching upward with his right hand, Arsadian pulled out the top carton of Charmin Ultra Soft until it balanced precariously with only an inch or two of carton still overlapping the cardboard box below it. With one motion he pulled the carton out the last couple of inches and stepped off the back of the trailer's deck, grabbing the carton with both hands as he fell over four feet down to the earth. He immediately dropped the carton to the ground and inserted his fingers under a flap to force it open. He let Sherazi enjoy the contents.

"You know, once the box is open, it has lost its value," said Arsadian with a twinkle in his eye. "Please tell your wife that not all of us Armenians are bad guys."

Sherazi bent over and pulled out a four roll package of Charmin. He was giddy. He squeezed the package and in very broken English said, "Please to squeeze the Charmin, mister

Whippy." It was the best his mind could remember from the days of his youth under the Shah when American products were still advertised on Iranian TV. He was like a young kid at his own birthday party.

Sherazi was grateful and he showed it. The usual 45 minute processing timeline only took him about 25 minutes. He returned to Arsadian with the standard paperwork. The driver was smoking a cigarette in his cab and listening to a CD of Armenian singer Arsen Grigoryan. Arsadian quickly turned down his system. "Drive safely, my friend," said the officer as he handed the clipboard up to Arsadian. The admonishment had particular import in Iran, where the death rate per mile driven was about 20 times greater than in the United States or Europe – a reflection of the national obsession with ignoring traffic laws and signals.

Among the paperwork delivered to the Armenian by Sherazi was the Green Jawaz, the official form under Iranian law that proved that all required customs duties had been paid by the importer, and the CMR, the international consignment note that needed to be kept by Arsadian while he had a loaded truck inside Iran. With these documents, Arsadian was free to travel the roads of Iran.

"Thank you."

"Khuda hafiz. I will see you soon. Be careful on the roads." The guard turned away from the truck, unaware of its hidden cargo and the importance of that cargo to the future of his country.

Arsadian started his eight cylinder diesel engine. He reached over to his CD/satellite radio/navigation system and, using the middle three fingers on his right hand, simultaneously pushed the "INFO", "CD" and "AUX" buttons along the bottom of the unit. On the unit's display, a red circle appeared in the lower left corner. He then pressed the "NAVI" and "MAP" buttons simultaneously. The red circle turned green. After 5 seconds, the circle turned off. For the next several minutes the truck's satellite GPS antenna broadcast a simple three digit code along with the GPS coordinates of the vehicle.

The signal was picked-up by Iridium 91, a commercial satellite in low earth polar orbit and one of 66 operating in the Iridium constellation. The satellite interpreted the truck's unique identifier code and routed a new signal to the Iridium satellite in orbit approximately 30 degrees to the east of Iridium 91. This satellite, in turn, routed the signal to the Iridium ground station in Beijing, which processed the signal and sent it via the Internet to Iridium's Satellite Network Operations Center in Landsdowne, Virginia. After passing through the system's commercial servers, the signal was routed via the internet to the servers of Fleet Management Solutions in California. Their servers quickly recognized the customer and forwarded the information to the servers of Yerevan Freight Forwarding, the company set up by Hamak Arsadian for his trucking operations – a company with only himself, his wife and his brother as employees. The company servers were maintained by an outsourced IT firm in Indonesia. As the information hit their servers, a small bit of software code recently inserted recognized the customer and forwarded the information to a server in the Netherlands, which published the information to a non-descript website.

In the Olympus bunker, a young Israeli soldier clapped his hands as he watched the progress of a tractor-trailer rig that was just leaving the Nordouz Customs Center. Next to the dot on the map which moved as information was updated via the Iridium GPS network, a pop up balloon contained a short message: "321". This was the simple code that meant that Arsadian had passed through customs and not been compromised. The soldier picked up the phone next to his screen and dialed Amit Margolis.

"Yes," said Amit curtly. The stress of what was being initiated was building very rapidly.

"The driver has cleared and is on his way to Point Kabob."

"Thank you." Amit hung up the phone and turned to General David Schechter. "We are green light. God be with us."

"Stay calm, Amit," responded the veteran of multiple military operations. "We are still a long way from the point of no return. But, yes, God be with us." The general's desk was next to Amit's. It was an arrangement that the experienced officer insisted on. He wanted all information freely shared between the senior decision makers of this operation. He picked up the phone and issued the command to execute the mission of Task Force Camel. On his computer, the date said Thursday, October 3.

36 – Task Force Camel

Almost three hours later a U.S. Air Force C-37A sat at the southeast end of runway 33 right at Tel Nof Air Force Base just south of Tel Aviv. The noon heat shimmered the horizon as the pilot began his take off roll. On board, in addition to the pilot and co-pilot, was a 12 member team of Sayeret Matkal, the elite special forces of the IDF. Also on board was a CIA agent whose job was to get this unit, referred to as Task Force Camel, on its way to completing its assigned mission, the details of which were kept from him.

The air force version of the Gulfstream 550 banked left and climbed rapidly as it headed west over the Mediterranean Sea. After flying 35 miles the plane started to turn left and completed a slow 180 degree turn. The plane finally leveled its wings as it headed back to the east, first over Israel, then over Jordan and finally over Saudi Arabia.

As the aircraft flew to the east at a true ground speed of over 580 miles per hour, it leveled out at 36,100 feet. The team of Israeli commandos sat in silence. A couple of men who had better English skills were flipping through various magazines that were on board, including Time and The Economist. This Gulfstream usually ferried senior American officers around the globe and was outfitted in a way that would leave any Fortune 100 executive happy. To pass the time, several men picked up newspapers on board, even though they could not read English, hoping that the photographs would be sufficient to convey the stories. No one had been allowed to bring anything connected to Israel other than what was inside their duffle bag. Experience had taught the men to take full advantage of the restroom on the plane. It would be the last functioning toilet they would encounter for some time. The CIA agent acted as flight attendant and passed water bottles and small snack packs of peanuts and Oreo cookies out to the men.

Two hours and twenty-eight minutes after takeoff, the Gulfstream touched down to the northwest on runway 30 right at Ali Al Salem Air Base, just to the west of Kuwait City. The plane decelerated gradually and turned right about two-thirds of the way down the long runway onto the Papa loop taxiway. The pilot was happy to see that no Blackhawk helicopters were parked nearby as the plane veered 45 degrees to the left and taxied almost one quarter mile to a section of tarmac that was larger than a soccer pitch. The plane came to a stop on the southern end of the tarmac. On the northern end sat a MH-47G Chinook twin-engine helicopter of the 160th Special Operations Aviation Regiment of the U.S. Army, known throughout the U.S. military as the Night Stalkers.

The 12 Israeli soldiers walked down the Gulfstream's short staircase and onto the tarmac as the sun was accelerating its descent to the west. They all wore standard U.S. Army combat uniforms in digital universal camouflage pattern complete with the insignia of the US 10th Mountain Division, topped off with the standard patrol cap. Each man carried an olive drab

Army duffle bag as he walked quickly and silently to the back of the Chinook helicopter and up the ramp into the sunlit shade of the helicopter interior.

The five man crew of the helicopter were all veterans. They averaged over five years of experience at inserting American SEALs, Rangers and Green Beret operators throughout the various countries of the Middle East, working closely with the "snake eaters" who risked their lives in secret missions as the absolute tip of the spear of American military power. None of the three crew members in the cabin recognized any of the men on this team. When they were told in their mission briefing earlier that afternoon that they were not to talk to anyone in this team other than their CIA handler, they knew this mission would be different. When they found out that the insertion was north of Halabja and only a few miles from the Iranian border, pulses quickened among an elite group of men renowned for their cool. The briefing officer, reading the minds of the men in front of him, had admonished them not to speculate and to forget about this mission once they got back to base.

The CIA operator was the last man on board. He stopped next to the crew chief. "Up ramp." The aft ramp of the helicopter was quickly closed.

The chief leaned into the CIA agent. "They are fast roping in, right?"

"Yes."

"They know what they are doing on that? Know the signals, right?"

"They know what they are doing."

"Just want to be sure." The crew chief looked at his payload for this mission. They were all young and in top physical condition. But what caught his eye is that they all had dark complexions, black hair and dark eyes. If not for the American uniforms, he thought, they looked just like the "Hajis" that he had to shoot at from time to time with his M240D machine gun. He was accustomed to the overwhelmingly northern European background of the men who make up America's Special Forces. He had no facts, but was sure of one thing: These men were not Americans.

The CIA agent offered his hand to the crew chief, who shook it firmly. "They will be fine. It's a standard insertion."

As the Israeli team found their spots, half the team on each side of the long cabin, men placed their duffle bags on the canvas bench seats. Captain Yoni Ben Zeev maintained his silence. He issued his command by lifting his right index finger straight upward and rotating it in the air. Each man removed his American uniform and placed it in a pile near the front of the helicopter. From inside their duffel bags, each pulled out a new uniform, the 3-color desert tan camouflage of the Iranian paramilitary border guards, a standard-issue Iranian winter coat, an AK-47 assault rifle, a holstered and suppressed SIG Sauer P226 9-millimeter pistol, a back pack and a pair of thin leather gloves. The men were under strict orders not to talk – there was to be nothing said or shown that would confirm the Israeli identity of the team.

At that moment, exactly 368 miles to the north at Joint Base Balad, an air base just north of Baghdad, an American major picked up a telephone. The Air Force officer was one of the small number of U.S. military personnel left in Iraq for advisory, training and liaison purposes. He called a senior Iraqi Air Force counterpart located in a building about 80 meters away. The two men knew each other well, the American officer being on his fourth tour in Iraq. They had taught each other much about the other's culture.

Colonel Walid picked up the phone. "Hello." The word was in excellent English and the greeting itself demonstrated the level of western influence on the Iraqi colonel.

"Hello, Mohammed," replied the American officer. "How is your family?"

"Healthy, Inshallah. How have you been? We have not talked in a few days. It is getting too slow." The Iraqi officer's comments reflected the lack of any functioning Iraqi Air Force more than the reality of life for Iraqis on the heels of the withdrawal of all American combat forces.

"You are always so eager, Mohammed." The major paused for a moment to gather his thoughts. "We have an issue. We have a UAV that crashed about forty klicks north of Halabja. We are sending a flight of helicopters north out of Kuwait to retrieve it. They will need in-flight refueling. The refueling will take place at Fueler three five." The grid reference by the major was for a patch of desert west of Baiji, Iraq that was an oft used spot for refueling operations.

"No problem, Mike. As always, we appreciate the communication. When will they be airborne?"

"Within the next hour."

"How many aircraft?"

"Three choppers and a single KC-130. CAP will be airborne over Turkey since they are going all the way to Kurd land." U.S. Air Force policy was to maintain a combat air patrol, or CAP, whenever American military aircraft were flying over potentially dangerous airspace. Halabja was adjacent to the Iranian border and no American officer wanted to be responsible for not having been prepared if American helicopters were suddenly set upon by Iranian warplanes.

"Okay I will send out your SSR codes in a few minutes along with a network flash update. Please route them west direct to Ralti, turning north direct to Tuben." Colonel Walid was directing the mission via VOR/DME navigational beacons that would take them west over the sparsely inhabited portions of Iraq. He wanted to bypass Baghdad airspace and he knew from experience this was the preferred route for the U.S. military. "I believe that takes them close to Fueler three five for refueling. Then they can turn east and continue VFR operations. Have them … um … hold on." The Iraqi officer checked his daily flight manual. "Have them squawk using mode three-a. They are assigned call sign 'Union Hotel four-five Tango'. Your tanker will be 'Union Kilo four-five'. Set hard ceiling at flight level one two zero for commercial traffic."

The American wrote the important information on his notepad and then repeated it back to the Iraqi officer for confirmation. "Thank you. Let's have tea tomorrow if you have some time." He would have the critical data typed into his computer and sent by email to American military air traffic control within a minute.

"Yes, Mike. I would enjoy to catch up with you."

Several minutes later an email arrived from the Iraqi colonel that provided the clearance code of "7011" to be squawked by all four aircraft and the fighter planes flying CAP, indicating to Iraqi air controllers that this was an authorized American military flight under visual flight rules. For the U.S. Air Force, which had spent two decades doing whatever it wanted to do over Iraq, the new clearance rules and process seemed humiliating. But the major told himself this was the price of peace and progress.

37 – Family History

Hamak Arsadian yawned as he slowed his truck to turn right from the four lanes of Iran Road 21 onto the two lanes of Iran Road 15. He used his turn signal – a rare courtesy in Iran. As he slowed he inched toward the left lane to maximize the amount of arc available to the big rig. Unknowingly, he caused the driver in the sedan next to him to get nervous and slow as well. For the driver of the Toyota pickup truck driving in the left lane at over 120 kph and coming up rapidly on the sedan, this inconvenience was not acceptable. The young driver accelerated and turned his wheel to steer his pickup through the right hand lane and onto the asphalt shoulder of the road. Arsadian was just starting to turn his wheel hard to the right as the pickup truck shot past him on the right hand shoulder at close to 130 kph.

"Fucking rabiz," blurted out Arsadian as his mind raced to interpret just how close he had come to a serious accident, using the Armenian slang word roughly equivalent to "redneck." The pickup truck passed by so fast that Arsadian was 20 feet further into his turn before he realized that his foot was no longer on the gas pedal. He pressed back down on the pedal to complete the turn and begin the last stretch of his journey to the rendezvous point. His heart was now racing and his face turned red the way it always did when anger overcame his ability to control it. Being tired now seemed a distant feeling. He took some deep breaths to calm himself, trying to think about anything other than how angry he was at that moment. The face of his mother popped into his mind, as it often did in times of stress.

She had died 27 years earlier when he was 15, and he was no longer sure if his image of her was from real memories or just a projection of one of the many photographs of her he kept in his possession at all times. But he knew for certain that her death changed everything about his life and his view of the world. The breast cancer that metastasized to her vital organs had made him hate at first. Hatred of God for taking his mother. Hatred of the medical profession in Armenia that he viewed as nothing better than primitive witch doctors. Hatred of his father for allowing this to happen, including yelling at his father one night for not taking the entire family to the U.S. where, the young Hamak was certain, his mother would be cured.

When his mother returned from her last visit to the clinic in Yerevan with a single bottle of pain killers, the teenage boy knew from his father's reaction that his mother was home to die in her own bed. Hamak stayed home from school for two weeks to take care of his mother as a growing tumor relentlessly attacked her liver. His father had to continue to work each day delivering goods by truck to the various businesses of Yerevan, giving up his lucrative Iranian excursions in order to be home every night for his wife. The family, always living day to day in the best of times, was struggling to pay bills resulting from his mother's illness – despite ostensibly free medical care as a Republic of the Soviet Union. Like all families, the Arsadians had not planned or budgeted for the costs of unexpected death. Doctors and pharmacists who demanded bribes for real drugs. Bed pans and basic supplies to care for the bedridden. The cost of a burial plot and headstone – burial being the only option available under the beliefs of the Armenian Church. The bills mounted. But regardless of the growing debt, every night his father came home and took over the duties of caring for a woman facing death at the age of only 39.

The experience made Hamak grow into a man, the carefree days of youth now extinguished completely, ground into the dust of the harsh realities of life and death. But the moment that his understanding of the world changed was the day his mother summoned her fading reserves of energy to talk to her first born child. His father was working and his younger brother was in school. It was a few minutes after 9 in the morning on the second Friday after his mother's return from the clinic. "What can I get you, mother?" asked the teen as he approached the bed.

"Sit, my son." Her words were slow and labored. Hamak complied and sat down in an old wooden chair his grandfather had made. The sun's rays pierced the stale air of the small bedroom, illuminating myriad dust particles floating randomly about the room. The woman reached out with her left hand and Hamak placed his palm underneath hers, careful not to hurt the woman who had always been the pillar of strength in the family but was now as fragile as crystal. "You must do something for me."

"Of course, mother. What do you need?"

"Swear to me that what I tell you now you will keep secret. Swear on my soul."

"What? Why?" Hamak's reaction was typical for a teenager, whether in Yerevan or Atlanta.

"Just swear to me."

"Okay. I swear that I will keep what you say secret."

"On my soul. Swear on my soul."

"Mother?" The teen was confused and felt blind-sided. The mother gathered enough strength to give him "the look" that told her son that he was on his last chance to choose wisely.

"Okay, okay. I swear on your soul."

The mother managed a faint smile. "You must go and fetch a man and bring him here."

"Why?"

"Just listen. He lives close by. Go to the corner here," she raised her right arm to point in the correct direction, "and walk to Losifian Street. On that corner is a house with red awnings." The mother noticed her son's eyes react. "You know it?"

"Yes. But who do I ask for and why?" The boy had spent his whole life in this neighborhood. He knew every building and home for blocks in any direction.

The mother winced in pain. She had grown used to the constant dull aching in her abdomen, but occasional sharp throbbing pain hit her. She willed herself for the next few words. "Ask for Rabbi Rothstein."

"Rabbi? A Jew? Why?"

The mother looked her son in his eyes. "Because, Hamak, I am a Jew."

"What? That is crazy. We are Christians." The boy's voice was raised.

"Yes, son. Your father is Christian and you are baptized. But I was born a Jew and you were born a Jew, as was your brother."

Hamak let go of his mother's hand and stood up. "You are crazy in your head. It is the drugs." He began to pace the room. The Jewish community in Yerevan in the middle of the 1980s was very small, only about a thousand or so. Anti-Semitism existed but the country had always been fairly tolerant, especially when compared to the other Republics of the Soviet Union. Still, Hamak had friends who told him stories of Jews with devil horns hidden under their hats or scarves.

"Your father made me promise to never tell you this. But it is true and it is your right to know. Have you never wondered why we never see or discuss my family?" She struggled to reach for a cup of tea close to the bed. She was not thirsty, but she knew that her son would return to her side.

Hamak rushed over to pick up the cup for her as he thought about her last question. "Here." He handed her the cup. His voice was tender again.

"Thank you." She took the cup. "Now listen to me. Go and fetch Rabbi Rothstein. Tell him you are my son. He will come. He will tell you that I am not crazy. But do not tell your father. He will be angry."

Hamak just stood there looking at his mother. The weight of her pending death hung on him, threatening to crush his very soul. But now that weight seemed to double. The only thing worse, he thought, was if she had revealed that Rabbi Rothstein was his real father. The thought made him chuckle involuntarily.

"This is funny?" asked his mother.

"No, Mother. It's just that …" He took his mother's hand again. "It's just I am confused. I don't understand this."

"I know. This is not easy. When your brother is older, you will need to tell him. But you must wait. Now that you know the truth, you are free to decide the path you take in life. Just do not hurt your father. Now please go."

The teenager did go to find the middle-aged rabbi, who came to the small house without hesitating, the pair speaking no words as they walked back. Rabbi Rothstein had not seen Hamak's mother in many years, but he cried with her and comforted her as they prayed the Vidui. Hamak stood in disbelief as the rabbi of Sheik Mordecai Synagogue, the only synagogue in Yerevan, and his mother prayed in a language the teenager had never heard spoken before that moment. In that instant, he knew that every word his mother told him was the truth and he knew this truth would change his pathway in life.

His mother died the next day and received a funeral and burial under the auspices of the Armenian Apostolic Church. Hamak watched the priest place an icon of Saint Gregory into the dead hands of his mother as her body lay in an open coffin. As he watched, Hamak decided that he must know more about what it means to be Jewish. He kept his word to his mother and never said a word to his father, but his curiosity grew into obsession. He would look for books on

Judaism only to realize that the communist regime that controlled his country had long since cleansed the libraries of Jewish literature or culture.

His obsession grew as his thirst for knowledge went unsatisfied. Finally, almost three years after his mother's death, as the Soviet Union was entering its final death throes, he turned to the only source he could find. On a dark winter evening he knocked on the door of the home of Rabbi Solomon Rothstein. The rabbi recognized him and remembered every moment of the morning visit to his mother's deathbed three years earlier. Hamak spent two hours with the rabbi that night, consuming knowledge as fast as the rabbi and his wife could speak. That was the start of a growing friendship defined by unannounced visits from the young Armenian every few months or so.

That same year Hamak entered Yerevan Polytechnic Institute as an electrical engineering major. The cost of attendance was free, but he found himself in almost nightly arguments with his father, who wanted him to work as a truck driver and contribute money to the family. The economy was collapsing as it was throughout the old Soviet empire. His father was drinking and each day the prospects for earning money seemed to dim. Hamak's younger brother, then 14-years-old, increasingly turned to Hamak for emotional support. During the day Hamak was at school where he was free and thrived in the intellectual environment that was exploding as the heavy hand of the Soviet state was crumbling. On campus, various groups openly debated concepts like Democracy, private property ownership and free speech. Revolution was occurring and Hamak was in the middle of it all.

But every night, he would return to the realities of family life, reminding him always of the darkness and despair of the final weeks of his mother's life. Father's demands were intensifying, the stress of his financial situation aging him in front of his sons. Hamak finally agreed to drive a truck on weekends and some nights to help make money. He started in late October of his first year in University. This certainly helped with finances, stopping the worst of the bleeding, but the family was treading water at best. Hamak told his father that they would be okay in the end. Everything was in disarray in Armenia, but as far as Hamak could tell they were still in a better position than most. His father seemed to gain no solace from this argument. At least, Hamak told himself, he enjoyed driving a small straight truck around the streets of the city. From the start, he made his reputation by always being on time. At the tail end of seven decades of communist rule, showing up on time was a trait that made you famous.

In February, as the latest winter snowfall melted into a black mess, Hamak was studying at home for a midterm exam in calculus the following day. His father came home late that night. He had been drinking with his friends, arguing over the relative merits of communism, European socialism or American capitalism. He was already angry as he walked in the door. Seeing Hamak home instead of out earning money set him off and the pair spent the next five minutes yelling at each other before the father headed into his small bedroom, slamming the door behind him. Hamak drank a beer to calm himself before returning to his books. He had to be ready for his test at 11 the next morning. He finally went to the room he shared with his brother at three in the morning to get a few hours of sleep. When he awoke, it was 8:32. Hamak headed for the home's single bathroom. As he passed his father's bedroom it struck him that the door was still closed. His father never left the door closed and should have been long gone.

Hamak, standing in his underwear, knocked on the door. No response. He knocked again. "Father?" Nothing. He opened the door. During the night his father had died of a heart attack. Hamak and his younger brother were now alone and Hamak was now the head of the family. He dropped out of University that week and began his full-time career as a truck driver, always being sure to guard his reputation for being on time.

As the years passed by, Hamak brought his brother into the business, which grew enough to support them both – first alone and then later as they each married and began families of their own. When his little brother turned 21, Hamak revealed the family secret. But unlike Hamak, the brother never became curious or obsessed. As he told Hamak at the time, "I am Christian. I will stay a Christian."

For his part, Hamak had continued to learn about his secret faith. He visited his friend Rabbi Rothstein, always at night and always unannounced, until the night of September 11, 2001, when he came home to find his wife watching the news, something she never did. The attacks on New York and the Pentagon affected him in a way he could not anticipate. Living in a Christian country surrounded by Islam – and identifying more and more with his Jewish identity – Hamak had watched the rise of fundamental Islam with concern like most Armenians. His business had grown by developing connections in Iran and applying his reputation to the growing trade flowing through Yerevan. He found the Persians to be friendly and accepting, at least as long as they believed him to be a Christian. But when he made his occasional trips into Tehran he ran into the other side of Iran, the zealots who believed that everyone must convert to Islam and lead a pious Muslim life. These Persians scared him but he had to make a living and Iran was the key to his living. He would keep his mind focused on his job and let the rest of the world worry about radical Islam.

But for the second time in his life, he could feel his path changing as he watched the video of the World Trade Center towers collapsing. He knew immediately that radical Islamic terrorists were to blame, even if he had not previously heard of Osama bin Laden. And he knew immediately that he could not keep his head buried in his work as the world collapsed around him. He thought endlessly about the Jews of Europe during the 1930s who did nothing as the dark clouds of death enveloped them. He was a Jew. He had never called himself that prior to that day, but as the footage was repeated over and over, he screamed it to himself. *I am a Jew.*

The next evening he knocked one more time on the door of his rabbi, his mentor. What he told Solomon Rothstein that night was simple. He wanted to fight the terrorists. He wanted to fight for Israel. He was well placed to help his people. Rothstein told him to visit again in a week. A week later Rothstein told him to come back the night of October 3. When Hamak showed up that night, his rabbi simply gave him a note with the name and address of a coffee bistro downtown. Rothstein said simply, "Be there by nine tonight. There are booths in the back. Sit in one of those. Shalom." Rothstein smiled and shook the hand of the man he had come to love as a son.

Two hours later, Hamak's new life as an agent for Israel began when a man sat down across from him in the booth and introduced himself as a businessman in need of a logistics provider. This was not what the Armenian was expecting, but he found himself being sized up by a man wearing a nice business suit. For half an hour the man quizzed him about his business and his travels through Iran. He asked him about his contacts in the Persian nation and whether the Armenian could deliver "sensitive" cargo to the Iranian military. Hamak told him that he had only done business with civilian businessmen in Iran and had no contacts in the military other than the border guards and customs officers he had come to know over the years. The man asked Hamak what he thought of Iranians. Hamak was honest. Finally the man asked Hamak about his mother. What was her name? When Hamak responded, the man said "No, I want to know her maiden name." Hamak gave the man what he wanted. The man stood. "Are you in your office tomorrow morning?" Hamak nodded. "Good. I will visit. I want to see your operation." Hamak did not stand up, but he reached across the table top to shake the man's hand.

By the following morning Mossad agents in Tel Aviv had researched the family background of Hamak Arsadian. They had the history as supplied by Solomon Rothstein, but they wanted to verify the history of both Hamak's mother and his father. When the Mossad agent showed up at the Armenian's small office by Zvartnots International Airport, he had the green light from Tel Aviv to formally recruit Hamak Arsadian into the service of Mossad. For the next five years Arsadian provided routine intelligence to Mossad about his travels throughout Iran. Who he met. Where he went. What he delivered. It was very routine and, after the first few months, very boring. Arsadian wondered what the point was. He could not imagine that there was any value to the mundane information he provided.

But excitement finally came. He received a real mission in March of 2007. For the first time he was actually given a shipment from his Mossad contact. It came in from Pakistan, a shipment of computer parts – chips and circuit boards – that needed to be delivered to a company called Shahid Hemat Industrial Group. The delivery warehouse was inside a military facility known as Parchin, located just to the south and east of Tehran. The delivery was routine, but Hamak was smart enough to put the pieces of the puzzle together in his mind. He wasn't sure what the parts he delivered were for, but he was sure that he had just done something important for Israel. The rush of excitement he felt on this trip was addictive. He wanted more.

More came only six months later. For the first time his Mossad handler asked him to rendezvous with a specific person as he passed through Tabriz. The role he played was simple. He was told to be sure he stopped for fuel at the Behran Petrol Station on Road 32 just outside and to the west of Tabriz. He was to be there at one in the afternoon on the day he entered Iran from Armenia. Arsadian knew this station well. He always planned his travels so that he could stop there on the way into or out of Iran. The best part of travelling to the Islamic Republic was taking advantage of the subsidized cost of diesel fuel. Hamak never filled his tanks in Armenia.

On this trip he needed to make contact in the food store with a man named Hassan. When Hamak walked in, Hassan looked exactly as described and the two men exchanged simple and innocuous code phrases about driving conditions in the city that day. Hassan then went to the restroom and left. Hamak purchased some items and went to the restroom before going back outside to his truck. While in the restroom, which had only a single toilet, he lifted the lid on the toilet tank as he was instructed. Taped to the underside of the lid was a small package wrapped in plastic. Hamak removed the package and placed it in the small of his back, the bottom edge tucked under his waist band and the entire package underneath his shirt, further obscured by his windbreaker.

It was not until he was back on the road that Arsadian realized that, unlike the simple retelling of his travels that he had been providing the Mossad for years, he was now involved in real espionage. This was the type of activity that got men arrested and tortured in Iran. But what shocked the Armenian truck driver was the realization that thinking about what he was doing made his adrenaline surge. He was excited, not frightened or nervous. For the first time he felt like he was a warrior in the struggle against a regime that threatened Israel at every turn. He was contributing and the contribution was real and tangible. He loved it.

His delivery that day was a small load in Tabriz itself. He unloaded by 3 p.m. and was at his office in Yerevan by midnight, where a Mossad-supplied and installed safe was the final repository of the real payload on this trip. Sometime the next day his Mossad handler would stop by the office and use his own key to enter, open the safe and retrieve the contents before driving the short distance to the airport for a flight out of Yerevan to Istanbul, where the package would be delivered safely to the Israeli Embassy. Arsadian never opened the package and never knew its contents, but he had just spirited the latest construction plans for the underground Fordow Enrichment site, Complex I and II, out of Iran.

To his Mossad handler and his handler's superiors in Tel Aviv, Hamak was proving himself a real asset. He could handle the situations that made many people panic. When in 2011 Amit Margolis devised a way to get a small elite team of Israeli commandos to the Dehloran Radar Site, the men at Mossad who knew about Hamak Arsadian knew that he was the right asset for the job. For Hamak, he recognized that this new mission, when he first learned about it in early 2013, was something different, something hugely important. His payment was the tractor-trailer rig that he now piloted south down Iran Road 15. He already had title to both the tractor and the trailer in the name of his company with no liens attached. It was a nice rig, one of the nicest to be found in this region of the world. If Hamak made it home alive, the rig was his to keep, complete with its secrets.

But Hamak was a bright man who had become a news junkie as he aged. He had always been good at putting the pieces together. He guessed that this mission was the prelude to an Israeli assault on the Iranian nuclear program. He hoped he was right but knew better than to ask his handler even the most basic questions. The unstated rules were clear: Hamak was told only what he needed to know and any prying beyond that was both unprofessional and potentially dangerous to his health. When Yoni Ben Zeev was introduced to him in Yerevan several months earlier using the name Younis Mohammed, Arsadian was convinced that his suspicions about the importance of this mission were correct. The moment he laid eyes on Ben Zeev, he knew the young man in front of him was a special forces operator. Ben Zeev was straight out of central casting, a man who looked like he could be dropped into the middle of the Himalayas with nothing but a pair of shorts on and still find his way back to civilization no worse for wear.

So the journey that brought Hamak Arsadian to this day on a rural road in Iran began when he was 15 years old. It had been a journey of discovery and self-fulfillment for the Armenian. Now he prayed that he would live to someday tell his grandchildren about his exploits. But at this moment he still had 96 miles of driving ahead of him from the turn off of Road 21 to reach Point Kabob. The easy and relatively flat driving of the prior few hours was giving way gradually to the Zagros Mountain range. Soon he would be climbing up steep switchbacks, his tractor struggling in its battle against gravity, the length of his rig demanding every available inch of pavement – and more. Sporadic guardrails and crumbling road shoulders would test his mettle and his skills. As he thought about the coming drive, Hamak realized the wisdom of the load he carried that someone in the Mossad had dreamed up. The 449 remaining cartons of Charmin in his trailer weighed less than his typical load and the new MAN tractor he was driving had 175 more horsepower than his prior tractor. He was enjoying the combination. This tractor-trailer rig performed better loaded than his old one when it was empty.

At 7:58 p.m., Arsadian turned right around a sharp mountain corner. The drive had been uneventful since his near miss with the pickup truck. The nighttime weather was beautiful and the temperature was falling rapidly. He was only a mile from the Iranian Kurdish village of Dezli. That meant he was only a few miles from Point Kabob where he could pull over and get some sleep as he waited for Ben Zeev and his team to arrive.

Suddenly the Armenian slammed his foot on the brake pedal, engaging the engine braking system and forcing highly pressurized air into the push rods that rotated S-cams on both front wheels as well as the wheels on the single tractor axle and three trailer axles. In turn, each S-cam forced its mated brake pads against their braking drums, turning kinetic energy into heat. The brake management system of the MAN GTX took over to coordinate all of the numerous braking points, including implementing the anti-lock system for the inside wheels of the trailer brakes. The truck was going uphill at only 21 kph, but the small sedan in front of him was at a dead stop and Hamak had only a short distance to bring his rig to a full stop. He made it with about a meter to spare, much to the relief of the family sitting in the sedan.

Hamak looked down the road as is straightened out in front of him. There was a line of about a dozen cars all stopped. A single straight truck broke the silhouette of the cars in the line. The Armenian's eyes followed the line, expecting to see an accident at the front. What he saw made his pulse quicken. An Iranian military truck was placed perpendicular to the road, ensuring that no vehicle passed through. Several soldiers were mulling around the truck, each of them fondling his G3 assault rifle. As the air brakes released their pressure, loudly announcing the arrival of the big tractor-trailer rig, Arsadian saw a soldier walking on the road past each of the vehicles, clearly heading to the latest traveler to hit this roadblock. As the man grew larger, Hamak was not certain about his uniform. He was wearing a heavy dark olive pea coat. Once the soldier approached the tractor door, Arsadian recognized the patch of the Army of the Guardians of the Iranian Revolution, more generally known as the Iranian Revolutionary Guard or IRG for short, on the soldier's dark olive patrol cap. Arsadian's Mossad handler had given him a book to study the various uniforms of the Iranian military and police branches. The IRG emblem, a raised forearm clutching a stylized AK-47, was easy to spot. The driver could not tell the man's rank, but his bearing suggested he was an officer.

He lowered his window and smiled. The cold air hit the Armenian hard. He had climbed several thousand feet since he last exposed himself to the outside air and had paid no attention to the thermostat on his dashboard. He looked down quickly to see how cold it was. The readout said "39°F/4°C." His breath was instantly visible as condensation. The clear skies had come with the first cold front of the fall.

"As-salamu alayka." This officer was very different from the customs agent earlier in the day. He was young and in good shape. Hamak guessed his age to be only 24 or 25. There was an intensity in his eyes that immediately put the Armenian on notice: This was not a courtesy call.

"Wa' alayka s-salam. Has there been an accident?"

"No." The young officer was curt. He was not used to having questions asked of him by civilians. The tone of his answer was intended to make that fact clear to Arsadian, who absorbed the message. "You are not Persian." It was a statement, not a question.

"Armenian."

"You are Christian?"

"Yes." This question did not concern Arsadian. Most Iranians respected Christians as fellow believers in the one true God. Still, thought the driver, it was not the same as if he were Muslim and the man he was talking to now was a zealot – the patch on his cap proved that much.

"What are you doing here?"

"I am delivering my load to Ahvaz."

"Delivering what?"

"A shipment of toilet paper."

The IRG officer hesitated, not knowing how to respond to that information. "Let me see your papers."

Arsadian passed the same clipboard to this officer that he had passed to his friend Abdul Hamid, the customs officer in Nordouz, about nine hours earlier – only this time there was no money strategically placed for quick retrieval. The officer looked at the first two items and turned away to walk back to his comrades hanging around the military truck at the front of the line. The Armenian's passport was attached to the clipboard and this action by the IRG officer violated the first rule of international travel: Never let your passport out of your sight. Arsadian had no options, however. The power at this moment was completely on one side of the equation.

Almost 25 minutes had passed when Hamak noticed motion at the front of the line. A dark sedan had pulled up to the military truck and the Armenian estimated that almost twenty men were hanging around the IRG truck. He was struck by the realization that he had not noticed other than a handful of men before that instant. Arsadian was nervous for the first time since becoming a Mossad spy. He tried to tell himself that he was just one of many stuck in this line. But the more he thought about it, the more he realized just how much he stood out in this setting

– an Armenian Christian driving a large tractor-trailer rig through the mountains of eastern Iran just a couple of miles from the Iraqi border. It was not logical. With the exception of the other truck in the line, everyone else looked like normal Iranian civilians simply in the wrong place at the wrong time. He then noticed the dark sedan driving down the road toward him. A half dozen men from the IRG truck were walking in his direction as well. He felt his chest tighten.

The dark sedan stopped in the road beside his truck. An older officer of the IRG stepped out of the back door and paused for a moment to look at the tractor-trailer unit in front of him. Arsadian noticed that this man was holding the clipboard. Obviously he was superior to the first officer and appeared to be the man in charge. The man stood there waiting for the six soldiers to arrive on foot. As they did, the senior officer approached the driver door of the truck. "Mister Arsadian," he said hesitantly. "Did I pronounce your name correctly?" The Armenian nodded his head. "I am Captain Javed Samadi. Please step out of your truck."

Arsadian opened the door and stepped out of his cab, grabbing the down jacket that he kept draped over the passenger seat. He kept his engine running as did the straight truck driver up ahead of him. In this cold a diesel engine could be very hard to start if left off for too long. He was scared that his nervousness would show. The first thing he noticed as his feet hit the pavement was that the captain, at six feet tall, seemed to tower over him. The Armenian was four inches shorter, but the gap seemed to him to be at least a foot – the height difference magnified by the fact that the driver was on the downhill side of the pair. The captain extended the clipboard to Hamak. Inside the Armenian breathed a sigh of relief, interpreting the returned paperwork as a positive sign, the first one since he had stopped on this spot. Nevertheless, his right hand shook as he reached for the clipboard. The IRG captain noticed. "Why are you taking toilet paper to Ahvaz?"

"This is how I make my living. Iranian companies hire me to deliver goods. Today it is toilet paper. Next week it is machine parts. Next month it is computers. I never know until I am hired."

"Why do you take this route?"

Arsadian had practiced his response to this question. "Because this route to Ahvaz is faster than driving on twenty-one through Sanandaj. If I had driven that way I would have hit rush hour traffic. Either way I drive through the same mountains. No way for me to avoid that. I have been driving through Iran for many years."

"Do you know any Kurds in this area?"

"No. None."

"Do you have friends in any of the villages along your route?"

"No. I just drive and deliver my goods so I can get home to my family in Yerevan as I have done for over twenty years."

"I think maybe you are sympathetic to Kurdish rebels, no?"

"No, not at all. Kurds are no friends to Armenians."

The tall captain stood quietly in the dark night air studying the older truck driver. He wore no winter jacket, just his standard field tunic. The lights of his sedan lit up the left side of the truck. "We will inspect your cargo." Again, it was a statement, not a request. Arsadian was quickly learning to detest the IRG. This was the first time in his two decades that he had interacted with any of them. "Open your doors."

"At your service," replied Arsadian. The officer caught a hint of sarcasm in the driver's response even though Hamak was consciously trying to avoid that. The driver went to the rear and opened his trailer doors as the driver of the captain's sedan drove past the truck, executed a three point turn in the middle of the curved roadway and came back up the road behind the truck, shining his lights into the now open trailer.

The captain signaled his men and they began removing cartons of Charmin toilet paper onto the road. It seemed the IRG officer had a hunch and was determined to follow it. The soldiers unloaded the first couple of rows of cartons which gave them about six feet of trailer floor to work with. The IRG officer stood next to the Armenian driver, alternately watching him and his men. Finally he broke the tension. "You appear nervous."

Arsadian turned to the Iranian. "This is my livelihood, Captain Samadi. This shipment is my responsibility. I have never failed to deliver." His nervousness was rapidly being replaced by anger. He decided to play offense. "Why is this roadblock here? Why do you treat me this way?"

The captain did not respond. He next issued orders to his men, telling them to pull out a single column along the side until they reached the wall at the front of the trailer. His men complied with their orders, carefully pulling out cartons along the right hand sidewall. The captain was waiting for the void that his gut told him would turn up in the trailer.

When his men reached the front wall of the trailer, creating a lane that stretched from the back door 44 feet to the front wall, the captain became agitated. He walked among the now displaced cartons of Charmin stacked haphazardly on the mountain road. He grabbed several cartons and lifted them, judging the weight of each to determine if it approximated what he expected. After he returned the third carton to the ground, he ripped the carton open, pulling out its contents. Then he climbed on board the trailer, telling the few men still inside to move out of his way. He walked along the thin corridor created by the removed cartons and picked a row about a third of the way from the front. He pulled a carton from the top of the next column and yelled at his men to grab the cartons that he kept pulling out, working his way in from the corridor to the opposing sidewall. He kicked cartons on either side of this new perpendicular corridor, certain that he would find weapons or explosives hidden in the cardboard boxes. When he made it to the other side he realized that his hunch was wrong. The officer had to swallow his pride that night. He had not caught a Kurdish spy.

The IRG officer walked back out the corridor to the rear of the trailer and jumped down to the road pavement below. He barked orders to his men to repack the trailer as it was and started to walk to his sedan.

Hamak Arsadian interjected. "Is everything in order Captain?" The driver was rubbing salt in the man's wounded pride.

The captain paused. He had grown up in an upper middle class household in Tehran. He suddenly remembered the teachings of his mother and grandmother regarding Persian t'aarof, or hospitality. They would be displeased with him right now. He turned toward the driver. "My apologies. My men will return your cargo to the trailer."

Arsadian bent over and picked up the single carton that the IRG officer had opened moments before. "I understand that you are doing your job. Please take this box as an offering of respect for the job you do. I think your men will enjoy its contents." The Armenian knew that the contents would not wind up in the hands of the soldiers, but also knew that the captain would not accept the carton under any other pretense.

Samadi pondered for a moment before signaling for one of his men to carry the box to the trunk of his sedan. "For my men," he said. With those words the officer turned and was in the back of his sedan in moments. As soon as the trunk lid was shut, the sedan drove off up the mountain and past the roadblock. Arsadian had still not received an answer about why the roadblock was in place. Over the next twelve minutes the half dozen men remaining repacked the boxes into the trailer, now short two cartons from when Arsadian left Yerevan.

The soldiers left the Armenian standing behind his trailer and headed quickly back up the road, each one desperate to find some warmth. Hamak closed his trailer doors and walked 50 feet along the left side of the rig until he reached the driver side door. He began to reach for the handle when he stopped and walked another 20 feet further up the road to speak with the man who was driving the car in front of him. He learned that they had arrived about 15 minutes before Arsadian. The soldier who checked their papers told them that Kurdish rebel fighters had been operating in the area and that they would probably be able to pass in a couple of hours. The man and his family then offered water to Arsadian, but the truck driver politely refused and returned to his cabin to wait and get warm.

Arsadian pulled down the bed that stretched across the tractor cabin just behind the driver and passenger seats. He figured he might as well try to rest. The next few hours resulted in fitful periods of sleep, his eyes opening every half hour or so to check the dashboard clock that glowed red in the otherwise dark cabin. Finally he opened his eyes to see that midnight had arrived. During the prior two hours several cars had started up, only to turn around and head back down the mountain away from Dezli, each one waking him in the process. But like the straight truck driver that was waiting about 70 meters in front of him, Arsadian had no such option. He would wait out the IRG and their roadblock.

As he lay there wondering when he could proceed to Point Kabob, only a few frustrating miles further along Road 15, he noticed a blinking light on his navigation system panel. Arsadian quickly swung his legs over the edge of the bed and lowered himself into the passenger seat, from which access to the navigation system was easier. He turned the system's display panel on and pressed several buttons in combination. A menu appeared and the Armenian pressed the screen to cause a message to appear. The message said nothing, but only contained four digits. But the simple code told Arsadian what he needed to do once he was free to continue his journey.

38 - Insertion

"One hour out," shouted the chief as the formation of helicopters passed north of Baiji, Iraq and turned due east toward the drop zone. The local time was 9:36 p.m. Outside was complete darkness. The Night Stalkers were operating in their natural environment. Captain Ben Zeev pointed to two of his men, who each pulled out a device that looked like an iPad, only with a thick antenna attached and a rubber frame that was the tipoff that this device had been "ruggedized" to survive the rigors of combat. Each man powered up his unit and waited for about 30 seconds while the unit came to life. The man sitting next to the captain pushed several buttons on his screen and then handed it to his commander. The man with the other device, sitting on the opposite side of the helicopter, looked up at his commander and raised his right hand to give a fast thumbs up. He then turned his unit off.

The Israelis referred to the device as the tactical situation unit, or TSU. The TSU that was now in the hands of the Israeli captain was connected via satellite to an uplink in the Negev desert. The screen presented synthesized information being fed to Olympus from a single unmanned USAF RQ-4 Global Hawk flying at 64,000 feet above the eastern border between Iraq and Iran and a manned U.S. Rivet Joint electronic intelligence plane flying over Turkey. On the screen, the captain could see real-time infrared images of Iranian and Iraqi border guards and posts for a 20 mile radius around the drop zone. Periodic blinking lights pinpointed the approximate location of Iranian radio transmissions on frequencies used by the border guards and the military. Transmissions that were unencrypted or for which the code was easily broken on board the Rivet Joint aircraft were forwarded to Olympus, which analyzed them and decided which were relevant and important enough to send on to the device in the captain's hands. Ben Zeev could choose from his menu a chronological transcription of the communications, all presented to him in Farsi written in Arabic script.

On the Iraqi side, the image was as expected, with border guards in their static shelters scattered sporadically among the mountains about two miles inside the border. The primary drop zone was well chosen. It was in a high valley that was uninhabited and unobserved by any known border post either Iraqi or Iranian. But the initial relief was interrupted by tension as the captain looked at the Iranian side of the border. To his horror, he saw dozens of small red dots on the screen, most stationary but some moving south. All of the dots were close to the border and in the very valleys that he had planned to move through while crossing into Iran. They appeared to his experienced eye to be in ambush positions. On the screen, a light yellow star flashed in the lower left corner indicating that a message or messages were waiting for him. He pressed a button on the bottom of the device and a menu popped onto the lower left quadrant of the screen. He touched the screen and a message from Olympus opened up.

IRGC activity vicinity Dezli. Estimated company strength.

Of course, Yoni Ben Zeev thought, *tell me what I already know. I need to know why?* The captain reviewed his alternatives. His secondary drop zone was just to the north of the primary, which would route his men through the valley just north of the primary infiltration route. But on the Iran side, that valley was full of tiny red blips. During mission planning this scenario was discussed. Two more alternate drop zones had been identified, but both of them added miles of hiking for the team once inside Iran. More time on foot meant greater risk of bumping into unfriendly elements – or Kurdish goat herders. Contact with anyone other than Arsadian equaled danger and risk.

The captain had the authority to scrub the mission. *Are we compromised?* He thought about Hamak Arsadian, a man he had spent considerable time training in Yerevan. He had grown to like, respect and, most importantly, trust the Armenian. Had Arsadian been arrested? Iranian interrogators were not shy about the use of torture, especially in the case of anyone suspected of spying for Israel. Even worse, was he a double agent all along? The truck driver knew nothing about the mission other than that he was supposed to meet Ben Zeev and an undetermined group at Point Kabob sometime before the coming dawn. The driver would then continue on his route until told to pull over by the captain, at which time the Israelis would depart and go on their way.

The possibilities screamed through the head of the Israeli officer. Ben Zeev ran through the scenario that had gnawed at him for weeks. If Arsadian was compromised and the Iranians knew an Israeli team was on the way, then they could easily understand how this last minute helicopter mission to ostensibly retrieve a wayward American drone was an obvious cover for the insertion. It was common knowledge in the IDF that Iranian intelligence had deeply penetrated the Iraqi military since the Americans purged the mostly-Sunni Saddam Hussein loyalists in the aftermath of the 2003 invasion.

But the 28-year-old Israeli captain, as well as every member of his hand-picked team, also knew that this mission was perhaps the most important operation of Project Block G. If Task Force Camel failed for any reason, there was a back-up plan, but the cost to the Israeli military of having to turn to the alternative plan would be very steep. And the potential cost to Israel of failure could mean its very existence. Against that cost, Ben Zeev weighed the cost of the capture of any member of his team. Such an outcome could jeopardize all of Project Block G and the avoidance of capture under all scenarios was the first priority of the mission. This fact had resulted in a discussion with his men many months earlier in which a unanimous pact was made to fight to the death if the situation arose, including an oath to kill any wounded man if that man was unable to fight on and was in danger of capture.

All of these possibilities had been thought through in advance. In his final meeting with General Schechter a week earlier, the general had told Ben Zeev that scrubbing the mission and evading detection was a better outcome than a firefight with the Iranians. But none of these discussions made this decision any easier for Ben Zeev. As he thought through his alternatives, the captain looked at the number of enemy soldiers in and around the Iranian village of Dezli. Point Kabob was only a few kilometers south of the village on Road 15. He had expected no military presence in the village and now the amount of men was consistent with the entire mission being compromised. For the sake of security, in case anyone unintended was picking up and reading the same screen that Ben Zeev was looking at, the position of Arsadian's truck was not being broadcast. The captain suddenly cursed this decision. He was uncomfortable not knowing precisely where that truck was located. *I need more information.* Just as his mind began to entertain the unthinkable, a new message from Olympus popped up on the screen.

Confirmed negative AISR.

Flying just south of Hakkari, Turkey, about 200 miles north of the Chinook helicopter, a single USAF RC-135 Rivet Joint, a converted Boeing 707 with a 22 man crew and millions of dollars' worth of the latest electronic equipment and computing power, quietly vacuumed in every radio transmission over northern and western Iran. Over years of experience and intelligence gathering, the Americans had learned all of the frequencies used and characteristics emitted by the growing fleet of Iranian drones. While often hard to pick up on radar, drones had to communicate with their pilots on the ground and provide real time intelligence, which was their purpose. This meant that they had to broadcast either upward to overhead satellites or downward to listening stations on the surface. Either way, the Rivet Joint picked up their radio wave emissions. On this night, the crew on the Rivet Joint could locate the approximate location of four Iranian unmanned aerial vehicles. One was operating at high altitude just south of the Azerbaijan border, two were at medium altitude in circular patterns over the Iran-Afghanistan border and one had recently taken off from Mashhad Air Base in the northeastern corner of Iran. This fourth drone was climbing to the south, apparently heading for the Afghanistan or Pakistani border. No Iranian drone was airborne over the country's long border with Iraq.

Captain Ben Zeev immediately recognized the acronym for aerial intelligence, surveillance and reconnaissance and knew that the message meant that there were no Iranian drones operating in his area of concern. He processed this new information in a logical manner. Iran's operational drone fleet was growing, but its best reconnaissance drones were expensive to operate and the financial pressures on the Iranian regime limited their flight time. This had the practical effect that every mission had to be prioritized and approved by Revolutionary Guard headquarters in Tehran. As Ben Zeev reviewed this situation in his mind, he concluded that there could be no higher priority operation for the Islamic Republic of Iran than to catch or kill a group of Israeli commandos on Iranian soil. This would command all available resources and the fact that Iranian drones were looking for drug smugglers coming into the country from Afghanistan instead of his team coming in from Iraq meant to him that the Iranians must not know about his mission. Or so he reassured himself.

The captain shook the doubts from his mind and looked anew at the TSU device on his lap. His eyes scanned to Point Kabob on his screen. More good news. There were no soldiers indicated any closer to the rendezvous point than in the village of Dezli. Surely, he thought, they would have soldiers lying in wait around the rendezvous point if they knew about it. He had two more alternative landing zones that he and his team had reviewed, one to the north of the first two sites and one to the south. The northern route, designated drop zone four, made no sense. The Iranian unit in and around Dezli would be between his men and where they had to get to in order to successfully rendezvous with Arsadian. That left only drop zone three, which was a few miles south of the primary drop zone. This was less preferable to the drop zones to the north because there were a couple of small Kurdish villages that would each be within a mile of the drop. In addition, the southern route meant that the rendezvous with Arsadian would also have to be moved south to Kabob II, the back-up point. Ben Zeev didn't like changes to the plan, but he was out of options. He motioned for the CIA agent to come over. The American had a small pad that he handed to the Israeli, who wrote down his instructions in English in block letters.

CHANGE TO DZ-3 (SOUTH SARGAT)

As the CIA agent walked up to the cockpit to relay the change in plan, Ben Zeev opened up his backpack which was sitting at his feet. He pulled out a communication device that looked like a handheld GPS unit. He turned it on and entered a four digit code using the small keyboard. The keyboard filled up the bottom half of the device and the keys were marked in both English and Arabic letters. He pressed the send key and waited for confirmation of a successful transmission before turning the device off and repacking it. Six minutes later a message popped onto the screen of his TSU.

Confirmed 4033.

Olympus knew they were heading for drop zone three and that the rendezvous would therefore be at Point Kabob II. They would notify Arsadian.

What no one on board the helicopter or at Olympus knew was that something had occurred earlier that day that the Israelis had not planned for. A group of five men belonging to PJAK, the Party for a Free Kurdistan, had opened fire on an isolated Iranian border post only two miles north of the spot where Task Force Camel had planned to cross the border. As was usual with these events, no one on either side was hit. The Iranian border guards had returned fire with their AK's and a single U.S. built M2 .50 caliber machine gun left over from the days of the Shah. The latter was convincing enough to drive the Kurdish rebels back across the border into the safety of Iraq.

The news was greeted by the commander of the local Iranian Revolutionary Guards unit based in Biakara as a good reason to take his men into the field and set up some ambush positions for the night. The young commander was full of religious zeal, an outlier even by the standards of the IRG. He yearned for combat against the enemies of Islam and the Islamic Republic and dreamed of being recruited into the elite Quds Force. He needed to exhibit his zealotry to achieve that goal. Taking on PJAK guerillas was not exactly the same as the U.S. Army, but opportunity was opportunity. He knew the odds were against anyone coming along, but he was feeling lucky that day. Besides, the 165 men in his unit needed the field experience.

"Fifteen minutes to delta zulu three," stated the Chinook pilot into his helmet microphone. He was keyed into the internal system and the four other crew members simultaneously heard the communication. "Go dark." The co-pilot reached down and manipulated several switches, turning off the tactical formation navigation lights and infrared strobes and the helicopter's transponder. The three helicopters had for the past five minutes been flying in a very tight formation, much tighter than at any time in the prior five and a half hour flight. One Blackhawk was in front of the formation and maintaining an altitude about 100 feet higher than the other two choppers. The other Blackhawk flew at the same altitude as the Chinook, only off to the port side and slightly trailing the larger helicopter. When the pilot of the trailing Blackhawk helicopter saw the tactical formation lights of the Chinook go out, he immediately turned on a second transponder in his craft that mimicked the signal that had been being squawked by the Chinook. The pair of Blackhawks stayed in formation and began a slow turn to the north. They would spend the next 30 minutes executing a simulated search for a non-existent drone crash site about 15 miles north of the drop zone area. The Night Stalkers would not make it easy for any adversary to track the exact point where their elite cargo was being dropped off.

The pilot of the Chinook, looking at the mountainous terrain under him through a set of AN-AVS 6 night vision binoculars mated to his helmet, began a slow turn to the south and a faster descent down to an altitude only 100 feet above the undulating earth. The next quarter hour of flying was what he lived for and what distinguished him from the average helicopter jockey in the world. The cockpit of the advanced special operations helicopter had numerous flat panel displays that illuminated the earth ahead of them, including forward looking infrared and thermal imaging. But like most Night Stalker pilots, this man largely ignored these monitors and instead relied upon his helmet night vision system.

In the cabin, the crew chief lifted his left hand and flashed a single finger immediately followed by all five fingers. He then dimmed the soft green glow of the combat lights in the cabin to the lowest setting. The Israeli team began their final preparations for insertion into hostile territory. Several team members had to nudge the man next to him awake.

At 10:42 p.m. Iraqi time, the Chinook helicopter descended slowly toward a high mountain valley. The elevation of the earth beneath them was 3,978 feet. Every man in Task Force Camel had his backpack, winter coat and gloves on, his AK slung over his shoulder, a GPS device on his wrist and his patrol cap tucked firmly in his pocket. Finally, each man had put on head gear to mount the light weight AN/PVS-14 night vision monocle. The men were all cold but knew that they would soon be warmed by the exertion of hiking through the Zagros Mountain range, not to mention the accelerated heart rhythm that would come from stepping foot on Iranian soil.

At the back of the twin engine helicopter the ramp was down and a pair of two inch thick ropes, each 40 feet long, hung from giant eye bolts attached to box beams at the top of the helicopter interior. The ropes now hung in the black void. Every member of the helicopter's crew was wearing night vision goggles. Two of the crew, following standard operating procedure for a fast rope insertion, were on each side of the ramp on one knee with one hand firmly gripping the interior frame of the helicopter and their upper bodies thrust into the clear mountain air. Each man, secured by a thin cable tether, looked forward toward the drop zone as the Chinook maneuvered into a slow forward hover for insertion. Their job was to spot any obstacle that might damage the helicopter as it moved to hover approximately 15 feet above the valley floor. The crew chief watched his two men on the ramp and waited for the signal.

The big chopper flared briefly to scrub off speed and then leveled in hover, maintaining very slow forward motion. The man on the starboard side of the ramp rotated his upper body and extended his right arm out. With his palm open and facing upward, he raised his forearm toward the ceiling by bending his arm at the elbow. The crew chief signaled for everyone on the Israeli team to exit and all stood and moved to the ropes. Each man grabbed the rope and stepped off the platform into the Kurdish mountain blackness. The captain was the last, but took a moment to shake the hand of the crew chief and salute the CIA officer who had now succeeded in his part of this mission. It only took ten seconds for all twelve men of Task Force Camel to make it to the ground. Another thirty seconds later and the Chinook helicopter was already indistinguishable against the night sky, the sound of its counter-rotating blades fading rapidly into the dark as it headed for a reunion with its smaller partners and the long trip back to Kuwait.

The team had rehearsed this part of its mission dozens of times. The men all removed their night vision monocles from their backpacks and mounted them to their head gear. Every man on the team save one took the opportunity to relieve his bladder. It had been a long flight. One man, Yosef Hisami, the member of the team who was born and raised until the age of eight in the Kurdish city of Erbil, headed out to take point. He was moving rapidly to the east, bounding uphill to gain the advantage of a ridgeline that was one mile away. Yosef had proven his mountaineering skills to the team over the prior two years and the relatively gradual slopes of this terrain were like a casual stroll for the Kurdish Jew. The men on the team jokingly called him the "mountain goat." He was driven by his own paranoia – he hated being in a valley since he could never shake the feeling that he was being watched. At this moment, Yosef would not be comfortable until he could observe the valley on the other side of the ridge with his own eyes. Ben Zeev never let him see the screen of the TCU because he never wanted the mountain goat to relax. Yosef was the team's human early warning system. If anyone or anything was out there, he would see it first. Since the team was radio silent, he carried a small pen light that emitted an infrared flash when he pressed a button on the back. He could signal the team from a long distance with this device.

The main body of men followed at a distance that was initially a hundred meters. They had learned that they could not keep up with Yosef when he was obsessed on attaining a certain point on the map. They all knew that the gap would continually widen between them and Yosef by the time the Kurd made it to the ridgeline. The captain checked his GPS device to make sure he agreed with the direction of movement. The team had a two mile trek to reach the Iranian border. But their instant motivation was to get as far away from the insertion point as rapidly as possible. The village of Sargat was less than a mile to the north and no one wanted to run into a curious Kurd. Even worse, an Iraqi border post was only 4,000 feet away on the other side of the ridgeline that formed the southern edge of this valley that ran to the east toward Iran. However, Ben Zeev knew that since U.S. forces left this region during 2011, Iraqi border guards were never known to venture out of their posts at night. He prayed that tonight would not be a first.

Task Force Camel moved along the valley floor as quietly as possible. The terrain was barren and rocky with the exception of isolated wild pistachio trees that grew randomly throughout the valley along with patches of alpine milkvetch plants. The team set a pace that reflected their youth, fitness and level of training, which had included several extended visits during the prior two years into Kurdistan, the northern part of Iraq controlled by the Kurds and run as an autonomous part of Iraq. It took slightly more than an hour to reach the border where the mountain goat paused as had been practiced so many times in the past. The captain gathered his men about a hundred yards in front of the invisible line that formed the Iranian border. They had climbed more than 2,000 feet from the insertion point to this point that passed between two rocky pinnacles looming above them on each side. As the men gained altitude, the vegetation had become more scarce with the trees disappearing completely.

The captain told his men to rest, drink water and eat. Removing the TSU device from the backpack of the man standing next to him, the captain turned it on while two of his men used their open winter coats to ensure that no light emanating from the device gave their position away. The first thing the officer noticed was a dozen grouped blips in blue on the Iran-Iraq border. As he looked at his own men on the screen, Ben Zeev thought about how happy he was that the Iranians were not deploying this level of technology against him. Beyond that, the commander liked what he saw. The Iranian land in front of him was barren of human activity save for a lone border post over a mile away and in a direction that the team had no intention of heading. The absence of Iranians, Kurdish fighters, smugglers or the errant villager was the best possible outcome. The air was still, and the team was cognizant to the point of paranoia about how the sounds they made carried along the rocky valleys. Their isolation was welcome. No new messages from Olympus had been received so Ben Zeev shut down the device and placed it carefully back into the pack of his underling.

He called his point man over and together they discussed in hushed Farsi the path to Point Kabob II. They each set waypoints on their GPS units, making sure they stayed clear of the tiny Iranian village of Baharvas that lay in their path only a half mile ahead of them. The commander then synched up this set of waypoints with each man in the team. In case of separation in the darkness, each man now had the capability to navigate to Point Kabob II. Finally, Captain Yoni Ben Zeev motioned for all his men to gather together. He now did something that they had never rehearsed before. He spoke quietly in Hebrew. "This will be the last time any of us speaks or hears our language until this operation is complete. I ask you to bow your heads." The background of this team – reflecting the wide range of religious experience in Israel – varied greatly, but each man knew their leader was an observant Jew. And as all men do when combat was imminent, their hearts were open at this moment to their God. Six of the team bowed their heads. Four men continued to look at their leader. Yosef Hisami, suddenly nervous about the volume of his leader's voice combined with the use of Hebrew, scanned the valley around them.

The captain continued. "He who dwells in the covert of the Most High will lodge in the shadow of the Almighty. I shall say of the Lord that He is my shelter and my fortress, my God in Whom I trust. For He will save you from the snare that traps from the devastating pestilence. With His wing He will cover you, and under His wings you will take refuge. His truth is an encompassing shield. You will not fear the fright of night, the arrow that flies by day, pestilence that prowls in darkness, destruction that ravages at noon. A thousand will be stationed at your side, and ten thousand at your right hand, but it will not approach you. You will but gaze with your eyes and you will see the annihilation of the wicked. For you have said, 'The Lord is my refuge'. The Most High you have made your dwelling. No harm will befall you, nor will a plague draw near to your tent. For He will command His angels on your behalf to guard you in all your ways. On hands they will bear you, lest your foot stumble on a stone. On a young lion and a cobra you will tread and you will trample the young lion and the serpent. For he yearns for Me, and I shall rescue him. I shall fortify him because he knows My name. He will call Me and I shall answer him. I am with him in distress. I shall rescue him and I shall honor him. With length of days I shall satiate him and I shall show him My salvation."

Ben Zeev raised his head. Each man had heard these words at some point in their lives. Several recognized Psalm Chapter 91. For each man, the words had more meaning at this moment than they thought possible. "For two years we have trained. From this point we do not return without achieving our mission. Our forefathers watch our every step. I know that none of you will hesitate in your duty." Heads nodded in agreement.

The captain switched back to Farsi. "Now we go." The local time in Iran was now 11:57 p.m., 30 minutes ahead of Iraqi time – the difference the result of Iran maintaining its own time zone a half hour ahead of Iraq. The easy part of their journey was now behind them and what lay ahead was a drop into the valley just underneath Baharvas followed by a further climb in elevation of over 3,000 feet amid steeper mountains. They only had 2.4 miles to go as the crow flies, but their path would require them to climb a steep 2,500 feet over the last half mile, a portion of the western slope of Kuh-e Takht-e Uraman, one of the higher peaks in the area. Their destination, designated Point Kabob II, was a section of switchback on Road 15 that was only about four hundred feet below the point where the road passed its zenith over the mountain at just over 8,500 feet. Thankfully, they were still too early in the season for any significant snowfall. The captain worried about whether Arsadian had gotten the message on the change in rendezvous point. Only time would tell him for sure if the Armenian had succeeded in reaching Kabob II.

Ben Zeev took one more look at his watch, which had been on Iran time since given the mission go ahead earlier in the day. Midnight. He estimated that they would not arrive at Point Kabob II before 3:00 am.

39 – Point Kabob II

Task Force Camel crossed Road 15 on foot at 3:05 in the morning. The sun's ascent was still three hours away and the only natural light on this moonless night was the cloud-like consistency of the Milky Way as it stretched from horizon to horizon. The temperature was just under freezing as Captain Ben Zeev crossed the two lane road and headed quickly up the rocky slope on the eastern side. At this altitude, the mountain was completely barren of vegetation, comprised only of rock and the sand created from eons of the actions and reactions of wind, water and temperature on that same rock. The sand and rock was the color of dark grayish tan, as if the hand of God had pushed these jagged mountain rocks upward through an ancient desert.

Climbing up the final 300 feet of his journey, the commander came upon his point man crouched behind a large boulder that stood alone and formed an intermediate crest. Yosef was quiet, one of his true gifts. He used hand signals to direct his commander's vision. Fifty feet below them, on the other side, was a flat sandy area about fifty yards wide and at points as much as twenty five yards deep. The pavement of Road 15 bent through the northern edge of the area like a snake, forming a 180 degree turn. To the east, or uphill side, the road followed the mountain contours and continued up to the next switchback about half a mile further along and 410 feet higher in elevation. On the western side, the road ran downhill slightly for only a hundred yards before it turned back on itself and headed back to the south, passing below the spot where Ben Zeev and Yosef now crouched. At the western edge of the flat parking area was a thatched hut that formed a makeshift Kurdish tea house. In the summer, local villagers sold tea to the many families and tourists who travelled this road to enjoy the spectacular mountain views.

Both men had the same first impression as they looked through their monocles at the parking area below. There was no truck parked there, only a single sedan. Ben Zeev signaled his man to continue to scan the area, looking for anything or anyone that could threaten the team. He then turned and walked back a small distance to join the rest of the team. Sending a man to keep his point man company at the observation rock, the captain pulled out the TSU device and turned it on for the first time since crossing into Iran. The team had not rested during the prior three hours. The plan called for them to be on board the truck and underway to their target before dawn. The timetable was in jeopardy. As the device powered up and established its satellite link, the yellow star indicating that a message was waiting immediately began blinking. The captain entered the proper commands to display two new messages.

> Delayed. Close.
> Confirmed 2002.

The messages had been sent a couple of hours earlier. Ben Zeev did not know what to make of the first message. But the second message confirmed that the mission was still green lighted and that the rendezvous was still Point Kabob II, located 50 feet below their current position. Ben Zeev shut down the unit. Following mission protocol, he sent no messages nor did any man on his team emit any radio wave transmissions. They wore no tracking devices and their authorization to broadcast from inside Iran was contingent upon emergency or absolute necessity.

The captain set up pickets and told his men who were not on watch to rest and sleep if possible. The lack of motion would quickly make them cold, so each man removed a camouflaged blanket that he carried in his backpack, white on one side and on the other, the light gray digital pattern that had been perfected by the U.S. military in nearby Afghanistan. The blanket doubled as an infrared and thermal suppressor, making the men virtually invisible if necessary to hide from Iranian eyes. They had brought minimal supplies – just enough to either meet the truck or make it back across the border into Iraq. But the blanket was an item that they had learned was necessary during their first mission rehearsal in the Kurdish mountains 18 months earlier when Ben Zeev had cancelled the practice session early to save two of his men from the danger of frostbite.

An hour later and seven and a half miles to the north in Dezli, Captain Javed Samadi of the Iranian Revolutionary Guard was gently nudged by his driver as he slept in the back seat of his sedan. "Sir, it is past zero four hundred. We have had no contact."

The IRG captain shook his head to wake himself. He wiped the sleep from his eyes and straightened the cap on his head. "Nothing?" His voiced cracked in the dry air.

"No, sir."

The captain was disappointed. He wondered why God would not bless him with glory. Had he not been faithful to Allah in his heart? Yet, it seemed that no matter where he took his unit, action was elsewhere. He had spent most of the overnight hours checking on his men who lay in wait along the valley approaches just north of Dezli, the valleys that the locals swore to him were the favorite entry points for Kurdish rebels. Two hours earlier he had walked back to the sedan to warm up and rest, telling his driver to communicate contact status every hour. Now he opened the door and emerged from the car to stretch and let the cold air wake all of his senses.

Nearby a dozen of his trucks were parked – the vehicles that moved his unit around the mountains of western Iran. The truck closest to his sedan contained his radio communications unit. He walked over and the sergeant in charge stood to salute his officer, simultaneously kicking the man next to him awake. The officer spoke first. "Tell all units to abort operations and return. I want to be out of here by sunrise."

"Yes, sir." The sergeant saluted his commanding officer. He started to sit and then stopped and addressed the captain. "What about the roadblock?"

"Oh. Yes. Lift the roadblock."

Five minutes later, the sound of starting car engines awakened Hamak Arsadian. He looked out his windshield and saw the straight truck that had been stuck in the line ahead of him moving forward. "Yes," he stated loudly as he pumped his fist. He looked at the clock on his dashboard. It was 4:28 a.m. and the Armenian had about twelve miles of driving to reach the rendezvous point, the last five miles of which would be a treacherous climb up and over the snowcapped peak of Kuh-e Takht-e Uraman. He swung his legs down and lowered himself into the driver's seat. He was in a race against the dawn.

Forty-six minutes later Yoni Ben Zeev heard the sound that made him smile for the first time since parting company with the Night Stalkers. The sound was the unmistakable rumble of a large diesel engine being used to help manage the downhill momentum of a truck. The noise travelled clearly in the pre-dawn darkness. The captain looked up the mountain and saw the artificial light of a pair of tractor headlights as they swept around a switchback. He alerted the man next to him and the team was awake with their blankets packed away within seconds, every man now like a racehorse with Ben Zeev the jockey. A minute later and the commander could finally confirm the shape of the tractor-trailer rig as it negotiated the last hair-pin turn half a mile up the road. He stood and walked to the rock that overlooked the parking area. He looked down to see that the single sedan was still parked in the same spot as when they had arrived. They only had about 45 minutes of darkness left.

Hamak Arsadian recognized Point Kabob II with no problem. He had stopped for tea twice before at this spot while driving Road 15. It was he who had suggested this location as a backup if needed. As the roadway started a sharp turn on itself to the right, he under steered his rig onto the flat sandy parking area. Swinging the truck to the right to park roughly parallel to the curved pavement, he came to a stop with his headlights shining into the parked sedan. "Shit," said the Armenian, lamenting the further bad luck. He let his lights linger on the car, the interior now lit up as if an enemy plane caught in a World War II searchlight.

On the rock above, Ben Zeev reached up with his right hand to turn off his night vision monocle and flip it upward, freeing his right eye to join his left in natural vision. He could clearly see that two men were sleeping in the front seats, which had been reclined. The captain was not sure, but the car looked like a mid-90s vintage Toyota Corolla. As he thought about what to do, the man in the driver's seat raised his head up, covering his eyes from the intense glare of the tractor headlights. He looked toward the source of the light, obviously hearing the diesel engine and correctly deciphering the source of this annoyance. Just as abruptly he put his head back down on the reclined seat and rolled onto to his right side to turn his eyes and head away.

In the cab, Arsadian did not know what to do. But he knew that Ben Zeev would handle the situation. He turned off his headlights and settled down to await the next event. Up on the rock, the captain tapped his point man on the shoulder and the pair headed back to the rest of the team. He pointed to Manuchehr Moresadegh, who everyone on the team called Manu. "You and Yosef go down and get rid of them. Just tell them to move on. Tell them it's not safe due to Kurdish rebel activity." Manu shook his head in consent. "Leave your NVGs and backpacks here," ordered the commander, referring to the night vision monocles each man wore. Both were happy to comply as the units had long since begun to irritate. For Manu the headgear that mounted the monocle was giving him a headache. For Yosef, it had been the plastic eye cup rubbing his skin as he walked. "Take your flashlights," Ben Zeev commanded. "Go back down to the road there." The commander was pointing toward the spot below them where the team first crossed Road 15 about two hours earlier, "and walk up the road to the car." The two men understood their assignment.

Manu had lived in Tehran until his parents immigrated to Israel when he was 10. His Farsi was flawless and, more importantly for this assignment, very authoritative. Ben Zeev could not imagine any civilian failing to obey him. But Manu was also critical to the success of the mission. Everyone on the team knew that. Obviously the captain assessed the two men in the sedan to be low risk. He was sending Yosef for two reasons. The first was that the men in the car likely were Kurds who may not speak Farsi. The second was revealed when Manu headed down the mountain. Ben Zeev grabbed Yosef by the arm and spoke quietly in his ear. "Don't let anything happen to Manu."

Yosef looked his commander in the eye. "No worries, boss." The Israeli commando from Erbil turned and bounded down the mountain, catching up with his partner in seconds.

For the first time on this mission Yoni Ben Zeev pulled his AK-47 rifle off his shoulder, chambering a round in the process. He headed back to the rock to provide cover fire for his team mates if needed. It took three minutes for the pair of Israeli commandos to walk up the road, around the switchback that was just below Point Kabob II and up to the sedan. The small four-door Corolla was pointing away from them as they approached. Manu walked up the driver side of the car. The strap on his AK rifle was slung over his left shoulder and across his back, allowing the weapon to hang conspicuously across the front of his body at waist level, his right hand holding the gun's pistol grip tightly. In his left hand he held a small flashlight. He shined it into the back seat. It was full of junk, as far as Manu could tell, but no humans. He walked another step to the driver side window. On the other side of the car Yosef stood quietly, his SIG pistol drawn and cocked in his hand. He did not take his eyes off of the two occupants.

Manu Moresadegh tapped on the window with the muzzle of his assault rifle while he shined the flashlight at the back of the head of the man in the driver's seat. "Open your window," he ordered. In the tractor parked only 30 feet away, Hamak Arsadian watched the men standing outside the sedan. He assumed they were part of Ben Zeev's team, but he had never been told any specifics so could not be sure. He had not noticed their presence until Manu switched on his flashlight.

The man in the driver seat rolled over to look into the flashlight beam. He could see the muzzle of the AK pointed at him on the other side of the glass, which Manu made sure he couldn't miss. Manu repeated his command and the man reached down along his left side and rolled down the window. Simultaneously he raised his upper body and reached back with his right hand to release the mechanism that allowed the reclined seat to snap upward into a normal driving position. "What are you doing here?" demanded the commando in perfect Farsi.

The man was scared, the inescapable reaction to having the business end of an assault rifle only a foot from your head. His partner in the passenger seat was now awake and could also make out the muzzle of the assault rifle and nothing more. The driver spoke. Manu recognized his words as Kurdish, but could not understand him. Manu spoke to both men. "Do you understand Persian?" The driver continued to talk. The passenger was now wide awake but said nothing, the fear on his face being his only obvious commentary. Manu decided that he didn't care what they had to say as long as they got on their way. "Leave. You must leave." Again, the driver continued to talk, his voice now gaining in volume. Manu tried once more. "You need to leave the area. Drive on." The native of Tehran took his right hand off his weapon and waved it in a motion that suggested departure while he shined his flashlight on his right arm.

The driver said more that Manu could not understand. This time the passenger added his voice. Suddenly Manu heard a voice coming from the behind the car. "He is saying that he is the owner of this tea hut." Yosef was walking around the car to the driver side. "Perhaps we should switch sides." Manu stepped toward the rear of the car as Yosef passed by, moving forward until his body was even with the side view mirror. Yosef turned and shined his flashlight into the car. The driver was speaking the Kermanshah dialect of Kurdish. Yosef's native Kurdish was the Kurmanji dialect. Communication would be difficult, but not impossible.

Yosef spoke slowly. "You must move on. You cannot stay here."

"This is our tea stand. This is our living. We cannot leave." The tea hut was a family business. Family members took turns manning the location. It was very late in the season, but the family expected traffic the coming weekend and the two men were there to make the last bit of money before the winter hiatus. "Why do you ask us to leave? Who are you?"

"Border Guard," responded Yosef. "Kurdish rebels are in the area. It is not safe. You must move on."

"We are from Kermanshah. We cannot leave. The drive is too long. This is our livelihood."

"I am telling you to go now. I will not tell you again."

"You have no authority. Go tell the truck driver to leave. This is our business. We do not leave." Kurds were famous for two things: a hatred of authority and the stubbornness to back that hatred. Yosef understood these two foundational facts only too well.

Behind the rock Yoni Ben Zeev could not hear the discussion and would not be able to understand even if he could. Yosef was the only Kurdish speaker on the team. The captain expected the car to start up and leave any moment. The fact that it had not made him nervous. Daylight was approaching rapidly and with daylight came traffic. No one could witness the team boarding the truck. *What is taking so …* The captain's Generation III intensifier tube included technology to protect him at moments like this. Two bright flashes lit the parking area for brief instants in quick succession. The technology in the advanced night vision monocle cut the intensification within several nanoseconds in response to the intense flashes of light, sparing the vision of Ben Zeev and each of his team watching the car at that moment. The captain instantly realized what he had just witnessed. "Everyone advance," he yelled to his team, leading the way down from their perch above the parking area.

It took Ben Zeev only half a minute to reach the car. Yosef was already inside the vehicle looking for phones or any other communication devices. In the front seats were two dead Iranian Kurds from Kermanshah, each with a single bullet hole just on the left edge of their sternums. The men had died instantly within a second of each other, a single 9-millimeter round piercing each heart. Yosef emerged out of the car with each man's wallet and the single cell phone he had found on the driver. "Manu, check the back seat for phones or radios." He then spoke to his commander. "No choice, boss. They weren't going to leave." He simultaneously leaned down to pull up the trunk release latch.

Ben Zeev did not want this, but the decision had been made and the results could not be changed. "Push that car down the road and off the end of that hair pin down there. Don't start it up, we don't need an explosion right now. In fact, wait until we are ready. The car will be the last thing we do. Yosef, you continue searching the car. Benny will help you. Manu, you come with us." The captain directed the rest of his team toward the truck, issuing orders to empty just enough cartons of Charmin from the back to get eleven men in the rear of the trailer. They had to carry the cartons up the mountain a small distance to dump them behind a rock formation. His men got to work as Yoni Ben Zeev turned back to Yosef. "Put those wallets back and take the battery out of any cell phones you find. I want to make it as hard as possible to find these guys … assuming we avoid a bon fire."

"Ahead of you, boss," replied Yosef. He checked each wallet to make sure these men were who they said they were. In the driver's wallet, a family photo of the man, his wife and four children stared back at the Israeli commando from Erbil. "You dumb bastard," he murmured under his breath before returning the wallets to each man's pockets. While Benny looked through the trunk, Yosef removed the battery from the only cell phone they could find. He tossed the phone, the battery and its displaced cover into the rear seat.

Captain Ben Zeev walked over to the tractor, opened the passenger door and got in to greet a now very frightened Hamak Arsadian.

"What just happened?" asked the Armenian, his voice trembling noticeably. He knew the answer but somehow expected a reassuring response.

"We had no choice, Hamak." The captain reached across the center console of the cab to hold the Armenian's upper arm in an effort to calm the man. "It is great to see you. How are you?" Yoni retrieved his left hand and extended his right hand to the truck driver.

Arsadian shook the captain's hand. "I was okay." He took a deep breath. "Now I don't know."

"You will be fine. What happened to you?"

"The Iranians set up a roadblock in Dezli. I was stuck there until an hour ago along with a bunch of others."

"Well, we are all where we need to be now. We can get going in a minute." The captain looked around in the cab. "I have to change. Send the three two one code." As Ben Zeev stepped back out of the cab, Arsadian reached over and went through the same process of pushing buttons on his navigation system that he had done when he cleared customs the prior morning. At Olympus, which could track the truck and already knew that it had reached Point Kabob II, the simple code meant that the team and the driver were united and proceeding forward with the mission.

Captain Ben Zeev leaned into the tractor and opened a compartment behind the passenger seat. He pulled out a coverall and winter jacket. He removed his Iranian uniform and put on the clothes of a driver's helper, the ubiquitous assistant who accompanies truck drivers the world over, working for short wages and small tips. On the bottom of the small storage compartment was a rubber mat that kept items from rolling around. The Israeli officer lifted up the pad and removed an Iranian driver's license that featured his photograph. He was now a day laborer named Younis Mohammed who had been picked up by Arsadian in Tabriz to help unload the truck at its destination in Ahvaz.

As the captain changed, Yosef pushed the deceased body of the Kurdish tea stand operator to the side and wedged his small body into the left half of the driver seat. He started the Corolla, turned it around and drove it down the road to the first switchback where he pulled off the road. Benny ran down the road after him and quickly arrived by the car, the pair now waiting for their host vehicle to arrive before pushing the small Corolla over the edge of the mountain in front of them.

It took only a few minutes until the truck arrived and came to a stop on the downside leg of this particular switchback curve. The rear doors of the trailer were open, inviting the two remaining commandos to safety. Yosef got back in the driver seat and turned the key enough to allow him to place the shifter into neutral. He then turned the key back off and stepped out, closing the driver door behind him. "Okay," he said to Benny. The two men pushed the Corolla a few feet and it quickly gathered momentum. They turned toward the trailer, running to hop into the back. The Toyota gained speed and, after travelling ten more feet, the earth beneath it rapidly transitioned to a very steep downward pitch. The car began to careen down the mountain, travelling about 250 feet before smashing into a rock formation that instantly arrested its motion. Thankfully for the team, the car did not explode. Ben Zeev was grateful for the quality of Japanese engineering.

The captain, now acting as Arsadian's helper, was waiting for Yosef and Benny at the back of the trailer. He handed his AK and backpack, which now contained his border guard uniform and night vision equipment, up to his men and closed the trailer doors. He then ran up the side of the truck to take the passenger seat in the cab.

The Armenian drove the big rig with its elite cargo down the road for about 15 minutes. They were going downhill, and the main purpose of the tractor's big diesel engine now was to provide engine breaking to manage the speed of descent. Ben Zeev was not yet ready to relax. The team had more work to do in the trailer, work that was originally planned to occur while they were at Point Kabob. To the east, the first hints of orange began to appear on the horizon. Sunrise was only about fifteen minutes away. Finally the Armenian saw a lush area of vegetation and bushes on the left where a small stream intersected the road, passing underneath it through a man-made culvert. He slowed the truck and pulled over to the left hand side. "This looks good," he stated to the captain, the two men communicating in Farsi, the only common language they shared. The Armenian understood Hebrew no better than the day he first heard it spoken between his mother and Rabbi Rothstein.

"Agreed." Ben Zeev jumped out of the cab and ran to the back to liberate his men. He opened the doors. "Sunrise in fifteen minutes. You know what do. Let's move. Yosef on front point. Benny back here." The two men who had the dirty assignment of body disposal would sit this drill out, keeping watch over the road above and below them. Most of the rest of the team hopped out as Ben Zeev pulled himself up into the trailer. "Find a good spot," was the last order the captain gave as his men went to work. They had to dump 200 cartons of Charmin in the brush, hoping that the valuable waste would not be found for a couple of days at least.

The team accomplished its task efficiently. They had practiced this maneuver with empty cartons a half a dozen times. The weight of the loaded cartons, as Ben Zeev expected, did not slow his men down. The cartons were off loaded in under five minutes. Inside the trailer, the men rearranged the remaining cartons so that they were packed in all the way to the rear door, looking as they did 24 hours before when the truck left Yerevan. From the rear door moving forward, 248 remaining cartons of Charmin toilet paper were packed solidly, leaving an open void in the trailer about 20 feet deep at the front. The five men inside were now trapped by the cartons between them and the rear door. Along the ceiling, lights were flush mounted every six feet, providing a well-lit working environment.

Now one of the men did as he had rehearsed many times before and, using the blade of a combat knife, wedged up a single strip of two inch wide oak that lined the floor of the trailer. This specific strip of oak was easy for him to pick out because it had been intentionally stained with red paint at each end. It was right in the middle of the floor and, like all the oak strips, ran lengthwise along the trailer floor. After it was pried loose, another man grabbed it, lifted it up and placed it out of the way on the trailer floor. The man with the knife now dug his blade under a small metal plate on the subfloor, in the process cutting through security tape that had been placed over the plate after the trailer was loaded in Tel Aviv three weeks earlier. The plate raised up enough for him to put his fingers underneath and pull a wire handle upward, releasing a hidden latch and allowing the floor on the driver side of the trailer to pivot upward on a hinge.

Another man grabbed this floor and pivoted on its hinges into a vertical position until it came to rest perfectly against the sidewall. Two latches that looked like ordinary tie down points on the wall now were revealed to be clips that locked the false floor open. The first man now dug his fingers under the flooring on the passenger side of the trailer and the floor lifted, pivoted and was locked against the sidewall on the passenger side of the trailer. Two other men next took hold of two silvery blankets that were now exposed and lifted each up and away from the floor to reveal the secret cargo that Arsadian had been carrying from Yerevan. The newly revealed compartment was eight inches deep, eight feet wide and ten feet long. Inside this void, form fitting foam kept various weapons, ammunition, gear, food, computers and other devices secure. The team had all it needed to complete its mission.

A man reached down and grabbed a cargo net that was then unrolled and lashed to each sidewall to hold in place the wall of cartons that formed the rear of the newly created interior room. Reaching into the now exposed compartment, adjacent to the passenger sidewall, a commando unlatched a previously hidden hatch to open access to the ground underneath. The six other team members who would ride in the trailer were waiting to board. The last man in was Yosef, who closed the hatch behind him as Ben Zeev returned to the passenger seat of the tractor.

Sergeant Yosef Hisami was the man in charge whenever the captain, as now, was out of sight. This was despite the presence of three other officers inside the trailer. Hisami's leadership was by acclamation. It was earned through the respect of his comrades. The man who liked to call Ben Zeev "boss" was a natural leader at the age of 23 who stood only five feet seven inches. He would brawl with a man a foot taller to help his mate. But each man knew better than to call him "boss" – that moniker belonged only to Ben Zeev, he would retort.

Yosef reached into the compartment to pull out a sealed plastic bag full of blueberry crisp Clif Bars. He dug his finger into the plastic to create a tear and pulled the bag open. "We have blueberry, blueberry or blueberry," he joked in Farsi, maintaining the mission protocol that the team speak only in the native Persian tongue. He started to toss one energy snack at a time to each hand outstretched in his direction. Some of the men thought they saw his hand shaking. Everyone on the team tried not to think about what Yosef had just done, but each man could think of nothing else. For some, the incident only cemented their opinion that the "mountain goat" was the rock of the unit – the man that would be there for them when the situation was dark and in doubt, the man that each one would pick first to join them in battle. These were the professional soldiers, the men who knew that when you peeled away all of the platitudes and slogans, killing was what they did for a living. Others, especially the technical experts like Manu, could only think about the fact that two innocent civilians had been murdered in cold blood and the man who pulled the trigger seemed to never give it a second thought.

Each of these men grappled with his own complicity and each could only rest his own conscience by adding the enormous weight of this mission to their internal scales of justice. For the mountain goat himself, the photo of the driver's family ran through his brain like a movie caught in an endless loop. He wanted to cry, but that was his weak side. His inner will and drive, his strong side, would carry the moment as it always did. The weak side could wait for the days when he was no longer a warrior and when, he told himself, he would entertain bar patrons with alcohol fueled tales that no one would believe. For now, those days were somewhere in the distant future.

The mountain goat reached back into the compartment and pulled out a one liter bottle of water, the first of many in the compartment, to pass around as requested. Then he reached in and pulled out an M-4 carbine assault rifle with an eight inch suppressor attached to its muzzle. He laid the M-4 on its side and removed the AK that had been slung over his shoulder. He removed its magazine, cleared the chambered round, and placed the weapon into the now empty slot where the M-4 had been. He reached down again and pulled out several 30 round magazines for his M-4. "I already feel safer," said Hisami, a dangerous smile on his face. "Pass your AKs in." Each man on the team received an M-4 and the AK-47s were all placed into the vacated rack space. Everyone felt more comfortable with the weapon they always trained with. Two men on the team would exit the trailer at their destination with both an M-4 slung over their back and an Israeli Military Industries SR-99 sniper rifle with a very long suppressor extending from the end of its foregrip, along with an integrated night vision scope. The 7.62 millimeter weapon had the long range stopping power that the smaller caliber M-4 lacked.

In the tractor, the commander and the Armenian settled in for the drive ahead. "Let's go," said the captain, eager to put distance between the team and the Iraqi border. The commander understood that the discovery of the Toyota Corolla and its contents would result in a manhunt. As the truck moved south down Road 15, Yoni Ben Zeev slowly unwound, his body relaxing for the first time since he stepped foot on the American Chinook helicopter in Kuwait. He had not slept in almost 24 hours. He knew he needed to. He turned to his Armenian friend. "Head into Ilam. Wake me if you have any question. Wake me if we have trouble. Finally, wake me when we are closing in on Ilam. Okay?"

"Ilam. Got it."

"You okay? Good to drive?"

"I am good." The Armenian thought about his next words, debating different ways to phrase his point. "I am happy to have your team on board."

"Thank you, Hamak. It is mutual. You are a brave man." Ben Zeev reclined his seat the few inches available. He closed his eyes. The sleep washed over him. Even the lateral G-forces of the endless mountain curves could not diminish his body's desire to shut down and recover. In the hidden compartment only ten feet or so behind the captain, the men of Task Force Camel attempted to join their commander in sleep, some finding it easier than others.

Hamak Arsadian did not mind the deep sleep of his companion despite the occasional snoring that would start and last until the next hard mountain curve threw the Israeli's head to the opposite side and interrupted his snoring pattern. The captain's sleep allowed Hamak to smoke without enduring comment or dirty looks. He was not a chain smoker, but he needed a cigarette every hour or so. He had just finished his fifth cigarette since Point Kabob II when a sign for Ilam jogged his memory. He reached over and shook the left shoulder of the Israeli commando. "Younis. Wake up. We are nearing Ilam." He looked to his right for an instant. "Younis." He was almost shouting.

Ben Zeev's mind slowly found its way back to consciousness. He opened his eyes. "Where are we?"

"Close to Ilam. You wanted me to wake you up."

"What time is it?" In response, Arsadian simply pointed to the dashboard clock with his right hand. The time was 2:47 in the afternoon. "Good," replied the captain, his mind now regaining its full tactical awareness. "What road are we on now?"

"Seventeen."

"I want to take a different route."

The Armenian took the news in stride. He had fully bought into the adventure of this mission. He would drive that truck wherever Ben Zeev commanded. "Okay. Where?"

"Stay on Road 17 and follow the signs to the Ilam Airport. When we get to the Darreh Shahr Road, turn left. It's the same road that goes past the airport entrance. Take that road south to Darreh Shahr. Have you been this way?"

The driver shook his head. "Not that I recall. But we will find out soon what it's like. It can't be worse than Road 15 is south of Dezli." There was excitement in the driver's voice and Ben Zeev picked up on that. This was the same type of reaction from the Armenian that had caused the captain to grow to like him so much while they trained in Yerevan. If Arsadian were younger, thought the commander, he would recruit the man into Sayeret Matkal.

40 – Handshake Across the Desert

Sheikh Talal bin Walid walked into his fourth floor corner office in the sprawling Ministry of Foreign Affairs building on the corner of Prince Talal Road and Al Imam Abdulaziz bin Muhammad bin Saud Road in Riyadh, Saudi Arabia. The office was temporary for the Sheikh since the headquarters building of the agency he ran was undergoing renovation and reconstruction following a bombing the prior summer. On the wall hung a series of digital readouts that had the local time in eight of the world's largest and most important cities. In the middle of the city times, a single device read out two different dates. On the top, the date read '28 Dhu al-Qa'da 1434', which was the date according to the Hijri, or Islamic calendar. Underneath, the date read "04 October."

On his desk, Sheikh Talal's male aide had laid out the prior day's edition of the New York Times and Wall Street Journal, a morning reading ritual that dated from the days of his youth as a student at Columbia University. After thirty minutes of perusing the various articles, his aide entered the office with a tea setting and a red manila file. The file contained summarized reports of the key events that had occurred overnight.

"Don't forget your appointment with the King today for lunch," the aide said. The aide acted as the Sheikh's secretary and valet.

"Ah, yes. Thank you, Aziz," replied the Sheikh. The aide quietly left the office, closing the door behind him.

Sheikh Talal bin Walid, the head of Saudi Arabian intelligence, enjoyed a sip of his favorite tea, Earl Grey. He opened the red file, beginning the next portion of his morning routine. On his desk, a Blackberry cell phone sat in a cradle in a permanent state of recharging. It was not his regular cell phone. This phone never left his office.

The Sheikh noticed a red light blinking in the upper right corner of the phone. He returned his tea cup to its sterling silver tray and reached for the Blackberry. The phone had been provided to him by his internal communications group. The SIM card had been randomly and anonymously purchased in Paris. The phone had only one purpose: Every day or every other day – it didn't really matter – an innocuous text would come in. Every text was the typical type of text that a daughter who was off to college would send to a loving father.

He turned on the phone and opened the text messages icon on the screen. He then touched the single text to open it on the screen.

> Hi daddy. I'm flying home tomorrow and land at 17:00. Will you pick me up at the airport? Love you.

He typed a response.

      Yes, of course. See you tomorrow.

He hit send. The head of Saudi intelligence had just communicated with someone within Israeli Mossad who was based in Paris and using an equally anonymous cell phone. The Sheikh deleted the text and replaced the cell phone in its cradle. He then hit a button on his office phone. "Aziz, please have General Ratish come see me this afternoon."

"Yes, sir," replied the electronic voice. "What time?"

"Any time after I am back from seeing the King."

"Yes, sir."

41 – Midnight Flight

A formation of four IAF C-130 Karnafs leveled out at flight level 280 as it headed east over the northern Saudi desert. The mission was a routine training exercise and a continuation of the large formations flown by the IAF seemingly every month around the new moon. The formation flew with the full knowledge and approval of both the USAF and the Royal Saudi Air Force, but was still spread far apart to maximize its radar signature. The four planes maintained vertical separations of 200 feet, with the lowest airplane, the one trailing the formation, maintaining 28,200 feet.

The night of October 4 was the new moon. Over the desert sands of northern Saudi Arabia, with the few small towns offering almost no light, the view out of the cockpit window was the color that inspired the term "midnight black." With absolutely no visual horizon, the pilots of the trailing C-130 had to concentrate on their flight instruments. It was closing in on midnight local time and only the navigation lights of the other three transports were visible. Somewhere above them, a flight of three F-16C jet fighters that had just refueled behind a KC-707 aerial tanker was keeping watch over the four turboprop airplanes. But these welcome guardians were not visible to the crew of this C-130.

The formation of transports maintained a constant altitude and cruise speed of 290 knots. The flight continued toward the northeast on a heading of 52 degrees, passing over the Iraqi border at 11:50 p.m. local, or Juliet time. Just a minute after midnight, when the formation had flown a little over 50 nautical miles into Iraqi airspace, the two pilots overheard a conversation between the formation's lead aircraft and the Balad air control center. The air traffic controller was agitated and demanded that the formation of aircraft descend immediately to flight level 230 and begin a 180 degree turn to the south to exit Iraqi airspace as quickly as possible. The pilot of the lead aircraft offered his apologies at the inadvertent navigation error and confirmed the air traffic command to descend to 23,000 feet and begin a southward turn away from the prevailing traffic lanes over Iraq. The three lead C-130s all began the ordered maneuver.

The trailing C-130 began the same southward turn but maintained its altitude, the pilot lowering the plane's speed to 230 knots. The navigator reached to his left and rotated a small dial one click in a clockwise direction. In the cargo cabin, the white lights turned off and green nighttime cabin lights turned on. The navigator then leaned over and tapped the flight engineer on the shoulder. "Commence depressurization," he said into his microphone.

In the rear of the plane, six members of an elite IAF commando unit known as Shaldag and one loadmaster each put on oxygen masks. The loadmaster motioned for all of the men to stand. Each man began to perform a quick check of the equipment of the man in front of him, starting by ensuring that the valve on the small oxygen tank each man carried was fully open.

The loadmaster performed the check on the last man in line and then walked to the rear cargo ramp. He hooked a single tether strap to a harness he was wearing that wrapped around his shoulders and thighs. He then turned toward the six men and placed his right fist in the air.

All six men gathered near the ramp in a tight group. The loadmaster now raised his arm up and formed an 'A-OK' sign. Each man returned the sign. The loadmaster turned and waited. In the earpiece inside his helmet, he heard the navigator say "Two minutes." Thirty seconds later, he heard "Ramp down." Moments later the ramp door opened, an action which only took eighteen seconds to complete. As always, he was surprised at how calm it was to stand at the back end of a C-130 with its ramp open in flight.

The loadmaster turned to his men and put one finger in the air, giving them the one minute warning. The next fifty seconds passed by at different rates for each man. For the loadmaster, the time passed quickly. He suspected otherwise for the six Shaldag warriors by his side. Finally, the loadmaster heard a countdown in his ear. When the navigator said "Go", the loadmaster waved his right arm across his waist in an outward motion. Within two seconds, all six men had jumped off the end of the ramp and into the freezing black void. Now the loadmaster stepped back and pulled the release tab on two pallets that immediately rolled down the built-in rollers along the floor of the cargo cabin and out the door into the void. Static lines connected to an overhead cable deployed a sophisticated parafoil on each of the two cargo pallets.

The six men of Shaldag repeated what they had rehearsed on over 20 previous nighttime jumps. They used parafoils to "fly" over 10 kilometers to a point in the desert that was a little over one kilometer to the west of Mudaysis Airfield in the middle of Anbar Province, Iraq. They were the first Israeli soldiers to step foot on Iraqi soil. They would be the first of many.

After gathering their chutes, the unit commander sent two men ahead to reconnoiter Mudaysis, an airfield that satellite photos taken just twelve hours earlier indicated to be in the same abandoned condition as when Yosef Sayegh, disguised as a Kuwaiti engineer, had examined it over two years before. With his remaining men, the commander scanned the area with his night vision equipment. The night was so dark that his system used an infrared illuminator to make up for the lack of natural light available to amplify. Toward the south he saw what he was looking for: the two cargo pallets had landed about 150 meters apart and were only half a kilometer away.

The pallets had been delivered using an autonomous GPS-guided parafoil known as the Firefly Joint Precision Aerial Delivery System. The Shaldag unit needing only one of them, but two had been dropped under the assumption that at least one pallet would arrive at the designated location. The commander jogged to the nearer of the two pallets with his men. They cut open the thick webbed canvas strapping that held the cargo in place.

What was revealed looked something like a stripped down golf cart. There was just room enough for one man to drive it and its cargo of over six hundred pounds of pre-loaded equipment. The transport cart was powered by battery and very quiet. One of the men sat in the driver's seat and headed off slowly toward the airfield, the commander and one other man following in single file behind the vehicle, but only after they had gathered in the large parafoil to carry with them to the airfield. The last man headed toward the other pallet. His job was to gather up its parafoil and drape it over the pallet. Each parafoil had been designed to double as camouflage netting and was made of a fabric that had an effective desert camouflage pattern.

As the electric transport came within a hundred meters of the main landing strip, the commander ran ahead of it to gesture for the driver to stop. The commander got on his radio and spoke a single word in Arabic. Seconds later a single Arabic word came in response. The simple code, which told the commander that it was clear to come onto the airfield, would be innocuous chatter to any Iraqi picking up the broadcast. The commander gestured for the driver to continue and the transport headed off. The commander and the other soldier in the group were quickly on the runway and heading toward the tarmac located on the southeastern portion of the airfield.

Trailing behind, the sixth man who had placed the camouflage parafoil over the remaining pallet, came running to join his comrades. He took a more southerly route, cutting the distance to get from the drop site to the tarmac. The advance guard of two men had already taken up positions that allowed them to watch the single entrance road that led onto the airfield. They would spend the night guarding the only likely way for any Iraqi military vehicles to pay an unwanted and untimely visit to Mudaysis.

A sudden and sharp boom ripped the night air. *An explosion. We are under attack.*

The explosion that cracked through the still desert night did not produce any flash that any of the men noticed, but the sound was sharp and unexpected. All of the men of the Shaldag unit instinctively dropped into crouched positions and froze, each man desperately searching for the source of the attack. In the desert vastness of Iraq it was difficult to know which direction the explosion had come based on the sound alone. The commander was looking toward the entrance road when one of his men tapped his shoulder and pointed back in the direction they had just come from. Through his night vision system, the commander could see a cloud of dust that was already settling back to the desert floor.

The commander instructed the man who had been driving the cart to stay with it. He took the other soldier back with him toward the source of the explosion at a fast jog. Each man scanned the horizon as they moved, desperate to locate the enemy forces that were responsible for the blast. As they came nearer to the explosion site, the commander could make out the silhouette of his man on the ground, the same man he had just sent to cover the second pallet only minutes earlier. He was lying on his back in the sand only fifty meters or so off the edge of the runway. When the two men reached the runway's edge, the commander ordered the other soldier to stay where he was and provide cover. The commander now walked across the desert sand, unsure about what exactly had occurred.

As he came upon the man, the unmistakable sign of a landmine was apparent even in the greenish twilight world of night vision. The soldier had stepped on a mine and his right foot was blown off. The solder was still breathing but made no sounds. The commander kneeled at his side, quickly removing the man's fabric waist belt and placing it around his right calf, tightening it up as tight as it would go. The commander checked his soldier's pulse. It was weak.

"Uzi, can you hear me?" No response. The soldier was going into shock. The commander raised up the man's legs and maneuvered his own knee underneath the man's thighs to support them, trying to keep blood from leaving the soldier's vital organs. The commander looked at the stump. With his night vision goggles it was difficult to draw conclusions, but the commander correctly guessed that the shredded ankle was not bleeding heavily. The explosion had apparently cauterized the open blood vessels.

The mouth of the soldier named Uzi suddenly opened involuntarily and the muscles of his body went limp. The commander realized that the man was not breathing. He removed his leg from the support position and straddled Uzi's body. He spent the next two minutes compressing his soldier's chest at a rate of 100 beats per minute. He stopped to check Uzi's pulse. Nothing. His soldier was gone. What the commander would not realize until the sun rose the next morning was that a piece of shrapnel from a Soviet-built mine that had been buried in the sand for over a quarter century had severed the femoral artery in Uzi's left leg. The soldier had bled to death – the first combat casualty of the IDF during Project Block G.

Fourteen minutes later, the commander had dragged the body to the edge of the runway and removed his pack and M-4 carbine, giving each to the man standing watch. The commander then sent that man back to tell the cart driver to come over with the cart. The corpse was loaded on, now just another source of dead weight. The team headed to the same hardened aircraft shelter that the American unit had spent the night in two years earlier.

Among the items that had been unloaded from the battery-powered cart were two communication devices and a few body bags. The mission planners had planned for the loss of half the team and assumed that if more than half were killed, the entire team would be lost. What was not available to the team was any mine detection or clearing equipment. There was not supposed to be any landmines around this abandoned base and the contingency had not been planned for. Now within the relative protection of the hardened aircraft shelter, the commander operated one of the communication sets as two of his men placed the body of their friend into a bag that was then zippered shut.

The commander typed the following into the device's keyboard:

> Oscar Sierra. Equipment intact and operable. One KIA, UH – landmine.
> Send mine equipment. Shangri-La.

The simple code words at the start told Mount Olympus that the objective, Mudaysis Airfield, was secure. The third sentence informed them that Uzi Helzberg had been killed in action. The sign off was the codename given by the Olympus planners to this small patch of earth in the Iraqi desert that would play such a critical role in deciding whether or not Block G succeeded. The name had been christened by General Schechter, a World War II history buff who recalled that Franklin Roosevelt, when asked by reporters where the B-25 bombers that bombed Japan during the famous Doolittle Raid in April 1942 had come from, had simply replied "Shangri-La."

The communications device encrypted the message in a series of random digits and then waited to receive a signal from a passing satellite. With the satellite in line of sight, the device sent a burst signal that lasted less than one second. The message was decoded and read at Mount Olympus within two minutes.

The commander turned to the man who had been driving the cart. "We only have one thing to accomplish tonight, let's get to it. Uzi's gone. Let's make sure his death is for a reason." The driver was Uzi's close friend, the two having shared a bond built on common interests, complementary personalities and the shared hardships of life in a special operations unit. He was shaken but there was no time to mourn his friend – that would have to wait.

The soldier went to the cart and finished unloading the rest of the cargo, which included ammunition, food, tools, a range of push brooms, navigation lights, small flood lights, a small weather machine, four Shipon anti-tank missiles and a large rotating brush cylinder. He grabbed hold of the cylindrical brush, which was an attachment for the front of the cart. Kneeling down in front of the cart, he inserted two arms that extended from each side of the brush into sockets built into the cart. As soon as he was done, he hopped into the driver's seat. The commander grabbed his arm and offered unnecessary advice. "Stay only on the paved surfaces."

The driver headed off into the night. His job was to use the brush, which now was rotating along the ground as the cart moved, to sweep off the entire runway, taxiway and tarmac before morning light. The cart contained several extra batteries in series that provided enough power to keep it going for the next 12 hours. If necessary, they could retrieve the other cart in the second pallet left in the desert, an option that the commander was now hoping would not be necessary.

The commander grabbed two Shipon missile tubes and headed out to visit the two soldiers guarding the only road onto the airfield.

42 – The Road to Dehloran

The Iranian town of Derrah Shahr lies in middle of a high valley of the first range of the Zagros Mountains, known as the Folded Zagros. Along the long valley, which runs northwest to southeast parallel between the Folded Zagros and the High Zagros Mountain ranges, the high waters of the Karkheh River wind their way gracefully to the southeast. With a population of just over 60,000, the town itself is not on anyone's must-see list of destinations, but adjacent to the town are the ruins of the ancient city of Takht-e-Tavoos, dating from 5th century BC and the Archaemenid Empire of Cyrus the Great. The ruins attract Iranian and foreign tourists – those with either an adventurous side or a high level of interest in archaeology.

But it's the unrelenting beauty of the Zagros Mountain scenery that surrounds Derrah Shahr that has been a source of inspiration for Persians for centuries. Most people arrive into town using the well maintained valley road that runs north from Dezful, about an 80 mile drive away. Still others, as did Hamak Arsadian, come down from the north, along the Derrah Shahr road from the provincial capital city of Ilam.

The town of Derrah Shahr is arranged perpendicular to the main valley road, along a road that runs southwest through town and then into and over the Folded Zagros Mountain chain forming the southwestern flank of the high valley. A traveler on this road will eventually be delivered into the town of Abdanan at the foot of the Folded Zagros.

Along this route, only two and half miles outside of Derrah Shahr, lies a local tourist attraction, the fountains and modern bathhouse of the Sarab-e Derrah Shahr. The five acre site draws Iranians from near and far for a relaxing break among its well-manicured grounds in the clean mountain air.

Continuing along this same road, drivers heading for Abdanan would pass through the Kabir Kooh Gorge, land that had been a trail through this section of the Zagros Mountains for centuries. At the highest point of the gorge, as you drive along the eastern slope of the Kabir Kooh peak, you would be forgiven if you failed to notice a non-descript road about four meters wide that ran off to the east. The turnoff for this road was only seven miles driving distance from the fountains of Sarab-e Derrah Shahr.

The road has no markings to identify it, but if the curious turned onto it they would be soon met by ominous signs, written in Farsi, Arabic and English, that identified the road as Iranian military property, warning any vehicle that the use of deadly force was authorized if they continued any further. A single swinging metal pole – the type that guards the driveways of isolated farms the world over – acts as the sole barrier to progress. It is only twenty meters or so further past the sign and has no lock, just a simple latch.

Those who are authorized – or the foolhardy – need drive only one mile and four hairpin turns further to arrive at the site of the Dehloran early warning radar, an indigenous Iranian-built Ghadir radar system installed in the summer of 2012. Perched on a small knob at an altitude of 6,068 feet, the radar can pick up aircraft flying at a range of up to 450 kilometers from the installation, depending upon atmospheric conditions. The site is so strategically located that the Iraqi army had set its capture as one of its early objectives during the opening weeks of the Iran-Iraq war in 1980. The Iraqis failed in their attempt, stopped by the sacrifice and determined fighting of Iranian army and air force units.

The Ghadir radar is a new system built by Iran and based on the Russian Nebo UE "Tall Rack" radar system. The long wavelength of the system helps it to identify and track smaller targets such as drones, cruise missiles and – according to the Iranians – stealth aircraft. The system was a meaningful upgrade from the prior Russian built P-14 Tall King that had been inside the radar dome for many years prior to 2012.

But for the planners at Mount Olympus, the capabilities of the radar itself were not important. What was important was the integrated air defense network to which the radar was connected. The Iranians had learned the lessons of the preceding years well and they had spent handsomely to separate their radar network from the internet or any other network connected to the outside world. However, they also knew that a modern air defense network had to be connected across as many radars as possible to be effective and survive an intensive air assault.

Not only was the exchange of information across the network essential, but the ability to turn radars on and off intermittently – one radar tracking a target for a few seconds and then shutting down and handing the tracking off to another radar – has become a key tactic to survive the wave of incoming radar-homing missiles that is the standard opening air assault tactic of the U.S. or Israeli Air Force. Next to the nuclear program itself, there had been no higher defense priority in the Islamic Republic of Iran than the creation of a modern integrated radar network that was isolated from the outside world. The senior officers of the Olympus planning team were counting on the success of the Iranians in this effort.

After almost ten hours of hard mountain driving to cover only 342 miles of roadway, Hamak Arsadian turned his MAN tractor-trailer unit right as it entered the town of Derrah Shahr. He then drove another five and a half miles before turning into the large parking area of Sarab-e Derrah Shahr. Arsadian found a spot to turn around and then parked his rig. He and Yoni Ben Zeev – still in his guise as Younis Mohammed, the helper – stepped out of the tractor, each man stretching in the way that is automatic after a long road trip. They spent the next forty minutes walking around the grounds of the facility, enjoying the garden and the fountains as everyone was doing that was there on this beautiful fall day. They stopped in front of a cart vendor as the sun settled lower into the western horizon and purchased a Kurdish meal of lamb strips and tea.

Both men walked to a nearby masonry wall that was about a meter tall and capped with a granite cornice. They sat down to enjoy their meal and the setting sunshine. Yoni Ben Zeev thought about the beauty of this location and the coming storm that would engulf both Iran and Israel. He desperately tried to get the thought out of his mind, turning to Hamak to engage in small talk in Farsi. As he started to ask a question about the weather, a small trembler shook the ground and the wall the two men were sitting on. It successfully jolted Ben Zeev's mind out of his prior thoughts. "What was that?"

Arsadian smiled. "Earthquake. Not used to them?" The fact was that Ben Zeev was not used to feeling earthquakes, but in the Zagros Mountains, which were formed by the subduction of the Arabian sub-continental plate beneath the main Eurasian continental plate, they were a very common experience. The Israeli commando didn't respond. "You feel them all the time here in the Zagros."

The Israeli shivered. "Odd feeling," was all he added. He checked his watch. It was almost six in the evening Iranian time. The sun had set only minutes earlier. "Let's finish and get out of here."

Inside the trailer, the men of Task Force Camel opened their trap door and let the cool mountain air ventilate their temporary prison. They knew they still had six hours to wait. Some men continued to sleep, but others checked their weapons. Manu checked the status of several ruggedized laptop computers the team was carrying and the satellite communications gear they had available. One man read a novel he had sneaked into his backpack against orders. It was in English. When he pulled it out, he argued that it did not violate the rule against carrying anything Israeli. As he had correctly calculated, no one cared at this point.

Arsadian and Ben Zeev returned to the truck and started up the engine. The Armenian driver pulled back onto the Derrah Shahr-Abdanan road, now heading back toward the town of Derrah Shahr. He drove only about 300 meters – just enough to navigate a bend in the road. He pulled over onto a flat sandy section of runoff. Arsadian shut down the engine and reached back to pull down the bed that ran behind the rear of the cab. "You are welcome to it," he said to Ben Zeev.

"No. I am wide awake. Please." Ben Zeev motioned toward the bunk, officially ceding it to the Armenian. Hamak Arsadian slipped off his shoes and crawled into the small bunk rack. The Israeli captain entered the simple '3-2-1' code into the truck's SatNav unit, informing Mount Olympus that they were in position for the evening.

As darkness settled over the Folded Zagros Mountains on October 4, Captain Yoni Ben Zeev of the Israeli Defense Force leaned his head back against the passenger seat head rest and closed his eyes, searching for any way to make the time go by faster.

43 – The Climb to Dehloran

A little before 11 p.m., Captain Ben Zeev exited the tractor cab and walked back a few meters to slip underneath the trailer and up and through the trap door. He lifted himself into the trailer compartment. "Ready to do what we came here for?" asked the captain to his team as he closed the hatch underneath his feet.

He was greeted by a soft chorus of affirmative responses. He spent ten minutes changing into the uniform of the Iranian Revolutionary Guard Corps, the same uniform now worn by his team. He lifted up his new backpack and reached in to pull out a checklist. He spent the next fifteen minutes reviewing with each man the equipment in their possession to make sure that they departed this trailer with everything they would need.

When the captain was done, he returned the paper to his pack and grabbed the last M-4 carbine. Like all the others, it had a long suppressor on the muzzle threads in lieu of the standard issue flash hider. He then spent a half hour reviewing each step of the mission with his men, making absolutely sure that each man knew his role in the upcoming operation. When the time came, everyone would need to act as instinctively as possible.

With everything in place, one side of the hidden compartment cover was folded down and the other was released from the latch holding it against the side wall. Each man had a larger backpack than the prior night when they infiltrated the Iranian border. But like the prior night, each man wore the same AN/PVS-14 night vision monocle. Only now each member of the team added a tactical communication headset, allowing the team to communicate with each other up to about two kilometers apart.

Ben Zeev used the truck's intercom to talk to Arsadian, who would watch for any passing traffic. There were no cars on the road. Ben Zeev checked his watch. The time was 12:02 a.m. Iran time. "Okay. We go." He pointed to the mountain goat, who led the way as usual. "Remember, get cover from the road then get your bearings. Make sure you're heading in the right direction."

The captain watched eleven men drop through the hatch to the sandy earth below and quickly disappear. Finally, Ben Zeev lowered himself down as he pulled the heavy compartment cover down. After he had replaced and locked the hatch lid from underneath, he crawled out from under the trailer and walked to the tractor door. He reached in as Hamak Arsadian reached over to shake his hand. "You are on your own, my friend. God bless you."

"I don't know what your team is doing, but God be with you. If you need me, I will come."

Ben Zeev smiled. "The oak doors to the compartment are down, but the center oak strip is loose. You will want to fix that before you get too far down the road."

"Okay." Arsadian was nodding his head.

"You have a home in Israel with your family whenever you say the word. I will personally make it happen."

"I will see you there," smiled the Armenian.

Ben Zeev began to close the door, but pulled it back open. "Make your delivery as soon as you can and then get out of Iran the fastest way you can. I would waste no more time sleeping."

"I understand."

Task Force Camel budgeted two hours to cover 2.7 miles of uphill climbing that would take them from their current altitude of 2,657 feet at the truck up to 5,905 feet, a climb of more than 3,200 feet. Fortunately, their route would take them along the edge of a small stream bed that formed a gentle upward-sloping valley bordered by two ridge lines running away to the north from the Dehloran radar. The stream path would take them to a small plateau that was just below the ridgeline that held the Dehloran installation. The mountains in this area were little different from the mountains crossed by the team the night before. The land was rocky and largely barren, although the scattered trees were a little more numerous than along the border a couple hundred miles to the north as the crow flies.

A constant soft breeze came out of the northwest, carrying any sounds the team made to the southeast away from the radar station. The radar station at the top of the mountain had been under constant U.S. and Israeli satellite surveillance for over six months and the routine and disposition of the Iranian men who occupied the site were well known. Nothing in the routine had changed since concentrated surveillance had commenced the prior spring. About 8 a.m. each morning and 9 p.m. each night – the men at night being rewarded with a shorter stint for their graveyard shift duties – a white unmarked Ford passenger van and a white unmarked Chevy Suburban would pull off the Derrah Shahr-Abdanan road and drive the final mile to the station. The vehicles came from a military complex in the town of Abdanan on the opposite side of the mountain from the high valley town of Derrah Shahr. A single white crew cab pickup truck was kept parked on the grounds of the radar station so that crews had a way to get to town in an emergency.

At every shift change, four new technicians and six new IRGC guards arrived in the large passenger van. Another three guards accompanied the van in the Suburban during the drop off and then followed the van back to Abdanan with the ten men from the prior shift. The four radar technicians worked in shifts of two while they were on station, rotating two hours on and two off.

The IRGC guards tried to maintain four men on watch, with two overseeing the single road leading onto the site, two men walking the property and two men inside the middle of three white trailers set up along the ridge. This middle trailer acted as the sitting room, bunk room and kitchen for the men on station. But often the high resolution satellite photos showed that one or both of the men assigned to roam the property were actually in the sitting trailer, especially at night when it seemed that the roaming guards never ventured more than a hundred meters or so from the structures and the security of the lights mounted to them.

In addition to the sitting trailer in the middle, another trailer, the one closest to the large white radar dome, housed the radar operations and network communications equipment. The last trailer, furthest along the ridge, housed two diesel generators and an encrypted directional microwave transmitter and receiver that was aimed at a similar device 59 miles away on top of an 8,767 foot mountain peak located just to the northwest of the city of Khorramabad. About 80 meters past the last generator trailer and situated below the ridgeline, a large diesel storage tank was located. But the generators were only for backup. The radar complex was powered primarily by electrical wires that ran onto the site from higher voltage wires than ran alongside the Derrah Shahr-Abdanan road. From the first major structure on the ridge, the radar dome, to the diesel storage tank, the complex stretched for 262 meters, or 861 feet, following the ridgeline running to the northeast away from the radar dome.

With about a half mile to go to reach the diesel storage tank, the team stopped. They had reached the start of the plateau that was just underneath the radar station's ridgeline. There had been no man-made obstacles. No sensors. No barbed wire. No landmines. The Iranians relied on the guards and the natural isolation of the radar's location for defense. Off to the right from where the team stopped, Yosef Hisami had found their objective for the night. It was a spot along a sheer rise of rock wall averaging about 4 meters in height that ran for over 300 meters and formed the northern edge of the plateau. The particular spot where the Kurdish Jew now stood had been identified by space-based synthetic aperture radar surveys of the mountain top. It was underneath an overhanging rock that created a natural roof only two meters high at the opening and receding downward as it ran back so that the space formed underneath was in the shape of a wedge. At the rear of the space, the available height was only a few inches. But a number of men could lie down with their feet toward the rear and their weapons trained out the opening of the natural shelter, which faced north – away from the radar station.

Captain Yoni Ben Zeev directed nine of his men to take positions in the natural shelter. Two of those men immediately set to work erecting a camouflage net designed specifically for this mission. The net created a cloaking wall that effectively cut the men off from visible and infrared observation. Without saying a word, Hisami and Benny Stern headed off to another spot that had been pre-identified. The spot was almost a mile away and was on top of the next knob along the ridgeline that ran to the northeast and then turned east away from the radar station structures. The knob was actually at an elevation higher than the radar dome.

When the two men reached their destination they found a pair of large rocks, each about a meter in diameter, forming a barrier that was perpendicular to the radar complex. They spent the next hour taking turns digging a shallow ditch on the east side of the rocks. The finished trench was just deep and wide enough for the two men to lie down side by side, their weapons and binoculars trained between the two rocks toward the radar structures that were almost a mile away.

Benny Stern laid his M-4 in the ditch and positioned his primary weapon, one of the two SR-99 sniper rifles the team was carrying, on its bipod. Its powerful scope and integrated light intensifier allowed Stern to observe everything happening at the radar station within his line of sight. Finally, Hisami pulled out a camouflage net – a smaller version of the one being used to protect the main body of the team – and covered both men and all their gear including their weapons. This spot would be their "hide" for the next 17 hours. During the coming daylight hours, they would be unable to move out from under the netting. Any required bodily function would have to be taken care off within the claustrophobic confines of their enshrouded ditch.

They maintained sparse radio contact with the captain, using single Farsi words to let Ben Zeev know they were in position and had visual contact with their ultimate objective. The mountain goat put his M-4 down by his side and pulled out his suppressed SIG Sauer P226 9-millimeter pistol, holding it in his hand. He assumed that the only way they would be found before the next nightfall would be if someone happened to walk within a few meters of their hiding spot. If that misfortune were to occur, Hisami would make sure whoever it was did not live to reveal what they saw.

Stern told Hisami to get some sleep. Dawn was about four hours away. Stern would sleep sometime during the day.

Back underneath the natural overhang, Captain Ben Zeev pulled out a TSU and turned it on. While they were hiking up the mountain, the device had been passively receiving encrypted information. The captain tapped on the screen to open a specific file. A small number of high resolution photographs of the Dehloran radar station appeared on the screen in cascading files. The photos were in both visible and infrared light and spanned the prior 24 hours in four hour increments. He looked through the photos. They were no different than the ones he had been viewing for months. His conclusion was that the Iranians were not expecting his team.

44 – Morning in Iraq

The morning sun broke the horizon as seen from Mudaysis Airfield in Iraq at 5:59 a.m. A soldier shook the shoulder of the Shaldag commander, who had been able to get almost four hours sleep. The commander awoke to the cold desert air and worked his way out of the sleeping bag he was in. He was wearing his uniform from the night before, complete with his boots. Fortunately, no one had come to the airfield in response to the explosion. Either no one was close enough to hear the small blast or, thought the commander, perhaps the locals were accustomed to animals occasionally detonating old landmines from time to time. Either way, solitude was a very welcome condition. The commander wiped his eyes and looked to see that the cart was parked inside the aircraft shelter. "How did it go?" the commander asked of the soldier who woke him, the same man who had been driving the cart all night.

"Finished an hour ago. No problems."

"Any runway obstacles?"

"No."

"General condition?"

"Seems to be perfect to me."

"Did you remember the access road?"

"Yes, sir. It's in good shape as well."

"Good, good. Get some sleep if you can."

"Yes, sir."

The commander walked over to the meteorology machine that was lying in the middle of the pile of equipment and supplies unloaded the night before. He grabbed the machine, which was about the size of a microwave oven, and placed it outside the shelter in the clear path of the wind. He removed a plastic cover that exposed a weather vane and anemometer. He turned on the machine and pushed a button that quickly ran diagnostics to check the inner workings of the machine. I green LED lit up indicating that the machine was working properly. Finally, the commander opened a panel on the side of the machine, reached in and removed a long USB cable. He walked back to the communication device he had used the night before with the cable in his hand and plugged the cable into the device.

He sat down in front of the keyboard and typed in a cryptic message.

> Oscar Sierra. Quiet. Romeo condition alpha. Charlie clear. Victor unlimited. Shangri-La. +5.2C, 53.6P, 1.6K, W, 0307Z.

The update that Mount Olympus had been waiting for was received within a minute. The airfield was still secure and the condition of the runway, taxiway and tarmac was as good as anyone dared hope. The skies were clear with unlimited visibility. The commander did not enter the final set of numbers; they were automatically appended to the message by the meteorology machine through the USB cable, which was conveying temperature, humidity, wind speed, wind direction and the time of measurement in universal coordinated time, or UTC.

Now there was little to do until the afternoon except for updates to Mount Olympus every four hours. The commander headed out to relieve one of his men watching the entrance road. He wanted everyone to get as much sleep as possible. The commander's plan was that at around 3 that afternoon he would leave only one man on watch and he and the remaining three men would walk the taxiway, the runway and the tarmac in search of any objects, such as rocks, that could be sucked up into jet engines.

45 – The Midas Touch

A little after 1:20 in the afternoon of October 5, the first of three Ilyushin 78 Midas aerial refueling tankers operated by Swiss-Arab Air Cargo touched down on runway 33L at Kuwait International Airport just outside Kuwait City. The plane had departed from Ras Al-Khaimah airport about an hour earlier with a crew of five and more than 12,000 gallons of fuel. It had burned almost 8,000 gallons during the 577 mile flight. The plane slowed and taxied onto the commercial freight tarmac where it was directed to park. The pilot shut down his engines. He scanned the apron area and was very happy to see a line of 18 white refueling trucks of the Kuwait Petroleum Company waiting by the edge. Each truck held 5,000 gallons of JP-8 aviation fuel. Each of the three Ilyushin 78 tankers would require 30,000 gallons to reach their maximum fuel capacity.

The operations team at SAAC had no problem lining up the required fuel. The Kuwait Petroleum Company had become the largest supplier of JP-8 aviation fuel to the U.S. military in Iraq during the occupation, supplying millions of gallons of the fuel every month and billions of gallons over the prior decade. Kuwait Petroleum was now so eager for customers for its massive infrastructure that had been built to support the now departed U.S. military that it had offered SAAC a five percent price discount if it signed a contract to refuel its fleet of Ilyushin 78s on a regular basis. The operations leader at SAAC politely deferred a decision, stating that the service they received on this trip would be the key to deciding whether or not to enter into a long-term contract and pointing out that the airport in Doha was eager for their business.

As each of the other two Ilyushin tankers arrived and taxied to the tarmac, the refueling process began, with six trucks lining up to pump fuel at a rate of 500 gallons per minute into each plane. The entire refueling process would take almost 90 minutes to complete. The flight engineer of each of the Ilyushins walked out to oversee the refueling process while the crews took time to stretch their legs, the more adventurous looking for food or sodas in the nearby hanger area.

The captain of the first Ilyushin left his plane and walked over to speak with a representative of Kuwait Petroleum Company. The Russian pilot and the Kuwaiti manager shook hands and then spoke to each other in English. There was paperwork to be signed and the senior managers at Kuwait Petroleum Company wanted an authorized signer for Swiss-Arab Air Cargo FZE to attest to the actual delivery of 90,000 gallons of JP-8 fuel. Half of the payment for the fuel had been wired the prior day, but the other half was still due. When the paperwork was done, the Kuwaiti manager asked a question. "So what are you guys doing?"

"We have a contract to refuel Indian Air Force aircraft."

"The Indians are flying over the Gulf now?"

The captain shrugged his shoulders. "Hey, I don't ask too many questions. Refuel the Indians, the Saudis, the Americans. All the same to me. I just make sure that plane is where it's supposed to be at the time it's supposed to be there."

The Kuwaiti chuckled. "Inshallah. We are all just making a living."

The captain nodded his head in agreement. "Da. That's right."

46 – The Kingdom Sleeps

At 3:01 in the afternoon inside an underground bunker in Riyadh, Saudi Arabia, General Abdullah al-Ratish, the commander of the Royal Saudi Air Defense Forces, commenced a conference call with the air defense sector command officers located at the five main sector operating centers outside of Riyadh. The nation's "Peace Shield" early warning radar system was networked through the bunker that General Ratish was seated in at the moment. The bunker was staffed by both Saudis and a large number of American expatriates – many of whom were directly or indirectly employed by Lockheed Martin or Northrup Grumman, the manufacturers of the radars that were the backbone of the Peace Shield system.

Ratish, a member by marriage of the ruling al-Saud family – as were three of the five sector commanders on the phone – conducted the call in Arabic. "We are going to be upgrading the software on our 117 units tonight." Ratish was referring to the AN/FPS-117 phased array L-band radar built by Lockheed Martin that was the primary long-range radar used by the Saudis. "You must power down all 117 units by 1700 hours today. The upgrade will take ten hours and you will be notified by email when the work is done. As we have done in the past, we will have access to the American theater network." The Saudi Peace Shield network had been extended to link with Doha, Qatar, where the forward headquarters of the U.S. Central Command had its own computer network that centralized information from land-based radar, sea-based Aegis radar and various airborne AWACS systems. The information network between Riyadh and Doha could flow in both directions.

In the room with the general was Colonel Robert Peterson, the Land and Air Defense Forces liaison officer of the Joint Advisory Division of the United States Military Training Mission, or USMTM, in Saudi Arabia. USMTM has been in existence since 1953, when it was formed under the terms of the Mutual Defense Assistance Agreement between the Kingdom of Saudi Arabia and the United States. Colonel Peterson, the senior U.S. military officer based full time in Saudi Arabia, was known for his diplomatic skills and fluency in Arabic. He had become good friends with many important members of the Saudi royal family during his three years in the Kingdom – in a country in which friendships and blood ties were critical. It was well known that his next rotation would be a stint at U.S. Central Command forward headquarters and include a promotion to brigadier general – as soon as an officer with his skills could be found to replace him inside Saudi Arabia.

Colonel Peterson spoke. "I have recommended to General Ratish that, in addition to the CentCom electronic surveillance feed, two E-3 Sentries maintain airborne surveillance during this period." The Royal Saudi Air Force had purchased five E-3A Sentry airborne radar platforms many years earlier. "I recommend one maintain station hotel and the other maintain station yankee." This would place one Sentry in position to oversee the Strait of Hormuz and the other high over Saudi Arabia's tense southern border with Yemen.

"Thank you, Colonel Peterson. We will follow your advice." Ratish turned his attention back to the sector commanders on the phone call. "I want confirmation emails in my inbox from each of you when your units have powered down. Any questions?" The call ended without any further questions or comments.

After Robert Peterson left the general's office and returned to his own, only a small distance down the hall, Ratish picked up his phone again and pressed a single button that dialed the commanding officer of King Faisal Air Base located just outside of Tabuk in northwestern Saudi Arabia. The air base was the home of the Wing 7 of the Royal Saudi Air Force and had responsibility for the airspace bordering Israel, Jordan and Iraq. The commanding officer was technically the general's brother-in-law and their relationship was more cordial than otherwise.

"Yes, General," answered the base commander.

"How are you, my friend?"

"Good. Inshallah."

"I need you to put the second squadron on condition yellow tonight." The 2nd Squadron of Wing 7 was comprised of F-15 fighter interceptors and the best pilots in the Royal Saudi Air Force. Condition yellow meant that the squadron would remain grounded on stand-by for the night.

"Yes, yes." There was frustration in the base commander's voice. The general could hear it. "This is two nights in a row. Should we outsource our defense to the Zionists now?" There was no mystery among the senior officers on the air base about the many overflights of the Israeli Air Force. But every man with that knowledge knew that it was a state secret and that publicly disclosing it would risk a fate worse than simple demotion.

"Maintain your composure," replied Ratish. "I understand your frustration. Everything will be okay. You have your orders. Please keep your planes on the ground tonight unless you receive orders from here. I take responsibility."

"I apologize. My planes will be on the ground." The base commander had vented and knew better than to push the issue with the officer he was speaking to – General Ratish had married wisely, his wife was the daughter of the King.

"Thank you, my friend."

47 – Northwind by South

A CASA C-212 turboprop cargo aircraft belonging to Swiss-Arab Air Cargo called into the tower at Qaisumah Airport in Saudi Arabia. The airport was adjacent to the small town of Al Qaisumah in the northern Saudi desert about sixty miles south and a little west of Kuwait. Al Qaisumah and the nearby larger town of Hafar Al Batin were home to about 60,000 Saudis. The towns themselves were inconsequential but for the fact that they helped support the nearby King Khalid Military City, home to elements of three Saudi Royal Land Force brigades and a small number of American advisors.

In addition to the land forces, the military city was also home to an air base that was maintained primarily for the use of friendly air forces in time of crisis and an early warning radar facility just to the north of the city. The entire military facility was strategically located to impede any serious threat to the Kingdom from an enemy like Iran, but conveniently located far from any major Saudi city.

The small twin-engine C-212 landed to the northwest on runway 34 into the prevailing wind. The plane slowed quickly, using less than a quarter of the long runway. It turned around on the single runway, which doubled as the taxiway, and taxied back to turn onto the cargo apron. At 4:26 in the afternoon Saudi time, the plane came to a stop on the tarmac with its nose at a heading of precisely 246 degrees. The plane had left Ras Al-Khaimah earlier in the day and stopped for about an hour at Doha International Airport to refuel before continuing on to Qaisumah.

On board the plane were two pilots, four operations managers from SAAC and a single wooden crate that was wrapped in clear plastic. The two pilots carried passports from Germany and Spain and the four operations managers all held Russian passports. But every man on the plane was in reality an Israeli citizen. The men on board settled down to wait for a ramp agent to come out to the plane and inspect their paperwork. But in Saudi Arabia, nothing happened quickly and the men on board were counting on a long wait. The co-pilot exited the plane to go find a refueling truck. They had enough fuel to get out of Saudi Arabia, but to do so without first refueling, they would have to fly back to Kuwait instead of to their next planned stop, which was home to Israel. Each of the two pilots carried more than three thousand dollars' worth of Saudi riyals. The money had two purposes: to ensure the procurement of fuel and, if necessary, to make the judicious payment of "service taxes" that was often necessary to get paperwork and processes efficiently administered.

At the same moment, an Israeli Air Force RC-12D Kokiya, the military version of the twin-engine Beechcraft King Air 200, was flying a long oval circuit pattern over the Gulf of Aqaba. The plane was about 54 miles south of Ovda Air Base, where it would return once its mission was over. It had two pilots and was crammed with electronic sensors. Since the plane's initial delivery to the IAF in 1985, the electronic equipment it carried had been upgraded three times. The plane was a flying suction device, gathering in all of the communications and radar emissions that made their way to the aircraft as it flew at 22,000 feet. All of these data were then relayed by an encrypted spread spectrum microwave communications link to a ground station adjacent to Ovda.

On this day, the Kokiya had a very specific mission. Its latest upgrade fitted the plane with differential Doppler and time of arrival antennae that allowed the plane's sensors to determine the bearing of most of the signals it received. The plane's computers were looking for the specific L-band pencil beams of the Saudi AN/FPS-117 early warning radars. With its systems, it could identify each of seven AN/FPS-117 sites ranging from Jeddah far to the south to the unit operating just north of King Khalid Military City to the east. Over the next 25 minutes, one site at a time went off the air. At a few minutes before 5:00 in the afternoon, the last Saudi radar set still emitting, the one just outside of King Faisal Air Base adjacent to Tabuk, finally shut down. At the ground processing unit inside Ovda Air Base, a message was sent to Mount Olympus. The Saudi early warning radar network was down.

One minute later, at the Al Udeid Air Base just west of Doha, Qatar, American military personnel turned on an AN/TPS-77 phased array radar, the transportable version of the AN/FPS-117 radar used by the Saudis. The radar was programmed to use the same frequencies and search patterns utilized by the Saudis. The intention was to mimic the Saudi early warning radar site just to the west of King Abdulaziz Air Base outside of Dhahran.

Back on the cargo apron at Qaisumah Airport, the co-pilot had finally found the local fuel company. The plane needed 425 gallons to top off its tanks. The payment of cash for the fuel and a 500 riyal note to the office manager resulted in the procurement of an authorization form that allowed the company's truck driver to pump the required fuel. However, it was the payment of another 500 riyal note to the Indonesian truck driver to get him to "get around to do deliver" that finally ticked off the co-pilot. Now the co-pilot stood outside the plane waiting to direct the fueling truck to the where it needed to park.

Inside the plane, the pilot checked his watch. It was almost 5 p.m. and he needed to start one of the plane's engines to provide electrical power since the small plane had no auxiliary power unit. He reached up to his overhead console when he noticed the fueling truck approaching. Now he had to wait as the truck followed the co-pilot's instructions and came to a stop in front of the starboard side wing. The pilot impatiently drummed his fingers on the control yoke as he watched the young Indonesian driver fuel the plane. He caught the eye of the co-pilot, who was still outside on the tarmac, and rotated his right index finger in the air in the universal sign to speed things up. The co-pilot lifted his left hand palm upward and shrugged. There was nothing he could do; they needed the fuel.

After nine painful minutes, the driver finally reeled in the fueling hose, got in his truck and drove away. The co-pilot re-boarded the plane. The pilot was eager to start an engine. "Everyone on board?" he asked to the co-pilot as he climbed into the right seat.

"Affirmative," came the reply.

The pilot looked out the window to his left. "We are clear," he said. He reached up with his right hand and flipped a toggle downward to turn on the engine start batteries. Next he flipped the engine fuel pump toggle down into the open position and the air flow toggle from the normal to the ground position. He looked at a gauge on his instrument panel. "Batteries charged. Pressure good. Ready for ignition." The pilot reached up and used his finger to lift a red cover flap and push the left engine ignition button while he watched his gauges. The unmistakable whine of a turbine engine slowly built in volume and pitch. "Rotation check. Pressure twelve percent and climbing." He released his finger, bringing his arm back down to the left engine throttle. "Secondary ignition." As the engine built to the expected rotations per minute for the idle throttle setting, the pilot continued his mental checklist. "Pressure stabilized. We look good. Please lower the cargo ramp."

The co-pilot reached over to the center console with his left hand and turned a recessed dial clockwise one position. "Ramp down."

At the rear of the plane, the cargo ramp divided, with one portion lowering to the tarmac and the other portion raising up into the cabin roof. In the cabin, one of the operations men walked to the wooden crate, which was at the rear of the plane just inside the edge of the ramp. He kneeled down and pulled off a piece of wood, the only piece that was not covered by the clear plastic wrap that covered the rest of the crate. He reached in and pulled out a heavy cable that was over half an inch thick and had a male receptacle at the end. He stretched the power cable out and plugged the receptacle into a socket built into the side of the cabin. Almost immediately a hum emanated from the crate and it began to vibrate.

The rear of the crate was pointed in the direction of Kharg Island, which was 260 miles away. Inside the crate, a powerful L-band radar emitter was now sending a focused beam of invisible energy in the direction of the island. The emitter was programmed to mimic the frequencies and transmission pulse patterns – especially the pulse repetition rate – used by the Saudis. The plane was sitting in a position that was almost directly on the line formed between the fixed early warning radar site north of King Khalid Military City in Saudi Arabia and the Iranian listening post on Kharg Island in the Persian Gulf.

In the rear cargo cabin, the men joked about being cooked as if they were in a microwave oven despite the fact that the crate had a thin layer of lead that lined the bottom, the top and three of the four sides of the box. A betting pool formed on whether or not interference created by the emitter would cause befuddled Saudis to come out to the plane to investigate. The group was unarmed and their only method of escape would be to take off, head west toward Israel and hope that no fighter jets were vectored toward the slow plane before they could reach the protective umbrella of the IAF. In the cockpit, the co-pilot powered down the few flat panel displays, which were suddenly incapable of producing a clear image. Three of the four men in the back decided to exit the plane and pass the time by watching the comings and goings of civilian aircraft while seated in the shade underneath the starboard wing. They figured that the further they were from the crate, the better. The fourth man joked that he hoped they would all visit him when he was dying of cancer twenty years in the future.

Kharg Island measures three by five miles and is only twenty miles off the coast of Iran. The island is the main oil tanker fueling spot for Iranian crude oil exports. Its strategic importance to Iran is in great disproportion to the size of the island and it was the scene of fighting during the Iran-Iraq War in the 1980s. As a result, the island had long been militarized, with an airfield, a garrison, a Hawk missile SAM site and its own Tall King early warning radar.

Inside a dimly lit and humid bunker on the island, two technicians watched radar screens that synthesized the information gathered by the Russian built radar onto phosphorescent screens. Across from the radar technicians, a single man did double duty. He was the communications officer in charge of relaying any important information to Tehran, and he also operated electronic eavesdropping equipment placed on the island. Among the equipment was a radar receiving unit that picked up and analyzed the large volume of radar emissions aimed at Iran and traveling across the waters of the Persian Gulf. One of the man's jobs was to report to Tehran when the Saudi early warning radars were turned on and when they weren't. He had been on the job for several years and knew the signatures of all of the key permanently emplaced American and Saudi radar units in the line of sight of the island.

His electronic equipment had lost contact with the radar signal originating from King Khalid Military City about fifteen minutes earlier and he had quickly reported it. Now his equipment told him the radar was turned back on and operating normally. The unit at King Khalid was particularly important to the senior officers in Tehran since they had long assumed that the Saudis would turn the unit off if the Israeli Air Force was passing overhead on the way to Iran. A message was quickly sent to Tehran reporting that both the King Khalid and Dhahran radar sites were back online.

48 – Assault on Dehloran

The daytime hours passed uneventfully for Task Force Camel, each man dealing with his anxieties about the coming night as best he could. For soldiers heading into certain combat, this time was a heavy mix of apprehension, nervousness and fateful resolve – each man working out the relative balance of each emotion quietly as he did everything in his power to exude outward confidence and fearlessness.

Most of the men in this unit had combat experience somewhere inside Lebanon, Gaza or the West Bank, but all of those actions were in situations in which the main power of the Israeli Defense Force was an emergency call away. Here they were completely isolated. There would be no emergency helicopter pickup and no sortie from an F-16 or Apache helicopter to tilt the battlefield in their favor if they were discovered. There would be only a fight to the death and the lingering knowledge that their loved ones may never know their fate. Capture meant torture, humiliation, emotional isolation and, ultimately, execution – probably at the end of a hangman's noose. Success meant they would be national heroes. The utter juxtaposition of the two possible outcomes could drive the strongest man to despondency. Each man fought an internal war to keep the thoughts of defeat out of his mind. All the men had varying degrees of success.

The luckiest men of the team were Yosef Hisami and Benny Stern. They had something to do that occupied their minds professionally. The men took turns watching the complex, trying to steal precious hours of sleep when they could. It was easier for Benny Stern. The men joked that he could sleep at will – sleeping through an artillery barrage as long as he had a place to rest his head. True to form, once the morning came and he passed watch duty to Hisami, he fell fast asleep. Hisami was supposed to wake him after three hours, but the Kurd felt great when the scheduled time came and he let Benny Stern sleep until two in the afternoon. Besides, thought Hisami, his life might depend on Stern's aim later that night and he wanted the sniper to be as rested as possible.

The sun set at 5:43 p.m. Iranian time on the mountain. Two hours later, the main body of Task Force Camel had gathered the camouflage net and packed it away. Captain Ben Zeev had every man check his weapons and, for the first time since leaving Israel, told every man to chamber a round in his rifle, being careful to ensure that his weapon's safety was in the horizontal "Safe" position. After another ten minutes, with the darkness now total, Ben Zeev pointed to one of his team, a man named Isaac Mofaz. He had been born and raised in Israel, but his parents had both been born and raised in Tehran, immigrating to Israel three decades earlier.

"Almost ready," said Mofaz. He was completing the assembly of a small Unmanned Aerial Vehicle, or UAV, that was not much bigger than a radio-controlled airplane that any hobbyist would fly. The UAV was known as the Boomerang and it was built by an Israeli company called Bluebird Aero Systems Ltd. It was lightweight and, being powered by an electric motor, very quiet. Under its nose, a small gyro-stabilized infrared video camera could lock on a location and provide up to eight hours of continuous real-time video feed to its ground controller.

When he was done, Mofaz removed what looked like a large tablet computer from his backpack. He booted the machine up. After less than a minute, the tablet and the UAV established an encrypted radio link. The commando waited for the tablet control computer to establish its exact GPS coordinates and then to synchronize those coordinates into the miniature brain of the UAV. The Boomerang, which was painted flat black, was programmed to takeoff and climb to an altitude of 7,500 feet, or roughly half a kilometer above the radar station. Once there, it would establish a wide orbit around a target designated by Mofaz, which would be a point in the middle of the Dehloran Radar Complex. The UAV would then autonomously remain in orbit around that point until Mofaz told it to do something else or until its power source died and it fell from the sky.

Isaac Mofaz next unpacked a flat panel receiver and a tripod. The receiver, which resembled a very small phased array radar panel measuring a mere fourteen inches in diameter, would pick up the encrypted video feed from the Boomerang as it flew, so long as it maintained an unencumbered line of sight. A two foot long antenna extended above the receiver panel that enabled it to communicate with the control tablet that would remain with Mofaz. The Israeli checked to make sure that the tablet, the Boomerang and the flat panel receiver were all communicating with each other. He then turned to a team member kneeling beside him. "Take the receiver," he said. The man lifted the flat panel receiver and its tripod and headed out to place it at a location on the plateau that was above the rock wall formation the team was hiding under.

Finally, Mofaz placed the Boomerang UAV on a metal frame launch ramp that another man had set up. The launch ramp, which measured six feet in length with one end supported in the air by a bipod, looked like a slingshot on steroids. "Everybody stand clear," he said to the team. He touched a command on his tablet and the silent motor on the UAV came to life in an instant, only the whirr of the propeller indicating its motive force. He reached down and pulled a lanyard that trailed on the ground behind the launch rail, releasing a restraining catch. The UAV shot forward into the air. Within a second, only men using their night vision monocle could still see it. As it flew off, even the men with night vision could soon no longer make it out. The UAV climbed to its programmed altitude and started to circle above its launch point awaiting further direction from Mofaz.

"Situation?" Ben Zeev asked into his tactical microphone.

Almost a mile away, Yosef Hisami tapped the shoulder of his partner in the ditch. Benny Stern was once again using his night vision-enabled sniper scope to scan the radar complex. Stern raised up his left hand and put one finger in the air. The pair had worked out their code over the prior fourteen hours. "One man moving. Standard. Negative NVG," the mountain goat said into his microphone.

The captain understood what his sergeant was telling him – the guards standing outside had no night vision equipment. "Let's move," Ben Zeev commanded to the men around him after the UAV was on its way. Isaac Mofaz slung his M-4 over his shoulder and back and put on his backpack over the weapon's sling. He lifted the tablet, which had a cable attached to the backpack. Extending from the top of his backpack was an antenna that allowed communication between him and both the UAV and the flat panel receiver. The rest of the team followed their commander, who notified Hisami and Stern that they were on the move to the assault assembly point.

As the men moved onto the plateau, they first went to the spot where the flat panel receiver had been set up on its tripod. Isaac Mofaz and Manu Moresadegh took up a position by a large tree that was close to the flat panel receiver. The man who carried the flat panel receiver from the hide to where it now stood joined the rest of the team as they moved slowly in the direction of a clump of trees about 350 meters to the east of the diesel storage tank. Once they were in position, each man assumed a prone position to wait.

Mofaz commanded the UAV to widen its orbit. On one pass over the radar complex, he sent a command that locked a set of crosshairs in the center of the UAV's video feed onto the first trailer, the one that housed the radar's operational consoles. The UAV immediately adjusted its flight path to begin a quarter mile diameter orbit around that point. The software on the Boomerang handled the flying, freeing Mofaz to watch the video feed on his tablet. Mofaz zoomed the video focus out until he could see the two guards overlooking the access road and the one guard who was walking around. The mobile guard seemed to follow a path that formed a triangle between the diesel storage structure, the two guards watching the access road and the radar dome structure.

With the UAV now providing tactical reconnaissance, Ben Zeev ordered Stern and Hisami to leave their hide and join the assault team. It took the pair of men only eighteen minutes to reach the rest of the team at the assault assembly point. Benny Stern and the other sniper joined up and, along with one other man from the team, began to move out toward the southwest. The three men moved quietly and quickly, following the undulating eastern slopes that ran down from the radar complex ridge. Their destination was just over a kilometer of walking distance away. They continued toward the southwest, passing along the slopes underneath the radar dome and the trailers.

Suddenly the team heard the voice of Manu Moresadegh come over the tactical communication system, his flawless Farsi standing out among the team. "Mobile one approaching radar." Manu was passing along to the team what Mofaz pointed out to him on the tablet's screen.

Ben Zeev and the seven men remaining at the assembly point heard Manu clearly. But the captain wondered if the three men now maneuvering along the slope to the southwest of the IRGC guard could hear the communication. The assembly point was about half way between the three men on the slope and the spot where Mofaz and Moresadegh watched the UAV video feed. "Benny. Guard on the move. Copy?" Ben Zeev asked.

All three men heard their commander's voice at the same time and all three stopped in place and slowly dropped into a prone position. Benny Stern clicked his transmit button twice to signal the receipt of the message. "Hold," Captain Ben Zeev added.

On the video screen, Mofaz and Moresadegh watched as the guard walked past the radar dome structure, coming to a stop on the south side of the round foundation. Manu stared at the screen as the UAV's continued orbit placed the radar dome between the video camera and the IRGC guard, who disappeared behind the structure. As the Boomerang continued its silent orbit, the slope that the three Israeli commandos were on came into view and the camera's infrared imaging could distinguish the three men despite the near infrared reducing chemicals their uniforms had been treated with in Israel.

"Hold," the captain repeated into his transmitter as agonizing seconds stretched into a full minute. At the tablet screen, Manu and Isaac held their breath as the small UAV continued its counterclockwise orbit, finally sweeping around its northern arc and heading back south. There had been no sign of the guard. As the flying camera came around on its western arc, the southern side of the radar dome structure slowly came into view. Finally the men could see the side of the body of the Iranian. Seconds later his full body was in view. He was leaning against the radar's foundation, his back against the concrete wall.

Mofaz saw it first – the movement of the guard's arm, bending at the elbow as it dropped to his side. "The idiot is smoking," said Isaac. The red hot tip of the man's cigarette stood out brightly on the video screen.

Manu pressed the "push to talk," or PTT, button mounted to his belt. "The guy is smoking. Hold."

The team waited one more orbit for the guard to extinguish his cigarette and return to his usual patrol pattern. "Okay, clear," said Manu.

"Clear. Advance," said the captain into his system. Two clicks came back. The three man team continued on its way, soon turning uphill to climb to a small knob that was only 468 feet to the south and west of the radar dome. The men climbed 219 feet in altitude to take up positions that were a few feet higher than the level of ground where the guard smoked his cigarette.

The two snipers quickly assumed prone positions facing the northwest that were about three meters apart. Benny Stern was on the left, to the south of the other sniper. The second sniper was a couple of meters behind Stern such that if they altered their firing direction to the northeast, the second sniper would be clear of Stern's weapon. Each man folded down a bipod attached to the fore grip of their SR-99 sniper rifle just forward of the 25-round magazine.

The rifle typically fired a 7.62 millimeter caliber bullet weighing 172 grains with a muzzle velocity of 2,652 feet per second, making it deadly as far out as a kilometer in the hands of the two Sayeret Matkal snipers. The weapons were generally set to fire in a semi-automatic mode, but each man had selected single action mode. The result was that when they fired, the bolts would stay closed, reducing the amount of sound emitted. The sound from the business end of the weapon was reduced by a long suppressor attached to the muzzle.

But no suppressor could stop the "crack" of air produced by a bullet flying at supersonic speeds. For tonight's mission, that supersonic crack – a miniature sonic boom – was not acceptable. So each weapon was loaded with a round developed just for these circumstances, when the bullet needed to be subsonic but still deadly at range. To achieve this, each bullet was a long boat tail shaped projectile with a thin rod of depleted uranium comprising its central core. This increased the weight of the bullet to 269 grains and the added weight, combined with the energy-robbing effects of the suppressor, reduced the muzzle velocity of the round to 1,032 feet per second, just below the speed of sound at the elevation of the radar complex.

The third man lay down between and slightly behind the two snipers. He removed from his pack a small tripod and a device that looked like a cross between a scope and a pair of vertical binoculars. He mounted the device to the tripod and pressed a button on the side. The device was a powerful night vision scope with a built in laser rangefinder. He looked through the magnified spotting scope and scanned the ridgeline line across a small dell from their position. He found the access road and followed the road to the west toward its junction with the Derrah Shahr-Abdanan road.

After a few seconds of panning, the spotter came across his target: the two IRGC guards charged with maintaining watch over the access road. They were in the same spot always occupied by the two access road guards. It was a minor elevation that gave the guards a perfect view of the last major bend in the access road before it straightened out on the ridgeline's plateau. Unfortunately for the guards, the view from the position now occupied by three Israeli commandos gave them a perfect view of the guards. The Israeli reached up and pressed a button on top of his device. An invisible beam of light shot out and bounced off the back of one of the two men. "Four-three-three," whispered the man to the two snipers that flanked him. His range finder told him they were 433 meters, or 1,420 feet, away from the two guards.

The man on the range finder hit his PTT button. "Sandman is papa lima. Standing by."

"Affirmative. Stand by," replied Captain Ben Zeev.

The team now waited for the shift change. The wait was only a few minutes. At 8:46 p.m., the three men with scopes trained on the access road guards each saw the excitement of the two guards only moments before they noticed the movement of a passenger van as it passed by on the way to the trailers. One of the guards waved as the van passed. The trailing Suburban stopped for a moment at the guard post and words were apparently exchanged. The Suburban quickly continued on.

Isaac Mofaz, watching the video feed from the Boomerang, first noticed two men exit the middle trailer and then saw the two vehicles come to a stop just outside the middle trailer. He reached over and tapped Manu's back – the latter busy relieving himself onto the mountain dirt of the Zagros. After a moment Manu turned around to see the arrival of the new night shift. "Delivery now," said Manu into his microphone. At the assault assembly point, the pulses of seven men accelerated in varying amounts.

About five minutes later, following the exchange of men to and from the van and the exchange of a couple of boxes of food from the back of the Suburban with a large plastic bag of trash, the two vehicles began their journey back to Abdanan. The van stopped at the guard post and the two guards from the day shift got in. The two new IRGC soldiers who would take their place at the access road guard post were walking up the road from the second trailer, following in the tracks of the two vehicles.

"Delivery complete," commented Manu as he and Isaac watched the vehicles depart.

"Ten minutes," replied Ben Zeev into his microphone.

Twelve minutes later Manu initiated his transmitter with the PTT. "Two on access. Two mobile as a team. Settled."

"Report pattern," responded Ben Zeev.

A few minutes later, Manu replied. "Staying in the lights. Diesel to dome. Now leaving diesel."

The range finder at the sniper position keyed his radio. "Sandman is papa lima." The two IRGC soldiers were settled into their position.

"Sandman zero," said the captain over the tactical system. He talked next to the team around him. "Loaded?" Each man gave him a thumbs up. "Go to semi-auto." The captain and the six other men around him flipped the fire selection lever on their M-4 carbines so that it faced straight up, going from safe to semi-automatic. He then turned to Yosef Hisami, the mountain goat. "Lead us to the jump point." As Hisami moved out, Ben Zeev keyed his PTT. "Moving to jump."

At the sniper location, the man on the range finder shot his laser at one of the two men now standing in position to protect the access road. The two Iranians were talking to each other. "Four-three-three," he whispered. "Wind at one out of northwest." The men would be shooting almost directly into a one knot breeze. "Humidity is four-two. Forty-two. Temperature is one-seven. Seventeen."

Each sniper now referenced a small notepad and then adjusted, or "doped," their scope. Benny Stern spoke first. "Ready." The other sniper made the same statement seconds later.

"Sandman is active," said the range finder into his microphone.

As the two mobile IRGC guards walked at a leisurely pace toward the radar dome structure, the seven men with the captain moved quickly to cover 287 meters from their assembly point to the base of the largest of a grouping of three trees that was only a little more than a hundred meters from the diesel storage tank. The diesel storage tank was a vertical steel tank mounted on a concrete foundation. It held 4,000 gallons of fuel. The tank itself was ten feet in diameter and stood almost nine feet tall. It provided perfect cover for a couple of men.

Ben Zeev, reaching the designated jump point, took cover behind the largest tree in the stand and four other men assumed prone positions around him. Each man had his M-4 at his shoulder and aimed down the ridgeline. After the trees, there was nothing but the barren rock and dirt of the Zagros remaining along the ridge until the other side of the radar dome structure.

The mountain goat and one other man continued on toward the diesel storage tank, their shouldered M-4s leading their steps. After half a minute, the two men reached the round diesel storage tank. Yosef Hisami lowered his M-4. It now hung over his shoulder at his side, its muzzle facing the ground. He pulled out his suppressed SIG Sauer P226 pistol. The pair of men waited behind the storage tank. They were unable to see the mobile IRGC men, but they also knew the Iranians couldn't see them.

"Mobile at radar dome," said Manu about a minute later. "Now heading to diesel. Two still together."

"Sandman be ready. About three minutes," said Ben Zeev. Every man on the team tensed up. Some men concentrated on their breathing, making sure they did not hyperventilate.

About three minutes later, Manu updated the team. "Passing last trailer. Heading to diesel." The mountain goat raised his pistol. Behind him, his partner raised his M-4 to his shoulder, the suppressed muzzle extended past the right side of Yosef's head. The man held the M-4's fore grip in his left hand and leaned his left forearm into the right shoulder of the mountain goat. He wanted to feel when Yosef Hisami moved.

"Twenty meters. North side," said Manu, reporting the position of two mobile guards. As they usually did at night, they would be coming up to the diesel storage tank on its north side, the better lit side. It was the side that Hisami and his partner were facing.

Manu counted down the meters. "Ten. Nine. Eight. Seven. Six. Five ..."

Yosef Hisami advanced calmly from behind the diesel tank, his partner trailing along with him. The two Iranians were talking about their pay and the problems they were having with the rampant inflation in Iran. One man had a family and could not figure out how to pay for food anymore. He stopped in mid thought, his mind processing the man in an IRGC uniform who suddenly stepped into his view. It made him jump slightly, his mind first interpreting the movement as that of a wild animal leaping out. In less than a second, the reaction went from fright to fear to threat. He began to raise his AK-47. He was too late.

The mountain goat squeezed off two rounds into the man's chest. The second Iranian went to one knee, attempting to raise his rifle in a simultaneous movement. He got his weapon leveled using his left hand, which had a death grip on the magazine. But his right hand was still far from reaching the weapon's pistol grip when the first round directed at him hit his left shoulder, causing him to lose his grip on his weapon. Before the muzzle of his AK-47 hit the dirt, the next round from Hisami hit the man in the head. He was dead before his body collapsed. Hisami continued to advance. He arrived at the two motionless bodies and fired a round into each man's head from point blank range.

Captain Ben Zeev keyed his PTT. "Sandman engage." He led his men forward without issuing a command. The team of five ran to rejoin Hisami and his partner.

At the sniper position, the range finder began a countdown that had been rehearsed by the trio hundreds of times. Their next actions were simple muscle memory. "Three ... two ... one ... shoot."

The last word from the range finder was drowned out by the muffled explosions of two 7.62 x 51 mm rounds on each side of the man. The 269 grain bullets headed downrange, covering the distance to their targets in 1.5 seconds. Near the edge of the access road, in a position that had been used for years by Iranians without event, two men died quickly. The two snipers manually chambered their next rounds. Benny Stern continued to watch the two Iranian access road guards, ready to shoot either body if he detected signs of life. Another shot would not be necessary. The other sniper turned his weapon toward the structures on the ridgeline, ready to provide support as necessary.

Reunited with the mountain goat and his partner, the seven man team of commandos advanced to the southwest along the ridgeline. As he walked, Hisami replaced the magazine in his pistol despite having nine rounds still available. The last two men in the group stopped at the third trailer – the one housing two generators and the communication machinery. The remaining five men continued another thirty meters to the middle trailer. Ben Zeev pulled out his pistol. He took point for a four man entry. He and the mountain goat would be the shooters, using pistols. The two men trailing them would provide backup using M-4 carbines.

Captain Ben Zeev did not hesitate once the entry team was properly aligned in an entry stack. He walked up the three steps to the door and pulled it open. It was never kept locked. He walked in at a normal pace, but with intent. His pistol was drawn and pointed in his hands. As he entered, one man was warming up canned soup on an electric stove as two other men were seated at a table drinking tea. The trailer held two IRGC men and two radar technicians. The ability to distinguish between them was easy. The IRGC men wore camouflage while the radar technicians wore the light blue shirts of the Islamic Republic of Iran Air Force. The man warming the soup wore light blue. Ben Zeev's eyes scanned to the two men at the table. Both wore camouflage. He fired twice. The first round entered the back of the head of the man who was facing away from him. The man's forehead blew open, spewing blood and brain matter onto the man seated across from him. That man was too shocked to react. Yoni Ben Zeev fired again at the same time Yosef Hisami fired. Two rounds hit the chest of the Iranian Republican Guard Corps soldier facing the Israeli team.

The radar technician at the stove froze in fear, certain that his life was about to end. One of the men with an M-4 kept his weapon on him, approaching so that the radar technician lost all thought of engaging in any heroic action. Ben Zeev and Hisami continued past the table and walked down a narrow side hall. At the first door, the captain opened it and entered the room, the mountain goat behind him. The light in the room was off, the only illumination now coming from the hallway through the open door. An Iranian man who had just gotten to his feet from a top bunk was confused. "What the hell is ..." shouted the man.

"Quiet," responded the captain in Farsi. "Hands up." The man started toward the captain, who was closing the distance by continuing to advance. Ben Zeev was not sure of the man's intention, but he was not concerned. The man was wearing only a pair of boxer shorts. "Hands up," repeated the captain. The Iranian took another step and Ben Zeev lifted his right leg and kicked the man in his crotch, the Israeli's boot making solid contact with the man's testicles. The Iranian let out a groan and immediately sank to his knees, continuing his downward motion until he was doubled up on the floor. "Watch him," said Ben Zeev as he turned to exit the room and continue down the hall to the single restroom at the end of the trailer. He cleared the small bathroom. "All clear."

The Israeli commandos used plastic handcuffs to bind the arms of the two radar technicians behind their backs. As that was being done, the captain and the mountain goat walked back out of the trailer. As they stepped onto mountain dirt to head to the control trailer, they noticed that the two men who had stopped to clear the generator trailer were already covering the door of the final radar operations trailer. All six of the IRGC guards were now dead and two of the four radar technicians were in custody. Now only the two radar technicians on duty were left to secure, both men hopefully ignorant of the events of the last few seconds.

Ben Zeev and Hisami were at the door in under half a minute. The captain paused to catch his breath and relax. This entry would be different. He relaxed his arm and lowered his pistol to his side. The mountain goat did the same. Calmly, Yoni Ben Zeev opened the trailer door and walked in. Yosef Hisami followed. Inside the trailer, the room was dimly lit. Two Iranian radar technicians sat in front of control stations built into the center of the trailer. They were both busy and they both had their backs to the door. One man was doing what he would do for the rest of his shift if left interrupted – he was watching a flat panel display of the radar's information. The other, the man seated in front of both a radar display panel and the communications equipment, was reading a manual.

Captain Ben Zeev walked calmly up behind the man seated at the communications panel while Hisami walked up behind the man on primary radar watch. The two Israelis looked at each other and Ben Zeev nodded his head at the same time as the communications man started to ask why they were being bothered. The first word did not make it out of his mouth. At the same moment, each Israeli grabbed the collar of the man seated in front of him and pulled each swiftly backwards and away from their control panels and computer equipment. Both men were seated in wheeled chairs and both chairs instantly gathered momentum. The communications technician assumed this was a practical joke and got angry as he and his chair flew backwards across the trailer's linoleum tiled floor. He pressed the soles of his shoes down on the floor to arrest his momentum.

The radar watch officer had not noticed either man come in. He was wearing headphones that picked up Air Traffic Control communications from the regional center in Ahvaz. On his console, he could select the feed from any of the major ATC centers in Iran. He was reaching forward with his left hand to select another feed when he felt his hips move involuntarily underneath him. The sudden acceleration away from his console left him confused. His chair spun around as it travelled across the floor and the man fell out of his seat. Both Iranians started to curse the IRGC guards who they thought were responsible for this outrage.

"Quiet," shouted Ben Zeev. "Hands up." Hearing the commands, the two Israeli commandos still outside the trailer came through the open door and trained their M-4s on the two Iranians who slowly started to realize that this was no practical joke by their IRGC guards. The two men were placed in plastic cuffs and left in a seated position on the floor, their backs against the trailer wall opposite the control and communication consoles.

The captain keyed his PTT. "Secure. Secure. Everyone come home." At the spot where the flat panel receiver stood on its tripod, Manu Moresadegh lifted the tripod and headed out with Isaac Mofaz gathering his tablet and his backpack and following behind. At the sniper position, all three men were quickly on their feet and moving across the tiny dell – more a depression – between the knob and the ridgeline of the radar complex. No longer having to worry about stealth, they only needed to cover 250 meters to reach the operations trailer.

49 – Logging On

About twenty minutes after securing the Dehloran Radar Complex, all four of the Iranian radar technicians were handcuffed and seated on their own rear ends just outside of the radar operations trailer. Two Israeli commandos kept watch. One sniper and the laser range finding man were standing watch over the access road at the same position used by the IRGC. The two corpses were dragged about a dozen meters downhill and out of sight. Benny Stern found a place to set up where he could cover the men watching the access road and all of the structures. Isaac Mofaz set up the flat panel receiver at a random spot close to the trailers. He altered the orbit of the Boomerang so that it now orbited the junction of the access road and the Derrah Shahr-Abdanan road. He had handed the tablet off to the two men who were now guarding the access road.

Another Israeli commando was busy planting C-4 plastic explosive around the base of the radar dome structure. Still another had sent a message to Mount Olympus by burst transmission. The Olympus team now knew the complex was securely under the control of Task Force Camel.

But the real reason for this mission was taking place inside the radar operations trailer. Isaac sat in front of the communications console while Manu stood behind him looking over his shoulder. Captain Ben Zeev stood in the middle of the trailer. Yosef stood in the doorway, his pistol holstered and his M-4 draped across his front. He kept an eye on the four Iranians sitting outside and the three other Israelis sitting and standing inside. He had been calm through the entire process but was now nervous – the fact that he could no longer control events making him fidgety and anxious.

Isaac spent the next four minutes playing with the keyboard and the settings on the console. He seemed to be frustrated. The captain watched and listened to their conversation as best he could, but it had become quite technical and the military officer was no longer following the two computer geeks. Manu stepped over to his backpack and searched for something. He removed a small notepad and returned to his prior position. He began to flip through the pages and state word and number combinations to Isaac.

Finally Isaac stood up and Manu sat down. The Persian Jew began tapping on the keyboard as Isaac Mofaz made occasional suggestions, sometimes pointing at the computer screen both men were focused on.

After another six minutes, Ben Zeev stepped over. "What's going on?"

Manu kept looking at the screen as he replied. "We have a problem."

"What? Talk to me."

Manu hit enter and was still unsatisfied. "We expected that they would be logged onto the network. He was not logged on."

The captain felt a knot in his stomach. Failure to access the Iranian integrated air defense network would jeopardize a meaningful portion of the planning for Block G. It would not make their trip worthless – they had already achieved the base foundational requirement for the mission to go forward by taking control of the complex – but it meant that the losses suffered by the IAF this night would certainly be significantly higher than otherwise. "Okay, what does this mean?"

What the Olympus planners did not know was that the procedures followed by all crews manning Iranian early warning radar sites had been changed effective the first day of July. Since then, all communications officers had been required to log off the network at the end of every shift. The new shift crew had to log back on using a password that identified that team. The assault by Task Force Camel had occurred before the new communications officer had logged on. "We are trying all of the passwords provided to us. No luck so far." Aman and Unit 8200 had targeted Iranian military passwords and password methodology. But their ability to learn passwords relevant to the air defense network had been curtailed when the network was unplugged from the outside world.

"That will take forever. Damn, the man who knows the password is sitting outside," the captain commented. He turned around and walked to the door, looking outside at the four men sitting in the dirt. One man looked up at him and the captain recognized him as the man who had been at the communications console just minutes earlier. Ben Zeev turned to Hisami. "Bring that second man in here."

Moments later the Iranian stood in the middle of the trailer. He looked directly into the eyes of the captain. Manu asked him for the password. The man was silent. The captain repeated the request. The Iranian stayed silent. The captain stood directly in front of the captive. "This is my word to you. Give us the password and you and the men outside will live through this unharmed. You have my word. If you do not tell us, you and the men outside will suffer greatly and we will break into your network anyway before the night is through."

The man's gaze into Ben Zeev's eyes did not falter. If he was afraid, he did not show it. "Go to hell you Jew pig." The man knew exactly who he was dealing with.

The mountain goat stepped behind the Iranian and swung the butt of his M-4 into the man's right kidney. The man made no sound but his right knee buckled. Hisami followed his initial action by grabbing the man's hair and pulling down and back as he kicked his right boot into the rear of the Iranian's left knee. The communications officer dropped to his knees.

"Take him outside and gag all four of them," the captain commanded to Yosef Hisami. Ben Zeev did not want the two computer men in the trailer watching what was about to happen. The captain turned to Manu. "Keep working. If we get this guy to talk, I will be back in." Manu sat back down at the console.

Hisami grabbed the thick head of hair of the Iranian and dragged him across the floor and out the door. A couple minutes later, the captain stepped outside. All four men were now gagged by the insertion into their mouths of hand towels retrieved from the middle trailer. Three of the

Iranians were sitting as they had been before and the one who had been dragged out was lying on his stomach.

The captain addressed all four men. "Your friend has the password into the network. I need that password. When he gives it to me, at that point you will all be treated well and you have my word that you will all live through this ordeal. Until he gives me the password, you will suffer great pain." The captain studied the faces of the three seated men, looking for the weakest. He already knew the man that had been dragged out was very brave and very strong-willed. On the right, a young man, probably no older than 22 or 23, kept his head down. The man was shaking like a leaf. The captain walked to him and squatted down. Ben Zeev lifted the man's chin up and looked into his eyes. He pulled the gag from his mouth. "Do you want to die tonight?"

"No sir," replied the young Iranian, his voice quivering and breaking.

"Tell your friend to talk to us." The young man was too frightened to talk. "Go ahead, tell him to talk." The man just sat there shaking, his eyes looking down even as his chin was being held up.

The captain stood and directed a command to one of his men. "Get that one into a seated position." Ben Zeev was pointing at the communications officer. "I want him to watch this." The Iranian was flipped over onto his back and his shoulders raised up, bringing him into a sitting position.

Ben Zeev decided he could not outsource what he had to do next. He looked at the two other men. The one sitting next to the young man looked to be the stronger of the two. The captain stepped to him and grabbed the man's collar behind his neck, dragging him forward and onto his stomach. He pulled out his pistol and bent over to place the muzzle against the back of the man's left knee. He pulled the trigger and the bullet exploded into and through the man's kneecap, shattering the joint. The man screamed in pain, his gag seeming to make no difference to the volume coming from his vocal chords.

The young man lost control of bladder, wetting his pants. He began to cry. Ben Zeev stepped to him and squatted down. "Tell your friend to talk." No words came from the young man's mouth, only sobs. The captain stood up. "Now you all listen to me." He spoke loudly to be heard over the screams of the man who had just been shot. "When I am done with this man, I will move to each of you until I learn the password. But I will not use my pistol. Instead, I will cut every finger off your hands one at a time and then will I cut off your ears. Then I will cut off your balls. We will spend all night cutting you to pieces. This is your choice."

Captain Ben Zeev stood for a moment to let each of the men think about what was coming as they soaked in the screams and moans of the man whose left knee joint was now shattered beyond repair. Then the Israeli commander stepped over the man again and lowered his pistol down to the back of the man's right knee.

"Stop," yelled the young man.

Ben Zeev straightened up. "Then tell him to talk."

The young man was sobbing heavily and trying hard to catch his breath and gain control over his emotions. The Israeli recognized this and gave him time to compose himself. "He doesn't need to," the young man finally said.

At the other end of the line of four Iranians, the communications officer began screaming and shouting into his gag as he wildly shook his head side to side. He tried to lunge toward the young Iranian seated about two meters away but Hisami was all over the man, grabbing his shirt to restrain him in place. But the gagged words could still be made out. He was cursing the young man and telling him to be quiet.

"Shut him up," said Ben Zeev to Hisami. The mountain goat went down to one knee and placed the communications officer into a choke hold, squeezing with his arm until no more wind could pass through the Iranian's larynx. The captain turned to the young man, squatting down once again. "Tell me what you mean."

The young man continued to keep his head bowed down. He started to talk at a low volume. "Seven, four, dash, three, three, nine, underscore ..."

"You need to speak up," Ben Zeev inserted, but he had heard enough to look at one of his men and motion for him to write what was said. That man pulled a notepad and pencil from his breast pocket.

The young man took a deep breath. He spoke louder. "Seven, four, dash, three, three, nine, underscore, one, one, eight, capital H." Iranian military keyboards were western style qwerty boards.

The captain looked at the commando with the notepad, who nodded his head as he finished writing. He then handed the notepad to his commander. Ben Zeev walked into the trailer and handed the notepad to Manu. "Try this."

Within seconds, Manu pumped his fist into the air. "We are in."

The captain walked to the door. "Get that man medical treatment and remove their gags. Treat them well." Ben Zeev then sent a message to Mount Olympus.

50 – UAV Assault

Two IAF G550 Eitams of the 122nd Nachshon Special Missions Squadron, known in the IAF as the Dakota Squadron, lifted off from Navatim Airbase in the Negev within an hour of each other. Each plane was a Gulfstream business jet converted into an Airborne Warning and Control System, or AWACS, by the addition of ELTA Systems' EL/W-2085 radar and sensor package into large conforming blisters on the sides of the planes and a bulbous nose cone. Taking full advantage of the efficient long-range cruising capability of the base Gulfstream 550 jet, each plane could stay airborne for up to ten hours without refueling. With its advanced Active Electronically Scanned Array, or AESA, radar on the side of the fuselage, the Eitam can actively scan a massive area formed by a radius of over 300 miles in a 360° view around each plane. With its radar off, the plane doubled as a passive vacuum of any electromagnetic signals emissions that were within its line of sight.

The first Eitam took off only ten minutes after the Saudi early warning radar network went off the air. Trailing only minutes behind, two F-16B two-seat fighters of the 140th Golden Eagle Squadron, each loaded with long-range and short-range air-to-air missiles, departed Nevatim to escort the G550. The trio of planes headed to a point on the map over the northern Saudi desert designated as "Point Romeo." There they would spend the duration of Block G orbiting over Saudi Arabia. The G550 Eitam maintained an altitude of 47,000 feet, its crew acting as air traffic controllers for the coming waves of IAF aircraft that would all pass below it. But it also kept watch on the aircraft of all other nations in the area that could possibly interfere with Block G, including Saudi, Iraqi and American planes. The two F-16B fighters orbited in formation half a mile below the Eitam.

The second Eitam took off an hour later with an escort of four F-16Bs. It followed the same corridor over Saudi Arabia and took up a position over the Persian Gulf. The four F-16Bs would take turns breaking formation to return to Point Romeo to refuel.

On board an Israeli Air Force C-130 that was descending through 15,000 feet as it approached the Iraqi border, a technician had just finished checking the onboard satellite communications and avionics on the nineteenth of 23 disassembled unmanned aerial vehicles, or UAVs, inside the plane's cargo cabin. He would complete his diagnostics checks on the remaining four UAVs within the next ten minutes. The C-130 had been delivered to the Israeli Air Force only six months earlier. It was a brand new C-130J model nicknamed the "Samson" by the IAF. Its cargo cabin was 55 feet in length, a considerable increase from the 40 feet interior length of all other IAF C-130s. On this mission, all of that added length was being utilized.

Each UAV on board the plane was a Hermes 450 that had been modified specifically for this mission, the modified version referred to at Mount Olympus as the Hermes 450M. Each of these modified Hermes had a new 100 horsepower Wankel engine and a larger three-bladed pusher propeller on the back end of a 20 foot long fuselage. Each of the fuselages looked just like a torpedo, even in their diameter of just under 21 inches. The normally fixed tricycle landing gear system was now designed to fall away upon takeoff, making the UAV more aerodynamic in flight. Landing gear would not be necessary – all 23 Hermes 450Ms on board the four engine transport were on a one-way mission into Iran. The final modification was the addition of a high explosive warhead weighing 49 pounds in the nose of each fuselage. With the more powerful engines and upgraded propellers, these UAVs could cruise at a speed as high as 145 miles per hour, about 50% faster than their conventional cousins.

The torpedo shaped fuselages were arranged on two large racks that had been designed and built for this mission. The rack located forward in the plane, the second rack to be unloaded once on the ground, held twelve UAV fuselages that were placed four wide and stacked three high. Each other UAV fuselage in the rack was offset four feet forward to allow room for the V-shaped twin stabilizers mounted to the rear of the fuselage just in front of the rear-facing pusher propeller.

The rack in the rear of the plane, the first to be unloaded, held eleven fuselages and a device that would slide out and allow each fuselage to be lowered from the rack and mounted onto to its takeoff carriage. The fuselages were carefully arranged for the planned takeoff order, with their takeoff numbers painted on both the nose and the tail. Inside the cabin, 22 Israeli airmen were either standing along the sides of the cabin in the thin spaces between the UAV racks and the C-130 fuselage walls, or had found a small amount of space to sit on the floor at the front end of the cabin. Along the interior walls of the fuselage, the long wings of the Hermes UAVs, each only a little more than two feet wide, were stored on each side. Each man wore a helmet with its own flashlight mounted on it – in the style of a miner's helmet.

The plane continued to descend and turned off all emissions as it passed from Saudi into Iraqi airspace. This would be the sole planeload of UAVs to operate out of Mudaysis during Block G – the single exception to the plan's policy of redundancy. For this reason, the best C-130 pilots in the IAF had been chosen to make this flight from Palmachim Airbase to Mudaysis.

From the perspective of Mudaysis Airfield, the sun set below the western desert horizon at exactly 5:44 p.m. Iraqi time. The weather was perfect, with no clouds in the darkening sky and only a soft four knot breeze out of the northwest. The five surviving men of Shaldag had completed their preparations for the coming evening. Small lights with infrared strobes on the northwest face of their heavily weighted base were placed on each side of the runway about every 1,000 feet. They were not powerful, but were enough to provide a clear silhouette of the otherwise unlit runway from the air.

Almost one hour after sunset, the Shaldag commander was the first to hear the hum of distant turboprop engines. They grew rapidly in intensity but only slowly in volume, the westerly breeze carrying the sound from far off. Using night vision goggles, the plane first appeared as a dot more than five miles distant. Flying under 1,000 feet, the C-130 Samson had no set base leg vector to approach Mudaysis. Instead, the pilot turned slowly to the southeast to line up on the runway at a heading of 130 degrees magnetic. With a long runway to use, he maintained a landing glide slope of three degrees and an indicated air speed of 155 knots.

The pilot turned on his landing lights when he was a quarter mile off the end of the runway. The plane kissed the concrete at the gentle descent rate of only 200 feet per minute and slowed down gradually until the pilot could turn left on a short connector. He then turned the plane back to the northwest and taxied along the taxiway until he came to the Shaldag soldier who had swept the airfield the previous night. The soldier, using two orange coned flashlights, marshaled the C-130 to a stop just past the access road, which ran into the taxiway at a perpendicular angle.

The cargo ramp was lowered and a loadmaster pulled the quick release tab on two restraining straps that held the rear UAV rack in place. The loadmaster pulled out a stopwatch and clicked the start button. "Okay, we have ten minutes. Let's move."

Eight men, four on each side, pushed the rear rack down the cargo ramp and onto the taxiway, continuing to push the wheeled device off the taxiway and about one hundred yards down the access road. Eight other men pushed the second rack through the cargo cabin, down the ramp and onto the access road. The remaining men began to remove Velcro straps that held 35 foot long wings in place against the cabin sidewall. Three men handled each 152 pound wing, one on each end and one in the middle.

The first wing, painted with the number "1," was walked down the ramp and toward the front of the first rack. By the time the wing arrived, a fuselage had already been removed from the rack and mated to its takeoff carriage. The men with the wing walked around the fuselage and maneuvered the wing in place as the loadmaster placed floodlights outside the plane to light the work area.

The composite wing had two large bolts and two wiring harnesses protruding from the bottom of the wing directly in its center. The man in the middle rested the wing on his shoulder as he fed the two wiring harnesses into the opening in the central wing mount pedestal on the fuselage. He made sure that the bolts lined up with two receiving holes and the wing was then lowered into place. A missing access panel on the right side of the fuselage just behind the wing pedestal allowed necessary access.

The man who had been carrying the center of the wing now retrieved two large nuts and washers from a tool pouch worn around his waist. He reached into the fuselage and slid a washer around one bolt and used his hand to thread a nut onto the bolt. He repeated the process with the second bolt. He then pulled out a ratchet wrench and tightened each bolt in place. Next he reached in and connected a wiring harness that mated the wing's aileron and flap actuators to the flight control computers in the fuselage. He then clicked together a second wiring harness that connected the UAVs mission control and avionics modules to two launch rails mounted underneath the wing, one on each side of the fuselage.

"Done," yelled the man over the sound of the four idled engines of the C-130. On the edge of the road two Shaldag soldiers kept an inquisitive watch.

A second man stepped to the newly re-assembled UAV and looked into the opening in the side of the fuselage to inspect the connections using both a flashlight and his headlamp. In his left hand he held a curved sheet of aircraft aluminum that was two feet long and 18 inches wide along its arc. When he was satisfied that the connections were properly completed, he placed the aluminum sheet over the opening and snapped six latches which locked the panel in place. Behind him, the first man had folded up a hinged mast that was three feet in length and locked it into its operating position on top of the fuselage and just forward of the V-shaped tails. On top of the mast was a teardrop shaped pod that contained the UAV's satellite link system. Two other men walked to the wings. Each man had retrieved a single Hellfire missile from the rack and now mounted his Hellfire onto one of the launch rails underneath the wings.

As soon as the men had completed their roles, they each moved on to retrieve another Hermes fuselage from the rack and a wing from the C-130 cabin and repeat the process. Elsewhere on the access road, three other Hermes 450M UAVs – numbered "2," "3," and "4," – were completing their assembly, each one positioned slightly behind the one in front of it.

The senior C-130 loadmaster, one of four loadmasters now on the ground and assisting with the assembly of twenty-three drones, looked at his stopwatch as he walked through the busy team of men. He was counting out the minutes as they passed. "Four minutes," came the yell.

Finally the man who closed the wing mounting access hatch reached down along the side of the tubular fuselage. A single orange streamer about eighteen inches long and two inches wide flapped lazily in the dry desert breeze. It was connected to a pin that protruded from a small hole in the side of the UAV. The man grabbed hold of the streamer and yanked it and the pin it was attached to out of the UAV. Inside the Hermes, all of its systems came to life and a pre-programmed autonomous software routine commenced.

Over on the edge of the access road, just a few feet from where the Shaldag soldiers watched the process, the technician who tested the satellite communications while on board the C-130 had set up a small folding table that was waist high. On the table a laptop computer was open and connected by USB cable to a small plastic dome that was six inches in diameter and eight inches tall. The dome was communicating with each of the UAVs as they came online. On the computer screen, a status box indicated the number "1" and started to flash yellow. A series of boxes underneath turned from yellow to green as the UAV ran internal diagnostics to verify that all of its systems were online, communicating and in operating condition. The process took only eight seconds and when the last of the small boxes turned green, the main box on the screen also turned green and an "Engine Start" dialogue box appeared. The technician looked over at the first UAV to make sure the propeller was clear. He yelled "Clear One" as loud as he could and clicked the "Start" icon using his mouse.

The engine on the UAV turned on almost immediately, the three propeller blades spinning to life. On the screen of the laptop a new dialogue box opened with the query to "Initiate Mission." The technician clicked the "Initiate" icon. The Hermes 450M sat in its position for another half minute as the technician repeated the same process with the second UAV.

The senior loadmaster yelled out, "Five minutes." Suddenly the engine revolutions on the first UAV increased to full power and the flying machine started down the access road, rapidly gaining speed and autonomously taking off after a takeoff roll of 952 feet. Along with the next three UAVs, the flight of four was now on a journey to Tabriz in the northeastern corner of Iran. Their course would take them well north of Baghdad and cover over 450 miles, taking 3 hours and 22 minutes. The first UAV was on a mission to strike the Tall King early warning radar located near Tabriz International Airport, which shared its two parallel runways with a tactical airbase. The next UAV had no missiles, but carried the Skyjam electronic jamming system in its payload bay. Its mission was to suppress communications at the tactical airbase at Tabriz.

The last two of the four UAVs carried completely different payloads from the first two. Developed from the American BLU-114B, the payload of each of the last two UAVs was a series of two and a half inch wide by eight inch long cylinders that would be ejected downward on command. Each cylinder contained tens of thousands of hair-thin graphite filaments that uncoiled into strands twenty feet in length. A small explosive charge at the rear of the canister would detonate in the vicinity of their target and scatter the filaments. Each of the UAVs had a flat-bottomed protrusion underneath the fuselage that ran for five feet along its length and contained 140 of the cylindrical canisters. The target of these particular UAVs was the high voltage power lines leading from the Urmia Power Complex. The filaments would short these power lines, creating a catastrophic transmission failure and power blackout. One UAV would hit the power lines west of Tabriz and the other the power lines east of Tabriz. The American version of the weapon had been proven in combat over Iraq in 2003.

Over the next ten minutes, the remaining nineteen UAVs took off on their missions into Iran. In addition to the four UAVs flying to Tabriz, six UAVs were on missions to short high voltage electricity transmission lines carrying electricity from the main western Iranian power plants. Besides Urmia, this included the hydroelectric dams at Karoon and the fossil fuel plants at Khorramabad, Zanjan, Sultanyeh, Mahshahr, and Behistun. Five UAVs were sent on missions to jam communications at each of the main tactical air bases in western Iran. The eight other UAVs were all configured with two Hellfire missiles each to strike early warning radars located at Kabudrahang and Delbaran and command, control and communication centers located at the tactical air bases at Omediyeh and Kabudrahang and the heavy water nuclear plant complex at Arak.

The fourth Hermes 450M that departed Shangri-La that evening – the one headed for the power transmission lines on the east side of Tabriz – had the longest journey to its target. Assuming the prevailing winds, the planners had estimated that the trip would take 3 hours and 22 minutes at the modified UAV's top speed of 145 miles per hour. The time of arrival of this UAV would be 10:34 p.m. Iran time. The flight computer on all of the remaining UAVs, flying autonomously, would ensure their arrival at their targets within the same minute.

Each Hermes, painted a flat charcoal black, flew in the dark – emitting no light and no electromagnetic signals. The Hellfire armed drones would establish satellite contact with two-person flight crews waiting at Palmachim Airbase in Israel, but not until they were within two minutes of arrival over their target areas. The last three Hermes launched that night included one configured as a Hellfire armed drone, one as a jamming platform and one with the graphite filament submunitions. They were all carried as backups in case any one of the other UAVs failed to launch. Fortunately, all of the UAVs operated as designed and the three backups were each sent on secondary priority missions.

The senior loadmaster clicked his stopwatch off as the twenty-third Hermes 450M lifted off from the access road at Mudaysis airfield. The attack on Iran was underway. Hostilities were three hours away. The man checked his watch. The time was 1552 hours Zulu, 6:52 p.m. local Iraqi time. They took five minutes longer than his original charge. "Fifteen minutes," he yelled as men were congratulating themselves. "Not bad." He recalled the first nighttime exercise carried out at Palmachim sixteen months earlier. It had been conducted using only handheld flashlights, without the helmet mounted lights. It had taken the team 37 minutes to get all of the UAVs operational. They had come a long way.

He turned to walk back to the C-130. The technician joined him with his laptop computer and antenna dome in each hand and the folding table wedged under his arm. The two empty rack systems, now comparatively light at about 1,000 pounds each, were pushed back into the cargo cabin and secured in place. The four loadmasters and the technician found spots where they could sit down and relax on the flight home. Their role in Block G was now done. But for eighteen other men, there was still a lot more work to do before it would be their turn to board a C-130 and head home to Israel. They all headed off to wait for their next assignments on the tarmac at Mudaysis.

The rear ramp closed and the pilot of the C-130 immediately pushed all four throttles forward to full military power while he and his co-pilot held the brakes. Once the Allison turbine engines reached the desired rotation rate of 13,820 rpm, the pilots released the brakes and the C-130 leapt forward. It had half the length of the taxiway, or a little over 4,000 feet to achieve takeoff speed. The lightened aircraft needed only a third of that distance. It lifted off and began a slow turn to the west and home.

51 – Major Meyer Takes Charge

Twelve minutes after the departure of the C-130J Samson, an Israeli Air Force C-130 touched down 1,250 feet from the northwest end of the runway at Mudaysis Airfield, now known within Mount Olympus as Shangri-La. The C-130's pilot, despite the heavy cargo his plane carried, barely had to engage his brakes as he used another 7,460 feet of runway to slow down to five miles per hour, relying on reverse thrust from his propellers. Finally he turned the nose wheel and steered his plane to the left along a short concrete connector. He crossed the long taxiway that paralleled the runway and steered his plane onto the tarmac, a concrete rectangle that measured 1,380 feet in length by 380 feet wide. He taxied to the far side of the tarmac and brought his plane to a halt, simultaneously lowering the rear cargo ramp door.

The first man off the ramp was tall at six foot two inches. But it wasn't his height that made him stand out. He wore a German Afrika Korps pith helmet. He had worn it as a joke during the first small-scale daylight rehearsal exercise almost two years earlier. It had been passed down to him by his grandfather, a sergeant in the U.S. Army during World War II who had liberated the helmet from the body of a dead German officer in Tunisia in April 1943. Now the helmet, minus the Afrika Korps eagle and swastika emblem that had once been proudly worn by the original owner, was returning to wage war in the deserts of the Middle East. For the man who now wore the helmet, it served a practical purpose that became clear the first night he put it on – it made him easily identifiable in the midst of the chaos that would soon unfold around him. His name was Gideon Meyer and he was a major in the Israeli Defense Force. He would be the commander of Shangri-La for as long as Israeli forces were on the ground this night.

As he walked off the ramp, he was saluted by the Shaldag commander. "Welcome to Iraq, Major," said the Shaldag commander. "My men are under your command."

Meyer saluted back and smiled at the man who parachuted into this location the prior evening. "Happy to be here. I understand you had a loss." The two men discussed what had occurred the prior evening. The Shaldag commander pointed out the area where the mine had claimed his man. When he was done, Gideon Meyer instructed him to have his men bring the body bag over so they could load it aboard the C-130.

"Did you bring any mine clearing equipment?" asked the Shaldag commander.

Meyer looked at him as if caught in a lie, even though he had no reason to feel that way. "No. The decision was made at Olympus not to alter any of the load outs. We will just stay on the concrete."

"Except for the tankers."

"I have thought of that. The risk is acceptable."

The Shaldag commander was silent for a moment. "Have you told the men who will be walking in the sand?"

"No, and I will not. Where your man stepped on the mine is where I would expect the Iraqis to have laid them. The area around the tarmac would be illogical for mines. It seems to me that the Iraqis tried to clear the minefields and unfortunately the one that got your man was just missed."

The Shaldag commander did not agree with this assessment, but the point was now moot and he knew it. He changed the subject, asking what he could do to help. Major Meyer simply responded that they would repeat their numerous rehearsals one more time tonight and nothing would change. As they spoke, a second C-130 pulled onto the tarmac and came to a stop about two hundred yards behind Meyer's plane. It lowered its rear ramp. Both planes held identical loads, except that the first man off the ramp of the second plane was the second in command, a captain in the IDF.

Major Meyer knew exactly how the night would go. Like a top quarterback in the National Football League, every contingency he could think of occurring that evening was like a movie playing in his mind. He had personally led four previous full nighttime rehearsals where planes had flown into Ovda Air Base near the southern tip of the Negev. There, on a section of the base that had been laid out exactly like the Mudaysis Airfield, the teams had rehearsed their roles and made their mistakes when they could afford to make them. Every step in the choreographed process was burned into Meyer's mind.

But right now it was first things first. Two C-130s had to be unloaded and they only had fifteen minutes to get it done and get both planes on their way back to Israel, one carrying the body of Uzi Helzberg. Major Meyer wanted to think the young Shaldag soldier would be the only Israeli to die in Block G, but he knew better.

After Major Meyer, two John Deere Gator four-wheel utility vehicles drove down the ramp, each towing a telescoping set of floodlights with its own generator mounted on a single axle between two wheels. The wheeled floodlights, which would soon be telescoping 30 feet into the air, were each driven to a spot along the long northeastern edge of the rectangular tarmac and spaced about 400 feet apart. With identical lights from the other C130, four sets of floodlights were soon illuminating the tarmac.

After the Gator vehicles exited the aircraft, a Humvee was driven down the ramp, followed immediately by a Ford F-250 crew cab pickup truck. Each vehicle was painted the color of desert sand with intermittent splotches of brown, the camouflage scheme preferred by the Iraqi National Army. Iraqi flags and unit designations were prominently painted onto their front doors. In each vehicle were four members of Shaldag wearing the uniforms of the Iraqi National Army. The vehicles did not stop to allow for the exchange of any greetings. They drove across the tarmac back toward the main taxiway. There they turned to follow the taxiway northwest for half a mile until it intersected with the main airfield access road – the same access road where 23 UAVs had taken off minutes earlier. They turned right to drive the 11 mile distance to Highway 21. Two similar vehicles from the second plane were only a minute behind them.

Once the two faux Iraqi Army vehicles had cleared the cargo ramp, six men and the plane's loadmaster began to push eight pallets of equipment out of the cargo cabin and down the ramp. Each pallet was on its own manually operated pallet truck – a hand operated device seen in warehouses the world over and capable of lifting heavy palletized loads for movement across warehouse floors – or concrete tarmacs in the middle of the Iraqi desert. Six of the pallets held fuel pumps and hoses, each fuel pump powered by its own 12 horsepower generator. The remaining two pallets held electrical cords and various connectors with the tools necessary to properly connect all of this electrical plumbing. Next, two 750 gallon bladders of JP-8 aviation fuel, each weighing about 5,200 pounds, were man-handled off the ramp and out of the way as the Gator returned and backed into the cargo hold of the C-130. After thirty seconds, the Gator came back out, now towing a wheeled JP-8 fueled generator. The 102 kilowatt Pramac generator was placed next to the second telescopic floodlight.

The C-130's loadmaster walked to the end of the ramp and made eye contact with Major Meyer. He saluted the ground commander and quickly disappeared into the now empty cargo cabin of the C-130. The ramp closed and the four turboprop engines of the airplane powered up enough to begin to move the plane toward the long taxiway. The co-pilot turned on the navigation lights. Forty seconds later, the plane turned onto the main taxiway to face the northwest as the pilots pushed all four throttles forward to produce maximum power. The plane quickly accelerated, now unencumbered by the large load it had ferried to Shangri-La.

It only took 1,340 feet of taxiway for the C-130 to reach rotation speed and another 52 feet to lift off. As soon as the plane was airborne and the landing gear had been retracted, the plane banked to head due north in accordance with the departure protocol established for this mission. After thirty seconds, the co-pilot turned off the navigation lights. The plane leveled off at 1,000 feet and began a slow turn to the right, taking it toward central Iraq, but ensuring that in the blacked-out conditions – its transponder, radar and navigation lights all inactive – its flight path was deconflicted with incoming aircraft.

The plane continued its slow turn, taking it to the east and maintaining a distance no closer than eight miles to the tiny villages of Al Kasrah and Al Habariyah, before heading due south toward Saudi Arabia. After flying another 68 miles, the C-130, with its partner trailing about four miles behind, began a turn to the south west. Another 37 miles later, the plane crossed the border into Saudi Arabian airspace and began to climb slowly to 26,000 feet. The pilot's grip on the control wheel relaxed for the first time since departing Nevatim Air Base in the Negev almost three hours earlier.

52 – Securing Shangri-La

Underneath the two returning C-130s, four vehicles loaded with sixteen Shaldag soldiers sped along the access road from Mudaysis to Highway 21. The Humvee and Ford pickup from the first plane reached the highway and turned to the north, away from the two small villages. The two vehicles drove three kilometers along the two lane road and pulled over just before a 350 meter long section of bridge passing over the Wadi al Tubal. Two soldiers exited from the back seat of the Ford pickup and quickly walked across the road and through twenty meters of desert sand to the base of a telephone poll that carried both electrical and telephone lines from the main east-west artery of Highways 10 and 11 down to the villages of Al Kasrah and Al Habariyah.

One soldier was wearing a pole climbing belt and a pair of steel climbing spikes over his boots. He stopped at the base of the pole and wrapped a leather strap around it. He was ten meters up the pole in less than a minute. After setting his position on the pole just underneath the lowest wire, he reached down and pulled up a pair of bolt cutters that was hanging from his belt by a short tether. He cut through the cable that was attached to the pole just above the level of his head. The telephone service that connected the two villages to the rest of Iraq was now severed.

The soldier was back down on the ground within a handful of seconds. There was no intention of cutting the electrical service – the planners at Olympus were hoping that the inhabitants of the two villages would spend the evening watching their TVs. The young European football season's first "El Classico" was due to start in a few hours and Amit Margolis had incorporated this into his planning. Televisions all over Europe and the Middle East would be tuned in to watch Real Madrid and Barcelona – the two giants of Spanish soccer – square off for the first time this season. Minds would be focused on football, guards would be lowered.

The two men returned to the pickup and the two vehicles now parted ways. The Humvee continued on its way north for another twelve and a half miles, or twenty kilometers. The vehicle stopped and parked in the middle of the southbound land, its lights on. The men in this vehicle had a single job to do for the next several hours: They would turn away all traffic headed south on the road during that time. The men removed two stop signs and placed them in the road, each one had a flashing red light mounted on top of the sign. The pickup truck turned back south and parked at the turnoff onto the Mudaysis Airfield access road. Their secondary job was to stop any of the locals from turning down the access road.

The primary mission of the men in the Ford pickup truck was to use sophisticated jamming equipment mounted into the bed of the truck to stop any outbound transmissions from the two small villages to the south. The single phone line had been cut and the spreading cellular service in Iraq had not yet reached into these villages, but many of the homes had satellite phones to communicate with the outside world. More importantly, the single police station located on the southern edge of Al Kasrah had a two-way satellite connection to the provincial government in Ramadi.

The Shaldag soldiers retrieved a parabolic dish and mounted it on a pole swiveled upwards from the bed. They positioned it to point south toward the two villages. Then they opened a box and rotated what looked like a flat panel TV upward, swiveling it on its base until its business side was pointed south. The equipment in the pickup bed worked automatically, sending out signals which interfered with satellite phone frequencies and the frequencies used by the police satellite system. The parabolic dish listened for other suspicious signals and the computers in the system were programmed to respond to any known transmission frequencies other than those being used by the IAF.

Fifty kilometers to the south, the other two vehicle team of Shaldag soldiers set up a similar roadblock just to the south of Al Habariyah. At this location, the Ford pickup was parked on the edge of the southbound road, its jamming equipment quickly put into operation. Within fifteen minutes of their arrival, a sedan approached the Humvee from the south. It was stopped and its two occupants were searched. A cell phone was confiscated and the occupants were forced to turn around and head back to south, cursing the Iraqi Army the entire way.

At 7:23 p.m., one minute behind schedule and only four minutes after the second C-130 lifted off, a huge Ilyushin 78 Midas aerial tanker touched down on the runway. The plane was carrying over 25,000 gallons of JP-8 aviation fuel, having burned just over 9,000 gallons to fly from Kuwait International Airport. The plane had departed Kuwait one hour and forty-eight minutes earlier to fly to Mudaysis. The large tanker, carrying fuel weighing 170,660 pounds, needed most of the long runway to slow down. The pilot used his reverse thrusters and full braking, finally getting the plane slowed down to a speed that left the pilot comfortable, but doing so with less than three football fields of runway length left in front of him.

Like the C-130s before it, the Il-78 turned left at the last connecter and then made its way onto the tarmac. An Israeli soldier acted as the marshal for the plane, wielding two orange coned flashlights and signaling to the pilot from the far northern edge. The plane turned left and headed to the north-facing corner at the top of the tarmac. As it neared the corner, the pilot turned his nose gear to the right to taxi toward the northeast edge of the tarmac. The soldier acting as marshal walked backward, continuing into the desert sand and waving on the Ilyushin as he walked. The plane's nose tires went off the edge of the tarmac. The sand had the consistency of dirt, not as soft as a fine powdered beach but not as hard as compacted gravel. The pilot did not know what to expect since this aspect of his journey had never been rehearsed. He and his co-pilot each kept one hand on the four throttle levers located between them, ready to add power if the plane felt like it was bogging down.

After a few feet in the sand, the pilots increased throttle. The plane continued on deeper into the sandy desert. The soldier guiding them was backpedaling faster as he heard the jet engine whine increase. The plane continued on until the main landing gear tires left the tarmac.

The goal was to get the entire tail section clear of the tarmac and the pilot could feel the plane slow. He applied more power to drive the plane forward, but the nose tires were burying deeper into the sand. The plane was able to make it another thirty-seven feet before the pilot shut down the engines. The nose gear was now almost completely buried. This was a one-way trip for all three of the Il-78 Midas tankers. They would never leave the Iraqi desert.

The crew of the first Ilyushin lowered the rear ramp, allowing access to fuel pumping equipment in the cabin. The engines were shut down, but the plane's auxiliary power unit continued to run, providing power for the plane's fuel pumps and systems.

Over the next eight minutes, two other Ilyushin 78s landed. Each of these was guided into the sand off the long northeastern edge of the tarmac. The planes were maneuvered into the spaces between the telescoped floodlights that had been placed along the edge only minutes earlier. Once all three of the big Russian-built planes were in position, more than 30 men, along with the electric cart and its rotating brush attachment, set to work sweeping sand off the tarmac. They had a seventeen minute window.

The three large Ilyushin tankers held over 75,000 gallons – 500,000 pounds – of aviation fuel for the thirsty warplanes on their way. But that amount of fuel was still not enough for all of the aircraft that would be passing through Mudaysis. Before the night was over, 85 IAF warplanes would refuel on the outbound strike mission to various targets inside Iran and up to 45 on the return from Iran, the final number to be determined by the randomness of war.

53 – Flight of the Herons

Israeli Aircraft Industries and the IAF publicly unveiled a new UAV on October 8, 2007. As large as a Boeing 727, it was called the Eitan – Hebrew for "steadfast." The twin-tailed aircraft, also called the Heron TP, had been under development by IAI for several years and brought a new generation of UAV capabilities to the IAF. With a length of 43 feet and a wingspan of 86 feet, the Eitan could carry sizable payloads in its fuselage and stay airborne at high altitude for up to two days.

But to achieve this endurance, the Eitan relied on a propeller driven engine that allowed the UAV to cruise at a speed of only 145 knots, perfect for loitering over Lebanon but ill-suited for the requirements of the Olympus planning team. In early 2010, the IAF planners at Olympus approached IAI to create an upgraded version of the Eitan that could fly higher, faster and carry a heavier payload, including underwing mounted weapons.

Progress had been set back in January 2012 when an early version of the modified Eitan crashed during a test flight. But development continued and the resulting model was designated the Eitan-B. Its critical upgrade was the replacement of the propeller driven Pratt & Whitney engine with a new quiet and efficient small jet engine – the GE/Honda HF120 delivering over 2,000 pounds of thrust. The engine, combined with upgraded wing spars, allowed the Eitan-B to fly higher, carry more payload and, most importantly, fly much faster.

Israel had successfully kept the development of the Eitan-B secret for initial use on Project Block G – even to the extent of reprimanding those IDF officers who knew of its existence and asked for operational deployment over Syria, Lebanon and the Gaza Strip during the winter months of 2012-2013.

But now the time had come and the first Eitan-B to takeoff on a combat mission lifted off a runway at Tel Nof Airbase as the last of the big Ilyushins was maneuvered into place at Shangri-La. The UAV carried two Modular Stand Off Vehicles, or MSOVs, that each carried 36 runway denial submunitions. The MSOV was designed to create enough craters to keep enemy aircraft from using targeted runways until repairs were made. The MSOV itself was unpowered but able to glide for up to 75 miles on two wings that deploy from the delivery vehicle. The Eitan-B also carried two Spice 1000 gliding bombs that could autonomously glide up to 100 miles from the altitude that this UAV would be operating at.

The Eitan-B took off at 7:37 p.m. Israeli time to the northwest and climbed as it headed out over the Mediterranean Sea. The UAV flew to a point 87 miles off the coast and turned north. By the time it had reached its operating altitude of 59,000 feet, it turned again to head east over the northern portion of Syria, just inside its border with Turkey. The UAV's target was the two parallel runways and two connector strips that provided access to the runways at Tabriz

International Airport, an airport used jointly by civilian aircraft and the Islamic Republic of Iran Air Force. At the average cruise speed of 330 knots, the UAV would take just under two and a half hours to reach its weapons launch point. Once its weapons were launched, each of which operated autonomously, the UAV would fly to the southeast into Iran on a mission to jam radar and communications emissions in the area of Hamadan and Kermanshah.

Ten minutes later, two more Eitan-Bs lifted off the same runway. They carried no external weapons and were able to cruise at a speed of up to 405 knots. They would assume a tight formation with the lead UAV until they passed over the Iranian border. At that point, the two unarmed Eitan-Bs would turn north and then east again to pass well north of Tabriz before turning south and southeast to execute their missions. Each UAV was armed with chaff dispensers and electronic jamming gear that was designed to simulate the electronic emissions of a large force of aircraft. Chaff, a World War II innovation that is still effective to this day, involves the release of thousands of strips of aluminum foil into the air to create large radar echoes. It is used to create confusing radar returns and mask the approach of aircraft. The two UAVs were part of Operation Northwind, the plan to convince the Iranians that the attack was coming from Azerbaijan.

The planners at Olympus did not expect any of these three Eitan-B UAVs to make it back to Israel.

54 – Aircraft Carrier in the Desert

Eighteen minutes after the last of the three Ilyushin Midas tankers shut down its engines, the first of four C-130s landed at Mudaysis. The plane taxied to the upper northeast corner of the rectangular tarmac, heading toward one of the four telescopic floodlights. When the plane was about 80 feet from the light, the pilot turned its nose left, sweeping the plane around on its axis until it faced almost due south, its open rear cargo ramp now facing the floodlights. Two of the men on the ground acted as marshals, working as a team to act as the eyes for the pilots in the cockpit. The pilot altered the pitch of his propellers, causing them to reverse their thrust. He applied power until the plane and its heavy cargo reversed, the open ramp slowly moving toward the floodlight pedestal. The pilot continued to reverse as directed by a marshal standing off to his left side, out of the blast area of the reversed propellers. Just as the pilot was getting nervous, the marshal finally raised his hands over his head, forming an 'X' with his two orange-coned flashlights. The pilot stopped the plane.

In the cargo cabin, the loadmaster released the restraining straps and floor locks that held the cargo in place during flight. He walked to the front of the cabin and stood behind the last of three 2,500 gallon fuel bladders. Each bladder, weighing 17,900 pounds, sat inside an aluminum bath tub that rested on the C-130's floor roller system that ran the length of the cabin floor, including the cargo ramp. The loadmaster told the pilot he was ready.

The pilot set his propeller pitch to takeoff angle and applied military power to his throttles, holding the brakes. After three seconds, he released the brakes and the plane jolted forward. The forces of acceleration and inertia worked together, with the help of a push from the loadmaster, to slide the three large bladders and their aluminum tubs off the ramp and onto the tarmac of Mudaysis. Where they landed was where they would be used. There was no equipment big enough on the ground to move the bladders.

The pilot pulled his throttles back to idle just a couple of seconds after releasing the brakes, his timing based on dozens of rehearsals, all of which were done using bladders full of water. He could feel when the final bladder left the plane in the same way a bomber pilot could feel his plane lighten as the load exited the bomb bay. Over the intercom, the loadmaster simply said "Cargo free. Perfect."

The C-130 closed its rear ramp and continued on to the taxiway which served as the takeoff runway for this operation. As soon he turned onto the taxiway, he applied military power and began the journey home. Behind him, three other C-130s repeated the same maneuver at the base of the three other telescoping floodlights.

The entire process, from the touchdown of the first C-130 to the takeoff of the last, took only twelve minutes. Mudaysis now had 105,000 gallons of fuel awaiting the IAF strike force, with more fuel on the way.

Ten minutes later another C-130 landed at Mudaysis and taxied to a stop on the tarmac about 200 feet away from the northeastern edge, being careful to maintain a safe distance from the large fuel bladders that had just been dropped off. Within twenty seconds, a second C-130 stopped one hundred yards behind the first. Both aircraft held identical loads and within ten minutes each plane had dropped off an Air Traffic Control, or ATC, trailer with five trained ATC personnel. Following the ATC trailer, an airplane tug towing three wheeled carts full of spare parts and tools and twenty more ground personnel emerged. In addition, each plane unloaded an eight man IDF security team armed with four FIM-92 Stinger heat seeking surface to air missiles and a three man team of IDF demolition experts with enough C-4 plastic explosive and timed detonation triggers to accomplish their assignment to destroy all equipment left behind in the Iraqi desert, starting with the three Ilyushin aircraft. The last man out of each airplane was an officer, bringing the ground force command team for the night to four.

Each ATC trailer was quickly towed to a spot close to one of the two Pramac generators. Power cables were run to the trailers. Within minutes, the redundant trailers had established a communications link with the G550 Eitam orbiting about 120 miles to the south over Point Romeo. The trailers had no active radar and were reliant on the information being beamed to them via encrypted microwave link from the Eitam. One trailer took responsibility for aircraft inbound to Shangri-La and the other for aircraft outbound to Iran. But each trailer could perform both functions if either was unable to proceed.

After these two C-130s lifted off on their journey back to Israel, Gideon Meyer called all of the personnel left on the ground at Shangri-La, with the exception of the Shaldag and IDF soldiers on watch, over to the edge of the tarmac. The warplanes of the Israeli Air Force were on their way to this landing strip in the middle of the desert. In front of him stood 95 hand-picked men and women of the Israeli Defense Force. Everyone on that tarmac had been training for this evening for years and so far – with the exception of the mine that claimed the life of Uzi Helzberg – everything had gone as well as could be expected.

Gideon Meyer had been personally selected to command Shangri-La by General Schechter over two years earlier. His first job had been to think through how 85 F-15 and F-16 aircraft could land, refuel and takeoff from a deserted airbase with only one runway and one taxiway that was located in the middle of nowhere and over 600 miles away from Israel – all in the dead of night on a small tarmac and within the space of 45 minutes.

After a month of thinking about the challenge, Meyer had approached General Schechter with a request. He wanted permission to spend at least one month on a U.S. aircraft carrier operating at sea. He explained to Schechter that the tarmac at Mudaysis was only slightly larger than the flight deck of a U.S. carrier. The Americans had not only solved the dilemma, he argued to Schechter, but they had decades of experience and lessons learned. Schechter agreed and Meyer landed on the deck of the USS George H Bush in the back of a Grumman C-2 Greyhound cargo plane on October 12, 2011. He spent the next three weeks in the Persian Gulf soaking up the U.S. Navy's knowledge and experience on how to handle a large number of combat aircraft operating in a very confined space within extreme timetables. The flight deck of a carrier in the middle of combat operations was nothing short of controlled chaos and Meyer realized within the first 24 hours that he had made a wise decision. He returned to Israel with a clear picture of how he wanted to arrange and manage the Mudaysis airfield.

Among the 90 men and five women standing in front of him, 68 of the men were wearing colored shirts. All of these men wore the same helmets and hearing protection worn on the flight deck of U.S. carriers. In addition to the helmets, Meyer had borrowed the color coding scheme used on the USS George H Bush. Meyer had quickly realized the wisdom of making sure that every person operating within a tight space in which military jets were landing, taking off and moving about needed to know instantly the role of every other person.

Four men wore blue shirts. These were the men who would operate the two airplane tugs if needed. Six men wore red shirts. They were the ordinance experts who were there to handle any weapons that might come loose on the airplanes that landed that night. Ten men wore yellow shirts and were responsible for directing the aircraft that would be landing in rapid succession and queuing for fuel ten aircraft at a time. Another ten men wore white shirts. These men were responsible for quality control. They had to be sure that the airplanes that landed were ready for their missions and had to clear each plane for takeoff from Mudaysis. Each plane had to have the fuel it required, its access panels needed to be closed and properly latched and its weapons needed to be properly mounted and ready for action.

The next group of men numbered 14 and wore green. These men were all mechanics and included many of the most experienced mechanics in the Israeli military. Among this group were experts in the F-15, F-16 and C-130 and other men who were equally comfortable working on any plane – or fuel pump – that required their attention. Ideally, none of their services would be required, but prudence dictated their presence at Mudaysis on this night.

But the most numerous were the men wearing purple shirts. Onboard a U.S. carrier, these personnel are known as the "grapes." At Mudaysis, there were 24 of them and their job was certain to be necessary. They were responsible for refueling the planes and overseeing the fuel pumps that would deliver JP-8 jet fuel from the three Il-78 Midas aircraft, the twelve 2,500 gallon bladders deposited on the tarmac, and the four KC-130M aircraft that were then inbound, all at a rate of 1,000 gallons per minute. On their shoulders rested the timetable for Block G.

More than 200 men had volunteered to try out for this small group of fuelers under the cover story that the elite Unit 669 was looking for men to join the team. The tryouts had lasted for three days and included a sleepless night. In the end, the 24 men on the tarmac had been selected. They had been formed into six teams of four men each by Major Meyer and placed in competition against each other. Training progressed during the prior year at Nevatim Airbase. A chart kept the results of bi-weekly competitions to determine which teams could fuel four F-16s and four F-15s the fastest. The teams gave themselves nicknames based on Formula One racing teams, the observation having been made early on that they were like a Formula One pit crew. Team Mercedes had edged out Team Sauber to win the final competition conducted the preceding May.

Finally, four men – including Major Gideon Meyer – wore referee shirts, making them easily stand out. They were the senior officers on the ground at Shangri-La and the referee shirts were Meyer's idea. They seemed completely appropriate since, Meyer believed, the role of an officer was often to act as referee.

Meyer spoke to the assembled team of professional warriors in front of him. He removed his Afika Korps pith helmet. "First, give yourselves a hand." In the absence of any running aircraft engines, his voice was easily heard. He started to clap and within seconds was joined by 95 men and women. After about ten seconds, the clapping rapidly died off. "I am very proud of this team, but the easy work is done. We have four KC-130 tankers inbound and then, within fifteen minutes of their arrival, the real show begins."

Meyer held his right hand in the air and extended his index finger upward toward the sky. "One," he stated loudly with authority. "Less than one hour. That is the window we will have once the first F-16 lands. You have all been working your asses off for a long time for this forty-five minute window that is about to happen. Everyone here knows exactly what they are doing and exactly how to do it. Tonight is no different than the dozens of rehearsals. Just one more time. One." Major Meyer thrust his finger upward to reinforce his point.

"The KC-130s will be here in about ten minutes. Take this time to double check all of your systems, all of your connections. When you are done, check the connections and systems of the team next to you. Make sure you are ready to go. Plane directors – you should know exactly where each of the KC-130s is going. If you are not one hundred percent certain, then ask me.

"Finally, if you need help, if you have a problem, if you are not sure about something, then find me or any officer wearing a referee jersey. That is why we are here. That is why we are wearing these ridiculous outfits," he said as he waved his pith helmet in the desert air. The group laughed in unison. "Find us and tell us what you need or ask us what to do next. Always remember, the only stupid question is the one you don't ask. Now let's get to work."

Ninety-five professionals set about their tasks.

At 8:38 p.m. Iraqi time, the first of four KC-130H aerial refueling tankers, which itself had been refueled over the Gulf of Aqaba by another KC-130H, touched down at Mudaysis. The plane taxied to a position as close to the edge of the tarmac as the nerve of the pilot tolerated. The plane was parked close to the first of the beached Ilyushins. The pilot shut down his engines. The second plane landed and assumed its position.

The pilot of the third plane made his approach to Mudaysis only thirty seconds following the second plane. By now, darkness had completely swallowed the desert landscape. The pilot and co-pilot wore AN-AVS 6 night vision goggles inside the blacked-out plane. As they lined up on the infrared strobe lights that outlined the runway for their final approach, they turned on their landing lights about a half mile off the end of the runway. The pilots removed their night vision goggles and the co-pilot concentrated on the altimeter to call the rate of descent and the distance remaining to touchdown. The plane was very heavy, as were all of the planes that had landed before it. Its weight as it touched down would be just under 157,000 pounds, a weight that was tolerated only out of combat necessity.

The heavy weight of the plane put tremendous stress on the landing gear and all of the cargo planes landing that night had higher than usual air pressure in their tires to help compensate. But the most important factor was the individual skill of each pilot. The heavy loads meant that the pilot needed to land at as gentle a descent rate as practical. However, the same heavy load put a premium on landing as close to the start of the runway as possible to allow for the maximum amount of runway to slow down. As the third plane approached the runway threshold, the pilot was concentrating on his descent rate. He wanted to touchdown at a descent rate of somewhere around 200 feet per minute.

"One fifty-five," said the co-pilot as the plane passed over the end of the runway. The wheels were 155 feet above the runway. The co-pilot had concern in his voice. At their current speed of 170 knots, they were covering 1,150 feet of runway every four seconds they remained airborne. They had found through trial and error that they wanted to be about 30 feet above the runway as they passed over the runway threshold.

The pilot pushed forward on his control yoke slightly to force his plane down, but his throttle setting was still too high and his rate of descent barely changed. The plane was dropping too slowly. The pilots had been picked for their ability to land successfully on the first pass and the expectation was that no one would abort and go around – after all, there was another C-130 only thirty seconds behind him and blacked out planes were all over the area. The timetable had been drilled into their heads – it was sacrosanct.

"One forty. Need to get down," said the co-pilot. They were now 1,000 feet further down the runway and had already passed the point at which they wanted to touch down.

The pilot reduced throttle and the heavy plane instantly reacted, suddenly dropping at a rate of just over 518 feet per minute. Twenty feet over the runway, the pilot flared his plane to ensure that the four tires of the main landing gear touched down before the nose gear. The plane touched down 5,785 feet down the runway. The impact was hard but nothing that would have been a problem had their weight been more typical. Worse, a last minute course correction input from the pilot in response to a gust of wind caused the plane to land with most of its weight being borne by the main landing gear on the right hand side. One of the two tires on the right hand main gear struts was unable to handle the force. The tire blew apart and the other tire split slightly along the sidewall, its air pressure now escaping slowly into the desert night. The pilots felt and heard the tire explosion as they went to full power reverse thrust and heavy braking to slow their plane down in the 4,015 feet of runway they had left.

The co-pilot understood the real threat before the pilot did. Another C-130 was right behind them and more than likely there was now one or more large chunks of shredded tire on the runway – the type of debris that can destroy a propeller or an engine. After ten seconds of deceleration, the co-pilot took his hands off the control wheel and reached down to turn on the radio transmit button. The radio was set to the encrypted spread spectrum frequencies all inbound aircraft were using to communicate with the ATC trailers at Shangri-La.

"Abort, abort, abort," said the co-pilot into his mounted microphone. "Hold for clearance."

In the fourth KC-130, the pilot heard the transmission and recognized the voice. He was about to turn on his landing lights, but instead added power and turned his plane to the south to start a long oval "go-around" pattern.

On the ground, the KC-130 slowed and turned onto the last connector to make its way to the tarmac. The pilot knew he had a problem because he had to use more power than normal on his two starboard side engines to taxi. An alert plane director in his white shirt noticed the tires and decided to send the plane to the first available spot on the tarmac, which is where the last KC-130 was scheduled to be parked. The plane stopped as directed and the pilot opened his cockpit window and waved for the plane director as the co-pilot turned off the engines. The plane director ran to the side of the cockpit and lifted his ear muff away from his head to hear the words from the pilot.

"There is tire debris on the runway," shouted the pilot, pointing vigorously toward where they had just touched down. "We sent the next airplane around."

The plane director immediately talked into his microphone, utilizing the low power radio sets that everyone with a helmet had available for emergency communication. In one of the ATC trailers, the transmission from the plane director, which was directed to the second-in-command, was picked up on a handheld walkie-talkie. The final approach air traffic controller contacted the fourth KC-130 to hold in pattern.

Major Meyer heard the update from his second-in-command standing next to him. Ten purple shirted fuelers were standing nearby and Meyer told them what happened and sent them to the runway. All ten men left on the run and the runway was cleared within several minutes. The fourth and final KC-130 came in five minutes behind schedule, but the landing was uneventful.

Now there was more than 136,000 gallons of aviation fuel available at Shangri-La, all of the fuel that had been planned for by Mount Olympus. The first warplanes headed into Iran would land within ten minutes.

55 – The Hammers Fly

The town of Abasan al-Kabirah has a population of just over 23,000. It is located in the southern half of the Gaza Strip, but to its inhabitants, it feels a world away from the threat of conflict and sudden death that can often intrude into life in Gaza City neighborhoods like Rimal and Jibaliya to the north. Life in this town proceeds at a pace that has been set by centuries of Middle Eastern rural agricultural tradition. This tradition survives despite the influence of the nearby city of Khan Yunis. What Hamas activity goes on in the town is quiet and discrete.

But the town has a strategic distinction lost to all but the most interested observers. The highest point in town is 29 kilometers, or 18 miles, from the western end of the main runway of Hatzerim Airbase in the Negev desert. Hatzerim is perhaps the most important airbase of the IAF because of a simple reason: it is the base of the 69 Hammer Squadron. The Hammer Squadron flies all of the 25 F-15I Ra'am fighter-bombers of the Israeli Air Force, the single most potent strike weapon of the State of Israel. The prevailing winds, coming out of the west, mean that almost all takeoffs from Hatzerim are toward the west, almost in a straight line in the direction of Abasan al-Kabirah. For the nation of Iran, that made the town very important indeed, since knowledge of when the airplanes of Hammer Squadron were airborne, how many were airborne and which direction they headed, was the single most important early warning indicator of a strike on the Islamic Republic.

In order to observe the comings and goings of the Hammer Squadron, the Iranian Revolutionary Guard Corps, or IRGC, had quietly and secretly taken control of a three story apartment building on the highest hill in town. The eastern side of the building had an unobstructed view toward the east. During 2006 and 2007, the IRGC had moved undercover Iranian revolutionary fighters – some with their families – into each of the six apartments of the building as prior families moved out. Inside the top floor apartment, in a living room that had a large plate glass window facing east, the IRGC had set up very expensive optical equipment, night vision and infrared detectors. The passive instruments enabled the men in the room to affirmatively identify any F-15 departing or arriving at Hatzerim. No light was allowed in the room and no electronic messages were sent from the building. Observations were written down on paper in a simple code and taken by messenger to different safe houses in nearby Khan Yunis for transmission to Tehran by various methods that had evolved with technology. No one was involved in the chain who had not been recruited and trained in Iran by the IRGC.

The secret of the observation network had been so well maintained that the Israelis did not learn about the existence of the network until the NSA provided intercept data to Israel in late 2010. Even as of the date of the launch of Block G, despite the best efforts of Aman, the exact location of the observers was unknown to Israel. But the codes used to communicate with

Tehran had been broken and every message from Khan Yunis to Tehran was read by Unit 8200 at the same time as the IRGC was reading each message in Tehran.

The existence of the network had resulted in significant discussion among the Olympus planning team on how to eliminate the early warning notice that would go out to Iran when all of the planes of the Hammer Squadron left Hatzerim. Alternative ideas included jamming and having all of the F-15I aircraft spend a day or so prior to launch at dispersed airfields around Israel. But in the end, it was a suggestion by Amit Margolis that resulted in the plan finally adopted. Now that plan was in motion.

At 7:22 p.m. local time, one hour after sunset and before total darkness had set in, the first four of 24 F-15I Ra'ams of 69 Hammer Squadron took off in pairs in quick succession from parallel runways 28L and 28R at Hatzerim. Each plane had a pilot in the front seat and a weapons system officer, or "wizzo," in the back seat. Each plane was loaded to within one ton of the maximum takeoff weight of 81,000 pounds and used most of the available concrete of each of the two long runways.

The first plane to lift off was piloted by Gil Bar-Kokhba, call sign "Gadget," with his longtime partner Ronen Isser, call sign "Pacer," in the rear seat. Gadget's F-15I carried two GBU-121B thermobaric bombs, each weighing 2,000 pounds and mounted underneath the fuselage on each side of a centerline mounted 600 gallon external fuel tank. The bombs could not be dropped safely until the centerline fuel tank had been successfully jettisoned. The plane also carried two Python-5 air-to-air infrared missiles on underwing launch mounts located just to the outside of two 600 gallon external fuel tanks mounted under the wings. The plane's M61A1 Vulcan gun system had been removed to save weight, its right side wing root opening now covered for aerodynamic improvement – the mission of this plane was to deliver its GBU-121B bombs, not to engage in a dogfight. Gadget and Pacer would cover the longest distance of any the pilots involved in Block G and would explore the range limits of the F-15I.

All of the crews had been told only that morning that this was the day when Block G, for which they had all been training for years, was going to become a reality. As they had during the week long period running into the prior two new moons, they had been confined to base and following an enforced work-sleep pattern that had them waking at 4 in the afternoon, flying only nighttime training missions and going to sleep at 8 in the morning. The crews had begun to joke about the schedule as "Hammer Time."

The takeoff of the entire squadron, with the exception of a single plane, had been done many times over the prior two years. Tonight, the planes climbed toward the west, in the direction of Abasan al-Kabirah, and then banked to the north to continue their climb over Israel, being careful to stay clear of the airspace over the Gaza Strip. By the time the squadron turned west again, the planes were climbing through 18,000 feet as they passed over the coastal Israeli city of Ashdod. They continued to climb as they headed west over the Mediterranean Sea and started a slow turn to the north.

At 7:54 p.m. in Israel, equipment operated by Unit 8200 intercepted a telephone call originating from somewhere inside the Gazan city of Khan Yunis and going to a cell phone

number somewhere in the West Bank town of Nablus. The phone call was cryptic but was easy
to decode for the team assigned to this network. Once passed from the West Bank to Tehran, it
would inform the senior commander of Iran's air defense forces that the entire 69 Hammer
Squadron had departed Hatzerim at 1625 Zulu – 7:25 p.m. local time, 7:55 p.m. Iranian time –
headed to the west over the Mediterranean. The planes were heavily loaded with weapons
ordnance.

As Unit 8200 intercepted the call from Khan Yunis, the first six aircraft of a wave of 25 F-16s
took off to the northeast in pairs from three parallel runways at Ramon Airbase located south of
Hatzerim in the middle of the Negev desert. They would soon be joined by another 40 F-16s and
20 F-15s taking off from Ovda, Ramon and Nevatim Airbases, all within the Negev desert. All
85 of these aircraft flew south to the Gulf of Aqaba before turning to the east to head toward
Shangri-La by flying over northern Saudi Arabia. All of these aircraft were configured for
Suppression of Enemy Air Defense, or SEAD, missions. The majority of planes carried two
AGM-88D or E model high speed anti-radiation missiles, all of them designed to home into and
destroy sources of radar emissions. Half the planes carried a single Delilah missile. The Delilah
is an Israeli stand-off cruise missile that can travel over 200 miles to find and strike stationary
and mobile targets, including the ability to loiter over a target area and search for targets. Almost
all of the planes carried air-to-air missiles, including AIM-120 AMRAAM beyond visual range
missiles and Python 4 and 5 infrared missiles.

The twenty F-15Cs that took off from Nevatim Airbase were configured for SEAD and
Combat Air Patrol, or CAP, missions over Iran, some being armed with similar weapons as their
smaller F-16 partners. But the primary mission of all of the planes was CAP support in the event
that Iranian Air Force aircraft rose into the skies. Some of the planes carried the Spice 1000 or
Spice 2000 winged glide bomb for use against specific targets in route.

56 – The Madhatters Come Calling

Somewhere over the Mediterranean Sea, the F-15Is of 69 Hammer Squadron that took off from Hatzerim Airbase reached their cruising altitude of 37,000 feet and then turned back to southeast to fly back over Israel, turning due south until they had passed over the Israeli city of Eilat, situated on the Gulf of Aqaba. The planes flew in a tight trailing formation of four planes per group. About fifteen miles south of Eilat, they turned east to head over the northern desert of Saudi Arabia. Another 445 miles later, at a point in the sky designated Point Romeo, the planes of Hammer Squadron descended 10,000 feet to begin aerial refueling from seven IAF KC-707s. Each F-15I filled all available space within its internal fuel tanks, two conformal fuel tanks, two wing mounted external fuel tanks and one centerline mounted external fuel tank. After refueling, each plane left Point Romeo with 5,568 gallons, or 37,860 pounds, of JP-8 fuel, enough to fly about 3,870 kilometers, or 2,405 miles, depending on when the planes unloaded their lethal payloads. This was just enough for each plane to reach its target inside Iran, maneuvering as necessary to hit targets or evade air defenses, fly south to the Persian Gulf and then head west over the Saudi desert to return home to Hatzerim.

At 8:45 p.m. Israeli time, while the 24 planes of 69 Hammer Squadron were on their way to Point Romeo, the IRGC men inside the apartment in Abasan al-Kabirah were scanning the dark sky to the east with binoculars and night vision equipment when the man in next room started to call out. This man was looking at the flat panel display of a very sophisticated and expensive forward-looking infrared unit mounted on the roof of the building and cleverly concealed inside one of the six air conditioning condenser units. Even the fan on top of the faux unit would turn on when other units came on, but the east facing metal side wall would lower on command to allow the unit an unobstructed view toward Israel. The device enabled the man to see aircraft coming in from the north and apparently descending toward Hatzerim Airbase. The two men in the living room looked out the window in the indicated direction.

After half a minute, one man spoke out: He had acquired an F-15 moving slowly and descending. It had its navigation lights on and was following a standard landing approach route into Hatzerim that the IRGC had witnessed countless times in the past. He verbally directed the other man to the plane. The other man picked it out as well, along with several other F-15s. Over the next ten minutes, the two men counted twenty F-15 aircraft returning to Hatzerim and landing, all apparently with their heavy payloads still in place. The proper note was created and taken by runner to a nearby home, where another Iranian volunteer put the paper in his pocket and headed toward Khan Yunis on a motorcycle.

At that moment, 20 F-15E Strike Eagles of the U.S. Air Force's 492nd Fighter Squadron, the "Madhatters," which had departed Naval Air Station Sigonella in Sicily two and a half hours earlier, were directed to refueling tarmacs at Hatzerim. Lieutenant Colonel James "Slim Jim" Nolan, commanding officer of the squadron, exited his plane and was welcomed by the commanding officer of Hatzerim, who presented the squadron commander with the flag of Israel. None of the men of the 492nd knew why they were visiting Israel this particular evening, but they knew they had received orders earlier that day to be on standby at Sigonella ready to take off within ten minute's notice to proceed by the most direct route to Hatzerim. They also knew that they would be welcomed with food, soda, coffee and bathroom facilities, but that they would be taking off to return to Sigonella approximately 70 minutes after their arrival. Once back at Sigonella they would be free to get some sleep before returning the next day to their base at Lakenheath in England.

Thirty-two minutes later, as the 69 Hammer Squadron was refueling at Point Romeo, the team at Unit 8200's listening post just to the northeast of Urim, a kibbutz in the Negev not far from Hatzerim Airfield, intercepted another telephone call originating from the city of Khan Yunis to a number in the West Bank. The intercepted message was interpreted and forwarded to Mount Olympus by email. A young woman working at Mount Olympus as an IAF communications officer printed out the email and walked over to the adjacent desks of General Schechter and Amit Margolis. She was smiling broadly as she handed the printed email to Margolis. The co-commander of Block G stood and handed the paper to David Schechter, who looked at him expectantly.

Amit Margolis simultaneously punched his right fist in the air and loudly shouted, "Hell, yes."

General Schechter smiled and clapped his hands. "Amit, please do the honors. You earned it."

"Attention, please," Margolis shouted to the large team within the command room at Mount Olympus. Sixty-two men and women, many crammed into tiny cubicles just large enough to hold their computer screens, stopped and turned toward Margolis. "The Iranian command has been officially notified that twenty of the twenty-four aircraft of Hammer Squadron have now returned to Hatzerim."

In the room a round of applause erupted along with scattered whoops and yells. The senior air defense officials of Iran were now concluding that this night was going to pass without an Israeli attack. They would be proven wrong.

As expected by the Olympus planners, IRGC headquarters in Tehran sent an update of the status of 69 Hammer Squadron to the night watch commanders of the Islamic Republic of Iran's Air Force and the Air Defense Forces. But unknown to anyone at Mount Olympus, inside Iranian Air Force headquarters at Doshan Tappeh Air Base in Tehran, Brigadier General Hassan Shahbazi, the senior commander of the Iranian Air Force on duty that evening, sent along a coded message to the commander on duty at every air base in Iran. The message let the commanders know that 69 Hammer Squadron was at its home base in Israel and therefore unlikely to attack Iran this evening.

This communication, which took advantage of the valuable intelligence about 69 Hammer Squadron that came from the Gaza Strip, had been implemented by the Iranian Air Force fourteen months earlier. The extended periods of being on tripwire alert every night had resulted in meaningful fatigue among the crews and mechanics of the Air Force. Men who were highly trained had been leaving the service in numbers that threatened the viability of the Air Force if it persisted. So a decision had been made after much debate to limit the highest levels of alert readiness to those times when at least half of 69 Hammer Squadron was away from its home base.

At 8:22 p.m. Israeli time, exactly one hour after Gadget's F-15I lifted off, the first six of 55 F-16I Sufa strike aircraft lifted off from Ramon Airbase, taking off in pairs and using all three parallel runways. The planes had a one hour flight to Point Romeo where they would line up to refuel behind the seven KC-707s that had just finished refueling 24 F-15Is and 20 F-15Cs. Minutes later, a flight of 20 F-16Cs took off from Ovda Airbase, just north of the city of Eilat, to join the Sufas on the trip into Iran. The F-16Cs would be dedicated to Combat Air Patrol, or CAP, missions this evening. Refueling at Point Romeo in under two minutes per plane, the entire flight of 55 Sufas and 20 F-16Cs would take only nineteen and a half minutes to refuel behind seven KC-707s.

Like the F-15I, the F-16I Sufa represents the cutting edge development of the F-16 fighter-bomber, incorporating advanced Israeli electronic communications and counter-measure equipment and conformal fuel tanks that give the plane substantially more range than the typical F-16. All of the F-16Is were configured for strike missions, carrying a mix of guided bombs, Delilah missiles and the Popeye Lite standoff cruise missile. At 2,500 pounds, the Popeye Lite could be launched from as far away as 95 miles from its target, depending on the altitude of the F-16I at launch. For this night, all of the Popeye Lites were autonomous once launched, delivering their 776 pound high explosive warheads by a combination of GPS and inertial guidance.

Fourteen minutes after the Sufas began to depart from Ramon, two G550 Special Electronics Missions Aircraft, or SEMA, aircraft took off from Nevatim. They would soon join the growing wave of aircraft overflying Iraq to enter Iran at or near a point on the map that the Olympus planners referred to as Point Delta. Each plane was packed with the latest radar and communication jamming electronics – far more powerful and sophisticated than the jamming systems built into the Hermes 450Ms already on their way into Iran. These two planes would be in the line of fire, both flying deep into Iran before the night was over.

57 – Esther Loads Her Sling

On October 2, two Ilyushin 76 cargo aircraft bearing the insignia of Swiss-Arab Air Cargo landed a half hour apart after 10 p.m. at Nevatim Airbase in Israel. One plane had flown in from delivering cargo to Sarajevo and the other had delivered cargo to Kiev earlier in the day. The captains of each plane, Oleg Kolikov and Jim Miller, taxied their respective aircraft into two separate hanger buildings and then were driven, along with their crews, to a building where they could get some sleep. For Oleg Kolikov, a secular Russian Jew, this was the first time he had ever stepped foot in Israel. For Jim Miller, a secular American Jew, it was only the second time, the first time having been with his parents as a teenager almost five decades earlier. All of the other eight members of both crews were Jews, most of them Israelis, working for SAAC under false identities.

The crews spent most of the next day either in briefings or being introduced to their new planes. The briefings continued the day after that. The men had new systems to understand. At sunset on October 4, the crews boarded two Ilyushin 76 aircraft. They were each painted in the colors and logo of Swiss-Arab Air Cargo and carried the same tail numbers as the two planes the men had flown into Nevatim two nights before. But they were not the same planes. They were the two Ilyushins purchased by Sun d'Or II, the El Al subsidiary, which had first been flown to Nevatim during the last week of 2010 and the first week of 2011.

Captain Kolikov lifted off first, about 40 minutes after sunset. Captain Miller's plane left the runway just ten minutes later. Both planes headed out over the Mediterranean. Kolikov flew 395 miles to the west and then turned to the north into the air traffic lane he would have been on had he departed Bangui M'Poko International Airport in the Central African Republic as his filed flight plane claimed. He continued north for about a thousand miles and landed his plane at Luhansk International Airport in the Ukraine a little before 11 p.m. The crew spent an hour running diagnostic checks on the plane. A waiting corporate jet chartered by a Swiss company then flew Oleg Kolikov back to Israel, this time landing at Sde Dov Airport in the early morning hours.

Captain Miller flew his Ilyushin 76 about a hundred miles to the west and north over the Mediterranean before turning the big cargo plane around to head east over Israel, Jordan, Saudi Arabia and the Persian Gulf to finally approach Ras Al-Khaimah a little over three hours after he took off from the Israeli Air Force base at Nevatim. The plane followed the standard approach to the Ras Al-Khaimah Airport, entering the airspace of the United Arab Emirates to the south of the airport and then turning north to make its final approach to the single runway. At this late hour, Miller did not need to worry about any other traffic, but the tower was unable to give him any feel for wind conditions on approach. The best they could do is provide him an update from the anemometer on top of the tower and the lighted wind sock near the runway.

The big plane had its flaps and large leading edges extended to their maximum setting, Miller needed all the lift available with the large load he was carrying. The plane was descending gradually on final as it approached the runway threshold. With 9,800 feet of runway to work with and weighing more than he cared for, the American pilot was maintaining a higher than normal speed and a gentle glide slope, the high-winged aircraft maintaining an attitude that kept its nose level.

The plane passed over the threshold when an event occurred that is dreaded by all pilots – an event that could not be foreseen by Miller and for which he did not have the sophisticated Doppler radar that may have saved him from the what he was about to endure. The prevailing northwesterly wind coming in from its journey across the cool mountains of Iran and the Persian Gulf was colliding with a wave of air just above the ground that had worked its way north from the hot desert sands of the Arabian Peninsula. Miller was preparing to flare his aircraft when the modest headwind he had been flying into suddenly shifted into a swirling invisible mass of air that drastically reduced the air flow creating lift on his wings.

A sudden sinking feeling in the pit of his stomach was Miller's first physical notice of what was happening. The timing of the natural assault on his plane could not have been worse. The captain had no reserves of potential energy that gave good pilots the ability to fly their way through trouble. He had no altitude to work with and no time to apply power, the reaction time of the big jet's four engines being far too slow to make any difference at this point. Miller continued his flare maneuver instinctively, wanting to be sure that the impact that was coming was borne by the main landing gear. He adjusted his ailerons slightly to keep his wings level – he was fighting to ensure as even a distribution of the forces of touchdown as possible. "Brace. Brace," said the American, not even conscious of the words coming from his mouth – his decades of training and experience now combining into automatic responses.

The plane hit the runway hard, its heavy load absorbing many times the force of gravity at the moment of impact. The skill of the pilot had succeeded in distributing the force almost evenly among the 16 tires of the main landing gear. Miller winced as the plane touched down, the force hurting his back and reminding him of his age. But the plane held together, and, once the front gear and its four tires were on the runway, the deceleration was normal.

Miller taxied into the same hanger building he had departed from several days earlier. The four engines were shut down, and thick cables were plugged into a receptor port under the nose of the aircraft, providing power from a large generator parked outside the hanger.

The co-pilot looked at his captain. The much younger man was pale. He understood exactly what had just happened. "That was not fun at all," said the co-pilot. "You did a hell of a job getting this big son of a bitch to flair in time."

Miller shook his head. "Too close for comfort."

"You think anything is damaged?"

"I don't know," responded the captain. "That was pretty hard."

The crew began to perform a series of diagnostic checks, relying on a computer which had been installed directly into the cockpit by the engineers from Israel Aerospace Industries. Miller drank from a bottle of water as the flight engineer ran through a checklist he had on a clipboard at his station. Twenty minutes later the flight engineer made a comment that caught Miller's ear. "This isn't good." A discussion followed that lasted several minutes.

"Get through the rest of your checklist and then we can come back to this," Miller said. After another 45 minutes, the flight engineer repeated the routine that had prompted the earlier discussion.

"Negative function. It's not working."

Miller buried his forehead into his left palm, his large hand massaging his own scalp. "Talk to Olympus and let them know. I need to walk around." Jim Miller worked his body out of the captain's seat and was quickly onto the concrete floor of the hanger. He walked around the plane inspecting the landing gear and tires in particular. They had a full complement of skilled mechanics to address any problem – so long as it was a problem found on any normal Ilyushin 76.

After about ten minutes the flight engineer emerged from the fuselage and called the captain over. "They want you back. The jet is waiting outside. They are sending a couple of experts over in the morning."

Captain Jim Miller was airborne again within twenty minutes, this time as a passenger in the back of Dassault Falcon corporate jet. He slept on and off, short catnaps as the plane made its way west. The plane passed over Israel and headed out into the Mediterranean on a path that would take it to Italy, and then abruptly turned back to the east to land at Sde Dov Airport north of Tel Aviv.

Jim Miller walked into a conference room at Mount Olympus at one in the afternoon on October 5. It was a scheduled review for the two critical pilots of Block G on a day when everything that was occurring was scheduled down to the minute. Oleg Kolikov and four other men were in the small room seated around the table. All six were scheduled to fly the two Ilyushins – one now on a tarmac in Luhansk and the other in a hanger at Ras Al-Khaimah – later that night. Only they would fly the planes from remote control "cockpits" set up next to each other in a room just down the hall from the conference room they now occupied. Each plane would be flown by a flight engineer, a pilot and either Captain Kolikov in command of the Luhansk flight or Captain Miller in command of Ras Al-Khaimah flight. The role of each of the two captains was to use their experience over the last couple of years of flying in, over and around Iran to communicate with air traffic control personnel. The two flights later that night had to appear to be as routine as possible.

The men in the room welcomed the American who had become the respected father figure for all of the Ilyushin crews operating for Swiss-Arab Air Cargo out of Ras Al-Khaimah.

"Welcome to Israel, Captain Jim," said Oleg Kolikov as he stood and shook the American's hand. "I hear you had some turbulence."

Jim Miller shook his head as he shook hands with the other men in the room. "It was bad. Downdraft hit us just after we passed over the threshold. We probably had fifty, sixty feet to touchdown."

"Ouch," replied Kolikov. "Please tell me the plane is okay."

"The plane is fine except that when I left last night to fly here we still had no connection on the primary satellite control link. I heard that they sent a couple engineers out to fix it. I'm sure it's working by now." Miller sat down and the men talked about the coming night, waiting for Amit Margolis to show up.

After half an hour the room's door opened and General David Schechter walked in followed by Amit Margolis. They were both clearly concerned – Miller thought they were agitated and that made him nervous. Everyone in the room knew Margolis well, but it was the first time any of them had met the general. The Mossad agent introduced his co-commander to the group and then summarily asked everyone other than Kolikov and Miller to leave.

With just the two captains, the general and Margolis in the room, Amit took the lead. "We have a serious problem," he started. Miller felt his blood pressure drop involuntarily. He knew it involved the Ilyushin he had piloted the night before from Israel to the United Arab Emirates. "The primary flight control computer on Jim's plane is out of order."

"It was just the satellite communications module when we were running diagnostics last night," Miller protested.

"Yes, Jim, that is what the diagnostics said and that was confirmed by what we saw here. The two IAI technicians we flew to Ras Al-Khaimah early this morning took a replacement and switched it out. The communications now work but the real issue was being masked. The primary remote flight control computer is fried. The plane has to be flown back to Israel to fix and IAI says they need at least a day here to do the work. That plane cannot fly tonight as planned."

"What are we going to do?" asked Kolikov, beating Miller to the question.

"We are working on re-tasking strike packages now to replace Captain Miller's plane," responded Schechter. "This is a contingency we have planned on for some time."

Jim Miller interjected. "But a lot of targets will have to be scrubbed from the list and a lot of men may die or become prisoners in Iran tonight because of this. Can't we postpone for 24 or 48 hours?"

"We are past that point," stated Schechter. "Too many assets are in place or in motion already. We made the decision long ago that we would go so long as we have one of your two planes still in the show. At this point, the risk from postponing is much greater than the risk of going forward."

The room became quiet, each man reflecting on the change of plans at this eleventh hour of Block G. Jim Miller asked a question. "The plane still flies, right?"

"The plane is fine and all the systems are working other than the one system we need to fly it remotely from here," responded Margolis.

"From here," Miller repeated like a distant echo. Kolikov seemed to pick up on where the American pilot was going before either of the two co-commanders. "Amit, may I talk to you alone?" Miller asked.

Margolis looked at Schechter. The general didn't say a word or even look back at Margolis, he simply stood and walked out, holding the door for the trailing Kolikov. The door closed and now only the American and the Israeli spy remained. Jim Miller took a breath and looked Margolis in the eye. "Get me back to Ras Al-Khaimah this afternoon. I am going to fly that plane into Iran."

Margolis slowly shook his head. "We spent a lot of time and resources to enable us to fly those two planes from right here. We did that for a reason. I ..."

Miller raised up his hand, palm out in the signal to stop. "I understand fully why the money was spent to convert those planes into giant UAVs. But you – the man who conceived all of this – are forgetting why it is you had to come up with such a plan. If that plane doesn't fly tonight, then how many F-15 and F-16 crews are going to pay the price? Ten? Twenty? More?" The American stared Margolis in the eye inviting a response. None came. "Amit, I am 62 years old. I have no kids and no family. I am a gay man who lost the love of my life many years ago. How old are you?"

Margolis cleared his throat. His response was muted. "Thirty-eight."

"And if that plane doesn't fly, the men who will either die tonight or worse, spend God knows how long being tortured by the Iranians, are all younger than you. I could be their grandfather. They are in their prime. They have families and children – or they will in the future. I do not and I will not.

"Look, give me a chute and a survival kit. The last thing the Iranians will be looking for is a gray-haired old man. They will think I got separated from some tourist group." The attempt at humor fell flat under the circumstances.

Margolis lowered his head to think. After a few moments he stood up. "If you will excuse me, I have to discuss this with General Schechter."

"Of course." Jim Miller knew at that moment that he had won the argument. As Margolis walked out, the American slumped in his chair, the meaning of what he had just volunteered to do hitting him like a wave. *Dear God, what have I just done?*

Several minutes later, both co-commanders of Block G walked back into the room. Schechter walked straight to Jim Miller, who stood. "Are you absolutely sure you want to do this?"

"Yes."

"You understand that once you leave here to return to the UAE, we will revert to the original strike packages and assignments? The IAF crews will receive their final briefings and all mission computers will be set under the assumption that you are going. By eighteen hundred hours, those strike assignments will be fixed for the mission and we cannot change them back.

This is a final decision you are making here. Once you leave for the trip back, you have to go forward with your flight."

"General, I understand completely both what you are saying to me and what is at stake."

Schechter extended his hand and Miller grasped it. Schechter held on, looking into the American's eyes and judging the man in front of him. "Okay, we need to get you back to the UAE."

A little before four in the afternoon Swiss time, a Boeing 737-400F cargo plane, one of two that had been purchased by Swiss-Arab Air Cargo early in 2012, took off from Zurich Airport bound for Karachi, Pakistan. The flight was scheduled to cover over 3,500 miles and the plane had a scheduled stop at a small international airport located just outside the ancient Azerbaijani city of Ganja in order to refuel. The Ganja Airport was converted – salvaged really – from a Soviet era tactical airbase that had been wasting away in the often harsh weather. The crew planned for almost four hours of flying time from Zurich to Ganja.

The modern cockpit of the Boeing 737-400F required a crew of only two men. After their purchase, the two planes had undergone extensive renovation in Wichita, Kansas – at least according to the official logs kept by SAAC at its offices in Ras Al-Khaimah. In reality, the planes had been delivered to Nevatim Airbase in Israel to be worked on by the same engineers who had been working on the Ilyushin 76 cargo aircraft. The two planes had officially been added to the SAAC fleet only eleven months earlier.

58 - Slingshot

Inside the cockpit of the Ilyushin 76 that Captain Oleg Kolikov had flown to the Ukraine a day earlier, two men – a pilot and a flight engineer – taxied the giant cargo plane to the end of the single runway at Luhansk International Airport. The SAAC cargo carrier had filed its flight plan to return to its home base of Ras Al Khaimah Airport in the UAE, a flight path it had flown many times in the past under the command of Kolikov. The flight path would take it quickly over Russia, then briefly over Georgia and Azerbaijan before a long transit over Iran, passing south and west of Tehran as it flew towards the southeast on the path to the UAE. All of the required over flight rights, and the fees that went with them, had been paid for and acquired.

"SAAC seven fifteen heavy, you are cleared for takeoff. Runway niner," said the departure controller. Located in the airport's tower, the man spoke in English, the universal language of aviation. His accent was noticeable, but his mastery of the English language was nearly complete.

"SAAC seven fifteen heavy, cleared for takeoff," came the reply. The voice was that of Oleg Kolikov, a voice that many of the air traffic controllers recognized. The old timers in the area knew him for the Soviet war hero he was. But Captain Kolikov was not in the cockpit of the plane, he was sitting in front of several computer screens inside the command bunker at Mount Olympus on the edge of Sde Dov Airport just north of Tel Aviv. The computers gave him all the critical information on the Ilyushin 76 that would soon commence its takeoff roll, including position, horizon, altitude, heading and speed. The data link and the voice communications between Mount Olympus and the plane were being broadcast back and forth via encrypted satellite link – no different than the way any UAV is flown by a pilot half a world away.

"Contact Rostov departure on one two five point five. Have a nice evening."

"Rostov. One two five point five. SAAC seven fifteen. Thank you," replied Kolikov, repeating the frequency for the regional air traffic control center in Rostov-on-Don in Russia. The Russian pilot glanced at the clock on the wall, which showed Iranian and Zulu time. The time in Iran was 8:07 p.m.

The two men actually in the cockpit listened in on the routine communications between a captain, who would normally be in the left hand seat, and the airport tower. The pilot told the flight engineer to back his hand as he pushed four throttles forward to command maximum power. The plane was heavy and would need most of the long runway. The Ilyushin was airborne in under a minute and on its way. Twenty minutes later, the plane was at its cruising altitude of 32,000 feet when the two men in the cockpit, both of whom were experienced combat veterans of the IAF, turned control of the plane over to two men seated by Kolikov at Mount Olympus. Confirmation of remote control was made and the two men inside the plane removed their SAAC uniforms to reveal pressure suits. Each man put on a parachute and a helmet and oxygen mask, activating personal GPS devices in the process. They next depressurized the entire cabin and made their way to the rear of the main cargo cabin, at spots having to climb over or crawl under the cargo they were carrying.

When they were at the rear cargo door they waited for a signal that was programmed into the plane's mission computer. In less than ten minutes, a yellow light started to flash. After only a few seconds, the cargo doors opened and the two men jumped as soon as the doors gave them a clearing. They would land in a field somewhere north of Stavropol, Russia. On the ground, a Mossad team waited in a van to home in on their GPS signals.

Captain James Miller received clearance from the tower at Ras Al-Khaimah at 9:11 p.m. Iran time. The weather was nice in the UAE, with almost no clouds. The sky was dark and the moon was nowhere to be seen. In the cockpit, Miller sat in the left-hand seat. The plan had been for him to be seated about four meters away from Kolikov in the safety of the Mount Olympus bunker. Jim Miller's right hand shook as he pushed the four throttle levers of the Ilyushin forward. The co-pilot in the right-hand seat placed his left hand behind Miller's and applied pressure. The large plane was soon on its way.

After only ten minutes, the co-pilot and flight engineer each said goodbye to Miller, wishing him success. The two men soon jumped out of the depressurized cargo compartment and into the waters of the Persian Gulf where, by pre-arrangement, a U.S. Navy Seahawk helicopter soon homed into their GPS signals and plucked both men from the water.

Jim Miller continued north on the normal flight path for a SAAC flight from Ras Al-Khaimah to Imam Khomeini International Airport just south of Tehran. The plane's manifest showed that it was delivering medical supplies, but the authorities in Iran were actually expecting spare parts for Iran's civil aviation fleet. SAAC had made its name in Iran by reliably delivering machine tools and spare parts in violation of the trade embargo put in place by the U.S. and the European Union. The embargo was an effort to convince Tehran to abandon its goal of nuclear weapons. SAAC had been delivering illicit parts and supplies to Iran for over a year. As a result, when the company needed to overfly Iran or arrange for deliveries at odd hours in the middle of the night, it was easily able to do so. The material being delivered was valuable and had required the approval of Prime Minister Cohen. As long as they delivered nothing that could benefit Iran's nuclear program or air defense network, Amit Margolis had a green light.

Just minutes after Miller took off, the Boeing 737-400F that had left Zurich earlier in the afternoon landed at Ganja International Airport. The pilots taxied to the single tarmac and looked for an expected fuel truck. Azerbaijan was still on Daylight Savings Time and it was late, almost 11 p.m. The airport, other than the two people manning the tower, seemed to be closed. "Where is the fuel?" asked the pilot. The question was to himself as much as to his co-pilot.

"It should be here."

The captain talked to the tower in an attempt to learn the status of their fuel. The response was not helpful, the controller in the tower essentially telling the crew of the Boeing that fuel delivery was not part of his job description and they were on their own. The crew used its encrypted satellite communications system to discuss the situation with Mount Olympus. At the Sde Dov bunker, a junior IAF staff officer was assigned to contact the Mossad agents operating in Azerbaijan who had been responsible for arranging the fuel delivery. Money had been freely delivered and bonuses promised to ensure that the truck was waiting when the Boeing cargo plane arrived.

What the Mossad agents had not planned on was the Azeri truck driver stopping at his neighborhood pub to pass the time. The predominantly Muslim country still enjoyed a secular government, one of the positive things it inherited from its days inside the Soviet sphere. Despite the religious ban on alcohol, the driver accepted when several of his old friends bought the first round of vodka shots. Custom and honor dictated that each of the four men in the group pay for one round. Now the driver was telling drunken stories, each man attempting to outdo the others in their subject of choice. An argument broke out over the recent performance of the star striker for FC Kapaz, the local premier football club. The driver had not checked his watch in over an hour.

59 – Desert Pit Stop

In the Iraqi desert, at a spot that would be known as Shangri-La at least until the sun came up, 85 F-15 and F-16 fighter-bombers of the Israeli Air Force began to touch down on the main runway. Major Meyer felt very confident as the first warplane, an F-16C of 101 Squadron, the First Combat Squadron, touched down at 8:53 p.m. Iraqi time, 9:23 p.m. Iranian time.

Like all the planes coming into Mudaysis Airfield, this F-16 was outfitted for a SEAD mission, or Suppression of Enemy Air Defense. This particular plane was carrying four AGM-88D HARM, or High-speed Anti-Radiation Missiles, two AIM-120D AMRAAMs, or Advanced Medium Range Air-to-Air Missiles, and two Python 5 infrared air-to-air missiles. After using its HARM missiles, the plane would assume its secondary role of providing air combat cover. Other planes flying into Shangri-La – the two seat B and D models – carried the Delilah missile. The Delilah would be launched from a distance of one hundred miles or more to fly to its target area. It would then hunt for specific targets such as mobile missile launchers or truck-mounted radar and command centers. An optical feed to the back-seat weapons officer allowed for positive identification of targets before ordering the Delilah to home in on its kill. Still other aircraft were armed with guided bombs to target fixed command, control and communication nodes.

The Israeli men in yellow shirts guided the first F-16C to the front of ten refueling positions that had been established on the tarmac of Mudaysis. Two purple shirted refuelers pulled a high-volume type-4 hydrant fuel hose underneath the plane's left wing, opened a small access door, pushed the hydrant up onto the fuel nozzle and rotated the hydrant clockwise until it clicked. A flow of 1,000 gallons of JP-8 fuel per minute passed into the fuel tanks of the F-16. Next to the access door they had just opened, a number had been freshly painted. It told the two refuelers how many gallons needed to be pumped into this plane. It took less than two minutes to pump the 1,544 gallons, or 10,500 pounds, of fuel into the plane. By the time they were finished, three other F-16s were already parked in the line behind the lead F-16. Planes were landing every 30 seconds.

As soon as the hydrant was disconnected and the access door closed, a white shirted quality control officer checked the meter readings on the fuel pump, confirming the delivery of 1,551 gallons of fuel. He compared that against the number "1544" that was also painted very visibly on the nose of the aircraft. He then walked under the wing to confirm that the plane and its weapons were ready for flight. He stepped out from under the wings and to the side to salute the pilot, who knew he had been cleared.

The F-16 applied power to move away from the refueling spot and within seconds was on the long taxiway that ran parallel to the main runway. He applied military power and his afterburner to takeoff to the northwest directly into the path of oncoming aircraft. He turned on his navigation lights for the takeoff roll and immediately turned right as he lifted off the taxiway, turning off his navigation lights once he was about a kilometer off the end of the taxiway.

This same process was repeated 84 more times over the next 48 minutes. At Point Romeo over the northern Saudi desert, seven KC-707 refueling tankers of the IAF fueled 121 IAF warplanes during the same period of time. The planes refueling at altitude included 24 F-15I Ra'ams and 55 F-16I Sufas. Gadget's F-15I was the first plane to mate with the refueling boom of a KC-707.

A little before 10 p.m. Iranian time, thirty minutes later local time, two planes throttled up their engines to taxi to the end of the long runway at Ras Al-Khaimah Airport in the United Arab Emirates. The first plane was a SAAC Boeing 737-400F cargo plane identical to the one now waiting for fuel at the Ganja Airport in Azerbaijan. The second plane was a white C-130 without any markings other than a tail number.

The second plane had landed at Ras Al-Khaimah only forty minutes earlier. None of the Emirati employees working at SAAC, all of whom had become accustomed to the 24 hour pace of a rapidly growing cargo airline, took notice of the C-130 as it refueled on the tarmac. When a panel van pulled onto the tarmac and drove up the rear ramp of the plane, the process was so routine that nobody thought twice about it. What the Emirati employees didn't know is that the van held all of the records and computers of SAAC from the corporate office in Dubai.

A few minutes later, the Russian night manager finished loading his laptop computer and a handful of files into his briefcase and walked over to the desktop computer of one of the customer service women who worked standard daytime hours. He logged onto the company network using his user name and password and doubled clicked an icon that had been placed on everyone's desktop screen. A dialogue box opened up and the manager entered his user name and password once again. Now another box opened with a request for a second password. The Russian typed in the name of his childhood pet dog. A confirmation came back. In 25 minutes a virus would be unleashed in the computer network of Swiss-Arab Air Cargo FZE and every remaining computer linked into the network would have its hard drive wiped out. The manager grabbed his briefcase and walked out, telling the handful of Emirati employees that he passed that he would be back in under an hour.

He walked across the tarmac and up the ramp of the C-130. On board, in addition to the van, was every employee of SAAC left in the UAE who was a foreign national. Once the white C-130 took off, the only employees of SAAC left in the UAE were all local Emirati citizens, none of whom had any idea about the events of the coming minutes or the true purpose of Swiss-Arab Air Cargo.

The Boeing 737 cargo plane took off and headed due west over the Persian Gulf. After reaching altitude, it turned slightly to a more northerly heading, establishing itself in the normal air traffic corridor heading towards Kuwait City. The C-130 took off a couple of minutes later and turned in the opposite direction, heading out over the Arabian Sea on its way to Mumbai,

India. Somewhere over the ocean, the rear door of the C-130 was opened and the van – along with the computers and corporate records of Swiss Arab Air Cargo – was pushed out the back.

Inside the command buildings for the Iranian Air Force at Doshan Tappeh Air Base, General Hassan Shahbazi read through reports. The veteran F-4 Phantom pilot was bored as he caught up with his daily paperwork. He paused for a moment to think about what he would do if he were the commander of the Israeli Air Force. It was his favorite fantasy – the thought of having a real air force at his command. He ran through the scenario in his head that he had repeated over at least a hundred times before. He had Israeli planes coming into Iran in three waves from the north, south and over the central mountains. He shook his head to clear his secret fantasy. He had a lot of forms to fill out.

The message General Shahbazi sent earlier to each of the tactical air bases allowed pilots who had been close to their interceptors to relax for the night. As with all patterns of behavior that had gone unchallenged for long periods, the level of relaxation had gradually increased to a point where it was now routine for many pilots to go to bed or to even leave their base to return to their families in nearby homes. There was no reason for tonight to be any different – after all, the new moon had come and gone the previous evening and the Hammer Squadron was at its base in the middle of the Negev Desert.

After finishing a few more forms that would be couriered to the IRGC headquarters in the morning, General Shahbazi checked the clock on the wall. The time was 1825 hours Zulu time. Underneath the clock that displayed Zulu time, another clock gave the time in Iran, which maintains its own time zone. The local time was 2155 hours, 9:55 p.m. The country had returned to Standard Time from Daylight Savings Time on September 22.

Shahbazi stood up to walk around. The eighteen men on duty this night were all set up in temporary cubicles using computer monitors wired to servers that had all been placed temporarily in a vacant office. The entire operations center had recently been moved into the current building. The historical operations building was undergoing a wiring and telecommunications modernization being conducted by a Chinese contractor. The general stopped to chat with most of his men. The discussion was supposed to be about business, but everyone was focused on the Classico football match that was now in the 31st minute. Shahbazi enjoyed the chance to increase the bond with his men.

60 – Protocols

At the same moment that Shahbazi completed his rounds and headed back to his desk, the pilots of the Boeing 737-400F parked on the tarmac at Ganja Airport received a communication from Mount Olympus. Their window was closing. The pilot looked at his co-pilot. "It looks like we are not getting fueled tonight."

"Yeah, that seems to be the case."

"We have to go. How much fuel do we have?"

"We left Zurich with a full load. We have 11,070 pounds left."

"Enough to get us to Point Charlie. We are going. Figure out what airport we can make it to from Point Charlie."

"Tehran," said the co-pilot nervously in response.

"Don't be an asshole," replied the pilot as he glared briefly at his co-pilot. But the joke by the co-pilot had helped each man relax just a little.

The cargo plane was airborne within a few minutes and soon resuming its course for Karachi, Pakistan. The course took it to the southeast across Azerbaijan and then out over the Caspian Sea.

All 206 Israeli warplanes refueling over the Saudi desert or on the ground at Mudaysis would fly over Iraq and enter Iranian airspace in a gap that the Olympus planners knew would exist in the Iranian early warning radar network. They were headed for a spot on the map codenamed Point Delta. It was the airspace over the Dehloran radar station now in the hands of Ben Zeev's Sayeret Matkal team.

In the radar control trailer at Dehloran, Manuchehr Moresadegh looked at his commander with a smile. Twenty minutes had passed since network access had been achieved. On the console counter top, Manu had a laptop computer open and running. From a port on the laptop to a port located on the console, a USB cable connected the portable Israeli computer to the Iranian air defense network. Over the past fifteen minutes, Manu and Isaac Mofaz had been running diagnostic programs written by the software coders of Unit 8200. The programs had confirmed connectivity and returned all of the radar and surface to air missile systems now connected to the air defense network grid. The laptop's wireless card was also on and, without any intervention by the Sayeret Matkal operators, the laptop was communicating with the satellite burst communications device. Key information about the network was being transferred to the communications device, then being compressed, encrypted and sent in burst transmissions via satellite to Mount Olympus.

At the bunkers of Mount Olympus located on the edge of Sde Dov Airport, a team of specialists processed all of the information being received. Iranian radar frequencies were being analyzed and the status of surface to air missiles were being forwarded by satellite to three IAF G550 Eitams and two Eitan-B UAVs that would each play critical roles in Block G.

Now on the screen of Manu's laptop a single dialogue box was open. The box held three simple words: "Execute Block Protocol?" Manu looked at Captain Ben Zeev. "Ready to go on your command."

Ben Zeev checked his watch. "Execute the block protocol."

Manu smiled. "Yes, sir." He moved the cursor until it hovered over the small box that simply said 'Yes'. He clicked the mouse's left button. "Done," he said. The time in Iran was 10:00 p.m. on Saturday, October 5.

61 – Accidents Happen

Amit Margolis did something at his desk he never did, he started chewing his nails. Around him in the main operations command room for Block G, dozens of young men and women of the Israeli Defense Force sat in front of computer screens and TV monitors. Each one had a specific job: gathering and analyzing intelligence; communicating with units now moving into combat; tracking unit locations. Several hours earlier, all of the men and women of the Golani Infantry Brigade and the Barak and Saar Armored Brigades had been quietly notified to report immediately to their units. Margolis was in awe over all that had resulted from his simple idea. He had no idea what most of these young Israelis in uniform were even doing.

A few meters in front of the twin desks of Margolis and General Schechter, a white metallic board with the map of the Middle East held a number of small plastic stylized planes. A young man moved the magnetized plane figures every minute or so. Two large planes represented the main body of attack aircraft from Shangri-La and Point Romeo. They were now passing through a radar gap in Iraq and only minutes from entering Iranian airspace.

But Margolis' eyes focused on the four small plastic planes that were painted in red and white stripes. They represented the positions of the four aircraft that comprised Esther's Sling. One – Kolikov's plane – was over the northwestern portion of Iran and heading toward the underground enrichment facility north of Qom known as Fordow. A second plane – representing the Il-76 being piloted by James Miller – was now passing to the east of Isfahan and headed north toward Tehran. It would pass very close to the main Iranian enrichment facility at Natanz. Another plastic plane was being moved as Margolis watched. It had just passed over the coastline of Azerbaijan and the Caspian Sea and was heading toward Karachi. It would pass within a hundred miles of Tehran. The fourth plastic plane was over the Persian Gulf and heading west toward Kuwait City.

Margolis felt a push on his shoulder. He turned to look at David Schechter. The general tapped his watch with his right finger as he spoke. "Time for 8200 to implement Operation Accident."

"Yes." Margolis snapped his mind back to the tasks at hand. "Yes." He picked up a phone that connected him to the command center of Unit 8200. Located on the northeast edge of Ramat HaSharon, the underground command center was not far from Mount Olympus. Margolis was immediately connected to a senior officer of Unit 8200. "Execute Operation Accident now."

At the same moment, General Hassan Shahbazi was listening to a radio broadcast of the second half of the Classico match along with about half of his men. He would not have allowed this if the whereabouts of 69 Hammer Squadron was not known. But he drew the line at bringing in a television set, much to the chagrin of his men. A young adjutant had just asked the general if he wanted tea when Shahbazi's cell phone vibrated in his pocket. It was a text from his wife.

> Tahmineh in bad auto accident. I am on way to Arad Hospital. Meet me there.

Shahbazi's knees buckled. He had just read the text that every parent dreads. His daughter had been in an accident and was in the hospital. "Allahu Akbar," said the general under his breath. Like most officers in the Iranian Air Force, he was more secular than not, but he was now praying hard for his daughter. He headed to an empty office room, desperate to contact his wife and desperate to keep his men from seeing the tears welling in his eyes.

He pulled up his wife's number and pressed the dial button. After a moment, he heard the sound indicating that the call could not go through. He cursed silently. He tried the cell phone of his 16-year-old daughter. It was the same sound of non-connection. "What the hell is wrong?" he asked himself.

Shahbazi stuck his head out of the office and caught the eye of Colonel Alireza Askari, the night watch deputy commander. The general called him over by motioning his head. When Askari walked in, he saw his commander with a look on his face that he had never seen before. "What's wrong?" There was sincere concern in the colonel's voice. The two men had worked together for years and Shahbazi had long been Askari's mentor.

"My daughter has been in a car accident."

"Oh, no."

"She is apparently at Arad Hospital but I can't get through to my wife or to her."

"Let me call the hospital. We are talking about Tahmineh, right?" The general nodded his head in agreement. He was in no shape to leave the office. The colonel walked out of the barren office to find a phone.

Colonel Askari returned a few minutes later with a frustrated look. "They say they don't have a record of her. But they did say that they have admitted several people tonight who have been in accidents."

"Any a teenage girl?"

"They didn't know. Just go to the hospital. I can handle anything that comes up. Can you drive?"

"Yes." General Shahbazi thought for a moment, using the pause to gather himself. "Okay. Let me try to get my wife or my parents to see if I can learn anything. If not, I will leave in a few minutes."

"Yes, sir." Colonel Askari left the office.

Across Iran at that same moment similar texts were being read by senior officers and pilots of the Iranian military. All of the texts came from the phones of their spouses or children and all of the recipients were unable to get through if they called back. The planners at Unit 8200 had been careful to select the most important decision maker at each command node. They also picked out twelve pilots on stand-by that night who were rated as the most capable fighter pilots in Iran. The data necessary to pull off this diversion had been mined from the information sent to Israel by the Flame virus. It was the same virus that Yavi Aitan had informed the members of the Kitchen Cabinet was referred to internally as the Tunnel. Unit 8200 had been able to build a complete library of the key officers of the Iranian military and their families. This knowledge was now being put to use.

62 – Tally Ho

"SAAC six-two-two heavy, Isfahan."

"Isfahan control. This is SAAC six-two-two." Jim Miller's voice was recognized by the air traffic controller on duty at the Isfahan regional air traffic control center. Miller was worried that his voice was wavering, but to the ear of the Iranian controller, the American pilot sounded normal.

"Contact Tehran approach on one-nineteen point seven. Have a good night."

"Tehran approach on one-one-nine point seven. SAAC six-two-two heavy. Good night." Miller's mind was racing. He had to turn the plane sometime within the next few minutes. Mount Olympus would let him know the timing and when he did, he would be headed toward restricted airspace over the uranium enrichment facility of Natanz. Everything else would then be controlled automatically by the mission computer on board. The captain's hands were shaking. He had a parachute on and a helmet. An oxygen mask and small tank, enough for about 15 minutes of oxygen, was sitting on the co-pilot's seat. Soon the computer would depressurize the entire plane. With the mask on, Miller would find it difficult to respond to any radio communications.

Flying in the opposite direction at a point 234 miles to the north-northwest, SAAC 715 Heavy was at 32,000 feet and flying to the southeast toward Ras Al-Khaimah. In a conversation with the Tehran Air Traffic Control Center, Captain Kolikov had ironically just been handed off to the Isfahan center. The plane was on a course that would take it within 33 miles of the underground Fordow enrichment complex.

The Ilyushin 76 passed over a small town called Saveh that was just to the west of Fordow. With the plane depressurized, the mission computer took over. It was the equivalent of the pilot giving control of a World War II bomber to the bombardier. The rear cargo doors opened – two doors underneath the tail split in the middle and opened to each side. The main ramp just forward of those two doors lowered so that the ramp itself had a slight decline down toward earth.

Inside Mount Olympus, Amit Margolis stood in a soundproof room overlooking both of the remote control flight rooms. The rooms were just down the hall from the main operations center where the Block G co-commander had called Unit 8200 to initiate Operation Accident ten minutes earlier. On the left hand side, a room contained Captain Kolikov and two other men who had been remotely flying SAAC 715 Heavy. On the right hand side, a separate room that should have had Captain Miller plus two men, instead held only two men who were doing nothing other than monitoring the information coming from SAAC 622 Heavy. Within the next few minutes, the concept of Esther's Sling would meet success or failure.

SAAC 715 Heavy turned 85 degrees to its left. The Fordow complex was now 33 miles in front of the plane's nose as it covered one mile every seven seconds. On the ground underneath the plane, the air defenses of Fordow slept. No alerts had been issued and no radar systems were turned on. The overnight technicians – the centrifuges never stopped spinning – worked inside a mountain in the belief that they were impervious to attack. On the radar screens of the air traffic control centers in Tehran and Isfahan, the green triangle with the moniker "SA 715" next to it, continued to head toward Ras Al-Khaimah. The computer network that controlled the radar screens of the Iranian civilian air traffic control system had long been hacked into by Unit 8200.

Almost immediately after turning toward Fordow, 39 Spice 1000 flying bombs were ejected off the cargo ramp door. The Spice is a bomb with folded wings that deployed as soon as the weapon left the aircraft. From the altitude of the Ilyushin, the bombs could fly to targets as far as 100 miles away. Each bomb had a target programmed into its GPS guidance system. Eighteen of the bombs turned to the north to fly to targets in and around Tehran, including the headquarters of the IRGC and the Iranian Air Force and the basement room at Tehran University where Chinese IT specialists were engaged in a cyber-war with Israel. Two bombs turned south to head for the headquarters of the IRGC in the city of Qom. The remaining 19 Spice 1000 bombs flew straight ahead to targets around the Fordow complex, including eight SAM sites, five tunnel entrances and the uranium delivery and processing facility building that had not yet been buried under the mountain.

After the Spice 1000s left the plane, four MSOVs, each with 36 runway denial submunitions, were ejected. Like the Spice weapons, the MSOVs had wings that allowed them to fly long distances. They were essentially unpowered cruise missiles. Two MSOVs headed for Imam Khomeini International Airport and two for the runways at Doshan Tappeh Air Base. Then two more MSOVs were ejected, only these carried a new weapon developed by Boeing and being used for the first time in combat. The Counter-electronics High-powered Microwave Advanced Missile, or CHAMP, had been tested in the field for the first time the prior October. The weapon was able to emit targeted electromagnetic pulses that could fry the delicate internal circuits of unprotected computers. Each CHAMP had a programmed flight path over Tehran, including flying over the homes of Supreme Leader Ali Khamenei and numerous government and communications buildings.

The big cargo plane, now 53,460 pounds lighter than when it made its turn toward Fordow, continued onward. On the ground, there was still no idea that anything was happening out of the ordinary. When the plane was five and a half miles from Fordow, a large earth penetrating bomb, known in America as the Massive Ordnance Penetrator, or MOP, was released by parachute from the back of the plane. The plane climbed several hundred feet as the 30,455 pound bomb exited the rear cargo ramp.

The bomb's internal guidance computers knew exactly where it was above the earth to within a meter of error – and it knew precisely where it was going to strike the rocky ground of the mountain that housed the Fordow facility. Immediately after the huge MOP cleared the ramp, a second parachute inflated behind the plane and quickly extracted another MOP from the cargo hold. Its strike coordinates were precisely eighteen meters east of the strike point of the first MOP. It had been calculated that the second MOP would hit the eastern rim of the crater caused by the first MOP precisely 2.3 seconds after the first explosion.

The two MOPs had been secretly delivered to Israel during the summer of 2012. The delivery was the end product of extended behind the scenes maneuvering by Prime Minister Eli Cohen. In a late spring phone call with the President of the United States, he had agreed to stay quiet and become a "none factor" in the American presidential election in return for the two MOPs and assurance that the president would tacitly support Block G if he was re-elected. The agreements had been honored by all sides.

To the south, as the weapons of SAAC 715 Heavy were falling to earth, James Miller turned his plane to the left just after being prompted by Mount Olympus. He was now headed due west, directly toward the Natanz facility. As with the Fordow plane, the computer now took control of the plane and its cargo. A warning light and buzzer in the cockpit – as well as the popping of his ears – notified Miller that depressurization was underway. The American pilot quickly placed the oxygen mask on, making sure the valve on the tank was open. The plane automatically began the process of opening the cargo doors and dropping its preliminary cargo of Spice 1000, MSOV and CHAMP weapons on targets in and around Isfahan and Natanz.

On the ground, an Iranian sergeant manning a 5N62 "Square Pair" targeting and illumination radar for a surface to air missile battery consisting of SAM-5 Gammon missiles, turned on his radar. He was bored and had authorization to activate his radar if he had reason to believe that a threat existed, even though good electronics emission discipline dictated sparse use. He scanned the skies to the west and south, slowly rotating his radar between the two directions. He saw nothing unusual, just the standard commercial air traffic in well-established lanes – the same thing he always saw.

He was about to turn the radar off when he decided to try one 360 degree sweep. The radar swiveled on its turntable at its slew rate of 20 degrees per second. As it came through due south, it continued until it was pointed due east. The blip that appeared on his screen caused the sergeant to react immediately. Air traffic lanes out of Isfahan to the north were only about forty miles away to the east, but this blip was closer. The return was strong, the radar cross section of the big Ilyushin being easy for the Square Pair radar to analyze.

The sergeant stopped the radar's rotation and pointed the transmitting panel directly at Miller's Ilyushin 76. He studied the data now being fed to him by the Russian-built radar's computer system. The plane was at cruising altitude but was headed directly for Natanz at a speed of 420 knots. The sergeant picked up a phone mounted onto his console. It rang instantly in the command bunker located about 100 meters away. An officer picked up. "I have an unidentified bogey above flight level thirty, dead bearing ninety-three and closing at four-twenty. Distance is forty-eight. Negative squawk."

The officer was annoyed. He had a small portable radio in his hand and had been listening to the football match, which was now in its fiftieth minute. This interruption meant that he now had to follow protocol. "Just one target from the east?" The question was rhetorical. "Let me interrogate it. I'm sure it's just a commercial flight." The officer flipped a switch that turned on his IFF interrogator, a green light indicating the device was active. He pressed a button on his console and the radio device sent a coded message to the unidentified plane's transponder that was intended to trigger an automatic response. None came. He pressed the button again. The officer cursed his luck. "Hold on. I need to call him." The officer lowered the phone and called out to a radio technician sitting across the room. "Ahmed, wake up. You have work to do," said the officer sarcastically. He stood and walked a couple of meters across the floor to stand and look over the shoulder of the missile battery's communications technician.

"Open all civil air frequencies," the officer ordered. "Let me see the microphone." The officer reached out with his left hand and the communications technician flipped several switches and handed a microphone to his commanding officer. The officer held down the talk button. "Unidentified aircraft, you are entering restricted military airspace. Identify yourself." The challenge from the officer was in English.

In the cockpit of SAAC 622 Heavy, Captain Jim was just exiting the captain's seat, the chord connecting his helmet to the communications console just about to reach its full extension and get its plug pulled out by the egress motion of the American. At the last moment, Miller heard the Iranian officer's challenge. Miller stopped his motion and listened.

"Unidentified aircraft, you are entering a military area inside which deadly force is authorized. You must change course immediately."

James Miller thought through his options. He was not sure if all of the weapons had been launched yet. He was not even sure if any had been launched. Unlike the Fordow plane, there was no MOP on board that would announce its departure by creating sudden lift. In this case, the plane's primary weapons were 28 EGBU-28B earth penetrating GPS-guided bombs that each weighed 4,500 pounds, or 2,041 kilograms. Most of the bombs were targeted on Hall A at Natanz, which now had over 18,000 centrifuges installed and operating. Three bombs were targeted on the Pilot Enrichment Fuel Plant, a small underground chamber with almost 1,000 operating centrifuges. Five bombs were targeted on Hall B, which was as large as Hall A but as yet had no operating centrifuges.

Miller figured he would feel the main payload leaving the plane and he had not yet felt such a lightening of the airframe. The captain returned to his seat and picked up the microphone. With his left hand he released the oxygen mask he was wearing. He held the mask against his mouth and opened it just enough to talk into the microphone, replacing the mask as soon as he was done. "This is SAAC six-two-two Heavy. I am a commercial cargo flight."

"SAAC six-two-two you are entering restricted airspace. Alter your course immediately."

Miller thought for a few moments. He needed time. "Who are you? You are not Isfahan center."

The reply angered the Iranian officer. "SAAC six-two-two, this is an Iranian military facility. You must change course or you will be fired on."

Miller hesitated for as long as he dared. He heard noises from the cargo cabin. He was certain that weapons were being ejected, but he didn't think the main load of EGBU-28Bs had yet been released. "Whoever you are," continued the American pilot, "I am under the direction of Isfahan regional ATC. Please contact them for further commands."

"Listen to me," responded the officer, the anger no longer contained. "Alter your course immediately. You will be fired upon in thirty seconds if you have not altered course."

Miller started to feel a shuttering of the large plane – a feeling much different than before. The large bunker busting bombs were being ejected in pairs from the plane. "Okay, sir. I am happy to comply. Please allow me to check in with Isfahan center for vector guidance."

"You are on our radar. There is no other traffic. Turn immediately to bearing three six zero."

Again, Miller paused. Inside the SAM battery command post the officer yelled at his missile launch officer who was listening in on the conversation. "Prepare to fire bird one." Six SA-5 Gammon missiles were at the command of the officer. Each missile had a range of up to 300 kilometers at a top speed of Mach 4. The plane was now being illuminated by both the Square Pair radar and a second radar unit known as a PRV-17 "Odd Pair" that was used to pinpoint the altitude of the target.

"I am happy to comply. Just confirming with Isfahan center now," said Miller finally.

At the Isfahan regional air traffic control center, the man who had passed SAAC 622 Heavy onto Tehran approach minutes earlier was listening to the discussion. His radar showed the big plane on its usual course heading north toward Tehran. He was confused by the conversation. He keyed his transmitter. "SAAC six-two-two Heavy. Isfahan."

Miller reacted to the transmission as if it were a miracle. "Isfahan. SAAC six-two-two Heavy. Please provide course instruction."

"SAAC six-two-two Heavy. I show you at flight level three one heading three four five. Confirm."

"Affirmative. Confirmed, Isfahan. SAAC six-two-two at thirty-one thousand feet and heading three four five."

In the SAM command bunker, the Iranian officer was forced to decide between what he had just heard from the Isfahan ATC center or what his own radar sets were telling him. He choose the latter. "SAAC six-two-two, I don't give a damn about Isfahan control. Alter your course immediately. Confirm!"

Inside Mount Olympus, Amit Margolis and the other flight personnel listened to the exchange of radio communications between the American pilot, the Isfahan air traffic controller and the Iranian military officer. Each person was struck by the calmness in Miller's voice and the increasing desperation and anger in the Iranian officer's voice. Everyone realized that Jim Miller had to still be in the cockpit of the big plane, which would commence its final death dive any moment. The personnel of Mount Olympus already knew how this was going to end. No one spoke.

At Fordow to the north, relatively small explosions were the first sign that this was not another night. Spice 1000 bombs hit known and fixed SAM command bunkers and two static target acquisition radars. But just seconds later a muted flash lit the ink black night, for a fraction of a second illuminating the rocky mountain outlines around the Fordow enrichment site. The first MOP had penetrated 183 feet through the hardened lava flows that formed the mountain above the underground chambers. It exploded just past the void of the southwest corner of the decoy chamber. A shockwave instantly obliterated everything and everyone in the decoy chamber. Four Iranian technicians died without ever having a conscious knowledge of their fate.

Three seconds later, the second MOP hit the crater wall that had just been formed by the first explosion and penetrated 212 feet at an angle, exploding just inside the hidden main chamber. Everything in the chamber was evaporated. Only seconds later, four Spice 1000 bombs simultaneously hit the uranium reception building, destroying its interior and the four horizontal autoclaves that heated uranium hexafluoride into vapor for insertion into the Fordow centrifuge cascades.

At the same moment, SAAC 715 Heavy turned its nose down, gaining speed as it lost altitude. The plane was now a guided missile, its mass and remaining fuel comprising the primary destructive potential. But the engineers working at Nevatim had added a silent surprise. In the nose of the big plane, 150 kilograms of uranium enriched to 65% U-235 had been placed in hidden areas. Thin lead shielding had protected the engineers, mechanics and pilots who had been testing the plane during the prior weeks. The uranium, along with its lead shielding, would vaporize once the plane crashed, spreading highly radioactive debris all around the crash site – all around what was left of the Fordow enrichment facility.

The Ilyushin 76 met its end inside the massive crater created by the two MOPs. Its speed at impact was a supersonic 689 miles per hour. Within nanoseconds, the radioactivity at the site was deadly to unprotected human and animal life.

James Miller clicked on his microphone to speak. When he pulled his mask away, he felt the shuddering of the plane stop. The cargo plane was suddenly flying level and smooth, all of its weapons having now been expended. Miller released the button on his microphone, his body relaxing in the pilot seat. He said a prayer for the first time since he couldn't remember. He spoke to his God as if talking to his mother, seeking forgiveness for all he had done wrong in his life.

In the command bunker the Iranian officer shouted his order. "Fire bird one." A single SA-5 Gammon missile's solid rocket fuel ignited instantly, propelling it from a standstill to Mach 3.4 in under 20 seconds. Tracking in on the Ilyushin was easy. The big plane had a massive radar cross section and was taking no evasive action. The plane started to lower its nose to commence its final act – to fly into Natanz as a highly radioactive missile. The Ilyushin lost about 500 feet of altitude as James Miller closed his eyes and continued to pray to a God who he could not fault if He wasn't listening.

The Gammon missile was still in its boost phase when it exploded just thirty meters in front of the nose of the plane, spraying it with hundreds of ball bearings, each the size of double-aught buckshot. The supersonic shrapnel ripped through the nose, wings and engines of the Ilyushin, four pellets killing James Miller instantly. The plane exploded in flight, forming a fire ball that fell toward earth like a withering meteor.

Before the wreckage of SAAC 622 Heavy hit Iranian soil, 26 of 28 EGBU-28Bs punched through ten meters of dirt and four meters of reinforced concrete roofing and exploded within the voids of the enrichment halls of Natanz. Two of the sophisticated bombs failed, each one burying itself harmlessly into barren land before detonating at a depth that engulfed their warheads. Spice 1000 bombs hit their targets only moments later. One of the Spice bombs crashed through the relatively thin roof of the SAM battery command bunker. The Iranian officer who had just decided the fate of Jim Miller didn't live to enjoy the downing of the big attacking cargo plane – or to suffer the consequences of his failure to shoot the plane out of the sky before it had launched its weapons.

The ability of Natanz to enrich uranium had been eliminated at the cost of an aging Russian cargo plane and an aging gay American pilot who would soon be immortalized as a hero of the state of Israel.

63 – Northwind by North

Flying over the Caspian Sea toward the southeast at a point about 170 miles north of Tehran, the Boeing 737-400F from Zurich via Ganja was cruising at 36,000 feet. The plane had flown 465 kilometers from Ganja and had fuel left to fly only another 300 to 350 kilometers depending on when its payload was released and it began descending. The crew, in discussion with Mount Olympus, had decided that they would perform their mission and then turn around to land at Baku. But right now the plane was still flying away from that salvation.

The co-pilot spoke up. "We are inside the launch window. Baku is now 270 kilometers away and growing."

"I hear you," responded the captain. He switched his transmitter to the encrypted satellite link to Israel. "Executing Sierra November." The pilot then entered a code into the plane's flight computer.

The cargo cabin quickly depressurized. Underneath the fuselage, a door that had been added by IAI engineers opened up. Within 20 seconds, eight Delilah missiles had been ejected, each one with a pre-programmed target along the Iranian coast or in Tehran. Immediately after the last Delilah was launched, the first of 46 Miniature Air-Launched Decoys, or MALDs, was ejected from the plane. It took another two minutes for the process to complete.

Each MALD was programmed to fly an attack pattern that mimicked what the Iranians expected to see from the Israeli Air Force. This mission was the culmination of Operation Northwind and was designed to convince the Iranians that the attack this night was coming from the north. The Delilah missiles would do no strategic damage, but would add to the illusion of attack from Azerbaijan.

As soon as the last MALD was launched, the Boeing turned back around and headed for Baku, calling in an emergency after ten minutes of travel back toward the Azerbaijani capital.

At the same moment, General Hassan Shahbazi was exiting the building on Doshan Tappeh Air Base that was the temporary headquarters for the Iranian Air Force. He was headed to his car and once there, to Arad Hospital. He cursed the distance he had to walk to reach the parking area and started to jog. He had been unable to establish any communication with his family and with every step he fought an internal war to suppress the darkest thoughts that ran wild in his mind. He was half way when it happened. He heard the swoosh of an object flying at great speed and very close by. His mind had only a fraction of a second to process the sound.

The heat from a massive explosion hit the general's face a moment before the shockwave knocked him off his feet. The sound of the blast punctured his right ear drum. It would take him a couple of minutes to fully shake off the effect of the concussive forces that had just hit him. Debris rained down around him, one piece of lumber hitting his leg and cutting his thigh. One hundred and twenty meters away to his right, the building that was the permanent headquarters of the Iranian Air Force and that he would have been working in if not for the wiring renovation underway, lay in fiery ruins.

Before he realized where he was, two men from his staff were walking him back to the temporary building he had just exited. Inside, a junior officer trained in first aid started to wipe blood from the general's head and neck. Colonel Askari walked up to him. "Sir, we are under attack."

Shahbazi just looked back at his underling with incredulity. He put his hand up to the left side of his head and cupped it behind his ear.

Askari leaned forward and raised his voice. "Fordow, sir. Fordow has been bombed."

Suddenly the general understood everything. His daughter was unharmed, but his nation was under assault from Israel. "What comms do we have?" he shouted, his lack of hearing leaving him unable to judge his own volume. He received a quick summary of a situation that was pure confusion. The direct tactical communication link between the temporary command building and the air defense assets of Iran was out. This meant that both direct communications and the radar feeds from the early warning radar net were down. But the building still had a link to the country's internet backbone and email traffic was starting to flow.

As the general was being tended to, the colonel started receiving summaries of emails coming in from around the country. Critical news was being shouted to him from across the room as men read their computer screens.

"Natanz air defense reports that they have engaged and shot down an attacking plane," came a shout across the room.

"One plane?" the colonel shouted back. "Find out how many planes are attacking and where they came from."

"Germi reports thirty plus bogeys over the Caspian Sea inbound to Tehran," came another shout. Close to the northern Iranian mountain town of Germi, an early warning radar station similar to Dehloran kept watch over Azerbaijan and the Caspian Sea.

"Isfahan radar has nothing other than commercial traffic," responded the first man.

"Find out what the hell just hit us," shouted the colonel in an angry tone that every man in the room shared. Colonel Askari had been dreaming of one day taking command of the Iranian Air Force. Now as his commander was still unable to hear what was happening, Askari found himself temporarily in charge at a moment and in a situation he did not want. Men continued to shout updates as the lights went out. Battery back-ups kept the computers on as emergency lights flickered to life, casting a dull yellow glow over the room. Askari said a silent prayer for the generators, which had only been hooked into the temporary building a couple of days earlier, to turn on. About twenty seconds later his prayers were answered.

"Okay. Everyone be quiet," Askari shouted. "Send 'Alert Status Three – Attack Imminent' to all bases and air defense posts." He walked over to the man communicating with the Northern Defense Sector. "Get Tabriz and Mehrabad fighters up right now and vectored by Germi. I want two F-14s airborne for radar control right away." The Iranian Air Force still had

15 functioning F-14 Tomcat fighters and two were maintained on ready alert. Their AN/AWG-9 radars, despite being 1970s technology, were still powerful enough to act as de facto AWAC platforms for the other fighter aircraft of the IRIAF.

Askari returned to the side of General Shahbazi. The general's hearing in his left ear was slowly returning. Askari gave his commander a brief summary of what they knew. Shahbazi issued several orders. "Scramble all tactical bases. Get all fighters airborne. Get all commercial traffic on the ground at the nearest airport. Tell all tactical air bases and radar units to implement Code Blizzard." The last order would inform all air defense missile bases that attacks were underway and they should be scanning the skies for targets. Anything without proper IFF was now a legitimate target.

The general pulled Askari close to him. "Email the IRGC a status update. You must personally contact the Supreme Council. Try to get through to Imam Khomeini directly or his aide. We have to establish a direct link with him." The general was already thinking about the aftermath and repercussions of what was happening.

Over the Persian Gulf, the second Boeing 727-400F – the one that had departed from Ras Al-Khaimah 48 minutes earlier – began to execute its mission. It was several minutes behind schedule, the plane fighting heavy headwinds at its cruising altitude. At a point that was 326 miles west of the UAE, the recently installed door underneath of the plane opened up. Eight Delilah missiles were quickly ejected. As the wings of each Delilah missile cut into the cold thin air high above the Persian Gulf, its rocket motor ignited, sending the missile towards its target. The first six missiles, travelling in pairs, headed for three early warning radar installations along the Persian Gulf coastline: Kish Island, Siraf and a site known to the Olympus planners as Bushehr Southeast. The remaining two missiles, each carrying runway denial mines that scattered by the dozens and detonated if disturbed, heading due north for the Iranian airfield at Shiraz. The plane continued flying on toward the west as the door closed. It had another nine minutes of flying to reach its next release point 70 miles further along its route.

At 26,000 feet about 75 miles to the north of the Boeing, an Iranian Air Force MiG-29 Fulcrum fighter aircraft based out of Shiraz was flying a standard patrol pattern. For the pilot, it was another typical night in which the greatest excitement was the occasional encounter with the many U.S. Navy warplanes operating over the Persian Gulf. The protocols for these encounters were well established. He could "paint" an American plane with his targeting radar for about three seconds but no longer. Maneuvering to get your radar onto an enemy bandit was the fighter pilot's equivalent of puffing out your chest in a bar room showdown. A few seconds of illuminating your opposition was the way to keep score and was the basis for post-flight braggadocio once back at base.

There had been no encounters with the Americans this evening and the pilot was resigned to a quiet patrol. He was starting to look forward to returning to base for a shower when a radio transmission caught his ear. "Specter Five, alert status three. Confirm."

"Shiraz, Specter Five. Repeat status."

"Alert three. This is not a drill. Confirm."

The pilot, a veteran of over 4,000 hours in the single seat of the MiG-29, felt his face flush. This status meant war. "Specter Five. Alert three. No drill. Target eagles?" He was asking if Iran was at war with America.

"Negative. Assume defensive posture. Cleared to engage any penetration."

"Request vector," the pilot stated to his ground controller.

There was a pause in the response as the ground controller communicated with the nearby radar station at Siraf. "Vector one-nine-zero for bogey in civil lanes at angels three-four on course two-seven-five. Distance one-twenty. One-two-zero. Speed seven-three-eight. Confirm."

"One-nine-zero to angels three-four at one-two-zero. Cleared to engage?"

"Negative. Visual escort. Await further orders."

"Specter Five, on seek." The pilot turned his nose to the south and pushed his throttles forward through military power until his afterburners kicked in. Within seconds his speed was approaching 600 knots and his plane was climbing to 35,000 feet. Once at altitude, he throttled off his afterburners. He kept his search radar off until he closed the range. He only wanted to turn on the radar if the bogey he was chasing had no navigation lights on.

At its speed, the MiG closed the distance to the Boeing in under seven minutes. The night was crystal clear and the pilot easily spotted the blinking red navigation lights of the Boeing against the forest of stars from thirty kilometers away. The target was exactly where he expected. The Iranian pilot came in behind the Boeing and slowly descended until he was about a hundred feet above his target and trailing about a quarter mile behind and to the north of it. He turned on his forward-looking infrared and locked the target finder onto the Boeing jet flying in front of him.

The pilot's mind was racing as he thought through what was happening. He was now shadowing a cargo plane on a standard commercial flight while somewhere over Iran war was underway. He was frustrated. "Positive bogey identification," he reported to his ground controller. "Civil aviation. Boeing seven-three-seven or Airbus three-twenty class."

"Hold position," came the reply.

The MiG continued behind the Boeing for another two minutes. The pilot was antsy, sure that he was missing the chance to defend his country – his skills and training going to waste following a civilian plane high over the Persian Gulf. "Request alternate vector," he finally asked.

His timing was prescient. His ground controller at Shiraz was about to contact him. "We have lost contact with Kilo station." The controller was referring to the early warning radar at Kish Island. "We need visual fly by. Alter to course one-one-zero. Cleared to deck on VFR. Distance three-eight-five kilometers. Confirm."

The pilot was ecstatic. If Kish Island was under attack, he would be headed into the fray. "Course one-one-zero to deck. Specter Five disengaging." The pilot disengaged his forward-looking infrared sensor. He pulled his joystick to the left, eager to turn around and head back to the east toward Kish Island but careful to keep his plane clear of the vortices created by the Boeing's two large engines. As the nose of the MiG turned to the south, the pilot looked back at the cargo plane one last time to make sure he was clear of the bigger plane's turbulence. As he looked at the Boeing, its bottom navigation beacon flashed. The flash of red light reflected off something that caught the pilot's eye. He was certain he had seen something fall away from the plane.

"Turning back on bogey. Heavy G," said the pilot instinctively into his radio. He began his anti-G straining maneuver as he rotated his stick back to the right and applied power to quickly close the distance to several hundred meters. He turned on his infrared sensor and locked it on the cargo plane. What he saw shocked him. On the flat panel display he could see a door open underneath the Boeing. He watched as two Spice 1000 bombs slid out the doorway, their wings immediately deploying. The pilot got on his radio. "Bogey is hostile, not civil. Repeat hostile. Engaging target."

The pilot did not wait for authorization. He had found the war. He flipped a switch on the left side of the cockpit that activated his GSh-30-1 cannon in his left wing mount. "Cannon hot," he said into the radio. He raised the nose of his warplane and squeezed the trigger. Twenty rounds fired toward the Boeing's fuselage; each round held a small incendiary explosive charge. Every third projectile fired was a tracer round, its path clearly illuminated in the dark sky. The first six rounds were below the Boeing's fuselage and the pilot pulled back just slightly on the joystick to adjust his fire. The next rounds cut into the fuselage of the Boeing, penetrating its thin aluminum skin effortlessly and detonating just inside the fuselage. The third round that entered the plane collided with a MSOV and caused one of its runway munitions to detonate. Within a fraction of a second the remaining submunitions inside the MSOV detonated and the explosions caused the remaining Spice 1000 bombs to detonate. The MiG pilot reflexively pulled his stick up and right as he prayed to survive the rapidly expanding fireball in front of him. He opened his eyes after a few seconds and realized that he was still flying, the disintegrating Boeing now behind him. Allah had been with him.

"Splash one. Splash one. Turning to Kilo." His voice was calm, the years of training paying off.

64 – Through Point Delta

By the time the attack aircraft of the IAF were passing over Point Delta – the airspace above the Dehloran radar site – Fordow and Natanz were already in ruins. Esther's Sling had worked as Amit Margolis had envisioned it years before. But three pilots who had each been personally recruited by Margolis were now dead.

Now Block G turned to the conventional firepower of the Israeli Air Force. In the lead through Point Delta were the F-16 and F-15 aircraft operating in the SEAD configuration. The planes split into three main groups, one heading north toward the key targets in and around Arak and Tehran, one heading straight in for targets in and around Isfahan and the other turning toward the south for military targets between Isfahan and the Persian Gulf.

Inside the Iranian air defense network, software code written by programmers of Unit 8200 was busy issuing commands that were certainly not authorized. The software sought out the computer chips inside the command computers of the 29 Iranian Tor M-1E missile batteries that were the primary concern of the Olympus planners. The integrated circuit chips were receptive to the command – they were the same chips that Amit Margolis had exchanged in a hotel room next to the Shanghai Airport years earlier. The long code word – a series of digits and letters – activated an embedded command that caused the mobile target acquisition radars of each battery to broadcast a constant signal at 4.85 gigahertz. Nothing inside the radar control vehicles alerted the operators to the broadcast.

As planes reached designated spots that were an average range of forty miles from the primary targets of the IAF, SEAD aircraft launched AGM-88D HARM anti-radar missiles. In addition to their standard search protocols, each missile was programmed to find the 4.85 gigahertz signal being broadcast by the Tor M-1 batteries and home in on it. The radars that controlled the Tor batteries were among the first targets destroyed by the wave of Israeli aircraft now flying over Iran.

Behind the SEAD aircraft, fifty-two F-16I and twenty-four F-15I fighter-bombers followed. These aircraft had all refueled over the Saudi desert before forming in echelon for the entry into Iran through Point Delta. The leading F-15I was flown by Gadget, who, along with four other F-15Is, six F-16Is and four F-15Cs, had the longest to fly to strike their target this night. The group of fifteen warplanes was headed for the military complex known at Parchin about 24 miles southeast of downtown Tehran. Parchin was the center of Iranian research and development of both nuclear reaction initiators and high explosive lens for implosion weapons.

For the first part of the flight, Gadget had little to do other than fly his proscribed route, which took his aircraft through known radar gaps and around air defense nodes such as Natanz and Isfahan. But in the rear seat, Pacer was busy enough to be sweating inside his flight suit. The

Electronic Warfare Officer was monitoring all of the electronic equipment on board the F-15I that sniffed the airwaves for threats. All of the pilots and EWOs on this mission had been briefed about the viruses inserted into the Iranian defense network and the expected impact. If all went according to plan, the potent Iranian network would be severely degraded. However, everyone knew that operations as large as Block G rarely went according to plan. So Pacer never lifted his eyes off of the two key flat panel displays that summarized what the instruments on the plane were detecting. They had 33 minutes of flying from Point Delta until they could start their initial attack run, along with two other F-15Is, against three tunnel entrances in the hills just to the northwest of the Jajrud River valley that ran through the middle of Parchin.

As they flew over Iran, Pacer picked up radar frequencies being emitted from all directions surrounding the plane. Most of the signals were weak, indicating that the source was off in the distance – too far away to pose a threat to his plane. The signals would come alive for ten to twenty seconds and then go silent, only to be replaced by signals generated by different radar transmitters. This was the networked search pattern that had been developed around the world as a defensive measure against the type of sophisticated anti-radar missiles now being used by the IAF.

In the distance, Gadget could see the tracers of anti-aircraft artillery – most being the 23 millimeter rounds of dozens of ZU-23 gun emplacements – arcing through the dark sky. The Iranian air defenses were no longer sleeping. Pacer noticed that the number of radar emissions he was picking up seemed to be declining as they progressed. He was not sure if this was because they were moving away from the big defense nodes at Arak, Natanz and Isfahan or if radar transmitters were being destroyed by IAF action.

What Pacer didn't know was that the Block protocol now inside the Iranian air defense network was effectively neutering the ability of Iran's network of radars to do their job. Radars located in the northern defense sector – those along the coast line north of Tehran and along the borders of Azerbaijan – were left intact and operating normally. Those radars were sending information about aircraft attacking from the Caspian Sea to their operators. But the radars operating in the central and southern defense sectors – the radars protecting the heart of the Iranian nuclear program – had been compromised. These radars were now programmed to ignore any target that was emitting a specific code, and every IAF warplane now over Iran was emitting that coded signal. Worse, blips were showing up on the screens of the Iranian operators that showed aircraft flying from north to south. These were manufactured blips – simply lines of software code – that resulted in surface to air missiles shooting at ghost images and fighters being vectored toward Tehran and the airspace north of the city.

Around the center part of the nation, IAF aircraft struck electrical substations and major power lines. The lights were going out in central Iran.

But there were many Iranian officers who didn't believe the information being fed to them. They maintained their discipline and kept their defense assets close to home, avoiding the temptation to send fighters to the north. The smarter officers powered up mobile radar units and ordered their operators not to connect to the central defense network. Even though the Tor radar units had been destroyed, the major defense points had other mobile radar units, perhaps not as sophisticated as the Tor units, but still powerful enough to locate and track aircraft. These units allowed smart officers to order "snapshots," or surface to air missile launches toward an area of the sky where they had enough reason to believe that an enemy plane was passing through. This was the attack they had been preparing for over many years and there was no point in husbanding available missiles.

Gadget and Pacer continued on. In the distance they could occasionally see the track of a surface to air missile headed skyward. These were far away, but every missile track headed skyward still caused Gadget's heart rate to elevate slightly. About forty kilometers away from the target, the planes broke radio silence and began to coordinate their approaches. Flying ahead of Gadget's plane, the four F-15Cs each fired a single AGM-88E HARM missile and dropped a single Spice 1000 flying bomb. The Spice bombs had fixed targets pre-programmed, which included two communication and command nodes, the local electrical sub-station and an IRGC command bunker. The model E HARMs, the most advanced version of the missile, each began a search pattern, their internal computers set up with a hierarchy of targets. One missile homed in on the target acquisition radar of a Tor M-1 that was broadcasting at 4.85 gigahertz. The four F-15Cs then turned away from the target area to assume a Combat Air Patrol pattern, their recently upgraded APG-63v3 AESA radars taking turns searching for enemy aircraft.

Along with two other F-15Is, Gadget maneuvered to set himself up for his assigned bomb run on one of the three north-facing tunnel doors. His Tunnel Defeat system was now communicating with the two other F-15I Ra'ams. Pacer armed the first of two BLU-121B bombs underneath the fuselage. Over the Parchin site, "golden BBs" crisscrossed the valley. Gadget swallowed, using all his willpower to concentrate on the mission at hand. *I will not fail now. Not now.* The countless training missions were for this moment. The instinct to flee in the face of danger never disappears, but it can be made to assume a subservient role, the mind focusing on known tasks instead of unknown danger.

The approach was perfect and Gadget's ordnance released on the fourth and final tone he heard in his ear. The bomb flew horizontally through the concrete and steel blast door protecting the tunnel and penetrated 52 meters into the tunnel when it detonated at the same moment as two other BLU-121Bs that had been delivered into the other two tunnel entrances. The three blast waves converged to destroy an underground chamber that contained a factory for building high-explosive lenses – the lenses that are the key to imploding nuclear weapons.

Gadget pulled his nose around to the left and applied power to egress from the tunnel attack. Around him, F-16I Sufas were delivering their ordnance, including several Delilah missiles, on the facilities making up the Parchin base. Gadget looked to his right. He finally saw what he was expecting: the blinking infrared beacon of another F-15I, one of his partners in the tunnel attack. That plane formed up on his wing. The third F-15I that had just attacked the tunnel climbed and turned away from Parchin. Its role at this target was over and it now had two Spice 2000 bombs – the larger cousins of the Spice 1000 – left to send on their way toward the

Chinese-occupied cyber warfare center at Tehran University. One of the F-15Cs joined up with that Ra'am to accompany it as it dropped its two bombs and then headed home.

Gadget and his new wingman flew in a wide circle and came back around to line up on the Jajrud River heading due north. Twelve kilometers in front of them was the face of the Mamlo Dam. The Mamlo was a massive earthen dam across the Jajrud that formed a large lake.

The Mamlo was one of the large number of dams in Iran that collectively generate about five percent of the electrical power consumed by the country. This particular dam provided all of the electricity used by the researchers at Parchin and for that reason it had made the target list for Block G. Both Gadget and his wingman had a single BLU-121B left hanging beneath their planes. This would not be a difficult run, the main skill being that the backseat EWO in each plane needed to illuminate the right spot on the dam's face with their targeting laser. With that accomplished, each of the two thermobaric bombs would detonate at the precise spot inside the dam that physicists and engineers had calculated would cause catastrophic failure.

In front of the two F-15Is, a blanket of tracer fire lit the sky. This was heavier than Gadget faced earlier when his tunnel entrance target was on the edge of the worst fire. Now he had to fly through the teeth of it. He hoped to see explosions from Israeli weapons hit at the points of the tracer fire. His hopes were not met.

The two planes increased their speed to 545 knots and separated from each other about a hundred meters. Their run to the dam would be straight and would only take eleven seconds to pass through the last three kilometers of valley where the anti-aircraft fire was heaviest. The Tunnel Defeat computers on the two planes synched up as they began the final approach. The first of four tones sounded in Gadget's ear as the plane flew through the forest of tracer rounds.

Gadget felt the plane shudder as he released the second and final BLU-121B carried from Israel. The shudder felt different than every other time Gadget had released one of the big 2,000 pound bombs. His insides registered the difference before his brain could analyze the change.

Gadget pulled his joystick toward his stomach and to the left as his bomb flew true to its target. The plane that always moved as an extension of Gadget's desires banked left but otherwise didn't respond. In one of the random and capricious acts of war that separates survival from death, three rounds from a ZU-23 that had been fired off with nothing more than a hope and prayer, had hit the tail of Gadget's F-15I. One round had passed through the twin tails without detonating. But the other two rounds had destroyed the servo-cylinders that controlled the pitch angle of the two rear horizontal stabilators on the F-15I. Without the hydraulic cylinders, there was no longer any way for the angle of the stabilators to be changed – and without the stabilators, Gadget could not control the pitch, or angle, of the nose of his plane.

In the rear seat, Pacer watched his infrared targeting screen, making sure that his laser was locked onto the spot he wanted the bomb to hit. His trust in his partner's flying ability was complete and he had no feeling that anything was wrong with the plane. In the front seat, Gadget fought the onset of panic. The large earthworks of the Mamlo Dam was directly in front of the plane, which was flying at 627 miles per hour.

Gadget had only a couple of seconds to react. His nose would not turn upward even as he banked to the left. He increased his bank and pushed in the rudder pedal with his right foot, trying to get his nose pointed upward to climb over the dam by using his tail rudders.

The nose responded by turning to the right – which was toward the sky. But it was not enough. With a fraction of a second left, Gadget's mind conceded that his plane would not clear the earthen dam.

"Punch ou .." The last words of Gil Bar-Kokhba, known by his call sign "Gadget," were an attempt to save his partner. There was not enough time.

The leading edge of the plane's left wing dug into the top edge of the dam, the speed of the plane ripping the wing from the fuselage and pulling the nose of the plane down so that the fuselage skimmed over the top of the dam before slamming into the surface of the lake. At over 600 miles per hour, the impact on water was functionally no different than hitting solid ground. The F-15I disintegrated in a fraction of a second, the two men inside dying instantly from the effects of almost 100 Gs of acceleration. In the rear seat, Ronen Isser, known as "Pacer," died without ever realizing anything had gone wrong.

The two BLU-121Bs burrowed deep into the earthen dam and detonated in the spots that the planners intended. The large explosions created a liquefied void that resulted in a collapse of the side of the dam facing the lake. The water of the lake immediately rushed in to fill the void and the force of that water collapsed the dam above the void. The chain reaction continued until the Mamlo Dam had a V-shaped opening through which the waters of the lake gushed into the valley on the other side – the valley that contained many of the facilities of Parchin. Gadget and Pacer had not died in vain.

65 - Extraction

Two Blackhawk helicopters of Unit 669 of the Israeli Air Force – the Flying Cats – lifted off from Ali Al Salem Air Base just outside Kuwait City. The helicopters had no national identification and were easily lost in the myriad USAF Blackhawks that came and went at this hub of Persian Gulf military activity. They had a 237 mile flight almost due north, flying west of Basrah and skirting the Iraqi town of Amarah. At 10:46 p.m. Iran time, just a quarter hour after the start of Esther's Sling, the two helicopters banked right and flew the final 40 miles across the Meymeh River valley and into the western ranges of the Zagros Mountains of Iran. They touched down on the clearing that formed the parking lot for the Dehloran early warning radar complex.

"Now take your comrade and walk north. As soon as we are airborne, Israeli bombers will attack this site. You have only a few minutes to escape." The words were spoken by Yoni Ben Zeev and directed at the four Iranian radar technicians who had just had their plastic handcuffs cut off. Two of the Israeli commandos had jury-rigged a stretcher for the wounded radar technician. The Sayeret Matkal captain was determined to honor his word to the four men – it was his way to ease the guilt of having earlier shot one in the back of the knee, an act that he knew would haunt him in the coming years.

Ben Zeev was lying to the men, but he needed them to be motivated to leave the area as quickly as possible. There would be no Israeli airstrike. Instead the team had placed a large amount of high explosive around the base of the radar and in the command trailer. As soon as they saw the helicopters touchdown, five minute fuses were set. The team of Sayeret Matkal commandos had succeeded in their mission. Now all that was left was to get home.

The first helicopter took off with half the team as Ben Zeev stood on the mountain dirt shielding his eyes from the dust and small rocks kicked up as the rotors beat the wind to provide lift. After a moment, he lifted his head to see the Iranians moving away from the complex as fast as they could while carrying their stricken compatriot. Then the captain turned to see his demolition expert emerging from the command trailer and running at a dead sprint to board the remaining Blackhawk.

Slowly the captain walked up to the open door behind his demolition man and looked in to make a final head count. He spoke to the mountain goat, who was on the first Blackhawk, to confirm his head count. Ben Zeev was satisfied that no one was left behind. He climbed into the helicopter and closed the door.

"Let's get the hell out of here," he yelled toward the pilot, not sure if the man could hear him or not. The Blackhawk lifted off. Captain Ben Zeev sat by the door facing rearward, his eyes not wavering from the Dehloran complex. He was determined to witness the explosions that would come shortly. His helicopter was almost eight miles away when the flashes came. The first explosion destroyed the radar and its radome. Moments later, two more explosions occurred in quick succession, destroying the communications trailer and finally the radar operations trailer.

In under two hours, the team was safe at the same American military base where they had begun their journey two days earlier.

Fifteen KC-135 tankers registered to a shadowy company named AS-3 Air Lease Limited had taken off from Incirlik Air Base in Turkey earlier in the day. All of the planes had overflown Iraqi airspace to land and refuel at various American bases around the Middle East. All fifteen were now orbiting at 22,000 feet over the western end of the Persian Gulf. Israeli crews manned each plane and communicated with a nearby Eitam providing airborne warning and control. Ten F-16 Fighting Falcons were flying CAP.

The first planes to refuel behind the big tankers were not returning to Israel. Three F-16I Sufas and four F-15C Eagles refueled quickly and headed east at high speed. All of the Sufas and two of the Eagles descended to several hundred feet, while two Eagles stayed at altitude. The planes were heading due east across the waters of the Persian Gulf toward the Bushehr nuclear power plant.

Once the Bushehr attack aircraft had refueled, airplanes of the IAF returning from Iran began to take their turns being refueled. At 22,000 feet, over the course of the following hour, 146 thirsty Israeli warplanes refueled for the flight home over northern Saudi Arabia – but the plan had called for 150 planes to get refueled. In addition to Gadget's F-15I, two F-16Is and an F-15C had been shot down while executing their missions.

66 – A Visit to Bushehr

In the air over Bushehr, F-15 Eagles engaged several MiG-29 and F-4 Phantom fighters attempting to defend the nuclear reactor complex. The Iranians fought bravely but were drawn away from the real action. Flying under 500 feet, two of the Sufas lined up on their targets. The air defense radars around Bushehr had already been destroyed by the earlier attack from the Boeing B-737-400F – the last successful action taken by the cargo plane before being shot down 46 minutes earlier.

Each of the two Sufas had four GBU-32 laser-guided bombs weighing a little over 1,000 pounds. The bombs were general purpose bombs with no ability to penetrate reinforced concrete structures. The target of the one of the planes was the control room at Bushehr. The assignment of the other was to destroy the back-up generators that powered the nuclear plant's pressurized water pumps and the power sub-station that connected Bushehr to the electric grid.

The planning to destroy Bushehr had been the most debated aspect of Block G. Unlike Arak, which had not been operational and now lay in ruins with minimal radioactive impact, Bushehr was an operating nuclear power plant with a full fuel complement that had been running at its maximum design power since the summer of 2012. The same discussion between the President of the United States and Prime Minister Cohen during which the president agreed to send two MOPs to Israel, had become heated over the fate of Bushehr. The president thought he had elicited a promise of no attack on Bushehr. Now, the prime minister's view of what he had promised was being implemented. The key was to ensure no breach in the outer containment building of the nuclear reactor building made of up to three meters of reinforced concrete.

For the planners of Block G, Bushehr had only one purpose – it was a test bed to eventually provide Iran with plutonium for nuclear warheads. There had been no question of the need to target the facility, only intense discussion about how. Eventually, discussion gave way to planning and planning gained its own momentum.

Both F-16I Sufas designated their targets and dropped two bombs initially, then circled back to drop two more. The third Sufa pilot assessed the damage done before deciding to put two more bombs on the control room and two more on the electrical sub-station.

What was intentionally untouched was the emergency shutdown bunker and its two diesel generators. This room had only one function: to safely shutdown the reactor in the event of a complete failure of the main control room. Now the control room and its Iranian and Russian technicians was obliterated and on fire. The Israeli planners hoped that the emergency shutdown bunker was manned, as it was supposed to be at all times, but no one at Mount Olympus was sure.

The betting pool on a catastrophic core meltdown put the odds at 50-50. The scientists advising the prime minister had told him that the odds were high that the Iranians or their Russian advisors would successfully shut down the reactor, but if they didn't, any partial meltdown of the core should be contained within the main containment building. What the prime minister hoped for – and it was a hope not shared with any other person – was that the core would at least melt down partially, rendering the Bushehr Plant nothing but an expensive clean-up project.

Cohen was hoping for Three Mile Island, but everyone dreaded another Chernobyl. The fuse had been lit by Israeli bombs and only time and the courage and skill of surviving Iranian and Russian technicians would reveal the ultimate outcome.

67 – Going Home

At Shangri-La in the Iraqi desert, Major Gideon Meyer waited outside the rear ramp of the last remaining operational C-130 still on the ground. Over an hour long period, 45 planes of the IAF, all of which had been on SEAD missions, had passed through Mudaysis Airfield for refueling on their way home. During the 20 minutes since the last F-16 took off for home, two KC-130s had taken off with the air traffic control trailers and most of the men.

As Meyer stood there, the commander of a small demolition team walked up to him. "Everything is set," said the demolition expert. He held up a small radio transmitter to show the major. Once he pushed the button, all of the equipment they had wired to explode, which included the Ilyushin tankers and the KC-130 that had survived a rough landing but could not take off safely, would be on a two minute fuse.

Meyer motioned the demolition man into the cargo cabin of the KC-130. "Join your men. We shouldn't be much longer." They were now waiting only for the last of the four vehicles that had controlled traffic during the evening. About six minutes later, a Humvee painted in the colors of the Iraqi National Army pulled onto the tarmac and four men exited and ran to the back of the plane carrying all their portable equipment. Finally the major stepped away from the plane and pulled a small flare gun from his pocket. He fired a single orange flare into the sky. It was the last call. Anyone not on this plane was on his own.

Several minutes later, five remaining Shaldag soldiers, including their commander, emerged from the darkness and jogged to the KC-130. Meyer saluted each man as he boarded the plane and followed the Shaldag commander up the ramp.

While the plane was at the end of the taxiway preparing to start its takeoff roll, the demolition leader pushed the button on his radio transmitter. The plane took off and circled once to witness the expected explosions. Shortly after takeoff, six fireballs lit up the night. In addition to the four aircraft blown up, the two pickup trucks and their jamming equipment, which would have been flown home had the fourth KC-130 been operational, were blown.

The KC-130 headed home.

Epilogue

The sirens first sounded in Tel Aviv two hours after the concept codenamed Esther's Sling successfully destroyed Fordow and Natanz. Iran launched the first of a salvo of five Shahab-3 missiles before all of the aircraft of the IAF had returned to Israel. Only two of the medium range ballistic missiles were successfully intercepted by Arrow 2 missiles. The assurances of Defense Minister Avner had proven to be fleeting.

Two of the missiles landed in unpopulated spots – one in a field north of the city and one in the Mediterranean Sea. But one warhead, comprised of over 2,000 pounds of high explosive, detonated in the top floors of a tall condominium building not far from the Kirya. In the middle of the night – with most residents of Tel Aviv assuming that the sirens signaled yet another vain attempt by Hamas to strike Tel Aviv – few heeded the sirens. This was not a homemade rocket fired by Hamas. More than 90 died in the explosion and subsequent fire.

Worse came the next day. The shock of Project Block G had worn off and tens of thousands of Iranians marched the streets of Tehran burning Israeli and American flags and demanding revenge. The Iranian regime was equal to the request. A little after noon Iran time, the U.S. X-band radar site in Turkey detected the first of 98 Shahab 3 and 4 missiles launched within a two minute window. The launch had been long planned as the main retaliatory strike in the event of an Israeli attack.

Fifty-two of the missiles were aimed at targets in Tel Aviv, twenty-eight at Haifa and eighteen at the Israeli nuclear complex at Dimona in the Negev desert. The Iranian plan was to overwhelm the Israeli defenses. The plan was successful. Twenty-seven missiles landed within Tel Aviv, including two within the grounds of the Kirya, the IDF headquarters. Almost two dozen buildings were destroyed and over 1,000 Israelis would be pronounced dead once all the rubble was cleared. In Haifa, nine missiles eluded Israeli defenses and claimed the lives of seven civilians. But for Prime Minister Cohen and the IDF, the biggest blow came at Dimona. Six missiles landed within the sprawling complex, including a direct hit on the main containment building that blew a hole in the thick concrete shell of the building. The Dimona reactor had to be shutdown using emergency procedures. Only the skill of the engineers avoided a serious release of radiation.

On the same day, Hezbollah spun up its missile inventory on orders from its IRGC masters. The Israeli Air Force was back home and waiting for them. The next three days saw a repeat of the Second Lebanon War of 2006 as the IDF entered Lebanon in a measured manner to stop the rain of missiles. But the chaos in Syria and the collapse of the power of Bashar al-Assad had far more effect on Hezbollah than the raging warplanes of the IAF. The group was far too nervous about the developing war with Sunni Muslims in Syria to do anything other than make a showing on behalf of its benefactor Iran. A truce was agreed to late in the afternoon of October 8 as the IDF was completing the call up of 90,000 soldiers. In the end, it took the firing of just over 400 missiles into Israel to buy Hezbollah the level of respect it sought. None of these missiles had the impact of the Iranian Shahabs.

Late in the day on Sunday, October 6, in a bunker located on the outskirts of Jerusalem, the Kitchen Cabinet discussed the carnage that Shahab missiles had caused during the day. Defense Minister Avner offered his resignation even as he demanded a nuclear response. The meeting was interrupted by a long call between Cohen and the President of the United States. There would be no nuclear response. Avner's resignation would be accepted two weeks later. Despite the success of Block G, Zvi Avner would take the blame for the failure of Israel's ballistic missile defense system to protect the nation.

That same day, the world press tried to decipher what exactly had happened inside Iran and how much damage had been inflicted on the Iranian program. As was typical with the early reporting in an event like Block G, stories ranged from the use by Israel of nuclear weapons on Fordow, to reports of Israeli commando teams operating far and wide inside Iran. Initial speculation on the overnight airstrikes focused on the IAF operating from Azerbaijan despite adamant denials from Azerbaijani officials that they had anything to do with the prior night's events.

But by noon London time, the world's media became fixated on only one thing: the unfolding damage at the Bushehr Nuclear Power Plant and rumors of a meltdown of the core. It would take days of wild speculation and weeks of monitoring by American aircraft to confirm that Bushehr had experienced a partial meltdown of its core but that the resulting molten slag had been successfully contained within the concrete containment building. For Israel, it had been the biggest risk taken in Block G and it had paid off.

On Monday, October 7, stock markets around the world lost more than 2% of their value, the day starting particularly bad in Europe as Brent crude prices jumped more than $30 per barrel in the opening hour of trading. But a noontime drop in oil prices in reaction to the lack of hostilities in the Persian Gulf caused the European markets to rebound off their lows and helped limit the damage during early trading in the American markets.

Late in the day, as Iran continued to fire Shahab-3 missiles at Israel periodically, mines were discovered in the Straits of Hormuz. Skirmishes occurred sporadically between U.S. warships and IRG naval vessels in the Persian Gulf – the result typically being deadly for the Iranians. The president announced the deployment of two more American aircraft carriers in addition to the two already in the region. When an American F-22 Raptor operating out of Al Dafra Air Base in the UAE shot down a flight of three F-4 Phantoms that strayed too close to

U.S. naval forces in the Gulf, oil prices skyrocketed again and equity markets fell. But despite these "unfortunate incidents," no out-right war between the U.S. and Iran had yet begun.

During the day, two more Shahab-3 missiles evaded the Israeli missile defense system. One missile landed in a park, causing no damage. The other missile, targeted at Haifa, was a newer version of the Shahab with four independently targeted warheads. The missile struck home in downtown Haifa during the afternoon. One warhead detonated inside Rambam Medical Center, just above the ER waiting room. It killed 47 patients, medical professionals and employees. Among the more extreme pundits of the Israeli press, open calls for the deployment of nuclear weapons were discussed.

On October 8, the UN Security Council met to condemn Israel and the "war crime" of using civilian aircraft to attack Iran. The U.S. exercised its powers to keep the Security Council from passing the original resolution. Instead, a resolution was passed calling on all sides in the conflict to use restraint and stand-down. But the meeting that mattered on that day happened late in the evening in Geneva, Switzerland. After intervention by the Russians – who shared intelligence with the Iranians of U.S. preparations for an air campaign – the Iranian foreign affairs minister agreed to meet secretly with the American secretary of state.

The two men met in a small office room in the Palace of Nations on the Avenue de la Paix – the Avenue of Peace. The message delivered by the American official was blunt. The U.S. would not accept any action by Iran to close the Straits of Hormuz. This position was well known and had been oft repeated. What the Iranian did not expect was an equally unequivocal statement that the U.S. would not stand by while ballistic missiles were fired at Israel.

The dialogue between the men was unusually frank – the type of direct language demanded by the situation and emboldened by secrecy. "I am here to tell you" stated the secretary of state, "in clear and certain terms that any missile fired by your nation at any other nation after eight in the morning your time tomorrow will be considered an act of war by the Islamic Republic of Iran against the United States of America. The reaction will be the commencement of a full-scale and unrestrained aerial campaign to destroy the offensive capability of the Iranian military. Do you understand what I am saying?"

The foreign affairs minister, who had attended university in the U.S. and spoke fluent English, looked into the eyes of the American secretary of state. After a pause, he reacted. "Shock and awe. Yes, I understand this threat."

The next morning, Iran invited the UN secretary general to Tehran. The last missiles fired at Israel were all launched before sunrise on October 9. A de facto cease-fire took hold.

Hamak Arsadian reached the parking lot at the customs center in Nordouz, Iran at 9:15 p.m. on the evening of October 5. The guards had gone home and the border crossing over the Aras River was closed until morning. The Armenian parked his rig next to several other trucks waiting for the morning, turned his engine off and tried to sleep. He had been on an adrenaline high ever since he had dropped the Sayeret Matkal team in the middle of the Zagros Mountains the night before. Normally he would have spent the day dropping off his cargo and working on new connections for future business. But on this trip he had heeded the advice of Yoni Ben Zeev. He hastily made his delivery in Ahvaz early in the morning and immediately headed back north toward home.

Arsadian crawled into his bunk and did the one thing that would get him sleepy: He started to read a book.

The sound of a truck engine starting woke up the Armenian trucker the same way it often did. He wiped his eyes, pulled the blanket off and lowered himself into the driver's seat. All he wanted at that moment was a cup of coffee. As he gave into the temptation to yawn, he watched in shock as a border guard ran past his tractor. The border guards never ran – they were never in a hurry. Outside he noticed two IRGC soldiers walking toward the customs building. Each had an AK-47. But what struck Arsadian was that the guns were not slung over their shoulders, they were being held in their hands.

A group of drivers were talking nearby. Arsadian got out and joined them. He heard the news that apparently the Israeli Air Force had attacked Iran during the night. One man claimed that the Iranians had already destroyed Tel Aviv with a nuclear weapon in retaliation.

The border was closed for the time being.

During the next several hours, border guards – each with an IRGC shadow – questioned all of the drivers waiting to cross into Armenia. Arsadian's turn came a little before noon. He was interrogated about what he had done since passing through the crossing three days earlier. The guards looked into his now empty trailer before moving on to the next driver in the queue. Hamak returned to his tractor to wait. It seemed to him that the guards were more interested in the trucks that had loads they were transporting out of Iran. Several of those trucks were emptied in their entirety. As the Armenian thought through the action of the Iranians, it became clear to him that they were looking for men being spirited out of the country – spies, commandos, downed airmen.

Hamak Armenian and his truck had the opposite profile of where the Iranian suspicions were focused. At 3 in the afternoon, an Iranian border guard walked up to the Armenian's door and told him to he was cleared to go. He wished the Armenian a safe journey home. Hamak returned a warm thanks.

Hamak Arsadian crossed the Aras River bridge to the safety of his native country at 3:06 p.m. on October 6.

"Mazel tov!" shouted the guests as the groom smashed a wine glass with his right foot. It was a beautiful June weekend, perfect weather for an outdoor wedding on the shores of the Sea of Galilee.

The manager of Villa Melchett had never before seen security like this. The rough looking men in jackets with no ties were one thing, but when two IDF Blackhawk helicopters starting circling the estate about a half hour before the ceremony, she insisted on an explanation. The groom – whose name she did not recognize – calmly took her into her office.

"I have a special shomer," said the groom, referring to his best man.

"Who is he, the prime minister?" joked the manager. "He should be here already," she admonished.

The groom smiled. "You will understand once he arrives. In the meantime, you can take comfort that we are in the safest spot in Israel right now."

Fifteen minutes later several black SUVs pulled up in front of the villa, which had been rented by the groom for the weekend. Out of the first SUV, several men emerged. Like the advance crew, they were typically in their thirties or early forties. They wore jackets and were clearly in excellent condition. Each man wore sunglasses, a conspicuous earpiece, and none of them smiled. One man ran to the rear passenger door of the second SUV and opened it. Prime Minister Cohen stepped out in one of his finest suits. From the third SUV, Mossad Director Levy emerged wearing a suit that looked like it had been pulled out of a closet for the first time in a decade.

The manager rushed outside to welcome her guests. Cohen wondered why she was laughing. As he thought of it, he realized that his presence often provoked a wide range of unusual reactions. Of course, he was unaware of her speculation to the groom only minutes earlier.

Within the hour, Enya Govenin and Amit Margolis were a married couple. Cohen had drawn the line at dancing the Horah – too easy to be filmed on someone's phone he told Amit. But afterwards, as the bride danced with General David Schechter, the head of the state of Israel pulled the young Mossad agent aside. "I have something for you, Amit, something I bring in my official capacity."

Margolis drew closer to his commander in chief.

Cohen put his arm around the groom. "Your plan set back Iran's ambitions by at least a decade."

Margolis hoped that the prime minister was right. "I guess that gives me plenty of time to think up the next version of Esther's Sling," he joked.

Cohen smiled. "Seriously, the nation owes you much and yet you remain anonymous. This pains me."

"I wouldn't want it any other way. I like being able to go out and not worry."

Cohen pulled a small hinged gift box out of his pocket and opened it. "This is from a grateful country." Inside was the Medal of Valor – the Israeli equivalent of the Medal of Honor. "The Knesset approved this medal last week. I am sorry that this medal will, like everything about you, remain a secret. If I am not mistaken, you and your father are the only father-son recipients of this honor."

Amit Margolis exhaled. "I do not deserve this, sir."

"You most definitely do, Amit. Those Shahab missiles that hit Tel Aviv and Haifa would have come soon with nuclear warheads if not for your plan. Now the world respects our capabilities again – because of you. This medal is insufficient recognition. It is the least we can do."

"I am honored."

"The honor is mine."

Enya Margolis walked up at that moment, her right hand caressing the back of her new husband.

"You are a beautiful bride, Mrs. Margolis," Prime Minister Cohen said.

"Thank you, sir. Thank you for being at our wedding."

"You have married a national treasure. Take care of this man."

"You have my word on that, Mr. Cohen."

The prime minister laughed. "I am counting on it."

On the afternoon of Thursday, September 25, the start of the Hebrew year 5775, a ceremony took place on the compound of the Kirya in Tel Aviv. After a brief speech by Prime Minister Cohen, General David Schechter – the public face and public hero of the successful destruction of the Iranian nuclear program – reached up with his right hand and grabbed hold of a white sheet that enshrouded a new monument. In front of a crowd of over a hundred dignitaries and senior military officers, surrounded by construction equipment, Schechter pulled the sheet off as television cameras broadcast the event live in Israel. Photographers representing the major press agencies recorded the event in still images.

The edifice stood three meters high. The granite stone was topped with a stylized airplane soaring towards the heavens. Underneath the plane, a large Star of David had been carved. On the face of the six-pointed star, the names of the men of Mossad and the IDF who died in action during Block G were carved. At the top of the list – his place determined at the insistence of Amit Margolis – was the name "James L. Miller – Pilot."

Amit Margolis stood anonymously in the crowd and applauded.

– end -